This book belongs to

**Maheen
Ehtesham**

Twenty Thousand Leagues Under the Sea

Twenty Thousand Leagues
Under the Sea

JULES VERNE

WORTH PRESS

SIGNATURE CLASSICS

First published in 2019 by Worth Press Ltd, Bath, England
Email: worthpress@btconnect.com

Concept, design, introduction, reset text and coloured images of this edition
© Worth Press Ltd, 2019

British Library Cataloguing in Publication Data
A catalogue record for this book is available from the British Library

ISBN: 978-1-84931-165-6

10 9 8 7 6 5 4 3 2 1

Publisher's Note   Every effort has been made to ensure the accuracy of the
information presented in this book. The publisher will not assume liability for
damages caused by inaccuracies in the data and makes no warranty whatsoever
expressed or implied. The publisher welcomes comments and corrections from readers,
emailed to worthpress@btconnect.com, which will be considered for incorporation
in future editions. Every effort has been made to trace copyright holders and seek
permission to use illustrative and other material. The publisher wishes to apologize for
any inadvertent errors or omissions and would be glad to rectify these in future editions.

The images used in this book come from either the public domain or from the public
commons unless otherwise stated.

Page Resetting: IDSUK Ltd
Images coloured by Chandra Creative and Content Solutions
Cover and Front Matter Design: Jess Moon

Printed and bound in China

Contents

Matthew Booth is the author of *Sherlock Holmes and the Giant's Hand*, published by Breese Books and the co-author of *The Further Exploits of Sherlock Holmes*, a collection of new stories, commissioned by Sparkling Books in 2016. He contributed two original Holmes stories to *The Game is Afoot*, a collection of Sherlock Holmes short stories published in 2008 by Wordsworth Editions and contributed a story to Wordsworth Editions' collection of original crime tales, *Crime Scenes*. Matthew is the creator of Anthony Rathe, a disgraced former barrister seeking redemption by solving those crimes which come his way. The character first appeared in a series of radio plays produced and syndicated by Imagination Theatre in America. Rathe now appears in *When Anthony Rathe Investigates* published by Sparkling Books. A lifelong devotee of crime and supernatural fiction, Matthew has provided a number of academic talks on such subjects as Sherlock Holmes, the works of Agatha Christie, crime fiction, Count Dracula, and the facts and theories concerning the crimes of Jack the Ripper. He is also a member of the Crime Writers' Association and a contributor to their monthly newsletter, *Red Herrings*.

David Stuart Davies is an author, playwright and editor. His fiction includes six novels featuring his wartime detective Johnny Hawke, Victorian puzzle solver Luther Darke, and nine Sherlock Holmes novels, the latest being *Sherlock Holmes and The Ripper Legacy*. *Sherlock Holmes and the Instrument of Death* is due to be published in 2020. His most recent novel is *Oliver Twist and The Mystery of Throate Manor*. His non-fiction work includes *Starring Sherlock Holmes*, detailing the film career of the Baker Street sleuth. David is regarded as an authority on Sherlock Holmes and is the author of three Holmes stage plays, *Sherlock Holmes: The Last Act*, *Sherlock Holmes: The Death and Life* and *Sherlock Holmes: The Last Testament*. David has also penned three dark gritty crime novels set in Yorkshire in the 1980s. He is a committee member of the Crime Writers' Association and edits their monthly publication *Red Herrings*. His collection of ghost and horror stories, *The Halloween Mask*, appeared in 2015, championed by Mark Gatiss who said they were 'pleasingly nasty'. David is General Editor of Wordsworth's Mystery & Supernatural series and also contributes a monthly blog on classic novels for the Wordsworth website. He is a past Fellow of the Royal Literary Fund and has appeared at many literary festivals and the Edinburgh Fringe performing his one-man presentation *The Game's Afoot – an evening with Sherlock Holmes and Arthur Conan Doyle*. David is also a member of the famed Detection Club.

The Masterpiece of Masterpieces: An Examination of the *Nautilus*

Matthew Booth

Literature is filled with sea-going vessels whose names have become part of modern myth. There is the Russian schooner *Demeter* in Bram Stoker's *Dracula*, for instance; the *USS Caine* in Herman Wouk's *The Caine Mutiny*; the *Jolly Roger* in J.M. Barrie's *Peter Pan*; or the *Pequod* in Herman Melville's *Moby Dick*. All of these ships, and their numerous literary cousins, have all found their way into the collective consciousness of the public and, arguably, none more so than Captain Nemo's infamous submarine, the *Nautilus*, in Jules Verne's *Twenty Thousand Leagues Under the Sea*. Of all the vessels in literature, the *Nautilus* is perhaps the most spectacular, so much so that Verne himself describes it as 'a masterpiece containing masterpieces'. What sets the *Nautilus* apart from many of its literary companions, however, is not only its fantastic conception in Verne's novel, but also its basis in historical fact and its impact on future reality.

Details of the origins and mechanics of *Nautilus* are given by Nemo himself in the novel, when he is grandstanding its capabilities to Professor Pierre Aronnax. According to Nemo, the submersible's primary source of propulsion comes from electricity provided by sodium and mercury batteries, and its top speed is 50 knots. Its use of floodable tanks allows it to adjust buoyancy and control its depth, while the pumps which evacuate these tanks are so powerful that they produce immense jets of water when the vessel emerges rapidly from the surface of the sea. Not unsurprisingly, this mechanism and its resultant effect led many early observers of *Nautilus* to believe that the vessel is some species of whale, or even some other sea monster as yet undiscovered by science. As Nemo explains to M. Aronnax:

' "Here, M. Aronnax, are the several dimensions of the boat you are in. It is an elongated cylinder with conical ends. It is very like a cigar in shape, a shape already adopted in London in several constructions of the same sort. The length of this cylinder, from stem to stern, is exactly 70 m, and its maximum breadth is eight metres. It is not built on a ratio of ten to one like your long-voyage steamers, but its lines are sufficiently long, and its curves prolonged enough, to allow the water to slide off easily, and oppose no obstacle to its passage. These two dimensions enable you to obtain by a simple calculation the surface and cubic contents of the Nautilus. Its area measures 1011.45 square metres; and its contents 1,500.2 cubic metres; that is to say, when completely immersed it displaces 1500.2 cubic metres of water, or 1500.2 metric tons." '

These dimensions and measurements are the stuff of fantasy. They are Verne's imagination running wild, but they remain rooted in fact, so that the *Nautilus* becomes something more than the truth, a heightened depiction of reality. The best science fiction is that which is an exaggerated depiction of a recognizable reality. Too much fantasy in a novel will run the risk of alienating the reader, who will have no experience or knowledge to compare to an elaborate fiction and so he will be unable to empathize with the characters and situations in the novel itself. What Verne understood was that a degree of realism, presenting fantasy only as a heightened version of reality, would engage and satisfy the reader by maintaining the fantasy within the confines of reality. To put it another way, the incredible should never become the unbelievable. Against that background, it is important to note that, for all its exaggerations and fantastic abilities, the Nautilus has a fundamental basis in fact and, in particular, in two specific vessels.

Nemo's submarine is named after a real life *Nautilus* which was first tested in 1800. Designed between 1793 and 1797 by the American inventor Robert Fulton (1765–1815), the real *Nautilus* is widely accepted as being the first practical submarine. As might be expected, Fulton's prototype has far less impressive dimensions and capabilities than Verne's ideal. Whereas Nemo claims that his vessel is 70 metres (330 feet) long, Fulton's actual *Nautilus* was 6.48 metres (21.25 feet) long, consisting of copper sheets over iron ribs, but like its fictional counterpart, it flooded and emptied its ballast tanks in order to change buoyancy.

Its speed was less impressive than the 50 knots of Nemo's goliath, but the real *Nautilus* was still able to perform notable feats within its own capabilities. On 3 July 1801, at Le Havre, Fulton took a modified version of his *Nautilus* down to a depth of 7.6 metres (25 feet) which was then an impressive and unprecedented depth for such a vessel, and he maintained that depth for one hour without difficulty. Later, after some modifications, including the addition of a copper globe containing 5.7 cubic metres (200 cubic feet) of air, Fulton's vessel was able to maintain an underwater time of at least four and a half hours. Subsequent speed trials resulted in the vessel achieving two knots on the surface, and covering 400 metres (quarter of a mile) in 7 minutes.

It is perhaps not impossible to imagine an 1801 audience witnessing the *Nautilus* at work thinking that they were experiencing something out of a wild fiction. While speeds of two knots and a submerged time of four and a half hours might be child's play for the fictional depiction of Fulton's invention, which was capable of remaining submerged underwater for five days, the real life *Nautilus's* achievement is, for the confines of reality as opposed to the limitless possibility of fiction, not something to be dismissed without admiration. So impressed were Fulton's peers that an overseeing committee of the Admiralty recommended the building of two submarines based on *Nautilus's* design with the aim of increasing Fulton's crew of three men to a crew of eight and a proposed submersion time of eight hours. Perhaps a greater testament to Fulton's achievement was that Napoleon himself showed interest in the Nautilus, but the discovery of leaks and the subsequent dismantling of the vessel convinced the Emperor that the idea was not worth pursuing and that Fulton himself was little more than a charlatan.

Fulton was undeterred, as were the British. Fulton was paid the sum of £800 to come to England and build a second version of the submarine. However, the British victory at Trafalgar seemed to rob the underwater capability of the *Nautilus* of some of its edge of danger and Fulton found himself being ignored by the British, to the extent that he became frustrated and abandoned the project, returning to America in October 1806. He would never again mention or discuss his work and achievements on the *Nautilus* submarine. However, according to papers he had left behind, his British *Nautilus* was envisaged as something truly impressive for its time. Fulton's plan was for an 11-metre (36-foot) long seafaring boat with a crew of six, to be provisioned for 20 days at sea. The hull was designed to imitate a sloop with conventional-looking mast and sails that could be lowered for submersion. A two-bladed propeller was intended to fold up out of the water when surfaced in order to reduce drag. When submerged, air came through two streamlined ventilation pipes, and light from the conning tower. None of this was actually constructed, however, largely due to Fulton's treatment and rejection by the British.

How much of the *Nautilus's* achievements were known to Verne is not clear, but his use of the name suggests not only that he was aware of Fulton's work but that the author was influenced to some extent by it. What is known for certain is that Verne's fictional submarine was heavily influenced by a French vessel constructed by Siméon Bourgeois (1815–87), a captain in the French Navy, and Charles Brun (1821–97), a 1st Class engineer. Together, they developed and constructed the first mechanically propelled submersible. Their version of the submarine went by the name *Plongeur*, the French word for 'diver', and a model of it was displayed at the 1867 Exposition Universelle, the second world's fair to be held in Paris. It was this replica of the *Plongeur* which was studied closely by Verne and which, three years later, appeared as Nemo's *Nautilus*, albeit twisted by fantasy and imagination, in the pages of *Twenty Thousand Leagues*.

The idea that Verne took reality and heightened it for dramatic effect is perhaps most evident in his use of *Plongeur*. Nemo talks of *Nautilus'* *"elongated cylinder with conical ends...very like a cigar in shape"* and images of the French vessel show that Verne could easily have been describing *Plongeur* with those words. Already, the advancement in technology and science had enabled the French designers to create a vessel which, at a length of 43m, was considerably longer than Fulton's 6.48m long *Nautilus*, and it will be remembered that Nemo claimed that his *Nautilus* was 70m long. It is facts such as these which support the idea that what Verne was seeking to achieve with his fictional submarine was the idea that science fiction is best when it is a distorted reflection of reality rather than an overt denial of it. Fact demonstrates that the minds of men and an increased knowledge of science and technology had striven to refine an idea over 65 years in order to produce a larger, more efficient version of an earlier design. Fiction demonstrates that this increasing knowledge of the world around us can enable a man to create a further advanced, albeit incredible, version of the same idea.

How fiction exaggerates reality is further demonstrated by the fictional *Nautilus*. If the length of Nemo's vessel is not altogether divorced from the reality of *Plongeur*, his assertion regarding its displacement capabilities is a heavily dramatized version of the truth. It will be remembered that Nemo claimed that his *Nautilus* could displace 1500.2 metric tons, a far cry from *Plongeur's* 420 tons, but Verne accounts for the exaggeration by disguising it with supposed mathematic fact: *"...these two dimensions enable you to obtain by a simple calculation the surface and cubic contents of the Nautilus."* Still, it is this degree of exaggeration which ensures that the fiction can be entirely fantastical whilst retaining the basic foundations of fact. Even the immense size of the fictional vessel might have some basis in reality: *Plongeur* used a compressed-air engine, propelled by stored compressed air powering a reciprocating engine, and the air was contained in 23 tanks, which took up 153 square metres. As a result, *Plongeur* was a submarine of unprecedented size. Whilst Nemo's *Nautilus* might assign its size to the lavish dining rooms and libraries contained within it, as well as to the mechanisms and technology required to propel it, this idea of a submersible vessel whose advanced technology required it to be of considerable size is not the product of a writer's imagination but a simple matter of scientific fact, evidenced by the dimensions of Bourgeois and Brun's invention.

Plongeur shares another similarity with Verne's fantasy. In the novel, we are told that the world views the *Nautilus* as a sea monster, the evidence of which is her attacks on ships using a ramming prow to puncture target vessels below the waterline. As the book progresses, it becomes known that the *Nautilus* is a submarine after its attack on the Abraham Lincoln and Ned Land's striking of its metallic surface with a harpoon. Whilst this adds to the mystery and excitement of the novel, it should be borne in mind that *Plongeur* was armed with a ram to break holes in the hull of enemy ships. Again, fact and fiction become blurred within the pages of Verne's novel. *Plongeur* was also armed with an electrically fired torpedo, fixed at the end of a pole, so that its merits as a vessel of war are clearly stated. However, after his appointment as chairman of the Commission on Submarine Defences in 1871, Captain Bourgeois (then Admiral) opposed the use of torpedoes as a primary weapon in warfare. It is questionable whether Captain Nemo would share the same reservations.

Although Nemo's *Nautilus* shares much of the design and look of *Plongeur*, which was undoubtedly the primary influence on Verne's imagination, it is possible that the immense size of this submarine, in tandem with the scientific knowledge and capabilities of the era, were too much for the reality. Fiction can succeed where fact fails and this is perhaps true of the *Nautilus* and *Plongeur*. Where the former was in full command of its capabilities and was an underwater terror, the latter appears to have been less than impressive. *Plongeur* was commanded by Lieutenant de Vaisseau Marie-Joseph-Camille Doré and, on 6 October 1863, she undertook her initial trials by sailing down the Charente River, towards the harbour of the Cabane Carrée. The following month, on 2 November 1863, Plongeur was towed towards Port de Barques where her first underwater trials were planned. Poor weather conditions prevented the trials, however, and the submarine was eventually towed to harbour of La Rochelle. From there, on 14 February 1864, during trials in the Bassin à flot, an excessive admission of compressed air forced *Plongeur's* engine to race and the submarine bumped into the quay. Trials were stopped. It is impossible to imagine Nemo suffering such an embarrassment as Doré must have felt.

Nevertheless, on 18 February 1864, *Plongeur* was towed to La Pallice and dived to 9m but its massive size led to stability problems. The front of the submarine tended to dive first, hitting the bottom, so that the submarine would glide forward. Pumps were installed to compensate for the tilt, but they proved too slow to be effective. These difficulties meant that the submarine was limited to dives of a maximum depth of 10m. It will be remembered that Fulton's *Nautilus* had dived to 7.6m in 1801. It would seem that whilst the fictional Nemo could command the immense size of his submarine, his real-life counterparts could not. The passing of time might have enabled them to construct a far more impressive machine than Fulton, but it had not permitted them to control it. Such considerations and limitations were not factors with which the fictional *Nautilus* had to contend.

Perhaps as a direct result of these trials, *Plongeur* was struck by the French Navy on 2 February 1872, two years after she had been partly immortalized in Verne's novel. She was reactivated as an automotive water tanker on 1 January 1873, being assigned to the harbour of Rochefort where Charles Brun himself was stationed. She was equipped with a new engine in 1898, transferred from a torpedo boat and she remained in service there until 1927, when, upon the closure of the arsenal at Rochefort, she was transferred to the Mediterranean at Toulon. From there, *Plongeur* was used to supply the 1st and 3rd squadrons with water before being decommissioned on Christmas Day 1935. *Plongeur* had a serviceable career, but as a technological advance in submarine history it seems that the ideal was too much for the reality.

In some respects, both Fulton's *Nautilus* and *Plongeur* came to ignominious ends: abandoned as an idea because of her inventor's frustrations on the one hand; re-assigned and decommissioned on the other.

By contrast, Nemo's *Nautilus* is ensured the status of legend. At the conclusion of Verne's sequel to *Twenty Thousand Leagues*, entitled *The Mysterious Island*, the volcanic island in question erupts and Nemo dies aboard the *Nautilus*. The eruption of the volcano entombs him and the vessel for eternity. The destruction of the *Nautilus* and its captain means that such a vessel could never be replicated, imitated, or improved upon. The fictional ideal of the realism of both Fulton's *Nautilus* and Bourgeois and Brun's *Plongeur* will never be realized.

And yet, the legacy of Verne's work continued to influence science and technology. Just as Verne himself had taken ideas and achievements from historical fact, inventors and entrepreneurs were to take some inspiration from Verne's imaginary depiction of reality. *20,000 Leagues* suggests that the *Nautilus* achieved deep submersion in a short space of time by diving at a steep angle:

> *"I use an ordinary rudder fixed on the back of the stern-post, and with one wheel and some tackle to steer by. But I can also make the Nautilus rise and sink, and sink and rise, by a vertical movement by means of two inclined planes fastened to its sides, opposite the centre of flotation, planes that move in every direction, and that are worked by powerful levers from the interior."*

It is a technique known now as hydroplaning and it is a recognised aspect of submarine science, having been developed first by Simon Lake (1866-1945) of the Lake Torpedo Boat Company.

Lake himself was a great admirer of Verne's work, particularly *20,000 Leagues*, and he had been so captivated by the book's idea of underwater travel and exploration that it became his life's work. Amongst Lake's innovations were ballast tanks, divers' compartments, and the periscope; but it was his vessel the *Argonaut* which brought him lasting fame and the admiration of Verne himself.

The *Argonaut* was the first submarine to operate successfully in the open ocean. In 1898, with a crew of only four men, Lake undertook a 2000 mile journey in Chesapeake Bay and the Atlantic coast, travelling both on the surface and submerged. Lake and his crew retrieved fish, clams and oysters through the dive compartment in order to demonstrate the practicality of living and traveling underwater. It is not difficult to discern a comparison between Lake and his crew and that of Nemo and his men, who, as the novel tells us, gather and farm food from the sea. The fictional *Nautilus* has a galley to prepare such food, including a machine designed to convert seawater to drinking water. Nemo's vessel almost seems to champion the idea that the human race could live, travel, and survive beneath the waves.

In December 1898, Lake took the *Argonaut* to New York. His idea was to enlarge and improve it. He envisaged greater buoyancy, increased deck space, and living quarters for a crew of eight. This again recalls the library and dining room of the fictional Nautilus. This improved version of the *Argonaut* was 66 feet in length and capable of a non-stop voyage of 3000 miles, and submerging for 48 hours. For Verne, this was the closest a contemporary reality had come to his fantastic fiction, which, in itself, had been triggered by the achievements of truth. To Verne, Lake's work was not only of tremendous scientific interest, but it was a vindication of his own imagination. As he explained in a personal telegram to Lake:

"While my book 'Twenty Thousand Leagues Under the Sea' is entirely a work of imagination, my conviction is that all I said in it will come to pass. A thousand mile voyage in the Baltimore submarine boat (The Argonaut) is evidence of this. This conspicuous success of submarine navigation in the United States will push on under-water navigation all over the world. If such a successful test had come a few months earlier it might have played a great part in the war just closed. The next great war may be largely a contest between submarine boats. I think that electricity rather than compressed air will be the motive power in such vessels for the sea is full of this element. It is waiting to be harnessed as steam has been. It will then not be necessary to go to the land for fuel any more than for provisions. The sea will supply food for man and power without limit. Submarine navigation is now

ahead of aerial navigation and will advance much faster from now on.
Before the United States gains her full development she is likely to have
mighty navies not only on the bosom of the Atlantic and Pacific, but in
the upper air and beneath the water's surface."

Lake continued to work in the development of the submarine and he
became a pioneer in the field. Although he was forced to close the Lake
Torpedo Company in 1922, as a result of international treaties limiting
the size of navies, he continued designing maritime salvage systems.
He also advised the United States Navy on submarine technology and
maritime salvage during World War II, before his death on 23 June 1945.

But these examples are only a few of the illustrations of how Verne's
work foreshadowed the scientific advances of the present day. What is
impressive is Verne's ability to imagine a world far more advanced than
his own time, but one which still retained some degree of possibility, so
much so that much of what the author imagined came to pass, albeit
long after his mind had conceived them. It was not until the middle of
the twentieth century, for example, that actual submarines came close
to the performance of the fictional *Nautilus*. But, by combining the technological prowess of his age with his own creativity, Verne came within
the scope of some of the abilities of modern submarines.

It would be too simplistic to explain the *Nautilus'* advanced state as
being the product of some sort of futuristic power. In fact, Verne took
inspiration from what was within the confines of the scientific knowledge of his day. A major precursor of fact within the fiction is Verne's
suggestion that the *Nautilus* runs on electric power. As the Captain says
himself,

> *"There is a powerful agent, obedient, rapid, easy, which conforms*
> *to every use, and reigns supreme on board my vessel. Everything is*
> *done by means of it. It lights, warms it, and is the soul of my mechani-*
> *cal apparatus. This agent is electricity...electricity gives heat, light,*
> *motion, and, in a word, life to the Nautilus."*

As has been noted, the submersible's primary source of propulsion comes from electricity provided by sodium and mercury batteries. The *Nautilus* runs on these chemical batteries (Nemo refers to his "large and powerful" Bunsen batteries) and the vessel's engine room generates electricity by using large electromagnets which allow the various gears and levers of the submarine to function. Nemo explains that *"the electricity produced passes forward, where it works, by electro-magnets of great size, on a system of levers and cog-wheels that transmit the movement to the axle of the screw."*

To Verne and his contemporaries, batteries and electrical motors were in their infancy and it was not until the late nineteenth century that science began to catch up with Verne's imagination and begin to create efficient designs of electrical motors. However, Verne's suggestion that electrical batteries might power a vessel the size of the *Nautilus* was flawed. A failure to create an adequate power supply was a deficiency in all submarines until the close of the nineteenth century and in seeking to have his foundations in fact, Verne stumbled where his scientific counterparts did. Scientific research today suggests that only a nuclear reactor might enable a vessel of the size and dimensions of the *Nautilus* to function for extended periods of time at the speeds Verne envisaged.

And yet, Verne's idea that batteries might be the key to allowing the *Nautilus* to travel great distances over extended periods of time was not inconceivable. By the 1880s, underwater travel was being carried out in exactly this way. In Russia, Stefan Drzewiecki (1844-1938) had constructed the first electrically powered boats and, in 1884, he converted two mechanical submarines by installing batteries in them. Verne might have foreseen the use of batteries as a source of power in propelling underwater vessels, but he could not have foreseen the limited scope of such power. As time went on, the integral use of batteries as envisaged by Verne was swapped in favour of diesel electric propulsion. However, diesel submarines still required batteries to submerge, but they continued to limit the sped and range of the vessels. Nevertheless, this use of electrical power was a factor which Verne made central to the successful propulsion of the *Nautilus* and one which his scientific successors made fact.

Still, it cannot be said that Verne's predictions were altogether accurate. In discussing his electrical power, Nemo says that:

> "...my electricity is not everybody's. You know what sea-water is composed of. In a thousand grammes are found 96 1/2 per cent. of water, and about 2 2/3 per cent. of chloride of sodium; then, in a smaller quantity, chlorides of magnesium and of potassium, bromide of magnesium, sulphate of magnesia, sulphate and carbonate of lime. You see, then, that chloride of sodium forms a large part of it. So it is this sodium that I extract from the sea-water, and of which I compose my ingredients..."

Nemo has apparently enhanced his electrical batteries with this use of sodium from the sea. He extracts it from a remote island and combines it with sea coal, the resultant compound being used to recharge these fictional batteries. Verne's future scientific counterparts would know what he perhaps did not know: that sodium is explosive when brought into contact with water. Accordingly, any such use of sodium in the batteries might cause detonations, fires, and lethal gases to be expelled once they came into contact with the battery fluid.

Such quibbles should not detract from the central notion that Verne influenced future nautical technology, however, and his idea that the *Nautilus* was powered by electric batteries and motors was not simply the invention of a creative writer. It was to become a scientific fact. Nemo's apparatus also exceeds the technological capabilities of the day. *"This dial hanging in front of us indicates the speed of the Nautilus,"* says Nemo. *"An electric thread puts it in communication with the screw, and the needle indicates the real speed. Look! Now we are spinning along with a uniform speed of fifteen miles an hour."* It was not until the mid-twentieth century that electromagnetic logs were used on seafaring vessels but Verne has pre-empted its use with Nemo's electric thread and needle. For the majority of its design, whilst too large to be entirely practical, the

Nautilus can be recognized as a fictional blueprint for scientific reality and it has served as the creative impetus for technological advances in maritime and submarine travel.

As a result, whilst Captain Nemo and the *Nautilus* remain the stuff of fantasy, like all great literary legends, they endure because there is an element of truth behind their conception. In the case of Jules Verne and the *Nautilus*, however, their legacy extends beyond the literary. The *Nautilus*, itself a product of realism, has become the starting point for the development of underwater science and technology and the impact of Nemo's fictional submarine persists to this day. It is a testament to Verne's imagination and concepts, and his ability to enhance the realism of his own time, that his science fiction can be viewed equally as the precursor to science fact.

Jules Verne – The Founding Father of Science Fiction

David Stuart Davies

It always amuses me that numerous beginners' guides to writing fiction advise would-be scribes to 'write about what you know'. While there is an element of truth in this suggestion, it does seem to deny the power of the imagination so essential in creating an absorbing, challenging and entertaining narrative. If all authors just wrote exactly about what they knew, what a limited and rather dull selection of reads would be available to us on the bookshelf! Writers are artistic dreamers and while some dream of characters, plots and environments they are intimately familiar with, others reach beyond these confines into the unchartered terrain of the unknown. They become pioneers into realms of their own creation and, if successful, they convince us to join them on this ground-breaking journey. With the magic of carefully spun words and revolutionary ideas we are exposed to characters, situations and environments we ourselves could never have imagined without their help. Authors of fantasy and science fiction are our guides to these unique and very special worlds.

It was in the nineteenth century that writers very gradually began to construct what we would regard today as 'science fiction'. This was partly due, of course, to the great leaps that science made in all fields from medicine to industry during this remarkable period. The nineteenth century began with horse drawn carriages, gas-lamps and musical boxes and ended with motor cars, electric lighting, phonographs and numerous other inventions which would have been deemed incredible in an earlier age. The further and faster science and technology advances, the more it makes it possible for the writer to stretch his or her – and our – imaginations. Possible and necessary, for the fantastic becomes less fantastic as science supersedes fiction.

Isaac Asimov, the great exponent of the genre in the twentieth century, stated that, 'True science fiction, by its modern definition (or at least, my modern definition) could not have been written prior to the nineteenth century then, because it was only with the coming of the Industrial Revolution in the last decades of the eighteenth century that the rate of technological change became great enough to notice in a single lifetime – in those areas of the globe affected by that revolution.'

The growth of science fiction was not only due to the technological advances alone; it was also due to man's increasing curiosity about his world, its limits and its possibilities. There was a fascination with what constitutes life and what happens after death – it could be claimed that Mary Shelley's *Frankenstein* (1818), which encapsulates these concerns, is the first science fiction novel – and this in turn gave rise to the popularity of the ghost story. However, other writers looked not to the spirit world for their subject matter but other fantastic realms either in the future, or hidden from our view, or, indeed, beyond the confines of this mortal coil.

The greatest of all science fiction writers in the nineteenth century was Jules Verne (1828–1905). If imagination was a physical commodity, Verne would have had warehouses full of it. His fiction sparkles and fizzes with mind-blowing ideas, landscapes, plots and images. He remains one of the greatest of all fantasy writers and is generally regarded as the 'father of science fiction', although the actual term for the genre was not coined until the early twentieth century. Verne referred to his works as 'scientific romances'. In fact, he was the first professional writer who made a good living out of creating fantastic tales. He is well known for his novels such as *A Journey to the Centre of the Earth* (1864 1863), *From the Earth to the Moon* (1865), *Twenty Thousand Leagues Under the Sea* (1869–70), *Around the World in Eighty Days* (1873) and *The Mysterious Island* (1875). Verne has been the second most-translated author in the world since 1979, ranking between Agatha Christie and William Shakespeare.

Jules Gabriel Verne was born to bourgeois parents in Nantes, France in 1828. Legend has it that in 1839, at the age of 11, Verne secretly procured a job as cabin boy on the three-mast ship *Coralie*, with the intention of travelling to the Indies and bringing back a coral necklace for his cousin Caroline. The ship was all ready to depart for the Indies when Verne's father arrived just in time before the ship set sail, dragged his son on shore and made him promise that in future he would 'travel only in his imagination'. It is now known that the legend is an exaggerated tale invented by Verne's first biographer, his niece Marguerite Allotte de la Füye, although it may have been inspired by a real incident. One thing is true, Verne did travel extensively and wildly in his imagination.

Young Jules was trained to follow in his father's footsteps as a lawyer but, while in Paris, instead of immersing himself in the law, Verne found himself attracted to the theatre and, after obtaining his law degree and setting up a practice in 1850, he indulged in his passion for creative writing and began penning numerous plays, dramas and operettas for the Théâtre Lyrique.

Verne later recalled: 'I was greatly under the influence of Victor Hugo, indeed, very excited by reading and re-reading his works. At that time I could have recited by heart whole pages of *Notre Dame de Paris*, (*The Hunchback of Notre Dame*) but it was his dramatic work that most influenced me.'

In 1851, Verne met with a fellow writer from Nantes, Pierre-Michel-François Chevalier, the editor-in-chief of the magazine *Musée des familles* (*The Family Museum*). Chevalier was looking for articles about geography, history, science, and technology, and was keen to make sure that the educational component would be made accessible to large popular audiences using a straightforward prose style or an engaging fictional story. Verne, with his delight in diligent research, especially in geography, was a natural for the job. He first offered Chevalier a short historical adventure story, 'The First Ships of the Mexican Navy', which was published in July 1851, but more significantly in the same year there came a second short story, 'A Voyage in a Balloon' which, with its combination of adventurous narrative, travel themes, and detailed historical research, would later be described by Verne as 'the first indication of the line of novel that I was destined to follow'.

His later collaboration with the publisher Pierre-Jules Hetzel led to the creation of *Les Voyages Extraordinaires*, a widely popular series of scrupulously researched adventure novels. Hetzel, already the publisher of such authors as Balzac, George Sand and Victor Hugo, had long been planning to launch a high-quality family magazine in which entertaining fiction would combine with scientific education. He saw Verne, with his wild detailed imagination, as an ideal contributor for such a magazine. Verne's first effort, *Five Weeks in a Balloon*, an extended version of his earlier short story, was published by Hetzel in January 1863. It is with this first novel that Verne perfected the 'ingredients' of his later work, skilfully mixing a plot full of adventure and twists that hold the reader's interest with passages of technical, geographic, and historic description. The book gives readers a glimpse of the exploration of Africa, which as 'the dark continent' was still little known to Europeans of the time. Public interest in fanciful tales of African exploration was at its height, and the book was an instant hit; it made Verne financially independent.

For the rest of his lifetime, most of Verne's novels would be serialized in Hetzel's magazine before their appearance in book form, beginning with his second novel, *The Adventures of Captain Hatteras* (1864–5). This is one of the author's lesser known works but it has all the daring hallmarks of his more famous titles. The plot concerns Captain John Hatteras's obsession with the challenge of reaching the North Pole. Experiencing appalling cold and hunger, the captain treks across the frozen wastes encountering endless perils and adventures until he attains his goal. The novel contains well-researched fascinating details about the Arctic expeditions that captivated Verne's imagination. In 1912 a version of the book was filmed by the innovative French director, Georges Méliès.

When *The Adventures of Captain Hatteras* was published in book form, Hetzel publicly announced his literary and educational ambitions for Verne's novels by saying rather grandly in a preface that they would form an unusual sequence in which Verne's aim was 'to outline all the geographical, geological, physical, and astronomical knowledge amassed by modern science and to recount, in an entertaining and picturesque format that is his own, the history of the universe.' Late in life, Verne confirmed that this commission had become the running theme of his novels: 'My object has been to depict the earth, and not the earth alone, but the universe... And I have tried at the same time to realize a very high ideal of beauty of style. It is said that there can't be any style in a novel of adventure, but it isn't true.'

Exploration was also the theme of Verne's next novel, *Journey to the Centre of the Earth* (1864) but this time there was a strong fantasy element to the narrative and it can be regarded as his first true science fiction tale. The story involves German professor Otto Lidenbrock who believes there are volcanic tubes leading down toward the centre of the Earth. Along with his nephew Axel and their guide Hans, he descends into the Icelandic volcano Snæfellsjökull, encountering many adventures, including prehistoric animals and natural hazards, before eventually rising to the surface again in southern Italy, at the Stromboli volcano. It is a story that has continued to fascinate readers, and indeed film makers. There have been at least six film versions as well as a number of radio and TV adaptations, including an animated series for American television.

The range of Verne's books is remarkable. He wrote about space, air, and underwater travel before navigable aircraft and practical submarines were invented, and before any means of space travel had been devised. Verne himself flatly denied that he was a futuristic prophet, however, saying that any connection between scientific developments and his work was 'mere coincidence', attributing his indisputable scientific accuracy to his extensive research: 'even before I began writing stories, I always took numerous notes out of every book, newspaper, magazine, or scientific report that I came across.'

The third in his series of *Voyages Extraordinaires* novels was *From the Earth to the Moon* (1865). In this novel Verne really allowed his fantastic imagination full rein. The story concerns two Americans and a

Frenchman who are launched into orbit from the muzzle of an enormous gun embedded in the ground on the coast of Florida. The story has certain remarkable aspects to it. Verne attempted to do some rough calculations as to the requirements for the cannon and, considering the total lack of any data on the subject at the time, a great number of his calculations are surprisingly close to reality. The author shows amazing prescience in some of the details in the novel. Verne's cannon was called Columbiad and when the Apollo 11 space mission set off for the moon in 1969 the command module was named Columbia. This was manned by three astronauts including Neil Armstrong, the first man to set foot on the moon, the same complement as in the novel. Verne's rocket base is in 'Tampa Town' in Florida, just the other side of the peninsula to Cape Canaveral. *From the Earth to the Moon* is more of an adventurous romp than a gripping drama but it is a significant work in the annals of science fiction.

Surprisingly it took Verne three years to write a follow-up novel, *Around the Moon* (1868). Actually this work is less of a sequel, rather a completion of the original tale. It recounts the travellers' experiences on reaching the moon and how they returned to Earth.

One example of how Verne's creative visionary mind could break through the confines of his own time is found in his novel *Paris in the Twentieth Century*, written in 1863. It is about a young man who lives in a world of glass skyscrapers, high-speed trains, gas-powered automobiles, calculators, and a worldwide communications network, yet cannot find happiness and who comes to a tragic end. Hetzel thought the novel's pessimism would damage Verne's blossoming career, and suggested that he wait twenty years to publish it. Reluctantly Verne agreed, stored the manuscript away in a safe and appeared to have forgotten all about it. It was discovered by his great-grandson in 1989 and the long-lost novel was first published in 1994.

The relationship between publisher and writer changed significantly around 1869, when Verne and Hetzel were brought into conflict over the manuscript for *Twenty Thousand Leagues Under the Sea*. Verne had initially conceived the submariner Captain Nemo as a Polish scientist whose acts of vengeance were directed against the Russians who had killed his family during the January Uprising. Hetzel, not wanting to alienate the lucrative Russian market for Verne's books, demanded that Nemo be made an enemy of the slave trade, a situation that would make him an unambiguous hero. Verne, after fighting vehemently against the change, finally settled on a compromise in which Nemo's past was shrouded in mystery.

The plot of this novel concerns French naturalist Dr Aronnax who joins an expedition to hunt down a sea monster that is attacking ships, only to discover that the creature is in fact the *Nautilus*, a remarkable submarine built by the enigmatic Captain Nemo. Together Nemo and Aronnax explore the underwater marvels, undergo a transcendent experience among the ruins of Atlantis, and plant a black flag at the South Pole. Nemo reappeared in a later novel, *The Mysterious Island* (1875).

In 1873, Verne penned what some believe was his greatest novel, *Around the World in 80 Days*. It certainly has maintained its popularity over the years and has been the subject of numerous film versions – the earliest being produced in 1919 – as well as a number of stage adaptations and even a couple of musicals. In the novel, Phileas Fogg of London and his newly employed French valet Passepartout attempt to circumnavigate the world in eighty days on a £20,000 wager set by his friends at the Reform Club. Strictly speaking, the novel is an adventure yarn rather than a science fiction tale but does involve many of the innovations of the 19th century. In particular, the novel involves three technological breakthroughs which occurred in 1869–70 that made an around-the-world journey possible for the first time: the completion of the first Transcontinental Railroad in America (1869), the linking of the Indian railways across the sub-continent (1870), and the opening of the Suez Canal (1869). These were notable developments that marked the start of an age of fully global tourism that could be enjoyed in relative comfort and safety. The novel sparked the imagination, suggesting that anyone could sit down, draw up a schedule, buy tickets, and travel around the world, a feat previously reserved for only the most heroic and hardy of adventurers.

Verne remained prolific throughout the 1870s, writing *The Adventures of a Special Correspondent* (1872), *The Survivors of the Chancellor* (1875), *Michael Strogoff* (1876), and *Dick Sand, A Captain at Fifteen* (1878), among several others.

After Verne's long run with personal and professional success, the 1880s proved to be less kind. In 1886, Verne's favourite nephew, Gaston, attempted to murder him. He fired two shots from a pistol, and one stuck Verne's shin, giving him a limp for the rest of his life. Gaston turned out to be suffering from mental illness and was committed to mental institution. A week after Verne was shot, Hetzel died—an event that devastated the author. To add to his misery, Verne's mother died the following year.

Verne did, however, continue to travel and write. His last truly science fiction novels were *Robur the Conqueror* (1886) and its sequel *Master of the World* (1904). In the first novel, after a series of mysterious and fantastic planting of black flags on top of the world's tallest monuments, a man named Robur is revealed to have mastered the secret of flight. To demonstrate fully the capabilities of his huge rotocraft, the *Albatross*, Robur kidnaps three sceptics from a flight enthusiasts' club, the Weldon Institute. What follows is three-week trip around the world where the three kidnapped men come to realize that Robur's brilliance teeters dangerously close to madness. By turns an impassioned argument for aviation, a wild proto-steampunk adventure, and a jubilant celebration of the dream of flight, *Robur the Conqueror* ranks among Jules Verne's most iconic and influential works. Its technological speculations, including the unforgettable aircraft the *Albatross*, are a vibrant snapshot of nineteenth-century scientific innovation. In the sequel, *Master of the World*, Robur has perfected a new machine, which he has dubbed the *Terror*. It is a 10-metre (30-foot) long vehicle, capable of operating as a speedboat, submarine, automobile and aircraft. It can travel at the (then) unheard-of speed of 240 kilometres (150 miles) per hour on land and at more than 320 kilometres (200 miles) per hour when flying.

While writing this book Verne was suffering with diabetes, a disease that eventually overcame him. He died at his home in Amiens, France in 1905.

The works of Jules Verne continues to fascinate readers and, of course, the cinema has made full use of Verne's stories. So many fantasy films involving weird and wonderful locations, strange encounters and exciting incidents continue to be influenced by the magic pen of this great and innovative writer. Certainly Jules Verne did not just write about what he knew – he created fantastic narratives from his very fertile imagination and, although modern science has superseded much of what he wrote about, the stories, the landscapes, and the characters still manage to enthrall us today.

Principal Characters

Professor Pierre Aronnax is the novel's protagonist and narrator. This expert professor of marine biology now lives in New York but remains a loyal French citizen. He is an astute intellectual and scholar, totally fascinated by the oceans and sea life. He believes that the mysterious 'beast' plaguing the oceans is more likely to be a great narwhal than a monster or submarine. In general, Aronnax understands only what he knows for certain; anything beyond his knowledge and prior experience is deemed unlikely or unreal. Once aboard the Nautilus, he is torn: should he flee back to the surface or remain so he can learn more amazing underwater secrets? The professor's intent is not merely the acquisition of greater understanding but the opportunity to take this new knowledge to the world at large – and thus achieve fame and glory. He is paralysed by indecision, but ultimately Nemo's ruthless destruction of a warship spurs Aronnax into action, as the professor abhors this massacre of its innocent crew.

Captain Nemo is son of an Indian Raja, and a scientific genius; he roams the under-water ocean world in the *Nautilus*, the incredible submarine he has created. He is an extraordinarily multi-talented engineer, responsible for building the vessel's electric propulsion and navigation systems. He is expert at underwater navigation, able to negotiate submarine passages under the Suez isthmus and the Antarctic ice sheet. In Verne's original text, Captain Nemo is depicted as a Polish nobleman avenging his family slain by the Russians, but Verne's publisher

(for political reasons) insisted that Nemo's motivation become instead the 1857 suppression of the Indian Mutiny, in which the captain's family have been killed by the British. From his first appearance, it is clear that Captain Nemo is stern, reticent, sinister – and potentially dangerous. He is, however, clearly a champion of the natural world and willing to help the underdog. Aged some forty years, he is tall and swarthy, with wide-set eyes and a straight nose. He will use only products from the sea, whether as food, tobacco, clothing or furniture. Nemo believes that the laws of the world on the surface no longer apply to him. This is a mysterious and complex man, gradually revealed to be full of contra-dictions: a terrifying, vengeful maniac but also one who suffers great guilt over the deaths of enemy sailors as well as those of his own crew members.

Ned Land is originally from Quebec in Canada, and both a land hunter and a harpooner who has been on many fishing expeditions. He is a man of action; he is good with his hands and has excellent vision. Aboard the *Abraham Lincoln*, he makes friends with Professor Pierre Aronnax. Able to identify many fish species, he helps Aronnax with his underwater observations. He is constantly planning to escape from the *Nautilus*. He abhors Nemo's whale slaughter saying, 'This was just butchers' work.' Despite being Nemo's chief adversary, he saves the captain from a shark attack. Ned ends up suffering from claustrophobia, almost to the point of suicide, but then manages to escape when the *Nautilus* is caught in the Maelstrom tidal current swirl.

Conseil has been Professor Aronnax's incredibly loyal servant for ten years. He saves Aronnax from drowning when his beloved master is knocked overboard by the *Nautilus*. Aged thirty, Conseil is Flemish, very strong, in good health, practical and clever with his hands. He is hard working, down-to-earth, good-natured and stoical with a good sense of humour. He befriends Ned Land, whose cabin he shares on the *Nautilus*. Conseil takes part in expeditions outside the submarine and also spends much time trying to classify fish. Conseil eats an electric ray that had stung him – and enjoys this revenge, despite its tasting like leather! He is eager to escape and ends up being rescued by fishermen from the Norwegian Loffoden Islands.

Captain Farragut is an officer in the American Navy, captain of the *Abraham Lincoln*, a high-speed frigate. Aronnax tells us that the captain had one thing on his mind: 'Either [he] would kill the narwhal or the narwhal would kill [him]. There could be no middle course.' Believing that they're approaching a sleeping narwhal, Farragut orders: 'Damn the torpedoes – full speed ahead!' The *Abraham Lincoln* rams what turns out to be a double-hulled submarine but, despite their efforts, the crew cannot halt Nemo's mechanical monster.

Captain Anderson commands the *Scotia*, a passenger vessel that is damaged by the *Nautilus* (then thought to be a sea monster) on 13 April 1867 when a large hole is rammed into the ship's hull. The vessel does not sink and Anderson decides that the ship can continue her course, despite her paddles being half submerged. Captain Anderson remains calm in the crisis, reassuring his passengers and overseeing the ship's safe passage into harbour. This event is invoked by the US mission to search for the *Nautilus* in the *Abraham Lincoln*.

Sir Samuel Cunard is a renowned Canadian ship-owner and heads up the prestigious Cunard Line. When Cunard's vessel, *Scotia*, is attacked by the *Nautilus* this causes worldwide outrage. As Verne explains in the first chapter, 'No ocean-going company has been run with greater skill; no business crowned with greater success. During the past 26 years, Cunard ships have crossed the Atlantic 2,000 times, and never cancelled a journey, arrived behind schedule, or lost a letter, man, or vessel . . . Consequently no-one will be surprised at the stir produced by the accident to one of its finest steamships.'

A Jules Verne Timeline

1828 **1839** **1847** **1863**

Jules Verne

Enrols as a cabin boy
on the ship *Coralie*,
aged 11

*Five Weeks
in a Balloon*
published

Jules Verne born
on 8 February in Île
Feydeau, Nantes

Attends law school in
Paris; writes several
play scripts

UK and Ireland

First section
of London
Underground
Railway opens

Charles Darwin
elected fellow of
Royal Society

The Football
Association formed
in London

Charlotte Brontë's
Jane Eyre published

Europe

International
Committee of the
Red Cross founded
in Geneva

(1827)
Beethoven dies

First Daguerreotype
photographs of
Moon and a person

'Year of Revolutions',
with uprisings in
France, Germany,
Austria and Italy

President Abraham
Lincoln issues
Emancipation
Proclamation to free slaves

Rest of the World

First Opium War
between Britain
and China

President Lincoln gives
Gettysburg address

Devastating cyclone in
India destroys Coringa
city and 20,000 ships, kills
estimated 300,000 people

Liberia becomes first
African nation to
gain independence

1828 **1839** **1847** **1863**

1864

The Adventures of Captain Hatteras published

Charing Cross station opens in London

Second German–Danish War begins

Geneva Convention signed by 12 countries

1865

From the Earth to the Moon published

Lewis Carroll's *Alice in Wonderland* published

First ascent of Matterhorn

The 13th Amendment of US contitution ends slavery

1868

In Search of the Castaways published

Wilkie Collins's *The Moonstone* published

Constitution of Grand Duchy of Luxembourg adopted

First typewriter is patented in the US

1870

Twenty Thousand Leagues Under the Sea published

Married Women's Property Act allows wives to own property of their own

Franco–Prussian War begins

Guiseppe Verdi's *Aida* premieres at Cairo Opera

1864

1865

1868

1870

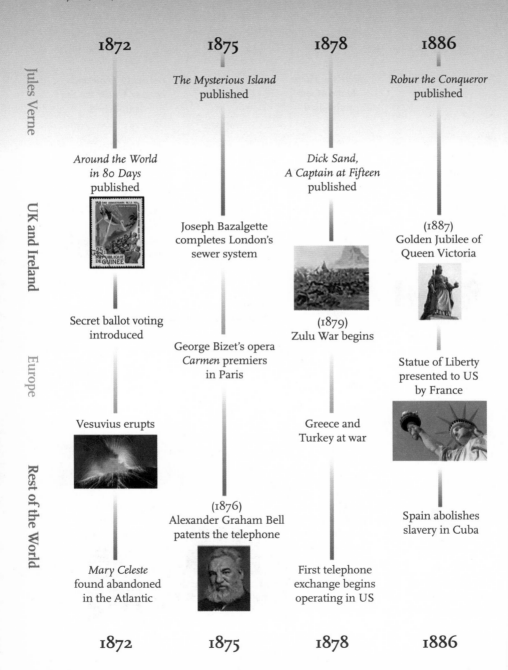

1872

Jules Verne

1875

The Mysterious Island
published

1878

1886

Robur the Conqueror
published

UK and Ireland

*Around the World
in 80 Days*
published

*Dick Sand,
A Captain at Fifteen*
published

Joseph Bazalgette
completes London's
sewer system

(1887)
Golden Jubilee of
Queen Victoria

Secret ballot voting
introduced

Europe

(1879)
Zulu War begins

George Bizet's opera
Carmen premiers
in Paris

Statue of Liberty
presented to US
by France

Vesuvius erupts

Greece and
Turkey at war

Rest of the World

(1876)
Alexander Graham Bell
patents the telephone

Spain abolishes
slavery in Cuba

Mary Celeste
found abandoned
in the Atlantic

First telephone
exchange begins
operating in US

1872

1875

1878

1886

1892

1897

An Antarctic Mystery published

1905

1994

Paris in the Twentieth Century published (written 1863)

Dies on 24 March and is buried in Amiens

Carpathian Castle published

Channel Tunnel opens

Oscar Wilde's *Lady Windermere's Fan* premieres

Guglielmo Marconi sends first ever wireless communication

Emmeline Pankhurst leads first public protest by suffragettes at Westminster

Last Russian troops leave Germany

Anti-Jewish violence in Bucharest, Romania

Allied occupation of Berlin ends

Vincent Van Gogh shoots himself

Bloody Sunday massacre of peaceful demonstrators in Russia

Yasser Arafat, Shimon Peres and Yitzhak Rabin awarded Nobel Peace Price

Klondike Gold Rush begins

Nelson Mandela inaugurated as South Africa's first black president

Thomas Edison patents first movie projector

Albert Einstein formulates theory of relativity

General Electrical Company incorporated in New York

Official opening of Trans-Siberian Railway

1892

1897

1905

1994

The route of the *Nautilus*

Twenty Thousand Leagues Under the Sea

PART 1

Chapter I
A Shifting Reef

The year 1866 was signalised by a remarkable incident, a mysterious and inexplicable phenomenon, which doubtless no one has yet forgotten. Not to mention rumours which agitated the maritime population, and excited the public mind, even in the interior of continents, seafaring men were particularly excited. Merchants, common sailors, captains of vessels, skippers, both of Europe and America, naval officers of all countries, and the Governments of several states on the two continents, were deeply interested in the matter.

For some time past, vessels had been met by "an enormous thing," a long object, spindle-shaped, occasionally phosphorescent, and infinitely larger and more rapid in its movements than a whale.

The facts relating to this apparition (entered in various log-books) agreed in most respects as to the shape of the object or creature in question, the untiring rapidity of its movements, its surprising power of locomotion, and the peculiar life with which it seemed endowed. If it was a cetacean, it surpassed in size all those hitherto classified in science. Taking into consideration the mean of observations made at divers times,—rejecting the timid estimate of those who assigned to this object a length of two hundred feet, equally with the exaggerated opinions which set it down as a mile in width and three in length,—we might fairly conclude that this mysterious being surpassed greatly all dimensions admitted by the ichthyologists of the day, if it existed at all. And that it *did* exist was an undeniable fact; and, with that tendency which disposes the human mind in favour of the marvellous, we can understand the excitement produced in the entire world by this supernatural apparition. As to classing it in the list of fables, the idea was out of the question.

On the 20th of July 1866, the steamer *Governor Higginson*, of the Calcutta and Burnach Steam Navigation Company, had met this moving mass five miles off the east coast of Australia. Captain Baker thought at first that he was in the presence of an unknown sandbank; he even prepared to determine its exact position, when two columns of water, projected by the inexplicable object, shot with a hissing noise a hundred and fifty feet up into the air. Now, unless the sandbank had been submitted to the intermittent eruption of a geyser, the *Governor Higginson* had to do neither more nor less than with an aquatic mammal, unknown till then, which threw up from its blow-holes columns of water mixed with air and vapour.

Similar facts were observed on the 23rd of July in the same year, in the Pacific Ocean, by the *Columbus*, of the West India and Pacific Steam Navigation Company. But this extraordinary cetaceous creature could transport itself from one place to another with surprising velocity; as, in an interval of three days, the *Governor Higginson* and the *Columbus* had observed it at two different points of the chart, separated by a distance of more than seven hundred nautical leagues.

Fifteen days later, two thousand miles farther off, the *Helvetia*, of the Compagnie-Nationale, and the *Shannon*, of the Royal Mail Steamship Company, sailing to windward in that portion of the Atlantic lying between the United States and Europe, respectively signalled the monster to each other in 42° 15' N. lat. and 60° 35' W. long. In these simultaneous observations, they thought themselves justified in estimating the minimum length of the mammal at more than three hundred and fifty feet, as the *Shannon* and *Helvetia* were of smaller dimensions than it, though they measured three hundred feet over all.

Now the largest whales, those which frequent those parts of the sea round the Aleutian, Kulammak, and Umgullich islands, have never exceeded the length of sixty yards, if they attain that.

These reports arriving one after the other, with fresh observations made on board the transatlantic ship *Pereira*, a collision which occurred between the *Etna* of the Inman line and the monster, a *procés verbal* directed by the officers of the French frigate *Normandie*, a very accurate survey made by the staff of Commodore Fitz-James on board the *Lord Clyde*, greatly influenced public opinion. Light-thinking people jested upon the phenomenon, but grave practical countries, such as England, America, and Germany, treated the matter more seriously.

In every place of great resort the monster was the fashion. They sang of it in the cafés, ridiculed it in the papers, and represented it on the stage. All kinds of stories were circulated regarding it. There appeared in the papers caricatures of every gigantic and imaginary creature, from the white whale, the terrible "Moby Dick" of hyperborean regions, to the immense kraken whose tentacles could entangle a ship of five hundred tons, and hurry it into the abyss of the ocean. The legends of ancient times were even resuscitated, and the opinions of Aristotle and Pliny revived, who admitted the existence of these monsters, as well as the Norwegian tales of Bishop Pontoppidan, the accounts of Paul Heggede, and, last of all, the reports of Mr Harrington (whose good faith no one could suspect), who affirmed that, being on board the *Castillan*, in 1857, he had seen this enormous serpent, which had never until that time frequented any other seas but those of the ancient "*Constitutionel.*"

Then burst forth the interminable controversy between the credulous and the incredulous in the societies of savants and scientific journals. "The question of the monster" inflamed all minds. Editors of scientific journals, quarrelling with believers in the supernatural, spilled seas of ink during this memorable campaign, some even drawing blood; for, from the sea-serpent, they came to direct personalities.

For six months war was waged with various fortune in the leading articles of the Geographical Institution of Brazil, the Royal Academy of Science of Berlin, the British Association, the Smithsonian Institution of Washington, in the discussions of the "Indian Archipelago," of the Cosmos of the Abbé Moigno, in the Mittheilungen of Petermann, in the scientific chronicles of the great journals of France and other countries. The cheaper journals replied keenly and with inexhaustible zest. These satirical writers parodied a remark of Linnaeus, quoted by the adversaries of the monster, maintaining "that nature did not make fools," and adjured their contemporaries not to give the lie to nature, by admitting the existence of krakens, sea-serpents, "Moby Dicks," and other lucubrations of delirious sailors. At length an article in a well-known satirical journal by a favourite contributor, the chief of the staff, settled the monster, like Hippolytus, giving it the death-blow amidst an universal burst of laughter. Wit had conquered science.

During the first months of the year 1867, the question seemed buried never to revive, when new facts were brought before the public. It was then no longer a scientific problem to be solved, but a real danger seriously to be avoided. The question took quite another shape. The monster became a small island, a rock, a reef, but a reef of indefinite and shifting proportions.

On the 5th of March 1867, the *Moravian*, of the Montreal Ocean Company, finding herself during the night in 27° 30' lat. and 72° 15' long., struck on her starboard quarter a rock, marked in no chart for that part of the sea. Under the combined efforts of the wind and its four hundred horse-power, it was going at the rate of thirteen knots. Had it not been for the superior strength of the hull of the *Moravian*, she would have been broken by the shock and gone down with the 237 passengers she was bringing home from Canada.

The accident happened about five o'clock in the morning, as the day was breaking. The officers of the quarter-deck hurried to the after-part of the vessel. They examined the sea with the most scrupulous attention. They saw nothing but a strong eddy about three cables' length distant, as if the surface has been violently agitated. The bearings of the place were taken exactly, and the *Moravian* continued its route without apparent damage. Had it struck on a sub-merged rock, or an an enormous wreck? they could not tell; but on examination of the ship's bottom when undergoing repairs, it was found that part of her keel was broken.

This fact, so grave in itself, might perhaps have been forgotten like many others, if, three weeks after, it had not been re-enacted under similar circumstances. But, thanks to the nationality of the victim of the shock, thanks to the reputation of the company to which the vessel belonged, the circumstance became extensively circulated.

The 13th of April 1867, the sea being beautiful, the breeze favour-able, the *Scotia* of the Cunard Company's line, found herself in 15° 12' long. and 45° 37' lat. She was going at the speed of thirteen knots and a half.

At seventeen minutes past four in the afternoon, whilst the passen-gers were assembled at lunch in the great saloon, a slight shock was felt on the hull of the *Scotia*, on her quarter, a little aft of the port-paddle.

The *Scotia* had not struck, but she had been struck, and seemingly by something rather sharp and penetrating than blunt. The shock had been so slight that no one had been alarmed, had it not been for the shouts of the carpenter's watch, who rushed on to the bridge exclaiming, "We are sinking! we are sinking!" At first the passengers were much frightened, but Captain Anderson hastened to reassure them. The danger could not be imminent. The *Scotia*, divided into seven compartments by strong partitions, could brave with impunity any leak. Captain Anderson went down immediately into the hold. He found that the sea was pouring into the fifth compartment; and the rapidity of the influx proved that the force of the water was consid-erable. Fortunately this compartment did not hold the boilers, or the fires would have been immediately extinguished. Captain Anderson ordered the engines to be stopped at once, and one of the men went down to ascertain the extent of the injury. Some minutes afterwards they discovered the existence of a large hole, of two yards in diameter, in the ship's bottom. Such a leak could not be stopped; and the *Scotia*, her paddles half submerged, was obliged to continue her course. She was then three hundred miles from Cape Clear, and after three days' delay, which caused great uneasiness in Liverpool, she entered the basin of the company.

The engineers visited the *Scotia*, which was put in dry dock. They could scarcely believe it possible; at two yards and a half below water-mark was a regular rent, in the form of an isosceles triangle. The broken place in the iron plates was so perfectly defined, that it could not have been more neatly done by a punch. It was clear, then, that the instrument producing the perforation was not of a common stamp; and after having been driven with prodigious strength, and piercing an iron plate 1¾ inches thick, had withdrawn itself by a retrograde motion truly inexplicable.

Such was the last fact, which resulted in exciting once more the torrent of public opinion. From this moment all unlucky casualties which could not be otherwise accounted for were put down to the monster.

Upon this imaginary creature rested the responsibility of all these shipwrecks, which unfortunately were considerable; for of three thousand ships whose loss was annually recorded at Lloyds', the number of sailing and steam ships supposed to be totally lost, from the absence of all news, amounted to not less than two hundred!

Now, it was the "monster" who, justly or unjustly, was accused of their disappearance, and, thanks to it, communication between the different continents became more and more dangerous. The public demanded peremptorily that the seas should at any price be relieved from this formidable cetacean.

Chapter II
Pro and Con

At the period when these events took place, I had just returned from a scientific research in the disagreeable territory of Nebraska, in the United States. In virtue of my office as Assistant Professor in the Museum of Natural History in Paris, the French Government had attached me to that expedition. After six months in Nebraska, I arrived in New York towards the end of March, laden with a precious collection. My departure for France was fixed for the first days in May. Meanwhile, I was occupying myself in classifying my mineralogical, botanical, and zoological riches, when the accident happened to the *Scotia*.

I was perfectly up in the subject which was the question of the day. How could I be otherwise? I had read and re-read all the American and European papers without being any nearer a conclusion. This mystery puzzled me. Under the impossibility of forming an opinion, I jumped from one extreme to the other. That there really was something could not be doubted, and the incredulous were invited to put their finger on the wound of the *Scotia*.

On my arrival at New York, the question was at its height. The hypothesis of the floating island, and the unapproachable sandbank, supported by minds little competent to form a judgment, was abandoned. And, indeed, unless this shoal had a machine in its stomach, how could it change its position with such astonishing rapidity?

From the same cause, the idea of a floating hull of an enormous wreck was given up.

There remained then only two possible solutions of the question, which created two distinct parties: on one side, those who were for a monster of colossal strength; on the other, those who were for a submarine vessel of enormous motive power.

But this last hypothesis, plausible as it was, could not stand against inquiries made in both worlds. That a private gentleman should have such a machine at his command was not likely. Where, when, and how was it built? and how could its construction have been kept secret? Certainly a Government might possess such a destructive machine. And in these disastrous times, when the ingenuity of man has multiplied the power of weapons of war, it was possible that, without the knowledge of others, a state might try to work such a formidable engine. After the chassepots came the torpedoes, after the torpedoes the submarine rams, then—the reaction. At least, I hope so.

But the hypothesis of a war machine fell before the declaration of Governments. As public interest was in question, and transatlantic communications suffered, their veracity could not be doubted. But, how admit that the construction of this submarine boat had escaped the public eye? For a private gentleman to keep the secret under such circumstances would be very difficult, and for a state whose every act is persistently watched by powerful rivals, certainly impossible.

After inquiries made in England, France, Russia, Prussia, Spain, Italy, and America, even in Turkey, the hypothesis of a submarine monitor was definitely rejected.

Upon my arrival in New York several persons did me the honour of consulting me on the phenomenon in question. I had published in France a work in quarto, in two volumes, entitled, "Mysteries of the Great Submarine Grounds." This book, highly approved of in the learned world, gained for me a special reputation in this rather obscure branch of Natural History. My advice was asked. As long as I could deny the reality of the fact, I confined myself to a decided negative. But soon finding myself driven into a corner, I was obliged to explain myself categorically. And even "the Honourable Pierre Aronnax, Professor in the Museum of Paris," was called upon by the *New York Herald* to express a definite opinion of some sort. I did something.

I spoke, for want of power to hold my tongue. I discussed the question in all its forms, politically and scientifically; and I give here an extract from a carefully-studied article which I published in the number of the 30th of April. It ran as follows:—

"After examining one by one the different hypotheses, rejecting all other suggestions, it becomes necessary to admit the existence of a marine animal of enormous power.

"The great depths of the ocean are entirely unknown to us. Soundings cannot reach them. What passes in those remote depths—what beings live, or can live, twelve or fifteen miles beneath the surface of the waters—what is the organisation of these animals, we can scarcely conjecture. However, the solution of the problem submitted to me may modify the form of the dilemma. Either we do know all the varieties of beings which people our planet, or we do not. If we do *not* know them all—if Nature has still secrets in ichthyology for us, nothing is more conformable to reason than to admit the existence of fishes, or cetaceans of other kinds, or even of new species, of an organisation formed to inhabit the strata inaccessible to soundings, and which an accident of some sort, either fantastical or capricious, has brought at long intervals to the upper level of the ocean.

"If, on the contrary, we *do* know all living kinds, we must necessarily seek for the animal in question amongst those marine beings already classed; and, in that case, I should be disposed to admit the existence of a gigantic narwhal.

"The common narwhal, or unicorn of the sea, often attains a length of sixty feet. Increase its size fivefold or tenfold, give it strength proportionate to its size, lengthen its destructive weapons, and you obtain the animal required. It will have the proportions determined by the officers of the *Shannon*, the instrument required by the perforation of the *Scotia*, and the power necessary to pierce the hull of the steamer.

"Indeed the narwhal is armed with a sort of ivory sword, a halberd, according to the expression of certain naturalists. The principal tusk has the hardness of steel. Some of these tusks have been found buried in the bodies of whales, which the unicorn always attacks with

9

success. Others have been drawn out, not without trouble, from the bottom of ships, which they had pierced through and through, as a gimlet pierces a barrel. The Museum of the Faculty of Medicine of Paris possesses one of these defensive weapons, two yards and a quarter in length, and fifteen inches in diameter at the base.

"Very well! suppose this weapon to be six times stronger, and the animal ten times more powerful; launch it at the rate of twenty miles an hour, and you obtain a shock capable of producing the catastrophe required. Until further information, therefore, I shall maintain it to be a sea-unicorn of colossal dimensions, armed, not with a halberd, but with a real spur, as the armoured frigates, or the "rams" of war, whose massiveness and motive power it would possess at the same time. Thus may this inexplicable phenomenon be explained, unless there be something over and above all that one has ever conjectured, seen, perceived, or experienced; which is just within the bounds of possibility."

These last words were cowardly on my part; but, up to a certain point, I wished to shelter my dignity as Professor, and not give too much cause for laughter to the Americans, who laugh well when they do laugh. I reserved for myself a way of escape: In effect, however, I admitted the existence of the "monster." My article was warmly discussed, which procured it a high reputation. It rallied round it a certain number of partisans. The solution it proposed gave, at least, full liberty to the imagination. The human mind delights in grand conceptions of supernatural beings. And the sea is precisely their best vehicle, the only medium through which these giants (against which terrestrial animals, such as elephants or rhinoceroses, are as nothing), can be produced or developed.

The industrial and commercial papers treated the question chiefly from this point of view. The *Shipping and Mercantile Gazette*, the *Lloyds' List*, the *Packet-Boat*, and the *Maritime and Colonial Review*, all papers devoted to insurance companies which threatened to raise their rates of premium, were unanimous on this point. Public opinion had been pronounced. The United States were the first in the field; and in New York they made preparations for an expedition destined to pursue this narwhal. A frigate of great speed, the *Abraham*

Lincoln, was put in commission as soon as possible. The arsenals were opened to Commander Farragut, who hastened the arming of his frigate; but, as it always happens, the moment it was decided to pursue the monster, the monster did not appear. For two months no one heard it spoken of. No ship met with it. It seemed as if this unicorn knew of the plots weaving around it. It had been so much talked of, even through the Atlantic cable, that jesters pretended that this slender fly had stopped a telegram on its passage, and was making the most of it.

So when the frigate had been armed for a long campaign, and provided with formidable fishing apparatus, no one could tell what course to pursue. Impatience grew apace, when, on the 2nd of July, they learned that a steamer of the line of San Francisco, from California to Shanghai, had seen the animal three weeks before in the North Pacific Ocean. The excitement caused by this news was extreme. The ship was revictualled and well stocked with coal.

Three hours before the *Abraham Lincoln* left Brooklyn pier, I received a letter worded as follows:—

"To M. ARONNAX, Professor in the Museum of Paris,
"Fifth Avenue Hotel, New York.

"SIR,
If you will consent to join the *Abraham Lincoln* in this expedition, the Government of the United States will with pleasure see France represented in the enterprise. Commander Farragut has a cabin at your disposal.

Very cordially yours, J. B. Hobson.
"SECRETARY OF MARINE."

Chapter III

I Form My Resolution

Three seconds before the arrival of J. B. Hobson's letter, I no more thought of pursuing the unicorn than of attempting the passage of the North Sea. Three seconds after reading the letter of the honourable Secretary of Marine, I felt that my true vocation, the sole end of my life, was to chase this disturbing monster, and purge it from the world.

But I had just returned from a fatiguing journey, weary and longing for repose. I aspired to nothing more than again seeing my country, my friends, my little lodging by the Jardin des Plantes, my dear and precious collections. But nothing could keep me back! I forgot all— fatigue, friends, and collections—and accepted without hesitation the offer of the American Government.

"Besides," thought I, "all roads lead back to Europe; and the unicorn may be amiable enough to hurry me towards the coast of France. This worthy animal may allow itself to be caught in the seas of Europe (for my particular benefit), and I will not bring back less than half a yard of his ivory halberd to the Museum of Natural History." But in the meanwhile I must seek this narwhal in the North Pacific Ocean, which, to return to France, was taking the road to the antipodes.

"Conseil," I called, in an impatient voice.

Conseil was my servant, a true, devoted Flemish boy, who had accompanied me in all my travels. I liked him, and he returned the liking well. He was phlegmatic by nature, regular from principle, zealous from habit, evincing little disturbance at the different surprises of life, very quick with his hands, and apt at any service required of him; and, despite his name, never giving advice—even when asked for it.

Conseil had followed me for the last ten years wherever science led. Never once did he complain of the length or fatigue of a journey, never make an objection to pack his portmanteau for whatever country it might be, or however far away, whether China or Congo. Besides all this, he had good health, which defied all sickness, and solid muscles, but no nerves; good morals are understood. This boy was thirty years old, and his age to that of his master as fifteen to twenty. May I be excused for saying that I was forty years old?

But Conseil had one fault, he was ceremonious to a degree, and would never speak to me but in the third person, which was sometimes provoking.

"Conseil," said I again, beginning with feverish hands to make preparations for my departure.

Certainly I was sure of this devoted boy. As a rule, I never asked him if it were convenient for him or not to follow me in my travels; but this time the expedition in question might be prolonged, and the enterprise might be hazardous in pursuit of an animal capable of sinking a frigate as easily as a nutshell. Here there was matter for reflection even to the most impassive man in the world. What would Conseil say?

"Conseil," I called a third time.

Conseil appeared.

"Did you call, sir?" said he, entering.

"Yes, my boy; make preparations for me and yourself too. We leave in two hours."

"As you please, sir," replied Conseil, quietly.

"Not an instant to lose;—lock in my trunk all travelling utensils, coats, shirts, and stockings—without counting, as many as you can, and make haste."

"And your collections, sir?" observed Conseil.

"We will think of them by and by."

"What! the archiotherium, the hyracotherium, the oreodons, the cheropotamus, and the other skins?"

"They will keep them at the hotel."

"And your live Babiroussa, sir?"

"They will feed it during our absence; besides, I will give orders to forward our menagerie to France."

"We are not returning to Paris, then?" said Conseil.

"Oh! certainly," I answered, evasively, "by making a curve."

"Will the curve please you, sir?"

"Oh! it will be nothing; not quite so direct a road, that is all. We take our passage in the *Abraham Lincoln*."

"As you think proper, sir," coolly replied Conseil.

"You see, my friend, it has to do with the monster—the famous narwhal. We are going to purge it from the seas. The author of a work in quarto, in two volumes, on the 'Mysteries of the Great Submarine Grounds' cannot forbear embarking with Commander Farragut. A glorious mission, but a dangerous one! We cannot tell where we may go; these animals can be very capricious. But we will go whether or no; we have got a captain who is pretty wideawake."

I opened a credit account for Babiroussa, and, Conseil following, I jumped into a cab. Our luggage was transported to the deck of the frigate immediately. I hastened on board and asked for Commander Farragut. One of the sailors conducted me to the poop, where I found myself in the presence of a good-looking officer, who held out his hand to me.

"Monsieur Pierre Aronnax?" said he.

"Himself," replied I; "Commander Farragut?"

"You are welcome, Professor; your cabin is ready for you."

I bowed, and desired to be conducted to the cabin destined for me.

The *Abraham Lincoln* had been well chosen and equipped for her new destination. She was a frigate of great speed, fitted with high-pressure engines which admitted a pressure of seven atmospheres. Under this the *Abraham Lincoln* attained the mean speed of nearly eighteen knots and a third an hour—a considerable speed, but, nevertheless, insufficient to grapple with this gigantic cetacean.

The interior arrangements of the frigate corresponded to its nautical qualities. I was well satisfied with my cabin, which was in the after part, opening upon the gunroom.

"We shall be well off here," said I to Conseil.

"As well, by your honour's leave, as a hermit-crab in the shell of a whelk," said Conseil.

I left Conseil to stow our trunks conveniently away, and remounted the poop in order to survey the preparations for departure.

At that moment Commander Farragut was ordering the last moorings to be cast loose which held the *Abraham Lincoln* to the pier of Brooklyn. So in a quarter of an hour, perhaps less, the frigate would have sailed without me. I should have missed this extraordinary, supernatural, and incredible expedition, the recital of which may well meet with some scepticism.

But Commander Farragut would not lose a day nor an hour in scouring the seas in which the animal had been sighted. He sent for the engineer.

"Is the steam full on?" asked he.

"Yes, sir," replied the engineer.

"Go a-head," cried Commander Farragut.

The quay of Brooklyn, and all that part of New York bordering on the East River, was crowded with spectators. Three cheers burst successively from five hundred thousand throats; thousands of handkerchiefs were waved above the heads of the compact mass, saluting the *Abraham Lincoln*, until she reached the water of the Hudson, at the point of that elongated peninsula which forms the town of New York. The the frigate, following the coast of New Jersey along the right bank of the beautiful river, covered with villas, passed between the forts, which saluted her with their heaviest guns. The *Abraham Lincoln* answered by hoisting the American colours three times, whose thirty-nine stars shone resplendent from the mizen-peak; then modifying its speed to take the narrow channel marked by buoys placed in the inner bay formed by Sandy Hook Point, it coasted the long sandy beach, where some thousands of spectators gave it one final cheer. The escort

15

of boats and tenders still followed the frigate, and did not leave her until they came abreast of the lightship, whose two lights marked the entrance of New York Channel.

Six bells struck, the pilot got into his boat, and rejoined the little schooner which was waiting under our lee, the fires were made up, the screw beat the waves more rapidly, the frigate skirted the low yellow coast of Long Island; and at eight bells, after having lost sight in the north-west of the lights of Fire Island, she ran at full steam on to the dark waters of the Atlantic.

Chapter IV

Ned Land

Captain Farragut was a good seaman, worthy of the frigate he commanded. His vessel and he were one. He was the soul of it. On the question of the cetacean there was no doubt in his mind, and he would not allow the existence of the animal to be disputed on board. He believed in it, as certain good women believe in the leviathan,—by faith, not by reason. The monster did exist, and he had sworn to rid the seas of it. He was a kind of Knight of Rhodes, a second Dieudonné de Gozon, going to meet the serpent which desolated the island. Either Captain Farragut would kill the narwhal, or the narwhal would kill the captain, There was no third course.

The officers on board shared the opinion of their chief. They were ever chatting, discussing, and calculating the various chances of a meeting, watching narrowly the vast surface of the ocean. More than one took up his quarters voluntarily in the cross-trees, who would have cursed such a berth under any other circumstances. As long as the sun described its daily course, the rigging was crowded with sailors, whose feet were burnt to such an extent by the heat of the deck as to render it unbearable; still the *Abraham Lincoln* had not yet breasted the suspected waters of the Pacific. As to the ship's company, they desired nothing better than to meet the unicorn, to harpoon it, hoist it on board, and despatch it. They watched the sea with eager attention.

Besides, Captain Farragut had spoken of a certain sum of two thousand dollars, set apart for whoever should first sight the monster, were he cabin-boy, common seaman, or officer.

I leave you to judge how eyes were used on board the *Abraham Lincoln.*

For my own part, I was not behind the others, and left to no one my share of daily observations. The frigate might have been called the *Argus,* for a hundred reasons. Only one amongst us, Conseil, seemed to protest by his indifference against the question which so interested us all, and seemed to be out of keeping with the general enthusiasm on board.

I have said that Captain Farragut had carefully provided his ship with every apparatus for catching the gigantic cetacean. No whaler had ever been better armed. We possessed every known engine, from the harpoon thrown by the hand to the barbed arrows of the blunder-buss, and the explosive balls of the duck-gun. On the forecastle lay the perfection of a breech-loading gun, very thick at the breech, and very narrow in the bore, the model of which had been in the Exhibition of 1867. This precious weapon of American origin could throw with ease a conical projectile of nine pounds to a mean distance of ten miles.

Thus the *Abraham Lincoln* wanted for no means of destruction; and, what was better still, she had on board Ned Land, the prince of harpooners.

Ned Land was a Canadian, with an uncommon quickness of hand, and who knew no equal in his dangerous occupation. Skill, coolness, audacity, and cunning, he possessed in a superior degree, and it must

17

be a cunning whale or a singularly "cute" cachalot to escape the stroke of his harpoon.

Ned Land was about forty years of age; he was a tall man (more than six feet high), strongly built, grave and taciturn, occasionally violent, and very passionate when contradicted. His person attracted attention, but above all the boldness of his look, which gave a singular expression to his face.

Who calls himself Canadian calls himself French; and little communicative as Ned Land was, I must admit that he took a certain liking for me. My nationality drew him to me, no doubt. It was an opportunity for him to talk, and for me to hear, that old language of Rabelais, which is still in use in some Canadian provinces. The harpooner's family was originally from Quebec, and was already a tribe of hardy fishermen when this town belonged to France.

Little by little, Ned Land acquired a taste for chatting, and I loved to hear the recital of his adventures in the polar seas. He related his fishing, and his combats, with natural poetry of expression; his recital took the form of an epic poem, and I seemed to be listening to a Canadian Homer singing the Iliad of the regions of the North.

I am portraying this hardy companion as I really knew him. We are old friends now, united in that unchangeable friendship which is born and cemented amidst extreme dangers. Ah, brave Ned! I ask no more than to live a hundred years longer, that I may have more time to dwell the longer on your memory.

Now, what was Ned Land's opinion upon the question of the marine monster? I must admit that he did not believe in the unicorn, and was the only one on board who did not share that universal conviction. He even avoided the subject, which I one day thought it my duty to press upon him. One magnificent evening, the 30th July—that is to say, three weeks after our departure—the frigate was abreast of Cape Blanc, thirty miles to leeward of the coast of Patagonia. We had crossed the tropic of Capricorn, and the Straits of Magellan opened less than seven hundred miles to the south. Before eight days were over, the *Abraham Lincoln* would be ploughing the waters of the Pacific.

Seated on the poop, Ned Land and I were chatting of one thing and another as we looked at this mysterious sea, whose great depths had up to this time been inaccessible to the eye of man. I naturally led up the conversation to the giant unicorn, and examined the various chances of success or failure of the expedition. But seeing that Ned Land let me speak without saying too much himself, I pressed him more closely.

"Well, Ned," said I, "is it possible that you are not convinced of the existence of this cetacean that we are following? Have you any particular reason for being so incredulous?"

The harpooner looked at me fixedly for some moments before answering, struck his broad forehead with his hand (a habit of his), as if to collect himself, and said at last, "Perhaps I have, Mr Aronnax."

"But, Ned, you, a whaler by profession, familiarised with all the great marine mammalia—you, whose imagination might easily accept the hypothesis of enormous cetaceans, *you* ought to be the last to doubt under such circumstances!"

"That is just what deceives you, Professor," replied Ned. "That the vulgar should believe in extraordinary comets traversing space, and in the existence of antediluvian monsters in the heart of the globe, may well be; but neither astronomers nor geologists believe in such chimeras. As a whaler, I have followed many a cetacean, harpooned a great number, and killed several; but, however strong or well-armed they may have been, neither their tails nor their weapons would have been able even to scratch the iron plates of a steamer."

"But, Ned, they tell of ships which the teeth of the narwhal has pierced through and through."

"Wooden ships—that is possible," replied the Canadian; "but I have never seen it done; and, until further proof, I deny that whales, cetaceans, or sea-unicorns could ever produce the effect you describe."

"Well, Ned, I repeat it with a conviction resting on the logic of facts. I believe in the existence of a mammal powerfully organised, belonging to the branch of vertebrata, like the whales, the cachalots, or the dolphins, and furnished with a horn of defence of great penetrating power."

"Hum!" said the harpooner, shaking his head with the air of a man who would not be convinced.

"Notice one thing, my worthy Canadian," I resumed. "If such an animal is in existence, if it inhabits the depths of the ocean, if it frequents the strata lying miles below the surface of the water, it must necessarily possess an organisation the strength of which would defy all comparison."

"And why this powerful organisation?" demanded Ned.

"Because it requires incalculable strength to keep one's self in these strata and resist their pressure. Listen to me. Let us admit that the pressure of the atmosphere is represented by the weight of a column of water thirty-two feet high. In reality the column of water would be shorter, as we are speaking of sea water, the density of which is greater than that of fresh water. Very well, when you dive, Ned, as many times thirty-two feet of water as there are above you, so many times does your body bear a pressure equal to that of the atmosphere, that is to say, 15 lbs. for each square inch of its surface. It follows then, that at 320 feet this pressure = that of 10 atmospheres, of 100 atmospheres at 3200 feet, and of 1000 atmospheres at 32,000 feet, that is, about 6 miles; which is equivalent to saying that, if you could attain this depth in the ocean, each square ¾ of an inch of the surface of your body would bear a pressure of 5600 lbs. Ah! my brave Ned, do you know how many square inches you carry on the surface of your body?"

"I have no idea, Mr Aronnax."

"About 6500; and, as in reality the atmospheric pressure is about 15 lbs. to the square inch, your 6500 square inches bear at this moment a pressure of 97,500 lbs."

"Without my perceiving it?"

"Without your perceiving it. And if you are not crushed by such a pressure, it is because the air penetrates the interior of your body with equal pressure. Hence perfect equilibrium between the interior and exterior pressure, which thus neutralise each other, and which allows you to bear it without inconvenience. But in the water it is another thing."

"Yes, I understand," replied Ned, becoming more attentive; "because the water surrounds me, but does not penetrate."

"Precisely, Ned: so that at 32 feet beneath the surface of the sea you would undergo a pressure of 97,500 lbs.; at 320 feet, ten times that pressure; at 3200 feet, a hundred times that pressure; lastly, at 32,000 feet, a thousand times that pressure would be 97,500,000 lbs.—that is to say, that you would be flattened as if you had been drawn from the plates of a hydraulic machine!"

"The devil!" exclaimed Ned.

"Very well, my worthy harpooner, if some vertebrate, several hundred yards long, and large in proportion, can maintain itself in such depths—of those whose surface is represented by millions of square inches, that is by tens of millions of pounds, we must estimate the pressure they undergo. Consider, then, what must be the resistance of their bony structure, and the strength of their organisation to withstand such pressure!"

"Why!" exclaimed Ned Land, "they must be made of iron plates eight inches thick, like the armoured frigates."

"As you say, Ned. And think what destruction such a mass would cause, if hurled with the speed of an express train against the hull of a vessel."

"Yes—certainly—perhaps," replied the Canadian, shaken by these figures, but not yet willing to give in.

"Well, have I convinced you?"

"You have convinced me of one thing, sir, which is that, if such animals do exist at the bottom of the seas, they must necessarily be as strong as you say."

"But if they do not exist, mine obstinate harpooner, how explain the accident to the *Scotia*?"

Chapter V

At a Venture

The voyage of the *Abraham Lincoln* was for a long time marked by no special incident. But one circumstance happened which showed the wonderful dexterity of Ned Land, and proved what confidence we might place in him.

The 30th of June, the frigate spoke some American whalers, from whom we learned that they knew nothing about the narwhal. But one of them, the captain of the *Monroe*, knowing that Ned Land had shipped on board the *Abraham Lincoln*, begged for his help in chasing a whale they had in sight. Commander Farragut, desirous of seeing Ned Land at work, gave him permission to go on board the *Monroe*. And fate served our Canadian so well that, instead of one whale, he harpooned two with a double blow, striking one straight to the heart, and catching the other after some minutes' pursuit.

Decidedly, if the monster ever had to do with Ned Land's harpoon, I would not bet in its favour.

The frigate skirted the south-east coast of America with great rapidity. The 3rd of July we were at the opening of the Straits of Magellan, level with Cape Vierges. But Commander Farragut would not take a tortuous passage, but doubled Cape Horn.

The ship's crew agreed with him. And certainly it was possible that they might meet the narwhal in this narrow pass. Many of the sailors affirmed that the monster could not pass there, "that he was too big for that!"

The 6th of July, about three o'clock in the afternoon, the *Abraham Lincoln*, at fifteen miles to the South, doubled the solitary island, this lost rock at the extremity of the American continent, to which some

Dutch sailors gave the name of their native town, Cape Horn. The course was taken towards the north-west, and the next day the screw of the frigate was at last beating the waters of the Pacific.

"Keep your eyes open!" called out the sailors.

And they were opened widely. Both eyes and glasses, a little dazzled, it is true, by the prospect of two thousand dollars, had not an instant's repose. Day and night they watched the surface of the ocean, and even nyctalopes, whose faculty of seeing in the darkness multiplies their chances a hundredfold, would have had enough to do to gain the prize.

I myself, for whom money had no charms, was not the least attentive on board. Giving but few minutes to my meals, but a few hours to sleep, indifferent to either rain or sunshine, I did not leave the poop of the vessel. Now leaning on the netting of the forecastle, now on the taffrail, I devoured with eagerness the soft foam which whitened the sea as far as the eye could reach; and how often have I shared the emotion of the majority of the crew, when some capricious whale raised its black back above the waves! The poop of the vessel was crowded in a moment. The cabins poured forth a torrent of sailors and officers, each with heaving breast and troubled eye watching the course of the cetacean. I looked, and looked, till I was nearly blind, whilst Conseil, always phlegmatic, kept repeating in a calm voice:

"If, sir, you would not squint so much, you would see better!"

But vain excitement! the *Abraham Lincoln* checked its speed and made for the animal signalled, a simple whale, or common cachalot, which soon disappeared amidst a storm of execration.

But the weather was good. The voyage was being accomplished under the most favourable auspices. It was then the bad season in Australia, the July of that zone corresponding to our January in Europe; but the sea was beautiful and easily scanned round a vast circumference.

The 20th July, the tropic of Capricorn was cut by 105° of longitude, and the 27th of the same month we crossed the equator on the 110th meridian. This passed, the frigate took a more decided westerly direction, and scoured the central waters of the Pacific.

Commander Farragut thought, and with reason, that it was better to remain in deep water, and keep clear of continents or islands, which the beast itself seemed to shun (perhaps because there was not enough water for him! suggested the greater part of the crew). The frigate passed at some distance from the Marquesas and the Sandwich Islands, crossed the tropic of Cancer, and made for the China Seas. We were on the theatre of the last diversions of the monster; and to say truth, we no longer *lived* on board. Hearts palpitated, fearfully preparing themselves for future incurable aneurism. The entire ship's crew were undergoing a nervous excitement, of which I can give no idea: they could not eat, they could not sleep—twenty times a day, misconception or an optical illusion of some sailor seated on the taffrail, would cause dreadful perspirations, and these emotions, twenty times repeated, kept us in a state of excitement so violent that a reaction was unavoidable.

And truly, reaction soon showed itself. For three months, during which a day seemed an age, the *Abraham Lincoln* furrowed all the waters of the Northern Pacific, running at whales, making sharp deviations from her course, veering suddenly from one tack to another, stopping suddenly, putting on steam, and backing ever and anon at the risk of deranging her machinery; and not one point of the Japanese or American coast was left unexplored.

The warmest partisans of the enterprise now became its most ardent detractors. Reaction mounted from the crew to the captain himself, and certainly, had it not been for resolute determination on the part of Captain Farragut, the frigate would have headed due southward. This useless search could not last much longer. The *Abraham Lincoln* had nothing to reproach herself with, she had done her best to succeed. Never had an American ship's crew shown more zeal or patience; its failure could not be placed to their charge—there remained nothing but to return.

This was represented to the commander. The sailors could not hide their discontent, and the service suffered. I will not say there was a mutiny on board, but after a reasonable period of obstinacy, Captain

Farragut (as Columbus did) asked for three days' patience. If in three days the monster did not appear, the man at the helm should give three turns of the wheel, and the *Abraham Lincoln* would make for the European seas.

This promise was made on the 2nd of November. It had the effect of rallying the ship's crew. The ocean was watched with renewed attention. Each one wished for a last glance in which to sum up his remembrance. Glasses were used with feverish activity. It was a grand defiance given to the giant narwhal, and he could scarcely fail to answer the summons and "appear."

Two days passed, the steam was at half pressure; a thousand schemes were tried to attract the attention and stimulate the apathy of the animal in case it should be met in those parts. Large quantities of bacon were trailed in the wake of the ship, to the great satisfaction (I must say) of the sharks. Small craft radiated in all directions round the *Abraham Lincoln* as she lay to, and did not leave a spot of the sea unexplored. But the night of the 4th of November arrived without the unveiling of this submarine mystery.

The next day, the 5th of November, at twelve the delay would (morally speaking) expire; after that time, Commander Farragut, faithful to his promise, was to turn the course to the south-east and abandon for ever the northern regions of the Pacific.

The frigate was then in 31° 15' north latitude and 136° 42' east longitude. The coast of Japan still remained less than two hundred miles to leeward. Night was approaching. They had just struck eight bells; large clouds veiled the face of the moon, then in its first quarter. The sea undulated peaceably under the stern of the vessel.

At that moment I was leaning forward on the starboard netting. Conseil, standing near me, was looking straight before him. The crew, perched in the ratlines, examined the horizon, which contracted and darkened by degrees. Officers with their night glasses scoured the growing darkness: sometimes the ocean sparkled under the rays of the moon, which darted between two clouds, then all trace of light was lost in the darkness.

In looking at Conseil, I could see he was undergoing a little of the general influence. At least I thought so. Perhaps for the first time his nerves vibrated to a sentiment of curiosity.

"Come, Conseil," said I, "this is the last chance of pocketing the two thousand dollars."

"May I be permitted to say, sir," replied Conseil, "that I never reckoned on getting the prize; and, had the government of the Union offered a hundred thousand dollars, it would have been none the poorer."

"You are right, Conseil. It is a foolish affair after all, and one upon which we entered too lightly. What time lost, what useless emotions! We should have been back in France six months ago."

"In your little room, sir," replied Conseil, "and in your museum, sir; and I should have already classed all your fossils, sir. And the Babiroussa would have been installed in its cage in the Jardin des Plantes, and have drawn all the curious people of the capital!"

"As you say, Conseil. I fancy we shall run a fair chance of being laughed at for our pains."

"That's tolerably certain," replied Conseil, quietly; "I think they will make fun of you, sir. And, must I say it?"—

"Go on, my good friend."

"Well, sir, you will only get your deserts."

"Indeed!"

"When one has the honour of being a savant as you are, sir, one should not expose one's self to"—

Conseil had not time to finish his compliment. In the midst of general silence a voice had just been heard. It was the voice of Ned Land shouting—

"Look out there! the very thing we are looking for—on our weather beam!"

Chapter VI

At Full Steam

At this cry the whole ship's crew hurried towards the harpooner,—commander, officers, masters, sailors, cabin boys; even the engineers left their engines, and the stokers their furnaces.

The order to stop her had been given, and the frigate now simply went on by her own momentum. The darkness was then profound, and however good the Canadian's eyes were, I asked myself how he had managed to see, and what he had been able to see. My heart beat as if it would break. But Ned Land was not mistaken, and we all perceived the object he pointed to. At two cables' lengths from the *Abraham Lincoln*, on the starboard quarter, the sea seemed to be illuminated all over. It was not a mere phosphoric phenomenon. The monster emerged some fathoms from the water, and then threw out that very intense but inexplicable light mentioned in the report of several captains. This magnificent irradiation must have been produced by an agent of great *shining* power. The luminous part traced on the sea an immense oval, much elongated, the centre of which condensed a burning heat, whose overpowering brilliancy died out by successive gradations.

"It is only an agglomeration of phosphoric particles," cried one of the officers.

"No, sir, certainly not," I replied. "Never did pholades or salpae produce such a powerful light. That brightness is of an essentially electrical nature. Besides, see, see! it moves; it is moving forwards, backwards, it is darting towards us!"

A general cry rose from the frigate.

"Silence!" said the Captain; "up with the helm, reverse the engines."

The steam was shut off, and the *Abraham Lincoln*, beating to port, described a semicircle.

"Right the helm, go a-head," cried the Captain.

These orders were executed, and the frigate moved rapidly from the burning light.

I was mistaken. She tried to sheer off, but the supernatural animal approached with a velocity double her own.

We gasped for breath. Stupefaction more than fear made us dumb and motionless. The animal gained on us, sporting with the waves. It made the round of the frigate, which was then making fourteen knots, and enveloped it with its electric rings like luminous dust. Then it moved away two or three miles, leaving a phosphorescent track, like those volumes of steam that the express trains leave behind. All at once from the dark line of the horizon whither it retired to gain its momentum, the monster rushed suddenly towards the *Abraham Lincoln* with alarming rapidity, stopped suddenly about twenty feet from the hull, and died out,—not diving under the water, for its brilliancy did not abate,—but suddenly, and as if the source of this brilliant emanation was exhausted. Then it reappeared on the other side of the vessel, as if it had turned and slid under the hull. Any moment a collision might have occurred which would have been fatal to us. However, I was astonished at the manoeuvres of the frigate. She fled and did not attack.

On the captain's face, generally so impassive, was an expression of unaccountable astonishment.

"Mr Aronnax," he said, "I do not know with what formidable being I have to deal, and I will not imprudently risk my frigate in the midst of this darkness. Besides, how attack this unknown thing, how defend one's self from it? Wait for daylight, and the scene will change."

"You have no further doubt, captain, of the nature of the animal?"

"No, sir; it is evidently a gigantic narwhal, and an electric one."

"Perhaps," added I, "one can only approach it with a gymnotus or a torpedo."

"Undoubtedly," replied the captain, "if it possesses such dreadful power, it is the most terrible animal that ever was created. That is why, sir, I must be on my guard."

The crew were on their feet all night. No one thought of sleep. The *Abraham Lincoln*, not being able to struggle with such velocity, had moderated its pace, and sailed at half speed. For its part, the narwhal, imitating the frigate, let the waves rock it at will, and seemed decided not to leave the scene of the struggle. Towards midnight, however, it disappeared, or, to use a more appropriate term, it "died out" like a large glow-worm. Had it fled? One could only fear, not hope it. But at seven minutes to one o'clock in the morning a deafening whistling was heard, like that produced by a body of water rushing with great violence.

The captain, Ned Land, and I, were then on the poop, eagerly peering through the profound darkness.

"Ned Land," asked the commander, "you have often heard the roaring of whales?"

"Often, sir; but never such whales the sight of which brought me in two thousand dollars. If I can only approach within four harpoon lengths of it!"

"But to approach it," said the commander, "I ought to put a whaler at your disposal?"

"Certainly, sir."

"That will be trifling with the lives of my men."

"And mine too," simply said the harpooner.

Towards two o'clock in the morning, the burning light reappeared, not less intense, about five miles to windward of the *Abraham Lincoln*. Notwithstanding the distance, and the noise of the wind and sea, one heard distinctly the loud strokes of the animal's tail, and even its panting breath. It seemed that, at the moment that the enormous narwhal had come to take breath at the surface of the water, the air was engulphed in its lungs, like the steam in the vast cylinders of a machine of two thousand horse power.

"Hum!" thought I, "a whale with the strength of a cavalry regiment would be a pretty whale!"

We were on the *qui vive* till daylight, and prepared for the combat. The fishing implements were laid along the hammock nettings. The second lieutenant loaded the blunderbusses, which could throw harpoons to the distance of a mile, and long duck-guns, with explosive bullets, which inflicted mortal wounds even to the most terrible animals. Ned Land contented himself with sharpening his harpoon—a terrible weapon in his hands.

At six o'clock, day began to break; and with the first glimmer of light, the electric light of the narwhal disappeared. At seven o'clock the day was sufficiently advanced, but a very thick sea fog obscured our view, and the best spy-glasses could not pierce it. That caused disappointment and anger.

I climbed the mizen-mast. Some officers were already perched on the mast heads. At eight o'clock the fog lay heavily on the waves, and its thick scrolls rose little by little. The horizon grew wider and clearer at the same time. Suddenly, just as on the day before, Ned Land's voice was heard:

"The thing itself on the port quarter!" cried the harpooner.

Every eye was turned towards the point indicated. There, a mile and a half from the frigate, a long blackish body emerged a yard above the waves. Its tail, violently agitated, produced a considerable eddy. Never did a caudal appendage beat the sea with such violence. An immense track, of a dazzling whiteness, marked the passage of the animal, and described a long curve.

The frigate approached the cetacean. I examined it thoroughly.

The reports of the *Shannon* and of the *Helvetia* had rather exaggerated its size, and I estimated its length at only two hundred and fifty feet. As to its dimensions, I could only conjecture them to be admirably proportioned. While I watched this phenomenon, two jets of steam and water were ejected from its vents, and rose to the height of 120 feet, thus I ascertained its way of breathing. I concluded definitely that it belonged to the vertebrate branch, class mammalia.

The crew waited impatiently for their chief's orders. The latter, after having observed the animal attentively, called the engineer. The engineer ran to him.

"Sir," said the commander, "you have steam up?"

"Yes, sir," answered the engineer.

"Well, make up your fires and put on all steam."

Three hurrahs greeted this order. The time for the struggle had arrived. Some moments after, the two funnels of the frigate vomited torrents of black smoke, and the bridge quaked under the trembling of the boilers.

The *Abraham Lincoln*, propelled by her powerful screw, went straight at the animal. The latter allowed it to come within half a cable's length; then, as if disdaining to dive, it took a little turn, and stopped a short distance off.

This pursuit lasted nearly three-quarters of an hour, without the frigate gaining two yards on the cetacean. It was quite evident that at that rate we should never come up with it.

"Well, Mr Land," asked the captain, "do you advise me to put the boats out to sea?"

"No, sir," replied Ned Lane; "because we shall not take that beast easily."

"What shall we do then?"

"Put on more steam if you can, sir. With your leave, I mean to post myself under the bowsprit, and if we get within harpooning distance, I shall throw my harpoon."

"Go, Ned," said the captain. "Engineer, put on more pressure."

Ned Land went to his post. The fires were increased, the screw revolved forty-three times a minute, and the steam poured out of the valves. We heaved the log, and calculated that the *Abraham Lincoln* was going at the rate of 18 ½ miles an hour.

But the accursed animal swam too at the rate of 18 ½ miles.

For a whole hour, the frigate kept up this pace, without gaining six feet. It was humiliating for one of the swiftest sailers in the American navy. A stubborn anger seized the crew; the sailors abused the monster, who, as before, disdained to answer them; the captain no longer contented himself with twisting his beard—he gnawed it.

The engineer was again called.

"You have turned full steam on?"

"Yes sir," replied the engineer.

The speed of the *Abraham Lincoln* increased. Its mast trembled down to their stepping holes, and the clouds of smoke could hardly find way out of the narrow funnels.

They heaved the log a second time.

"Well?" asked the captain of the man at the wheel.

"Nineteen miles and 3/10, sir."

"Clap on more steam."

The engineer obeyed. The manometer showed ten degrees. But the cetacean grew warm itself, no doubt; for, without straining itself it made 193/10 miles.

What a pursuit! No, I cannot describe the emotion that vibrated through me. Ned Land kept his post, harpoon in hand. Several times the animal let us gain upon it.—"We shall catch it! we shall catch it!" cried the Canadian. But just as he was going to strike, the cetacean stole away with a rapidity that could not be estimated at less than thirty miles an hour, and even during our maximum of speed, it bullied the frigate, going round and round it. A cry of fury broke from every one!

At noon we were no further advanced than at eight o'clock in the morning.

The captain then decided to take more direct means.

"Ah!" said he, "that animal goes quicker than the *Abraham Lincoln*. Very well! we will see whether it will escape these conical bullets. Send your men to the forecastle, sir."

The forecastle gun was immediately loaded and slewed round. But the shot passed some feet above the cetacean, which was half a mile off.

"Another more to the right," cried the commander, "and five dollars to whoever will hit that infernal beast."

An old gunner with a grey beard—that I can see now—with steady eye and grave face, went up to the gun and took a long aim. A loud report was heard, with which were mingled the cheers of the crew.

The bullet did its work; it hit the animal, but not fatally, and sliding off the rounded surfaces, was lost in two miles depth of sea.

The chase began again, and the captain, leaning towards me, said—

"I will pursue that beast till my frigate bursts up."

"Yes," answered I; "and you will be quite right to do it."

I wished the beast would exhaust itself, and not be insensible to fatigue like a steam engine! But it was of no use. Hours passed, without its showing any signs of exhaustion.

However, it must be said in praise of the *Abraham Lincoln*, that she struggled on indefatigably. I cannot reckon the distance she made under three hundred miles during this unlucky day, November the 6th. But night came on, and overshadowed the rough ocean.

Now I thought our expedition was at an end, and that we should never again see the extraordinary animal. I was mistaken. At ten minutes to eleven in the evening, the electric light reappeared three miles to windward of the frigate, as pure, as intense as during the preceding night.

The narwhal seemed motionless; perhaps, tired with its day's work, it slept, letting itself float with the undulation of the waves. Now was a chance of which the captain resolved to take advantage.

He gave his orders. The *Abraham Lincoln* kept up half steam, and advanced cautiously so as not to awake it adversary. It is no rare thing to meet in the middle of the ocean whales so sound asleep that they can be successfully attacked, and Ned Land had harpooned more than one during its sleep. The Canadian went to take his place again under the bowsprit.

The frigate approached noiselessly, stopped at two cables' lengths from the animal, and following its track. No one breathed; a deep silence reigned on the bridge. We were not a hundred feet from the burning focus, the light of which increased and dazzled our eyes.

At this moment, leaning on the forecastle bulwark, I saw below me Ned Land grappling the martingale in one hand, brandishing his terrible harpoon in the other, scarcely twenty feet from the motionless animal. Suddenly his arm straightened, and the harpoon was thrown; I heard the sonorous stroke of the weapon, which seemed to have struck a hard body. The electric light went out suddenly, and two enormous waterspouts broke over the bridge of the frigate, rushing like a torrent from stem to stern, overthrowing men, and breaking the lashing of the spars. A fearful shock followed, and, thrown over the rail without having time to stop myself, I fell into the sea.

Chapter VII

An Unknown Species of Whale

This unexpected fall so stunned me that I have no clear recollection of my sensations at the time. I was at first drawn down to a depth of about twenty feet. I am a good swimmer (though without pretending to rival Byron or Edgar Poe, who were masters of the art), and in that plunge I did not lose my presence of mind. Two vigorous strokes brought me to the surface of the water. My first care was to look for the frigate. Had the crew seen me disappear? Had the *Abraham Lincoln* veered round? Would the captain put out a boat? Might I hope to be saved?

The darkness was intense. I caught a glimpse of a black mass disappearing in the east, its beacon lights dying out in the distance. It was the frigate! I was lost.

"Help, Help!" I shouted, swimming towards the *Abraham Lincoln* in desperation.

My clothes encumbered me; they seemed glued to my body, and paralysed my movements.

I was sinking! I was suffocating!

"Help!"

This was my last cry. My mouth filled with water; I struggled against being drawn down the abyss. Suddenly my clothes were seized by a strong hand, and I felt myself quickly drawn up to the surface of the sea; and I heard, yes, I heard these words pronounced in my ear—

"If master would be so good as to lean on my shoulder, master would swim with much greater ease."

I seized with one hand my faithful Conseil's arm.

"Is it you?" said I, "you?"

"Myself," answered Conseil; "and waiting master's orders."

"That shock threw you as well as me into the sea?"

"No; but being in my master's service, I followed him."

The worthy fellow thought that was but natural.

"And the frigate?" I asked.

"The frigate?" replied Conseil, turning on his back; "I think the master had better not count too much on her."

"You think so?"

"I say that, at the time I threw myself into the sea, I heard the men at the wheel say, 'The screw and the rudder are broken.'"

"Broken?"

"Yes, broken by the monster's teeth. It is the only injury the *Abraham Lincoln* has sustained. But it is a bad look out for us—she no longer answers her helm."

"Then we are lost!"

"Perhaps so," calmly answered Conseil. "However, we have still several hours before us, and one can do a good deal in some hours."

Conseil's imperturbable coolness set me up again. I swam more vigorously; but, cramped by my clothes, which stuck to me like a leaden weight, I felt great difficulty in bearing up. Conseil saw this.

"Will master let me make a slit?" said he; and slipping an open knife under my clothes, he ripped them up from top to bottom very rapidly. Then he cleverly slipped them off me, while I swam for both of us.

Then I did the same for Conseil, and we continued to swim near to each other.

Nevertheless, our situation was no less terrible. Perhaps our disappearance had not been noticed; and if it had been, the frigate could not tack, being without its helm. Conseil argued on this supposition, and laid his plans accordingly. This phlegmatic boy was perfectly self-possessed. We then decided that, as our only chance of safety was being picked up by the *Abraham Lincoln's* boats, we ought to manage so as to wait for them as long as possible. I resolved then to husband our strength, so that both should not be exhausted at the same time; and this is how we managed: while one of us lay on our back, quite still, with arms crossed, and legs stretched out, the other would swim and push the other on in front. This towing business did not last more than ten minutes each; and relieving each other thus, we could swim on for some hours, perhaps till daybreak. Poor chance! but hope is so firmly rooted in the heart of man! Moreover, there were two of us. Indeed I declare (though it may seem improbable) if I sought to destroy all hope,—if I wished to despair, I could not.

The collision of the frigate with the cetacean had occurred about eleven o'clock the evening before. I reckoned then we should have eight hours to swim before sunrise, an operation quite practicable if we relieved each other. The sea, very calm, was in our favour. Sometimes I tried to pierce the intense darkness that was only dispelled by the phosphorescence caused by our movements. I watched the luminous waves that broke over my hand, whose mirrorlike surface was spotted with silvery rings. One might have said that we were in a bath of quicksilver.

Near one o'clock in the morning, I was seized with dreadful fatigue. My limbs stiffened under the strain of violent cramp. Conseil was obliged to keep me up, and our preservation devolved on him alone. I heard the poor boy pant; his breathing became short and hurried. I found that he could not keep up much longer.

"Leave me! leave me!" I said to him.

"Leave my master? never!" replied he. "I would drown first."

Just then the moon appeared through the fringes of a thick cloud that the wind was driving to the east. The surface of the sea glittered with its rays. This kindly light reanimated us. My head got better again. I looked at all the points of the horizon. I saw the frigate! She was five miles from us, and looked like a dark mass, hardly discernible. But no boats!

I would have cried out. But what good would it have been at such a distance! My swollen lips could utter no sounds. Conseil could articulate some words, and I heard him repeat at intervals, "Help! help!"

Our movements were suspended for an instant; we listened. It might be only a singing in the ear, but it seemed to me as if a cry answered the cry from Conseil.

"Did you hear?" I murmured.

"Yes! yes!"

And Conseil gave one more despairing call.

This time there was no mistake! A human voice responded to ours! Was it the voice of another unfortunate creature, abandoned in the middle of the ocean, some other victim of the shock sustained by the vessel? Or rather was it a boat from the frigate, that was hailing us in the darkness?

Conseil made a last effort, and leaning on my shoulder, while I struck out in a despairing effort, he raised himself half out of the water, then fell back exhausted.

"What did you see?"

"I saw"—murmured he; "I saw—but do not talk—reserve all your strength!"

What had he seen? Then, I know not why, the thought of the monster came into my head for the first time! But that voice? The time is past for Jonahs to take refuge in whales' bellies! However, Conseil was towing me again. He raised his head sometimes, looked before us, and uttered a cry of recognition, which was responded to by a voice that came nearer and nearer. I scarcely heard it. My strength was exhausted; my fingers stiffened; my hand afforded me support no longer; my mouth, convulsively opening, filled with salt water. Cold crept over me. I raised my head for the last time, then I sank.

At this moment a hard body struck me. I clung to it: then I felt that I was being drawn up, that I was brought to the surface of the water, that my chest collapsed:—I fainted.

It is certain that I soon came too, thanks to the vigorous rubbings that I received. I half opened my eyes.

"Conseil!" I murmured.

"Does master call me?" asked Conseil.

Just then, by the waning light of the moon, which was sinking down to the horizon, I saw a face which was not Conseil's, and which I immediately recognised.

"Ned!" I cried.

"The same, sir, who is seeking his prize!" replied the Canadian.

"Were you thrown into the sea by the shock of the frigate?"

"Yes, Professor; but more fortunate than you, I was able to find a footing almost directly upon a floating island."

"An island?"

"Or, more correctly speaking, on our gigantic narwhal."

"Explain yourself, Ned!"

"Only I soon found out why my harpoon had not entered its skin and was blunted."

"Why, Ned, why?"

"Because, Professor, that beast is made of sheet iron."

The Canadian's last words produced a sudden revolution in my brain. I wriggled myself quickly to the top of the being, or object, half out of the water, which served us for a refuge. I kicked it. It was evidently a hard impenetrable body, and not the soft substance that forms the bodies of the great marine mammalia. But this hard body might be a bony carapace, like that of the antediluvian animals; and I should be free to class this monster among amphibious reptiles, such as tortoises or alligators.

Well, no! the blackish back that supported me was smooth, polished, without scales. The blow produced a metallic sound; and incredible though it may be, it seemed, I might say, as if it were made of riveted plates.

There was no doubt about it! this monster, this natural phenomenon that had puzzled the learned world, and overthrown and misled the imagination of seamen of both hemispheres, was, it must be owned, a still more astonishing phenomenon, inasmuch as it was a simply human construction.

We had no time to lose, however. We were lying upon the back of a sort of submarine boat, which appeared (as far as I could judge) like a huge fish of steel. Ned Land's mind was made up on this point. Conseil and I could only agree with him.

Just then a bubbling began at the back of this strange thing, (which was evidently propelled by a screw), and it began to move. We had only just time to seize hold of the upper part, which rose about seven feet out of the water, and happily its speed was not great.

"As long as it sails horizontally," muttered Ned Land, "I do not mind; but if it takes a fancy to dive, I would not give two straws for my life."

The Canadian might have said still less. It became really necessary to communicate with the beings, whatever they were, shut up inside the machine. I searched all over the outside for an aperture, a panel, or a man-hole, to use a technical expression; but the lines of the iron rivets, solidly driven into the joints of the iron plates, were clear and uniform. Besides, the moon disappeared then, and left us in total darkness.

At last this long night passed. My indistinct remembrance prevents my describing all the impressions it made. I can only recall one circumstance. During some lulls of the wind and sea, I fancied I heard several times vague sounds, a sort of fugitive harmony produced by distant words of command. What was then the mystery of this submarine craft, of which the whole world vainly sought an explanation? What kind of beings existed in this strange boat? What mechanical agent caused its prodigious speed?

Daybreak appeared. The morning mists surrounded us, but they soon cleared off. I was about to examine the hull, which formed on deck a kind of horizontal platform, when I felt it gradually sinking.

"Oh! confound it!" cried Ned Land, kicking the resounding plate; "Open, you inhospitable rascals!"

Happily the sinking movement ceased. Suddenly a noise, like iron works violently pushed aside, came from the interior of the boat. One iron plate was moved, a man appeared, uttered an odd cry, and disappeared immediately.

Some moments after, eight strong men, with masked faces, appeared noiselessly, and drew us down into their formidable machine.

Chapter VIII

Mobilis In Mobili

This forcible abduction, so roughly carried out, was accomplished with the rapidity of lightning. I shivered all over. Whom had we to deal with? No doubt some new sort of pirates, who explored the sea in their own way.

Hardly had the narrow panel closed upon me, when I was enveloped in darkness. My eyes, dazzled with the outer light, could distinguish nothing. I felt my naked feet cling to the rings of an iron ladder. Ned Land and Conseil, firmly seized, followed me. At the bottom of the ladder, a door opened, and shut after us immediately with a bang.

We were alone. Where, I could not say, hardly imagine. All was black, and such a dense black that, after some minutes, my eyes had not been able to discern even the faintest glimmer.

Meanwhile, Ned Land, furious at these proceedings, gave free vent to his indignation.

"Confound it!" cried he, "here are people who come up to the Scotch for hospitality. They only just miss being cannibals. I should not be surprised at it, but I declare that they shall not eat me without my protesting."

"Calm yourself, friend Ned, calm yourself," replied Conseil, quietly. "Do not cry out before you are hurt. We are not quite done for yet."

"Not quite," sharply replied the Canadian, "but pretty near, at all events. Things look black. Happily, my bowie-knife I have still, and I can always see well enough to use it. The first of these pirates who lays a hand on me"—

"Do not excite yourself, Ned," I said to the harpooner, "and do not compromise us by useless violence. Who knows that they will not listen to us? Let us rather try to find out where we are."

"I groped about. In five steps I came to an iron wall, made of plates bolted together. Then turning back I struck against a wooden table, near which were ranged several stools. The boards of this prison were concealed under a thick mat of phormium, which deadened the noise of the feet. The bare walls revealed no trace of window or door. Conseil, going round the reverse way, met me, and we went back to the middle of the cabin, which measured about twenty feet by ten. As to its height, Ned Land, in spite of his own great height, could not measure it.

Half an hour had already passed without our situation being bettered, when the dense darkness suddenly gave way to extreme light. Our prison was suddenly lighted, that is to say, it became filled with a luminous matter, so strong that I could not bear it at first. In its whiteness and intensity I recognised that electric light which played round the submarine boat like a magnificent phenomenon of phosphorescence. After shutting my eyes involuntarily, I opened them and saw that this luminous agent came from a half globe, unpolished, placed in the roof of the cabin.

"At last one can see," cried Ned Land, who, knife in hand, stood on the defensive.

"Yes," said I; "but we are still in the dark about ourselves."

"Let master have patience," said the imperturbable Conseil.

The sudden lighting of the cabin enabled me to examine it minutely. It only contained a table and five stools. The invisible door might be hermetically sealed. No noise was heard. All seemed dead in the interior of this boat. Did it move, did it float on the surface of the ocean, or did it dive into its depths? I could not guess.

A noise of bolts was now heard, the door opened, and two men appeared.

One was short, very muscular, broadshouldered, with robust limbs, strong head, an abundance of black hair, thick moustache, a quick penetrating look, and the vivacity which characterises the population of Southern France.

The second stranger merits a more detailed description. A disciple of Gratiolet or Engel would have read his face like an open book. I made out his prevailing qualities directly:—self-confidence,—because his head was well set on his shoulders, and his black eyes looked around with cold assurance; calmness,—for his skin, rather pale, showed his coolness of blood; energy,—evinced by the rapid contraction of his lofty brows; and courage,—because his deep breathing denoted great power of lungs.

Whether this person was thirty-five or fifty years of age, I could not say. He was tall, had a large forehead, straight nose, a clearly cut mouth, beautiful teeth, with fine taper hands, indicative of a highly nervous temperament. This man was certainly the most admirable specimen I had ever met. One particular feature was his eyes, rather far from each other, and which could take in nearly a quarter of the horizon at once.

This faculty—(I verified it later)—gave him a range of vision far superior to Ned Land's. When this stranger fixed upon a object, his eyebrows met, his large eyelids closed around so as to contract the range of his vision, and he looked as if he magnified the objects lessened by distance, as if he pierced those sheets of water so opaque to our eyes, and as if he read the very depths of the seas.

The two strangers, with caps made from the fur of the sea otter, and shod with sea boots of seals' skin, were dressed in clothes of a particular texture, which allowed free movement of the limbs. The taller of the two, evidently the chief on board, examined us with great attention, without saying a word: then turning to his companion, talked with him in an unknown tongue. It was a sonorous, harmonious, and flexible dialect, the vowels seeming to admit of very varied accentuation.

The other replied by a shake of the head, and added two or three perfectly incomprehensible words. Then he seemed to question me by a look.

I replied in good French that I did not know his language; but he seemed not to understand me, and my situation became more embarrassing.

"If master were to tell our story," said Conseil, "perhaps these gentlemen may understand some words."

I began to tell our adventures, articulating each syllable clearly, and without omitting one single detail. I announced our names and rank, introducing in person Professor Aronnax, his servant Conseil, and master Ned Land, the harpooner.

The man with the soft calm eyes listened to me quietly, even politely, and with extreme attention; but nothing in his countenance indicated that he had understood my story. When I finished, he said not a word.

There remained one resource, to speak English. Perhaps they would know this almost universal language. I knew it, as well as the German language,—well enough to read it fluently, but not to speak it correctly. But, anyhow, we must make ourselves understood.

"Go on in your turn," I said to the harpooner; "speak your best Anglo-Saxon, and try to do better than I."

Ned did not beg off, and recommenced our story.

To his great disgust, the harpooner did not seem to have made himself more intelligible than I had. Our visitors did not stir. They evidently understood neither the language of Arago nor of Faraday.

Very much embarrassed, after having vainly exhausted our philological resources, I knew not what part to take, when Conseil said—

"If master will permit me, I will relate it in German."

But in spite of the elegant turns and good accent of the narrator, the German language had no success. At last, nonplussed, I tried to remember my first lessons, and to narrate our adventures in Latin, but with no better success. This last attempt being of no avail, the two strangers exchanged some words in their unknown language, and retired.

The door shut.

"It is an infamous shame," cried Ned Land, who broke out for the twentieth time; "we speak to those rogues in French, English, German, and Latin, and not one of them has the politeness to answer!"

"Calm yourself," I said to the impetuous Ned, "anger will do no good."

"But do you see, Professor," replied our irascible companion, "that we shall absolutely die of hunger in this iron cage?"

"Bah," said Conseil, philosophically; "we can hold out some time yet."

"My friends," I said, "we must not despair. We have been worse off than this. Do me the favour to wait a little before forming an opinion upon the commander and crew of this boat."

"My opinion is formed," replied Ned Land, sharply. "They are rascals."

"Good! and from what country?"

"From the land of rogues!"

"My brave Ned, that country is not clearly indicated on the map of the world; but I admit that the nationality of the two strangers is hard to determine. Neither English, French, nor German, that is quite certain. However, I am inclined to think that the commander and his companion were born in low latitudes. There is southern blood in them. But I cannot abide by their appearance whether they are Spaniards, Turks, Arabians, or Indians. As to their language, it is quite incomprehensible."

"There is the disadvantage of not knowing all languages," said Conseil, "or the disadvantage of not having one universal language."

As he said these words, the door opened. A steward entered. He brought us clothes, coats and trousers, made of a stuff I did not know. I hastened to dress myself, and my companions followed my example. During that time, the steward—dumb, perhaps deaf—had arranged the table, and laid three plates.

"This is something like," said Conseil.

"Bah," said the rancorous harpooner, "what do you suppose they eat here? Tortoise liver, filleted shark, and beefsteaks from seadogs."

"We shall see," said Conseil.

The dishes, of bell metal, were placed on the table, and we took our places. Undoubtedly we had to do with civilised people, and had it not been for the electric light which flooded us, I could have fancied I was in the dining-room of the Adelphi Hotel at Liverpool, or at the Grand Hotel in Paris. I must say, however, that there was neither bread nor wine. The water was fresh and clear, but it was water, and did not suit Ned Land's taste. Amongst the dishes which were brought to us, I recognised several fish delicately dressed; but of some, although excellent, I could give no opinion, neither could I tell to what kingdom they belonged, whether animal or vegetable. As to the dinner service, it was elegant, and in perfect taste. Each utensil, spoon, fork, knife, plate, had a letter engraved on it, with a motto above it, of which this is an exact facsimile:—

$$\textit{Mobilis in Mobili}$$
$$\textit{N}$$

The letter N was no doubt the initial of the name of the enigmatical person, who commanded at the bottom of the seas.

Ned and Conseil did not reflect much. They devoured the food, and I did likewise. I was, besides, reassured as to our fate; and it seemed evident that out hosts would not let us die of want.

However, everything has an end, everything passes away, even the hunger of people who have not eaten for fifteen hours. Our appetites satisfied, we felt overcome with sleep.

"Faith! I shall sleep well," said Conseil.

"So shall I," replied Ned Land.

My two companions stretched themselves on the cabin carpet, and were soon sound asleep. For my own part, too many thoughts crowded my brain, too many insoluble questions pressed upon me, too many fancies kept my eyes half open. Where were we? What strange power carried us on? I felt—or rather fancied I felt—the machine sinking down to the lowest beds of the sea. Dreadful nightmares beset me; I saw in these mysterious asylums a world of unknown animals, amongst which this submarine boat seemed to be of the same kind, living, moving, and formidable as they. Then my brain grew calmer, my imagination wandered into vague unconsciousness, and I soon fell into a deep sleep.

Chapter IX

Ned Land's Tempers

How long we slept I do not know; but our sleep must have lasted long, for it rested us completely from our fatigues. I woke first. My companions had not moved, and were still stretched in their corner.

Hardly roused from my somewhat hard couch, I felt my brain freed, my mind clear. I then began an attentive examination of our cell. Nothing was changed inside. The prison was still a prison,—the prisoners, prisoners. However, the steward, during our sleep, had cleared the table. I breathed with difficulty. The heavy air seemed to oppress my lungs. Although the cell was large, we had evidently consumed a great part of the oxygen that it contained. Indeed, each man consumes, in one hour, the oxygen contained in more than 176 pints of air, and this air, charged (as then) with a nearly equal quantity of carbonic acid, becomes unbreathable.

It became necessary to renew the atmosphere of our prison, and no doubt the whole in the submarine boat. That gave rise to a question in my mind. How would the commander of this floating dwelling-place proceed? Would he obtain air by chemical means, in getting by heat the oxygen contained in chlorate of potash, and in absorbing carbonic acid by caustic potash? Or, a more convenient, economical, and consequently more probable alternative, would he be satisfied to rise and take breath at the surface of the water, like a cetacean, and so renew for twenty-four hours the atmospheric provision?

In fact, I was already obliged to increase my respirations to eke out of this cell the little oxygen it contained, when suddenly I was refreshed by a current of pure air, and perfumed with saline emanations. It was an invigorating sea breeze, charged with iodine. I opened my mouth wide, and my lungs saturated themselves with fresh particles.

At the same time I felt the boat rolling. The iron-plated monster had evidently just risen to the surface of the ocean to breathe, after the fashion of whales. I found out from that the mode of ventilating the boat.

When I had inhaled this air freely, I sought the conduit-pipe, which conveyed to us the beneficial whiff, and I was not long in finding it. Above the door was a ventilator, through which volumes of fresh air renewed the impoverished atmosphere of the cell.

I was making my observations, when Ned and Conseil awoke almost at the same time, under the influence of this reviving air. They rubbed their eyes, stretched themselves, and were on their feet in an instant.

"Did master sleep well?" asked Conseil, with his usual politeness.

"Very well, my brave boy. And you, Mr Land?"

"Soundly, Professor. But I don't know if I am right or not; there seems to be a sea breeze!"

A seaman could not be mistaken, and I told the Canadian all that had passed during his sleep.

"Good!" said he; "that accounts for those roarings we heard, when the supposed narwhal sighted the *Abraham Lincoln*."

"Quite so, Master Land; it was taking breath."

"Only, Mr Aronnax, I have no idea what o'clock it is, unless it is dinner-time."

"Dinner-time! my good fellow? Say rather breakfast-time, for we certainly have begun another day."

"So," said Conseil, "we have slept twenty-four hours?"

"That is my opinion."

"I will not contradict you," replied Ned Land. "But dinner or breakfast, the steward will be welcome, whichever he brings."

"Master Land, we must conform to the rules on board, and I suppose our appetites are in advance of the dinner hour."

"That is just like you, friend Conseil," said Ned, impatiently. "You are never out of temper, always calm; you would return thanks before grace, and die of hunger rather than complain!"

Time was getting on, and we were fearfully hungry; and this time the steward did not appear. It was rather too long to leave us, if they really had good intentions towards us. Ned Land, tormented by the cravings of hunger, got still more angry; and, notwithstanding his promise, I dreaded an explosion when he found himself with one of the crew.

For two hours more, Ned Land's temper increased; he cried, he shouted, but in vain. The walls were deaf. There was no sound to be heard in the boat: all was still as death. It did not move, for I should have felt the trembling motion of the hull under the influence of the screw. Plunged in the depths of the waters, it belonged no longer to earth:—this silence was dreadful.

I felt terrified, Conseil was calm, Ned Land roared.

Just then a noise was heard outside. Steps sounded on the metal flags. The locks were turned, the door opened, and the steward appeared.

Before I could rush forward to stop him, the Canadian had thrown him down, and held him by the throat. The steward was choking under the grip of his powerful hand.

Conseil was already trying to unclasp the harpooner's hand from his half-suffocated victim, and I was going to fly to the rescue, when suddenly I was nailed to the spot by hearing these words in French—

"Be quiet, Master Land; and you, Professor, will you be so good as to listen to me?"

Chapter X

The Man of the Seas

It was the commander of the vessel who thus spoke.

At these words, Ned Land rose suddenly. The steward, nearly strangled, tottered out on a sign from his master; but such was the power of the commander on board, that not a gesture betrayed the resentment which this man must have felt towards the Canadian. Conseil interested in spite of himself, I stupified, awaited in silence the result of this scene.

The commander, leaning against a corner of the table with his arms folded, scanned us with profound attention. Did he hesitate to speak? Did he regret the words which he had just spoken in French? One might almost think so.

After some moments of silence, which not one of us dreamed of breaking, "Gentlemen," said he, in a calm and penetrating voice, "I speak French, English, German, and Latin equally well. I could, therefore, have answered you at our first interview, but I wished to know you first, then to reflect. The story told by each one, entirely agreeing in the main points, convinced me of your identity. I know now that chance has brought before me M. Pierre Aronnax, Professor of Natural History at the Museum of Paris, entrusted with a scientific mission abroad, Conseil his servant, and Ned Land, of Canadian origin, harpooner on board the frigate *Abraham Lincoln* of the navy of the United States of America."

I bowed assent. It was not a question that the commander put to me. Therefore there was no answer to be made. This man expressed himself with perfect ease, without any accent. His sentences were well turned, his words clear, and his fluency of speech remarkable. Yet, I did not recognise in him a fellow-countryman.

He continued the conversation in these terms:

"You have doubtless thought, sir, that I have delayed long in paying you this second visit. The reason is that, your identity recognised, I wished to weigh maturely what part to act towards you. I have hesitated much. Most annoying circumstances have brought you into the presence of a man who has broken all the ties of humanity. You have come to trouble my existence."

"Unintentionally!" said I.

"Unintentionally?" replied the stranger, raising his voice a little; "was it unintentionally that the *Abraham Lincoln* pursued me all over the seas? Was it unintentionally that you took passage in this frigate? Was it unintentionally that your cannon balls rebounded off the plating of my vessel? Was it unintentionally that Mr Ned Land struck me with his harpoon?"

I detected a restrained irritation in these words. But to these recriminations I had a very natural answer to make, and I made it.

"Sir," said I, "no doubt you are ignorant of the discussions which have taken place concerning you in America and Europe. You do not know that divers accidents, caused by collisions with your submarine machine, have excited public feeling in the two continents. I omit the hypotheses without number by which it was sought to explain in inexplicable phenomenon of which you alone possess the secret. But you must understand that, in pursuing you over the high seas of the Pacific, the *Abraham Lincoln* believed itself to be chasing some powerful sea-monster, of which it was necessary to rid the ocean at any price."

A half-smile curled the lips of the commander: then, in a calmer tone—

"M. Aronnax," he replied, "dare you affirm that your frigate would not as soon have pursued and cannonaded a submarine boat as a monster?"

This question embarrassed me, for certainly Captain Farragut might not have hesitated. He might have thought it his duty to destroy a contrivance of this kind, as he would a gigantic narwhal.

"You understand then, sir," continued the stranger, "that I have the right to treat you as enemies?"

I answered nothing, purposely. For what good would it be to discuss such a proposition, when force could destroy the best arguments?

"I have hesitated for some time," continued the commander; "nothing obliged me to show you hospitality. If I chose to separate myself from you, I should have no interest in seeing you again; I could place you upon the deck of this vessel which has served you as a refuge, I could sink beneath the waters, and forget that you had ever existed. Would not that be my right?"

"It might be the right of a savage," I answered, "but not that of a civilised man."

"Professor," replied the commander quickly, "I am not what you call a civilised man! I have done with society entirely, for reasons which I alone have the right of appreciating. I do not therefore obey its laws, and I desire you never to allude to them before me again!"

This was said plainly. A flash of anger and disdain kindled in the eyes of the Unknown, and I had a glimpse of a terrible past in the life of this man. Not only had he put himself beyond the pale of human laws, but he had made himself independent of them, free in the strictest acceptation of the word, quite beyond their reach! Who then would dare to pursue him at the bottom of the sea, when, on its surface, he defied all attempts made against him? What vessel could resist the shock of his submarine monitor? What cuirass, however thick, could withstand the blows of his spur? No man could demand from him an account of his actions; God, if he believed in one—his conscience, if he had one,—were the sole judges to whom he was answerable.

These reflections crossed my mind rapidly, whilst the stranger personage was silent, absorbed, and as if wrapped up in himself. I regarded him with fear mingled with interest, as, doubtless, OEdipus regarded the Sphinx.

After rather a long silence, the commander resumed the conversation.

"I have hesitated," said he, "but I have thought that my interest might be reconciled with that pity to which every human being has a right. You will remain on board my vessel, since fate has cast you there. You will be free; and in exchange for this liberty, I shall only impose one single condition. Your word of honour to submit to it will suffice."

"Speak, sir," I answered. "I suppose this condition is one which a man of honour may accept?"

"Yes, sir; it is this. It is possible that certain events, unforeseen, may oblige me to consign you to your cabins for some hours or some days, as the case may be. As I desire never to use violence, I expect from you, more than all the others, a passive obedience. In thus acting, I take all the responsibility: I acquit you entirely, for I make it an impossibility for you to see what ought not to be seen. Do you accept this condition?"

Then things took place on board which, to say the least, were singular, and which ought not to be seen by people who were not placed beyond the pale of social laws. Amongst the surprises which the future was preparing for me, this might not be the least.

"We accept," I answered; "only I will ask your permission, sir, to address one question to you—one only."

"Speak, sir."

"You said that we should be free on board."

"Entirely."

"I ask you, then, what you mean by this liberty?"

"Just the liberty to go, to come, to see, to observe even all that passes here,—save under rare circumstances,—the liberty, in short, which we enjoy ourselves, my companions and I."

It was evident that we did not understand one another.

"Pardon me, sir," I resumed, "but this liberty is only what every prisoner has of pacing his prison. It cannot suffice us."

"It must suffice you, however."

"What! we must renounce for ever seeing our country, our friends, our relations again?"

"Yes, sir. But to renounce that unendurable worldly yoke which men believe to be liberty, is not perhaps so painful as you think."

"Well," exclaimed Ned Land, "never will I give my word of honour not to try to escape."

"I did not ask you for your word of honour, Master Land." answered the commander, coldly.

"Sir," I replied, beginning to get angry in spite of myself, "you abuse your situation towards us; it is cruelty."

"No, sir, it is clemency. You are my prisoners of war. I keep you, when I could, by a word, plunge you into the depths of the ocean. You attacked me. You came to surprise a secret which no man in the world must penetrate,—the secret of my whole existence. And you think that I am going to send you back to that world which must know me no more? Never! In retaining you, it is not you whom I guard—it is myself."

These words indicated a resolution taken on the part of the commander, against which no arguments would prevail.

"So, sir," I rejoined, "you give us simply the choice between life and death?"

"Simply."

"My friends," said I, "to a question thus put, there is nothing to answer. But no word of honour binds us to the master of this vessel."

"None, sir," answered the Unknown.

Then, in a gentler tone, he continued—

"Now, permit me to finish what I have to say to you. I know you, M. Aronnax. You and your companions will not, perhaps, have so much to complain of in the chance which has bound you to my fate. You will find amongst the books which are my favourite study the work which you have published on 'the depths of the sea.' I have often read it. You have carried your work as far as terrestrial science permitted you. But you do not know all—you have not seen all. Let me tell you then, Professor, that you will not regret the time passed on board my vessel. You are going to visit the land of marvels."

These words of the commander had a great effect upon me. I cannot deny it. My weak point was touched; and I forgot, for a moment, that the contemplation of these sublime subjects was not worth the loss of liberty. Besides, I trusted to the future to decide this grave question. So I contented myself with saying—

"By what name ought I to address you?"

"Sir," replied the commander, "I am nothing to you but Captain Nemo; and you and your companions are nothing to me but the passengers of the *Nautilus*."

Captain Nemo called. A steward appeared. The captain gave him his orders in that strange language which I did not understand. Then, turning towards the Canadian and Conseil—

"A repast awaits you in your cabin," said he. "Be so good as to follow this man."

"And now, M. Aronnax, our breakfast is ready. Permit me to lead the way."

"I am at your service, captain."

I followed Captain Nemo; and as soon as I had passed through the door, I found myself in a kind of passage lighted by electricity, similar to the waist of a ship. After we had proceeded a dozen yards, a second door opened before me.

I then entered a dining-room, decorated and furnished in severe taste. High oaken sideboards, inlaid with ebony, stood at the two extremities of the room, and upon their shelves glittered china, porcelain, and glass of inestimable value. The plate on the table sparkled in the rays which the luminous ceiling shed around, while the light was tempered and softened by exquisite paintings.

In the centre of the room was a table richly laid out. Captain Nemo indicated the place I was to occupy.

The breakfast consisted of a certain number of dishes, the contents of which were furnished by the sea alone; and I was ignorant of the nature and mode of preparation of some of them. I acknowledged that they were good, but they had a peculiar flavour, which I easily became accustomed to. These different aliments appeared to me to be rich in phosphorus, and I thought they must have a marine origin.

Captain Nemo looked at me. I asked him no questions, but he guessed my thoughts, and answered of his own accord the questions which I was burning to address to him.

"The greater part of these dishes are unknown to you," he said to me. "However, you may partake of them without fear. They are wholesome and nourishing. For a long time I have renounced the food of the earth, and I am never ill now. My crew, who are healthy, are fed on the same food."

"So," said I, "all these eatables are the produce of the sea?"

"Yes, Professor, the sea supplies all my wants. Sometimes I cast my nets in tow, and I draw them in ready to break. Sometimes I hunt in the midst of this element, which appears to be inaccessible to man, and quarry the game which dwells in my submarine forests. My flocks, like those of Neptune's old shepherds, graze fearlessly in the immense prairies of the ocean. I have a vast property there, which I cultivate myself, and which is always sown by the hand of the Creator of all things."

"I can understand perfectly, sir, that your nets furnish excellent fish for your table; I can understand also that you hunt aquatic game in your submarine forests; but I cannot understand at all how a particle of meat, no matter how small, can figure in your bill of fare."

"This, which you believe to be meat, Professor, is nothing else than fillet of turtle. Here are also some dolphin's livers, which you take to be ragout of pork. My cook is a clever fellow, who excels in dressing these various products of the ocean. Taste all these dishes. Here is a preserve of holothuria, which a Malay would declare to be unrivalled in the world; here is a cream, of which the milk has been furnished by the cetacea, and the sugar by the great fucus of the North Sea; and lastly, permit me to offer you some preserve of anemones, which is equal to that of the most delicious fruits."

I tasted, more from curiosity than as a connoisseur, whilst Captain Nemo enchanted me with his extraordinary stories.

"You like the sea, Captain?"

"Yes; I love it! The sea is everything. It covers seven-tenths of the terrestrial globe. Its breath is pure and healthy. It is an immense desert, where man is never lonely, for he feels life stirring on all sides. The sea is only the embodiment of a supernatural and wonderful existence. It is nothing but love and emotion; it is the "Living Infinite," as one of your poets has said. In fact, Professor, Nature manifests herself in it by her three kingdoms, mineral, vegetable, and animal. The sea is the vast reservoir of Nature. The globe began with sea, so to speak; and who knows if it will not end with it? In it is supreme tranquillity. The sea does not belong to despots. Upon its surface men can still exercise unjust laws, fight, tear one another to pieces, and be carried away with terrestrial horrors. But at thirty feet below its level, their reign ceases, their influence is quenched, and their power disappears. Ah! sir, live—live in the bosom of the waters! There only is independence! There I recognise no masters! There I am free!"

Captain Nemo suddenly became silent in the midst of this enthusiasm, by which he was quite carried away. For a few moments he paced up and down, much agitated. Then he became more calm, regained his accustomed coldness of expression, and turning towards me—

"Now, Professor," said he, "if you wish to go over the *Nautilus*, I am at your service."

Captain Nemo rose. I followed him. A double door, contrived at the back of the dining-room, opened, and I entered a room equal in dimensions to that which I had just quitted.

It was a library. High pieces of furniture, of black violet ebony inlaid with brass, supported upon their wide shelves a great number of books uniformly bound. They followed the shape of the room, terminating at the lower part in huge divans, covered with brown leather, which were curved, to afford the greatest comfort. Light moveable desks, made to slide in and out at will, allowed one to rest one's book while reading. In the centre stood an immense table, covered with pamphlets, amongst which were some newspapers, already of old date. The electric light flooded everything; it was shed from four unpolished globes half sunk in the volutes of the ceiling. I looked with real admiration at this room, so ingeniously fitted up, and I could scarcely believe my eyes.

"Captain Nemo," said I to my host, who had just thrown himself on one of the divans, "this is a library which would do honour to more than one of the continental palaces, and I am absolutely astounded when I consider that it can follow you to the bottom of the seas."

"Where could one find greater solitude or silence, Professor?" replied Captain Nemo. "Did your study in the Museum afford you such perfect quiet?"

"No, sir; and I must confess that it is a very poor one after yours. You must have six or seven thousand volumes here."

"Twelve thousand, M. Aronnax. These are the only ties which bind me to the earth. But I had done with the world on the day when my *Nautilus* plunged for the first time beneath the waters. That day I bought my last volumes, my last pamphlets, my last papers, and from that time I wish to think that men no longer think or write. These books, Professor, are at your service besides, and you can make use of them freely."

I thanked Captain Nemo, and went up to the shelves of the library. Works on science, morals, and literature abounded in every language; but I did not see one single work on political economy; that subject appeared to be strictly proscribed. Strange to say, all these books were irregularly arranged, in whatever language they were written; and this medley proved that the Captain of the *Nautilus* must have read indiscrimately the books which he took up by chance.

"Sir," said I to the Captain, "I thank you for having placed this library at my disposal. It contains treasures of science, and I shall profit by them."

"This room is not only a library," said Captain Nemo, "it is also a smoking-room."

"A smoking-room!" I cried. "Then one may smoke on board?"

"Certainly."

"Then, sir, I am forced to believe that you have kept up a communication with Havannah."

"Not any," answered the Captain. "Accept this cigar, M. Aronnax; and though it does not come from Havannah, you will be pleased with it, if you are a connoisseur."

I took the cigar which was offered me; its shape recalled the London ones, but it seemed to be made of leaves of gold. I lighted it at a little brazier, which was supported upon an elegant bronze stem, and drew the first whiffs with the delight of a lover of smoking who has not smoked for two days.

"It is excellent," said I, "but it is not tobacco."

"No!" answered the Captain, "this tobacco comes neither from Havannah nor from the East. It is a kind of sea-weed, rich in nicotine, with which the sea provides me, but somewhat sparingly."

At that moment Captain Nemo opened a door which stood opposite to that by which I had entered the library, and I passed into an immense drawing-room splendidly lighted.

It was a vast four-sided room, thirty feet long, eighteen wide, and fifteen high. A luminous ceiling, decorated with light arabesques, shed a soft clear light over all the marvels accumulated in this museum. For it was in fact a museum, in which an intelligent and prodigal hand had gathered all the treasures of nature and art, with the artistic confusion which distinguishes a painter's studio.

Thirty first-rate pictures, uniformly framed, separated by bright dra-
pery, ornamented the walls, which were hung with tapestry of severe
design. I saw works of great value, the greater part of which I had
admired in the special collections of Europe, and in the exhibitions
of paintings. The several schools of the old masters were represented
by a Madonna of Raphael, a Virgin of Leonardo da Vinci, a nymph of
Corregio, a woman of Titian, an Adoration of Veronese, an Assump-
tion of Murillo, a portrait of Holbein, a monk of Velasquez, a martyr
of Ribeira, a fair of Rubens, two Flemish landscapes of Teniers, three
little "genre" pictures of Gérard Dow, Metsu, and Paul Potter, two specimens of Géricault and Prudhon, and some sea-pieces of Backhuysen
and Vernet. Amongst the works of modern painters were pictures with
the signatures of Delacroix, Ingres, Decamp, Troyon, Meissonnier,
Daubigny, &c.; and some admirable statues in marble and bronze, after
the finest antique models, stood upon pedestals in the corners of this
magnificent museum. Amazement, as the Captain of the *Nautilus* had
predicted, had already begun to take possession of me.

"Professor," said this strange man, "you must excuse the uncer-
emonious way in which I receive you, and the disorder of this room."

"Sir," I answered, "without seeking to know who you are, I recognise in you an artist."

"An amateur, nothing more, sir. Formerly I loved to collect these
beautiful works created by the hand of man. I sought them greedily,
and ferreted them our indefatigably, and I have been able to bring
together some objects of great value. These are my last souvenirs of
that world which is dead to me. In my eyes, your modern artists are
already old; they have two or three thousand years of existence; I confound them in my own mind. Masters have no age."

"And these musicians?" said I, pointing out some works of Weber,
Rossini, Mozart, Beethoven, Haydn, Meyerbeer, Hérold, Wagner,
Auber, Gounod, and a number of others, scattered over a large model
pianoorgan which occupied one of the panels of the drawing-room.

"These musicians," replied Captain Nemo, "are the contemporaries of Orpheus; for in the memory of the dead all chronological differ-

ences are effaced; and I am dead, Professor; as much dead as those of your friends who are sleeping six feet under the earth!"

Captain Nemo was silent, and seemed lost in a profound reverie. I contemplated him with deep interest, analysing in silence the strange expression of his countenance. Leaning on his elbow against an angle of a costly mosaic table, he no longer saw me,—he had forgotten my presence.

I did not disturb this reverie, and continued my observation of the curiosities which enriched this drawing-room.

Under elegant glass cases, fixed by copper rivets, were classed and labelled the most precious productions of the sea which had ever been presented to the eye of a naturalist. My delight as a professor may be conceived.

The division containing the zoophytes presented the most curious specimens of the two groups of polypi and echinodermes. In the first group, the tubipores, were gorgones arranged like a fan, soft sponges of Syria, ises of the Moluccas, pennatules, an admirable virgularia of the Norwegian seas, variegated umbellulairae, alcyonariae, a whole series of madrepores, which my master Milne Edwards has so cleverly classified, amongst which I remarked some wonderful flabellinae, oculinae of the Island of Bourbon, the "Neptune's car" of the Antilles, superb varieties of corals, in short, every species of those curious polypi of which entire islands are formed, which will one day become continents. Of the echinodermes, remarkable for their coating of spines, asteri, sea-stars, pantacrinae, comatules, astérophons, echini, holothuri, &c., represented individually a complete collection of this group.

A somewhat nervous conchyliologist would certainly have fainted before other more numerous cases, in which were classified the specimens of molluscs. It was a collection of inestimable value, which time fails me to describe minutely. Amongst these specimens, I will quote from memory only the elegant royal hammer-fish of the Indian Ocean, whose regular white spots stood out brightly on a red and brown ground, an imperial spondyle, bright-coloured, bristling with spines, a rare speciment in the European museums—(I estimated its value at not less than £1000); a common hammer-fish of the seas of New Holland, which is only procured with difficulty; exotic buc-cardia of Senegal; fragile white bivalve shells, which a breath might shatter like a soap-bubble; several varieties of the aspirgillum of Java, a kind of calcareous tube, edged with leafy folds, and much debated by amateurs; a whole series of trochi, some a greenish-yel-low, found in the American seas, others a reddish-brown, natives of Australian waters; others from the Gulf of Mexico, remarkable for their inbricated shell; stellari found in the Southern Seas; and last, the rarest of all, the magnificent spur of New Zealand; and every description of delicate and fragile shells to which science has given appropriate names.

Apart, in separate compartments, were spread out chaplets of pearls of the greatest beauty, which reflected the electric light in little sparks of fire; pink pearls, torn from the pinna-marina of the Red Sea; green pearls of the haliotyde iris; yellow, blue, and black pearls, the curious productions of the divers molluscs of every ocean, and certain mussels of the water-courses of the North; lastly, several specimens of inestima-ble value which had been gathered from the rarest pintadines. Some of these pearls were larger than a pigeon's egg, and were worth as much, and more than that which the traveller Tavernier sold to the Shah of Persia for three millions, and surpassed the one in the posses-sion of the Imaum of Muscat, which I had believed to be unrivalled in the world.

Therefore, to estimate the value of this collection was simply impos-sible. Captain Nemo must have expended millions in the acquirement of these various specimens, and I was thinking what source he could have drawn from, to have been able thus to gratify his fancy for collect-ing, when I was interrupted by these words—

"You are examining my shells, Professor? Unquestionably they must be interesting to a naturalist; but for me they have a far greater charm, for I have collected them all with my own hand, and there is not a sea on the face of the globe which has escaped by researches."

"I can understand, Captain, the delight of wandering about in the midst of such riches. You are one of those who have collected their treasures themselves. No museum in Europe possesses such a collection of the produce of the ocean. But if I exhaust all my admiration upon it, I shall have none left for the vessel which carries it. I do not wish to pry into your secrets; but I must confess that this *Nautilus*, with the motive power which confined in it, the contrivances which enable it to be worked, the powerful agent which propels it, all excite my curiosity to the highest pitch. I see suspended on the walls of this room instruments of whose use I am ignorant."

"You will find these same instruments in my own room, Professor, where I shall have much pleasure in explaining their use to you. But first come and inspect the cabin which is set apart for your own use. You must see how you will be accommodated on board the *Nautilus*."

I followed Captain Nemo, who, by one of the doors opening from each panel of the drawing-room, regained the waist. He conducted me towards the bow, and there I found, not a cabin, but an elegant room, with a bed, dressing-table, and several other pieces of furniture.

I could only thank my host.

"Your room adjoins mine," said he, opening a door, "and mine opens into the drawing-room that we have just quitted."

I entered the Captain's room: it had a severe, almost a monkish, aspect. A small iron bedstead, a table, some articles for the toilet; the whole lighted by a skylight. No comforts, the strictest necessaries only.

Captain Nemo pointed to a seat.

"Be so good as to sit down," he said. I seated myself, and he began thus.

Chapter XI

All by Electricity

"Sir," said Captain Nemo, showing me the instruments hanging on the walls of his room, "here are the contrivances required for the navigation of the *Nautilus*. Here, as in the drawing-room, I have them always under my eyes, and they indicate my position and exact direction in the middle of the ocean. Some are known to you, such as the thermometer, which gives the internal temperature of the *Nautilus;* the barometer, which indicates the weight of the air and foretells the changes of the weather; the hygrometer, which marks the dryness of the atmosphere; the storm-glass, the contents of which, by decomposing, announce the approach of tempests; the compass, which guides my course; the sextant, which shows the latitude by the altitude of the sun; chronometers, by which I calculate the longitude; and glasses for day and night, which I use to examine the points of the horizon, when the *Nautilus* rises to the surface of the waves."

"These are the usual nautical instruments," I replied, "and I know the use of them. But these others, no doubt, answer to the particular requirements of the *Nautilus*. This dial with the moveable needle is a manometer, is it not?"

"It is actually a manometer. But by communication with the water, whose external pressure it indicates, it gives our depth at the same time."

"And these other instruments, the use of which I cannot guess?"

"Here, Professor, I ought to give you some explanations. Will you be kind enough to listen to me?"

He was silent for a few moments, then he said—

"There is a powerful agent, obedient, rapid, easy, which conforms to every use, and reigns supreme on board my vessel. Everything is done by means of it. It lights it, warms it, and is the soul of my mechanical apparatus. This agent is electricity."

"Electricity?" I cried in surprise.

"Yes, sir."

"Nevertheless, Captain, you possess an extreme rapidity of movement, which does not agree well with the power of electricity. Until now, its dynamic force has remained under restraint, and has only been able to produce a small amount of power."

"Professor," said Captain Nemo, "my electricity is not every body's. You know what sea-water is composed of. In a thousand grammes are found 96 ½ per cent. of water, and about 2 ⅔ per cent. of chloride of sodium; then, in a smaller quantity, chlorides of magnesium and of potassium, bromide of magnesium, sulphate of magnesia, sulphate and carbonate of lime. You see, then, that chloride of sodium forms a large part of it. So it is this sodium that I extract from sea-water, and of which I compose my ingredients, I owe all to the ocean; it produces electricity, and electricity gives heat, light, motion, and, in a word, life to the *Nautilus*."

"But not the air you breathe?"

"Oh! I could manufacture the air necessary for my consumption, but it is useless, because I go up to the surface of the water when I please. However, if electricity does not furnish me with air to breathe, it works at least the powerful pumps that are stored in spacious reservoirs, and which enable me to prolong at need, and as long as I will, my stay in the depths of the sea. It gives a uniform and unintermittent light, which the sun does not. Now look at this clock; it is electrical, and goes with a regularity that defies the best chronometers. I have divided it into twenty-four hours, like the Italian clocks, because for me there is neither night nor day, sun nor moon, but only that factitious light that I take with me to the bottom of the sea. Look! just now, it is ten o'clock in the morning."

"Exactly."

"Another application of electricity. This dial hanging in front of us indicates the speed of the *Nautilus*. An electric thread puts it in communication with the screw, and the needle indicates the real speed. Look! now we are spinning along with a uniform speed of fifteen miles an hour."

"It is marvellous! and I see, Captain, you were right to make use of this agent that takes the place of wind, water, and steam."

"We have not finished, M. Aronnax," said Captain Nemo, rising; "if you will follow me, we will examine the stern of the *Nautilus*."

Really, I knew already the anterior part of this submarine boat, of which this is the exact division, starting from the ship's head:—the dining-room, five yards long, separated from the library by a water-tight partition; the library, five yards long; the large drawing-room, ten yards long, separated from the Captain's room by a second water-tight partition; the said room, five yards in length; mine, two and a half yards; and lastly, a reservoir of air, seven and a half yards, that extended to the bows. Total length thirty-five yards, or one hundred and five feet. The partitions had doors that were shut hermetically by means of india-rubber instruments, and they ensured the safety of the *Nautilus* in case of a leak.

I followed Captain Nemo through the waist, and arrived at the centre of the boat. There was a sort of well that opened between two partitions. An iron ladder, fastened with an iron hook to the partition, led to the upper end. I asked the Captain what the ladder was used for.

"It leads to the small boat," he said.

"What! have you a boat?" I exclaimed, in surprise.

"Of course; an excellent vessel, light and insubmersible, that serves either as a fishing or as a pleasure boat."

"But then, when you wish to embark, you are obliged to come to the surface of the water?"

"Not at all. This boat is attached to the upper part of the hull of the *Nautilus*, and occupies a cavity made for it. It is decked, quite water-tight, and held together by solid bolts. This ladder leads to a man-hole made in the hull of the *Nautilus*, that corresponds with a similar hole made in the side of the boat. By this double opening I get into the small vessel. They shut the one belonging to the *Nautilus*, I shut the other by means of screw pressure. I undo the bolts, and the little boat goes up to the surface of the sea with prodigious rapidity. I then open the panel of the bridge, carefully shut till then; I mast it, hoist my sail, take my oars, and I'm off.'.'

"But how do you get back on board?"

"I do not come back, M. Aronnax; the *Nautilus* comes to me."

"By your orders?"

"By my orders. An electric thread connects us. I telegraph to it, and that is enough."

"Really," I said, astonished at these marvels, "nothing can be more simple."

After having passed by the cage of the staircase that led to the platform, I saw a cabin six feet long, in which Conseil and Ned Land, enchanted with their repast, were devouring it with avidity. Then a door opened into a kitchen nine feet long, situated between the large storerooms. There electricity, better than gas itself, did all the cooking. The streams under the furnaces gave out to the sponges of platina a heat which was regularly kept up and distributed. They also heated a distilling apparatus, which, by evaporation, furnished excellent drinkable water. Near this kitchen was a bath-room comfortably furnished, with hot and cold water taps.

Next to the kitchen was the berth-room of the vessel, sixteen feet long. But the door was shut, and I could not see the management of it, which might have given me an idea of the number of men employed on board the *Nauilus*.

At the bottom was a fourth partition that separated this office from the engine-room. A door opened, and I found myself in the compartment where Captain Nemo—certainly an engineer of a very high order—had arranged his locomotive machinery. This engine-room, clearly lighted, did not measure less than sixty-five feet in length. It was divided into two parts; the first contained the materials for producing electricity, and the second the machinery that connected it with the screw. I examined it with great interest, in order to understand the machinery of the *Nautilus*.

"You see," said the Captain, "I use Bunsen's contrivances, not Ruhmkorff's. Those would not have been powerful enough. Bunsen's are fewer in number, but strong and large, which experience proves to be the best. The electricity produced passes forward, where it works, by electro-magnets of great size, on a system of levers and cog-wheels that transmit the movement to the axle of the screw. This one, the diameter of which is nineteen feet, and the thread twenty-three feet, performs about a hundred and twenty revolutions in a second."

"And you get then?"

"A speed of fifty miles an hour."

"I have seen the *Nautilus* manoeuvre before the *Abraham Lincoln*, and I have my own ideas as to its speed. But this is not enough. We must see where we go. We must be able to direct it to the right, to the left, above, below. How do you get to the great depths, where you find an increasing resistance, which is rated by hundreds of atmospheres? How do you return to the surface of the ocean? And how do you maintain yourselves in the requisite medium? Am I asking too much?"

"Not at all, Professor," replied the Captain, with some hesitation; "since you may never leave this submarine boat. Come into the saloon, it is our usual study, and there you will learn all you want to know about the *Nautilus*."

Chapter XII
Some Figures

A moment after we were seated on a divan in the saloon smoking. The Captain showed me a sketch that gave the plan, section, and elevation of the *Nautilus*. Then he began his description in these words:—

"Here, M. Aronnax, are the several dimensions of the boat you are in. It is an elongated cylinder with conical ends. It is very like a cigar in shape, a shape already adopted in London in several constructions of the same sort. The length of this cylinder, from stem to stern, is exactly 232 feet, and its maximum breadth is twenty-six feet. It is not built quite like your long-voyage steamers, but its lines are sufficiently long, and its curves prolonged enough, to allow the water to slide off easily, and oppose no obstacle to its passage. These two dimensions enable you to obtain by a simple calculation the surface and cubic contents of the *Nautilus*. Its area measures 6032 feet; and its contents about 1500 cubic yards; that is to say, when completely immersed it displaces 50,000 feet of water, or weighs 1500 tons.

"When I made the plans for this submarine vessel, I meant that nine-tenths should be submerged: consequently, it ought only to displace nine-tenths of its bulk, that is to say, only to weigh that number of tons. I ought not, therefore, to have exceeded that weight, constructing it on the aforesaid dimensions.

"The *Nautilus* is composed of two hulls, one inside, the other outside, joined by T-shaped irons, which render it very strong. Indeed, owing to this cellular arrangement it resists like a block, as if it were solid. Its sides cannot yield; it coheres spontaneously, and not by the closeness of its rivets; and the homogenity of its construction, due to the perfect union of the materials, enables it to defy the roughest seas.

"These two hulls are composed of steel plates, whose density is from .7 to .8 that of water. The first is not less than two inches and a half thick, and weighs 394 tons. The second envelope, the keel, twenty inches high and ten thick, weighs alone sixty-two tons. The engine, the ballast, the several accessories and apparatus appendages, the partitions and bulkheads, weigh 961.62 tons. Do you follow all this?"

"I do."

"Then, when the *Nautilus* is afloat under these circumstances, one-tenth is out of the water. Now, if I have made reservoirs of a size equal to this tenth, or capable of holding 150 tons, and if I fill them with water, the boat, weighing then 1507 tons, will be completely immersed. That would happen, Professor. These reservoirs are in the lower parts of the *Nautilus*. I turn on taps and they fill, and the vessel sinks that had just been level with the surface."

"Well, Captain, but now we come to the real difficulty. I can understand your rising to the surface; but diving below the surface, does not your submarine contrivance encounter a pressure, and consequently undergo an upward thrust of one atmosphere for every thirty feet of water, just about fifteen pounds per square inch?"

"Just so, sir."

"Then, unless you quite fill the *Nautilus*, I do not see how you can draw it down to those depths."

"Professor, you must not confound statics with dynamics, or you will be exposed to grave errors. There is very little labour spent in attaining the lower regions of the ocean, for all bodies have a tendency to sink. When I wanted to find out the necessary increase of weight required to sink the *Nautilus*, I had only to calculate the reduction of volume that seawater acquires according to the depth."

"That is evident."

"Now, if water is not absolutely incompressible, it is at least capable of very slight compression. Indeed, after the most recent calculations this reduction is only .000436 of an atmosphere for each thirty feet of depth. If we want to sink 3000 feet, I should keep account of the reduction of bulk under a pressure equal to that of a column of water of a thousand feet. The calculation is easily verified. Now, I have sup-plementary reservoirs capable of holding a hundred tons. Therefore I can sink to a considerable depth. When I wish to rise to the level of the sea, I only let off the water, and empty all the reservoirs if I want the *Nautilus* to emerge from the tenth part of her total capacity."

I had nothing to object to these reasonings.

"I admit your calculations, Captain," I replied; "I should be wrong to dispute them since daily experience confirms them; but I foresee a real difficulty in the way."

"What, sir?"

"When you are about 1000 feet deep, the walls of the *Nautilus* bear a pressure of 100 atmospheres. If, then, just now you were to empty the supplementary reservoirs, to lighten the vessel, and to go up to the surface, the pumps must overcome the pressure of 100 atmospheres, which is 1500 lbs. per square inch. From that a power"—

"That electricity alone can give," said the Captain, hastily. "I repeat, sir, that the dynamic power of my engines is almost infinite. The pumps of the *Nautilus* have an enormous power, as you must have observed when their jets of water burst like a torrent upon the *Abraham Lincoln*. Besides I use subsidiary reservoirs only to attain a mean depth of 750 to 1000 fathoms, and that with a view of managing my machines. Also, when I have a mind to visit the depths of the ocean five or six miles below the surface, I make use of slower but not less infallible means."

"What are they, Captain?"

"That involves my telling you how the *Nautilus* is worked."

"I am impatient to learn."

"To steer this boat to starboard or port, to turn, in a word, follow-ing a horizontal plan, I use an ordinary rudder fixed on the back of the stern-post, and with one wheel and some tackle to steer by. But I can also make the *Nautilus* rise and sink, and sink and rise, by a verti-cal movement by means of two inclined planes fastened to its sides, opposite the centre of flotation, planes that move in every direction, and that are worked by powerful levers from the interior. If the planes are kept parallel with the boat, it moves horizontally. If slanted, the *Nautilus*, according to this inclination, and under the influence of the screw, either sinks diagonally or rises diagonally as it suits me. And even if I wish to rise more quickly to the surface, I ship the screw, and the pressure of the water causes the *Nautilus* to rise vertically like a balloon filled with hydrogen."

"Bravo, Captain! But how can the steersman follow the route in the middle of the waters?"

"The steersman is placed in a glazed box, that is raised above the hull of the *Nautilus*, and furnished with lenses."

"Are these lenses capable of resisting such pressure?"

"Perfectly. Glass, which breaks at a blow, is, nevertheless, capable of offering considerable resistance. During some experiments of fishing by electric light in 1864 in the Northern Seas, we saw plates less than a third of an inch thick resist a pressure of sixteen atmospheres. Now, the glass that I use is not less than thirty times thicker."

"Granted. But, after all, in order to see, the light must exceed the darkness, and in the midst of the darkness in the water, how can you see?"

"Behind the steersman's cage is placed a powerful electric reflector, the rays from which light up the sea for half a mile in front."

"Ah! bravo, bravo, Captain! Now I can account for this phosphorescence in the supposed narwhal that puzzled us so. I now ask you if the boarding of the *Nautilus* and of the *Scotia*, that has made such a noise, has been the result of a chance rencontre?"

"Quite accidental, sir. I was sailing only one fathom below the surface of the water, when the shock came. It had no bad result."

"None, sir. But now, about your rencontre with the *Abraham Lincoln*?"

"Professor, I am sorry for one of the best vessels in the American navy; but they attacked me, and I was bound to defend myself. I contented myself, however, with putting the frigate *hors de combat*: she will not have any difficulty in getting repaired at the next port."

"Ah, Commander! your *Nautilus* is certainly a marvellous boat."

"Yes, Professor; and I love it as if it were part of myself. If danger threatens one of your vessels on the ocean, the first impression is the feeling of an abyss above and below. On the *Nautilus* men's hearts never fail them. No defects to be afraid of, for the double shell is as firm as iron; no rigging to attend to; no sails for the wind to carry away; no boilers to burst; no fire to fear, for the vessel is made of iron, not of wood; no coal to run short, for electricity is the only mechanical agent; no collision to fear, for it alone swims in deep water; no tempest to brave, for when it dives below the water, it reaches absolute tranquillity. There, sir! that is the perfection of vessels! And if it is true that the engineer has more confidence in the vessel than the builder, and the builder than the captain himself, you understand the trust I repose in my *Nautilus;* for I am at once captain, builder, and engineer."

"But how could you construct this wonderful *Nautilus* in secret?"

"Each separate portion, M. Aronnax, was brought from different parts of the globe. The keel was forged at Creusot, the shaft of the screw at Penn & Co.'s, London, the iron plates of the hull at Laird's of Liverpool, the screw itself at Scott's at Glasgow. The resevoirs were made by Cail & Co. at Paris, the engine by Krupp in Prussia, its beak in Motala's workshop in Sweden, its mathematical instruments by Hart Brothers, of New York, &c.; and each of these people had my orders under different names."

"But these parts had to be put together and arranged?"

"Professor, I had set up my workshops upon a desert island in the ocean. There my workmen, that is to say, the brave men that I instructed and educated, and myself have put together our *Nautilus.* Then, when the work was finished, fire destroyed all trace of our proceedings on this island, that I could have jumped over if I had liked."

"Then the cost of this vessel is great?"

"M. Aronnax, an iron vessel costs £45 per ton. Now the *Nautilus* weighed 1500. It came therefore to £67,500, and £80,000 more for fitting it up, and about £200,000 with the works of art and the collections it contains."

"One last question, Captain Nemo."

"Ask it, Professor."

"You are rich?"

"Immensely rich, sir; and I could, without missing it, pay the national debt of France."

I stared at the singular person who spoke thus. Was he playing upon my credulity? The future would decide that.

Chapter XIII

The Black River

The portion of the terrestrial globe which is covered by water is estimated at upwards of eighty millions of acres. The fluid mass comprises two billions two hundred and fifty millions of cubic miles, forming a spherical body of a diameter of sixty leagues, the weight of which would be three quintillions of tons. To comprehend the meaning of these figures, it is necessary to observe that a quintillion is to a billion as a billion is to unity; in other words, there are as many billions in a quintillion as there are units in a billion. This mass of fluid is equal to about the quantity of water which would be discharged by all the rivers of the earth in forty thousand years.

During the geological epochs, the igneous period succeeded to the aqueous. The ocean originally prevailed everywhere. Then by degrees, in the silurian period, the tops of the mountains began to appear, the islands emerged, then disappeared in partial deluges, reappeared, became settled, formed continents, till at length the earth became geographically arranged, as we see in the present day. The solid had wrested from the liquid thirty-seven million six hundred and fifty seven square miles, equal to twelve billions nine hundred and sixty millions of acres.

The shape of continents allows us to divide the waters into five great portions: the Arctic or Frozen Ocean, the Antarctic or Frozen Ocean, the Indian, the Atlantic, and the Pacific Oceans.

The Pacific Ocean extends from north to south between the two polar circles, and from east to west between Asia and America, over an extent of 145 degrees of longitude. It is the quietest of seas; its currents are broad and slow, it has medium tides, and abundant rain. Such was the ocean that my fate destined me first to travel over under these strange conditions.

"Sir," said Captain Nemo, "we will, if you please, take our bearings and fix the startingpoint of this voyage. It is a quarter to twelve, I will go up again to the surface."

The Captain pressed an electric clock three times. The pumps began to drive the water from the tanks; the needle of the manometer marked by a different pressure the ascent of the *Nautilus*, then it stopped.

"We have arrived," said the Captain.

I went to the central staircase which opened on to the platform, clambered up the iron steps, and found myself on the upper part of the *Nautilus*.

The platform was only three feet out of water. The front and back of the *Nautilus* was of that spindle-shape which caused it justly to be compared to a cigar. I noticed that its iron plates, slightly overlaying each other, resembled the shell which clothes the bodies of our large terrestrial reptiles. It explained to me how natural it was, in spite of all glasses, that this boat should have been taken for a marine animal.

Towards the middle of the platform the long-boat, half buried in the hull of the vessel, formed a slight excrescence. Fore and aft rose two cages of medium height with inclined sides, and partly closed by thick lenticular glasses; one destined for the steersman who directed the *Nautilus*, the other containing a brilliant lantern to give light on the road.

The sea was beautiful, the sky pure. Scarcely could the long vehicle feel the broad undulations of the ocean. A light breeze from the east rippled the surface of the waters. The horizon, free from fog, made observation easy. Nothing was in sight. Not a quicksand, not an island. A vast desert.

Captain Nemo, by the help of his sextant, took the altitude of the sun, which ought also to give the latitude. He waited for some moments till its disc touched the horizon. Whilst taking observations not a muscle moved, the instrument could not have been more motionless in a hand of marble.

"Twelve o'clock, sir," said he. "When you like"—

I cast a last look upon the sea, slightly yellowed by the Japanese coast, and descended to the saloon.

"And now, sir, I leave you to your studies," added the Captain; "our course is E.N.E., our depth is twenty-six fathoms. Here are maps on a large scale by which you may follow it. The saloon is at your disposal, and with your permission I will retire." Captain Nemo bowed, and I remained alone, lost in thoughts all bearing on the commander of the *Nautilus*.

For a whole hour was I deep in these reflections, seeking to pierce this mystery so interesting to me. Then my eyes fell upon the vast planisphere spread upon the table, and I placed my finger on the very spot where the given latitude and longitude crossed.

The sea has its large rivers like the continents. They are special currents known by their temperature and their colour. The most remarkable of these is known by the name of the Gulf Stream. Science has decided on the globe the direction of five principal currents: one in the North Atlantic, a second in the South, a third in the North Pacific, a fourth in the South, and a fifth in the Southern Indian Ocean. It is even probable that a sixth current existed at one time or another in the

Northern Indian Ocean, when the Caspian and Aral seas formed but one vast sheet of water.

At this point indicated on the planisphere one of these currents was rolling, the Kuro-Scivo of the Japanese, the Black River, which, leaving the Gulf of Bengal where it is warmed by the perpendicular rays of a tropical sun, crosses the Straits of Malacca along the coast of Asia, turns into the North Pacific to the Aleutian Islands, carrying with it trunks of camphor-trees and other indigenous productions, and edging the waves of the ocean with the pure indigo of its warm water. It was this current that the *Nautilus* was to follow. I followed it with my eye; saw it lose itself in the vastness of the Pacific, and felt myself drawn with it, when Ned Land and Conseil appeared at the door of the saloon.

My two brave companions remained petrified at the sight of the wonders spread before them.

"Where are we, where are we?" exclaimed the Canadian. "In the museum at Quebec?"

"My friends," I answered, making a sign for them to enter, "you are not in Canada, but on board the *Nautilus* fifty yards below the level of the sea."

"But, M. Aronnax," said Ned Land, "can you tell me how many men there are on board? Ten, twenty, fifty, a hundred?"

"I cannot answer you, Mr Land; it is better to abandon for a time all idea of seizing the *Nautilus* or escaping from it. This ship is a masterpiece of modern industry, and I should be sorry not to have seen it. Many people would accept the situation forced upon us, if only to move amongst such wonders. So be quiet and let us try and see what passes around us."

"See!" exclaimed the harpooner, "but we can see nothing in this iron prison! We are walking—we are sailing—blindly."

Ned Land had scarcely pronounced these words when all was suddenly darkness. The luminous ceiling was gone, and so rapidly that my eyes received a painful impression.

We remained mute, not stirring, and not knowing what surprise awaited us, whether agreeable or disagreeable. A sliding noise was heard: one would have said that panels were working at the sides of the *Nautilus*.

"It is the end of the end!" said Ned Land.

Suddenly light broke at each side of the saloon, through two oblong openings. The liquid mass appeared vividly lit up by the electric gleam. Two crystal plates separated us from the sea. At first I trembled at the thought that this frail partition might break, but strong bands of copper bound them, giving an almost infinite power of resistance.

The sea was distinctly visible for a mile all round the *Nautilus*. What a spectacle! What pen can describe it? Who could paint the effects of the light through those transparent sheets of water, and the softness of the successive gradations from the lower to the superior strata of the ocean?

We know the transparency of the sea, and that its clearness is far beyond that of rock water. The mineral and organic substances, which it holds in suspension heightens its transparency. In certain parts of the ocean at the Antilles, under seventy-five fathoms of water, can be seen with surprising clearness a bed of sand. The penetrating power of the solar rays does not seem to cease for a depth of one hundred and fifty fathoms. But in this middle fluid travelled over by the *Nautilus*, the electric brightness was produced even in the bosom of the waves. It was no longer luminous water, but liquid light.

On each side a window opened into this unexplored abyss. The obscurity of the saloon showed to advantage the brightness outside, and we looked out as if this pure crystal had been the glass of an immense aquarium.

"You wished to see, friend Ned; well, you see now."

"Curious! curious!" muttered the Canadian, who, forgetting his ill-temper, seemed to submit to some irresistible attraction; "and one would come further than this to admire such a sight!"

"Ah!" thought I to myself, "I understand the life of this man; he has made a world apart for himself, in which he treasures all his greatest wonders."

For two whole hours an aquatic army escorted the *Nautilus*. During their games, their bounds, while rivalling each other in beauty, brightness, and velocity, I distinguished the green labre; the banded mullet, marked by a double line of black; the round-tailed goby, of a white colour, with violet spots on the back; the Japanese scombrus, a beautiful mackerel of these seas, with a blue body and silvery head; the brilliant azurors, whose name alone defies description; some banded spares, with variegated fins of blue and yellow; some aclostones, the woodcocks of the seas, some specimens of which attain a yard in length; Japanese salamanders, spider lampreys, serpents six feet long, with eyes small and lively, and a huge mouth bristling with teeth; with many other species.

Our imagination was kept at its height, interjections followed quickly on each other. Ned named the fish, and Conseil classed them. I was in ecstacies with the vivacity of their movements and the beauty of their forms. Never had it been given to me to surprise these animals, alive and at liberty, in their natural element. I will not mention all the varieties which passed before my dazzled eyes, all the collection of the seas of China and Japan. These fish, more numerous than the birds of the air, came, attracted, no doubt, by the brilliant focus of the electric light.

Suddenly there was daylight in the saloon, the iron panels closed again, and the enchanting vision disappeared. But for a long time I dreamt on till my eyes fell on the instruments hanging on the partition. The compass still showed the course to be N.N.E., the manometer indicated a pressure of five atmospheres, equivalent to a depth of twenty-five fathoms, and the electric log gave a speed of fifteen miles an hour. I expected Captain Nemo, but he did not appear. The clock marked the hour of five.

Ned Land and Conseil returned to their cabin, and I retired to my chamber. My dinner was ready. It was composed of turtle-soup made of the most delicate hawksbills, of a surmullet served with puff paste (the liver of which, prepared by itself, was most delicious), and fillets of the emperor-holocanthus, the savour of which seemed to me superior even to salmon.

I passed the evening reading, writing, and thinking. Then sleep overpowered me, and I stretched myself on my couch of zostera, and slept profoundly, whilst the *Nautilus* was gliding rapidly through the current of the Black River.

Chapter XIV

A Note of Invitation

The next day was the 9th of November. I awoke after a long sleep of twelve hours. Conseil came, according to custom, to know "how I had passed the night," and to offer his services. He had left his friend the Canadian sleeping like a man who had never done anything else all his life. I let the worthy fellow chatter as he pleased, without caring to answer him. I was pre-occupied by the absence of the Captain during our sitting of the day before, and hoping to see him to-day.

As soon as I was dressed I went into the saloon. It was deserted.

I plunged into the study of the conchological treasures hidden behind the glasses. I revelled also in great herbals filled with the rarest marine plants, which, although dried up, retained their lovely colours. Amongst these precious hydrophytes I remarked some vorticellae, pavonariae, delicate ceramies with scarlet tints, some fan-shaped agari, and some natabuli like flat mushrooms, which at one time used to be classed as zoophytes; in short, a perfect series of algae.

The whole day passed without my being honoured by a visit from Captain Nemo. The panels of the saloon did not open. Perhaps they did not wish us to tire of these beautiful things.

The course of the *Nautilus* was E.N.E., her speed twelve knots, the depth below the surface between twenty-five and thirty fathoms.

The next day, 10th of November, the same desertion, the same solitude. I did not see one of the ship's crew: Ned and Conseil spent the greater part of the day with me. They were astonished at the inexplicable absence of the Captain. Was this singular man ill?—had he altered his intentions with regard to us?

After all, as Conseil said, we enjoyed perfect liberty, we were delicately and abundantly fed. Our host kept to his terms of the treaty. We could not complain, and, indeed, the singularity of our fate reserved such wonderful compensation for us, that we had no right to accuse it as yet.

That day I commenced the journal of these adventures which has enabled me to relate them with more scrupulous exactitude and minute detail. I wrote it on paper made from the zostera marina.

11th November, early in the morning. The fresh air spreading over the interior of the *Nautilus* told me that we had come to the surface of the ocean to renew our supply of oxygen. I directed my steps to the central staircase, and mounted the platform.

It was six o'clock, the weather was cloudy, the sea grey but calm. Scarcely a billow. Captain Nemo, whom I hoped to meet, would he be there? I saw no one but the steersman imprisoned in his glass cage. Seated upon the projection formed by the hull of the pinnace, I inhaled the salt breeze with delight.

By degrees the fog disappeared under the action of the sun's rays, the radiant orb rose from behind the eastern horizon. The sea flamed under its glance like a train of gunpowder. The clouds scattered in the heights were coloured with lively tints of beautiful shades, and numerous "mare's tails," which betokened wind for that day. But what was wind to this *Nautilus* which tempests could not frighten!

I was admiring this joyous rising of the sun, so gay, and so life-giving, when I heard steps approaching the platform. I was prepared to salute Captain Nemo, but it was his second (whom I had already seen on the Captain's first visit) who appeared. He advanced on the platform not seeming to see me. With his powerful glass to his eye he scanned every point of the horizon with great attention. This examination over, he approached the panel and pronounced a sentence in exactly these terms. I have remembered it, for every morning it was repeated under exactly the same conditions. It was thus worded—

"Nautron respoc lorni virch."

What it meant I could not say.

These words pronounced, the second descended. I thought that the *Nautilus* was about to return to its submarine navigation. I regained the panel and returned to my chamber.

Five days sped thus, without any change in our situation. Every morning I mounted the platform. The same phrase was pronounced by the same individual. But Captain Nemo did not appear.

I had made up my mind that I should never see him again, when, on the 16th November, on returning to my room with Ned and Conseil, I found upon my table a note addressed to me. I opened it impatiently. It was written in a bold, clear hand, the characters rather pointed, recalling the German type. The note was worded as follows:—

"To PROFESSOR ARONNAX, on board the *Nautilus*.
"16th of *November* 1867.

"Captain Nemo invites Professor Aronnax to a hunting-party, which will take place tomorrow morning in the forests of the island of Crespo. He hopes that nothing will prevent the Professor from being present, and he will with pleasure see him joined by his companions.

"CAPTAIN NEMO,
COMMANDER OF THE *NAUTILUS*."

"A hunt!" exclaimed Ned.

"And in the forests of the island of Crespo!" added Conseil.

"Oh! then the gentlemen is going on *terra firma?*" replied Ned Land.

"That seems to me to be clearly indicated," said I, reading the letter once more.

"Well, we must accept," said the Canadian. "But once more on dry ground, we shall know what to do. Indeed, I shall not be sorry to eat a piece of fresh venison."

Without seeking to reconcile what was contradictory between Captain Nemo's manifest aversion to islands and continents, and his invitation to hunt in a forest, I contented myself with replying—

"Let us first see where the island of Crespo is."

I consulted the planisphere, and in 32° 40' north lat., and 157° 50' west long., I found a small island, recognised in 1801 by Captain Crespo, and marked in the ancient Spanish maps as Rocca de la Plata, the meaning of which is "The Silver Rock." We were then about eighteen hundred miles from our starting-point, and the course of the *Nautilus*, a little changed, was bringing it back towards the south-east.

I showed this little rock lost in the midst of the North Pacific to my companions.

"If Captain Nemo does sometimes go on dry ground," said I, "he at least chooses desert islands."

Ned Land shrugged his shoulders without speaking, and Conseil and he left me.

After supper, which was served by the steward, mute and impassion, I went to bed, not without some anxiety.

The next morning, the 17th of November, on awakening I felt that the *Nautilus* was perfectly still. I dressed quickly and entered the saloon.

Captain Nemo was there, waiting for me. He rose, bowed, and asked me if it was convenient for me to accompany him. As he made no allusion to his absence during the last eight days, I did not mention it, and simply answered that my companions and myself were ready to follow him.

We entered the dining-room, where breakfast was served.

"M. Aronnax," said the Captain, "pray, share my breakfast without ceremony; we will chat as we eat. For though I promised you a walk in the forest, I did not undertake to find hotels there. So breakfast as a man who will most likely not have his dinner till very late."

I did honour to the repast. It was composed of several kinds of fish, and slices of holothuridae (excellent zoophytes), and different sorts of sea-weed. Our drink consisted of pure water, to which the Captain added some drops of a fermented liquor, extracted by the Kamschatcha method from a sea-weed known under the name of *Rhodomenia palmata*. Captain Nemo ate at first without saying a word. Then he began—

"Sir, when I proposed to you to hunt in my submarine forest of Crespo, you evidently thought me mad. Sir, you should never judge lightly of any man."

"But, Captain, believe me"—

"Be kind enough to listen, and you will then see whether you have any cause to accuse me of folly and contradiction."

"I listen."

"You know as well as I do, Professor, that man can live under water, providing he carries with him a sufficient supply of breathable air. In submarine works, the workman, clad in an impervious dress, with his head in a metal helmet, receives air from above by means of forcing pumps and regulators."

"That is a diving apparatus," said I.

"Just so, but under these conditions the man is not at liberty; he is attached to the pump which sends him air through an india-rubber tube, and if we were obliged to be thus held to the *Nautilus*, we could not go far."

"And the means of getting free?" I asked.

"It is to use the Rouquayrol apparatus, invented by two of your own countrymen, which I have brought to perfection for my own use, and which will allow you to risk yourself under these new physiological conditions, without any organ whatever suffering. It consists of a reservoir of thick iron plates, in which I store the air under a pressure of fifty atmospheres. This reservoir is fixed on the back by means of braces, like a soldier's knapsack. Its upper part forms a box in which the air is kept by means of a bellows, and therefore cannot escape unless at its normal tension. In the Rouquayrol apparatus such as we use, two india-rubber pipes leave this box and join a sort of tent which holds the nose and mouth; one is to introduce fresh air, the other to let out the foul, and the tongue closes one or the other according to the wants of the respirator. But I, in encountering great pressures at the bottom of the sea, was obliged to shut my head, like that of a diver, in a ball of copper; and it is to this ball of copper that the two pipes, the inspirator and the expirator, open."

"Perfectly, Captain Nemo; but the air that you carry with you must soon be used; when it only contains fifteen per cent. of oxygen, it is no longer fit to breathe."

"Right! but I told you, M. Aronnax, that the pumps of the *Nautilus* allow me to store the air under considerable pressure, and on those conditions, the reservoir of the apparatus can furnish breathable air for nine or ten hours."

"I have no further objections to make," I answered; "I will only ask you one thing, Captain—how can you light your road at the bottom of the sea?"

"With the Ruhmkorff apparatus, M. Aronnax; one is carried on the back, the other is fastened to the waist. It is composed of a Bunsen pile, which I do not work with bichromate of potash, but with sodium. A wire is introduced which collects the electricity produced, and directs it towards a particularly made lantern. In this lantern is a spiral glass which contains a small quantity of carbonic gas. When the apparatus is at work this gas becomes luminous, giving out a white and continuous light. Thus provided, I can breathe and I can see."

"Captain Nemo, to all my objections you make such crushing answers, that I dare no longer doubt. But if I am forced to admit the Rouquayrol and Ruhmkorff apparatus, I must be allowed some reservations with regard to the gun I am to carry."

"But it is not a gun for powder," answered the Captain.

"Then it is an air-gun."

"Doubtless! How would you have me manufacture gunpowder on board, without either saltpetre, sulphur, or charcoal?"

"Besides," I added, "to fire under water in a medium eight hundred and fifty-five times denser than the air, we must conquer very considerable resistance."

"That would be no difficulty. There exist guns, according to Fulton, perfected in England by Philip Coles and Burley, in France by Furcy, and in Italy by Landi, which are furnished with a peculiar system of closing, which can fire under these conditions. But I repeat, having no powder, I use air under great pressure, which the pumps of the *Nautilus* furnish abundantly."

"But this air must be rapidly used?"

"Well, have I not my Rouquayrol reservoir, which can furnish it at need? A tap is all that is required. Besides, M. Aronnax, you must see yourself that, during our submarine hunt, we can spend but little air and but few balls."

"But it seems to me that in this twilight, and in the midst of this fluid, which is very dense compared with the atmosphere, shots could not go far, nor easily prove mortal."

"Sir, on the contrary, with this gun every blow is mortal; and however lightly the animal is touched, it falls as if struck by a thunderbolt."

"Why?"

"Because the balls sent by this gun are not ordinary balls, but little cases of glass (invented by Leniebroek, an Austrian chemist), of which I have a large supply. These glass cases are covered with a case of steel, and weighted with a pellet of lead; they are real Leyden bottles, into which the electricity is forced to a very high tension. With the slightest shock they are discharged, and the animal, however strong it may be, falls dead. I must tell you that these cases are size number four, and that the charge for an ordinary gun would be ten."

"I will argue no longer," I replied, rising from the table; "I have nothing left me but to take my gun. At all events, I will go where you go."

Captain Nemo then led me aft; and in passing before Ned and Conseil's cabin, I called my two companions, who followed immediately. We then came to a kind of cell near the machinery-room, in which we were to put on our walking dress.

Chapter XV

A Walk on the Bottom of the Sea

This cell was, to speak correctly, the arsenal and wardrobe of the *Nautilus*. A dozen diving apparatuses hung from the partition, waiting our use.

Ned Land, on seeing them, showed evident repugnance to dress himself in one.

"But, my worthy Ned, the forests of the Island of Crespo are nothing but submarine forests."

"Good!" said the disappointed harpooner, who saw his dreams of fresh meat fade away. "And you, M. Aronnax, are you going to dress yourself in those clothes?"

"There is no alternative, Master Ned."

"As you please, sir," replied the harpooner, shrugging his shoulders; "but as for me, unless I am forced, I will never get into one."

"No one will force you, Master Ned," said Captain Nemo.

"Is Conseil going to risk it?" asked Ned.

"I follow my master wherever he goes," replied Conseil.

At the Captain's call two of the ship's crew came to help us to dress in these heavy and impervious clothes, made of india-rubber without seam, and constructed expressly to resist considerable pressure. One would have thought it a suit of armour, both supple and resisting. This suit formed trousers and waistcoat. The trousers were finished off with thick boots, weighted with heavy leaden soles. The texture of the waistcoat was held together by bands of copper, which crossed the chest, protecting it from the great pressure of the water, and leaving the lungs free to act; the sleeves ended in gloves, which in no way restrained the movement of the hands. There was a vast difference noticeable between these consummate apparatuses and the old cork breastplates, jackets, and other contrivances in vogue during the eighteenth century.

Captain Nemo and one of his companions (a sort of Hercules, who must have possessed great strength), Conseil, and myself, were soon enveloped in the dresses. There remained nothing more to be done but to enclose our heads in the metal box. But before proceeding to this operation, I asked the Captain's permission to examine the guns we were to carry.

One of the *Nautilus* men gave me a simple gun, the butt end of which, made of steel hollow in the centre, was rather large. It served as a reservoir for compressed air, which a valve, worked by a spring, allowed to escape into a metal tube. A box of projectiles, in a groove in the thickness of the butt end, contained about twenty of these electric balls, which, by means of a spring, were forced into the barrel of the gun. As soon as one shot was fired, another was ready.

"Captain Nemo," said I, "this arm is perfect, and easily handled; I only ask to be allowed to try it. But how shall we gain the bottom of the sea?"

"At this moment, Professor, the *Nautilus* is stranded in five fathoms, and we have nothing to do but to start."

"But how shall we get off?"

"You shall see."

Captain Nemo thrust his head into the helmet, Conseil and I did the same, not without hearing an ironical "Good sport!" from the Canadian. The upper part of our dress terminated in a copper collar, upon which was screwed the helmet. Three holes, protected by thick glass, allowed us to see in all directions, by simply turning our head in the interior of the headdress. As soon as it was in position, the Rouquayrol apparatus on our backs began to act; and, for my part, I could breathe with ease.

With the Ruhmkorff lamp hanging from my belt, and the gun in my hand, I was ready to set out. But to speak the truth, imprisoned in these heavy garments, and glued to the deck by my leaden soles, it was impossible for me to take a step.

But this state of things was provided for. I felt myself being pushed into a little room contiguous to the wardrobe-room. My companions followed, towed along in the same way. I heard a water-tight door, furnished with stopper-plates, close upon us, and we were wrapped in profound darkness.

After some minutes, a loud hissing was heard. I felt the cold mount from my feet to my chest. Evidently from some part of the vessel they had, by means of a tap, given entrance to the water, which was invading us, and with which the room was soon filled. A second door cut in the side of the *Nautilus* then opened. We saw a faint light. In another instant our feet trod the bottom of the sea.

And now, how can I retrace the impression left upon me by that walk under the waters? Words are impotent to relate such wonders! Captain Nemo walked in front, his companion followed some steps behind. Conseil and I remained near each other, as if an exchange of words had been possible through our metallic cases. I no longer felt the weight of my clothing, or of my shoes, of my reservoir of air, or my thick helmet, in the midst of which my head rattled like an almond in its shell.

The light, which lit the soil thirty feet below the surface of the ocean, astonished me by its power. The solar rays shone through the watery mass easily, and dissipated all colour, and I clearly distinguished objects at a distance of a hundred and fifty yards. Beyond that the tints darkened into fine gradations of ultramarine, and faded into vague obscurity. Truly this water which surrounded me was but another air denser than the terrestrial atmosphere, but almost as transparent. Above me was the calm surface of the sea. We were walking on fine even sand, not wrinkled, as on a flat shore, which retains the impression of the billows. This dazzling carpet, really a reflector, repelled the rays of the sun with wonderful intensity, which accounted for the vibration which penetrated every atom of liquid. Shall I be believed when I say that, at the depth of thirty feet, I could see as if I was in broad daylight?

For a quarter of an hour I trod on this sand, sown with the impalpable dust of shells. The hull of the *Nautilus*, resembling a long shoal, disappeared by degrees; but its lantern, when darkness should overtake us in the waters, would help to guide us on board by its distinct rays.

Soon forms of objects outlined in the distance were discernible. I recognised magnificent rocks, hung with a tapestry of zoophytes of the most beautiful kind, and I was at first struck by the peculiar effect of this medium.

It was then ten in the morning; the rays of the sun struck the surface of the waves at rather an oblique angle, and at the touch of their light, decomposed by refraction as through a prism, flowers, rocks, plants, shells, and polypi were shaded at the edges by the seven solar colours. It was marvellous, a feast for the eyes, this complication of coloured tints, a perfect kaleidoscope of green, yellow, orange, violet, indigo, and blue; in one word, the whole palette of an enthusiastic colourist! Why could I not communicate to Conseil the lively sensations which were mounting to my brain, and rival him in expressions of admiration? For aught I knew, Captain Nemo and his companion might be able to exchange thoughts by means of signs previously agreed upon. So, for want of better, I talked to myself; I declaimed in the copper box which covered my head, thereby expending more air in vain words than was perhaps expedient.

Various kinds of isis, clusters of pure tuftcoral, prickly fungi, and anemones, formed a brilliant garden of flowers, enamelled with prophitae, decked with their collarettes of blue tentacles, sea-stars studding the sandy bottom, together with asterophytons like fine lace embroidered by the hands of naiads, whose festoons were waved by the gentle undulations caused by our walk. It was a real grief to me to crush under my feet the brilliant specimens of molluscs which strewed the ground by thousands, of hammerheads, donaciae (veritable bounding shells), of staircases, and red helmet-shells, angel-wings, and many others produced by this inexhaustible ocean. But we were bound to walk, so we went on, whilst above our heads waved shoals of physalides leaving their tentacles to float in their train, medusae whose umbrellas of opal or rose-pink, escalloped with a band of blue, sheltered us from the rays of the sun and fiery pelagiae, which, in the darkness, would have strewn our path with phosphorescent light.

All these wonders I saw in the space of a quarter of a mile, scarcely stopping, and following Captain Nemo, who beckoned me on by signs. Soon the nature of the soil changed; to the sandy plain succeeded an extent of slimy mud, which the Americans call "ooze," composed of equal parts of silicious and calcareous shells. We then travelled over a plain of sea-weed of wild and luxuriant vegetation. This sward was of close texture, and soft to the feet, and rivalled the softest carpet woven by the hand of man. But whilst verdure was spread at our feet, it did not abandon our heads. A light network of marine plants, of that inexhaustible family of seaweeds of which more than two thousand kinds are known, grew on the surface of the water. I saw long ribbons of fucus floating, some globular, others tuberous; laurenciae and cladostephi of most delicate foliage, and some rhodomeniae palmatae, resembling the fan of a cactus. I noticed that the green plants kept nearer the top of the sea, whilst the red were at a greater depth, leaving to the black or brown hydrophytes the care of forming gardens and parterres in the remote beds of the ocean.

We had quitted the *Nautilus* about an hour and a half. It was near noon; I knew by the perpendicularity of the sun's rays, which were no longer refracted. The magical colours disappeared by degrees, and the shades of emerald and sapphire were effaced. We walked with a regular step, which rang upon the ground with astonishing intensity; the slightest noise was transmitted with a quickness to which the ear is unaccustomed on the earth; indeed, water is a better conductor of sound than air, in the ratio of four to one. At this period the earth sloped downwards; the light took a uniform tint. We were at a depth of a hundred and five yards and twenty inches, undergoing a pressure of six atmospheres.

At this depth I could still see the rays of the sun, though feebly; to their intense brilliancy had succeeded a reddish twilight, the lowest state between day and night; but we could still see well enough; it was not necessary to resort to the Ruhmkorff apparatus as yet. At this moment Captain Nemo stopped; he waited till I joined him, and then pointed to an obscure mass, looming in the shadow, at a short distance.

"It is the forest of the Island of Crespo," thought I;—and I was not mistaken.

Chapter XVI

A Submarine Forest

We had at last arrived on the borders of this forest, doubtless one of the finest of Captain Nemo's immense domains. He looked upon it as his own, and considered he had the same right over it that the first men had in the first days of the world. And, indeed, who would have disputed with him the possession of this submarine property? What other hardier pioneer would come, hatchet in hand, to cut down the dark copses?

This forest was composed of large treeplants; and the moment we penetrated under its vast arcades, I was struck by the singular position of their branches—a position I had not yet observed.

Not a herb which carpeted the ground, not a branch which clothed the trees, was either broken or bent, nor did they extend horizontally; all stretched up to the surface of the ocean. Not a filament, not a ribbon, however thin they might be, but kept as straight as a rod of iron. The fuci and Ilianas grew in rigid perpendicular lines, due to the density of the element which had produced them. Motionless, yet, when bent to one side by the hand, they directly resumed their former position. Truly it was the region of perpendicularity!

I soon accustomed myself to this fantastic position, as well as to the comparative darkness which surrounded us. The soil of the forest seemed covered with sharp blocks, difficult to avoid. The submarine flora struck me as being very perfect, and richer even than it would have been in the arctic or tropical zones, where these productions are not so plentiful. But for some minutes I involuntarily confounded the genera, taking zoophytes for hydrophytes, animals for plants; and who would not have been mistaken? The fauna and the flora are too closely allied in this submarine world.

These plants are self-propagated, and the principle of their existence is in the water, which upholds and nourishes them. The greater number, instead of leaves, shoot forth blades of capricious shapes, comprised within a scale of colours;—pink, carmine, green, olive, fawn, and brown. I saw there (but not dried up, as our specimens of the *Nautilus* are) pavonari spread like a fan, as if to catch the breeze; scarlet ceramies, whose laminaries extended their edible shoots of fern-shaped nereocysti, which grow to a height of fifteen feet; clusters of acetabuli, whose stems increase in size upwards; and numbers of other marine plants, all devoid of flowers!

"Curious anomaly, fantastic element!" said an ingenious naturalist, "in which the animal kingdom blossoms, and the vegetable does not!"

Under these numerous shrubs (as large as trees of the temperate zone), and under their damp shadow, were massed together real bushes of living flowers, hedges of zoophytes, on which blossomed some zebrameandrines, with crooked grooves, some yellow caryophylliae; and, to complete the allusion, the fish-flies flew from branch to branch like a swarm of humming-birds, whilst yellow lepisacomthi, with bristling jaws, dactylopteri, and monocentrides rose at our feet like a flight of snipes.

In about an hour Captain Nemo gave the signal to halt. I, for my part, was not sorry, and we stretched ourselves under an arbour of alariae, the long thin blades of which stood up like arrows.

This short rest seemed delicious to me; there was nothing wanting but the charm of conversation; but, impossible to speak, impossible to answer, I only put my great copper head to Conseil's. I saw the worthy fellow's eyes glistening with delight, and to show his satisfaction, he shook himself in his breastplate of air, in the most comical way in the world.

After four hours of this walking I was surprised not to find myself dreadfully hungry. How to account for this state of the stomach I could not tell. But instead I felt an insurmountable desire to sleep, which happens to all divers. And my eyes soon closed behind the thick glasses, and I fell into a heavy slumber, which the movement alone had prevented before. Captain Nemo and his robust companion, stretched in the clear crystal, set us the example.

How long I remained buried in this drowsiness. I cannot judge; but, when I woke, the sun seemed sinking towards the horizon. Captain Nemo had already risen, and I was beginning to stretch my limbs, when an unexpected apparition brought me briskly to my feet.

A few steps off, a monstrous sea-spider, about thirty-eight inches high, was watching me with squinting eyes, ready to spring upon me. Though my diver's dress was thick enough to defend me from the bite of this animal, I could not help shuddering with horror. Conseil and the sailor of the *Nautilus* awoke at this moment. Captain Nemo pointed out the hideous crustacean, which a blow from the butt end of the gun knocked over, and I saw the horrible claws of the monster writhe in terrible convulsions. This accident reminded me that other animals more to be feared might haunt these obscure depths, against whose attacks my diving-dress would not protect me. I had never thought of it before, but I now resolved to be upon my guard. Indeed, I thought that this halt would mark the termination of our walk; but I was mistaken, for, instead of returning to the *Nautilus*, Captain Nemo continued his bold excursion. The ground was still on the incline, its declivity seemed to be getting greater, and to be leading us to greater depths. It must have been about three o'clock when we reached a narrow valley, between high perpendicular walls, situated about seventy-five fathoms deep. Thanks to the perfection of our apparatus, we were forty-five fathoms below the limit which nature seems to have imposed on man as to his submarine excursions.

I say seventy-five fathoms, though I had no instrument by which to judge the distance. But I knew that even in the clearest waters, the solar rays could not penetrate further. And accordingly the darkness deepened. At ten paces not an object was visible. I was groping my way, when I suddenly saw a brilliant white light. Captain Nemo had just put his electric apparatus into use; his companion did the same, and Conseil and I followed their example. By turning a screw I established a communication between the wire and the spiral glass, and the sea, lit by our four lanterns, was illuminated for a circle of thirty-six yards.

Captain Nemo was still plunging into the dark depths of the forest, whose trees were getting scarcer at every step. I noticed that vegetable life disappeared sooner than animal life. The medusae had already abandoned the arid soil, from which a great number of animals, zoophytes, articulata, molluscs, and fishes, still obtained sustenance.

As we walked, I thought the light of our Ruhmkorff apparatus could not fail to draw some inhabitant from its dark couch. But if they did approach us, they at least kept at a respectful distance from the hunters. Several times I saw Captain Nemo stop, put his gun to his shoulder, and after some moments drop it and walk on. At last, after about four hours, this marvellous excursion came to an end. A wall of superb rocks, in an imposing mass, rose before us, a heap of gigantic blocks, an enormous steep granite shore, forming dark grottos, but which presented no practicable slope; it was the prop of the Island of Crespo. It was the earth! Captain Nemo stopped suddenly. A gesture of his brought us all to a halt; and however desirous I might be to scale the wall, I was obliged to stop. Here ended Captain Nemo's domains. And he would not go beyond them. Further on was a portion of the globe he might not trample upon.

The return began. Captain Nemo had returned to the head of his little band, directing their course without hesitation. I thought we were not following the same road to return to the *Nautilus*. The new road was very steep, and consequently very painful. We approached the surface of the sea rapidly. But this return to the upper strata was not so sudden as to cause relief from the pressure too rapidly, which might have produced serious disorder in our organisation, and brought on internal lesions, so fatal to divers. Very soon light reappeared and grew, and the sun being low on the horizon, the refraction edged the different objects with a spectral ring. At ten yards and a half deep, we walked amidst a shoal of little fishes of all kinds, more numerous than the birds of the air, and also more agile; but no aquatic game worthy of a shot had as yet met our gaze, when at that moment I saw the Captain shoulder his gun quickly, and follow a moving object into the shrubs. He fired;—I heard a slight hissing, and a creature fell stunned at some distance from us. It was a magnificent sea-otter, an enhydrus, the only exclusively marine quadruped. This otter was five feet long, and must have been very valuable. Its skin, chestnut-brown above, and silvery underneath, would have made one of those beautiful furs so sought after in the Russian and Chinese markets; the fineness and the lustre of its coat would certainly fetch £80. I admired this curious mammal, with its rounded head ornamented with short ears, its round eyes, and white whiskers like those of a cat, with webbed feet and nails, and tufted tail. This precious animal, hunted and tracked by fishermen, has now become very rare, and taken refuge chiefly in the northern parts of the Pacific, or probably its race would soon become extinct.

Captain Nemo's companion took the beast, threw it over his shoulder, and we continued our journey. For one hour a plain of sand lay stretched before us. Sometimes it rose to within two yards and some inches of the surface of the water. I then saw our image clearly reflected, drawn inversely, and above us appeared an identical group reflecting our movements and our actions; in a word, like us in every point, except that they walked with their heads downward and their feet in the air.

Another effect I noticed, which was the passage of thick clouds which formed and vanished rapidly; but on reflection I understood that these seeming clouds were due to the varying thickness of the reeds at the bottom, and I could even see the fleecy foam which their broken tops multiplied on the water, and the shadows of large birds passing above our heads, whose rapid flight I could discern on the surface of the sea.

On this occasion, I was witness to one of the finest gun-shots which ever made the nerves of a hunter thrill. A large bird of great breadth of wing, clearly visible, approached, hovering over us. Captain Nemo's companion shouldered his gun and fired, when it was only a few yards above the waves. The creatures fell stunned, and the force of its fall brought it within the reach of the dexterous hunter's grasp. It was an albatross of the finest kind.

Our march had not been interrupted by this incident. For two hours we followed these sandy plains, then fields of algae very disagreeable to cross. Candidly, I could do no more when I saw a glimmer of light, which, for a half mile, broke the darkness of the waters. It was the lantern of the *Nautilus*. Before twenty minutes were over we should be on board, and I should be able to breathe with ease, for it seemed that my reservoir supplied air very deficient in oxygen. But I did not reckon on an accidental meeting, which delayed our arrival for some time.

I had remained some steps behind, when I presently saw Captain Nemo coming hurriedly towards me. With his strong hand he bent me to the ground, his companion doing the same to Conseil. At first

I knew not what to think of this sudden attack, but I was soon reassured by seeing the Captain lie down beside me, and remain immovable.

I was stretched on the ground, just under shelter of a bush of algae, when raising my head, I saw some enormous mass, casting phosphorescent gleams, pass blusteringly by.

My blood froze in my veins as I recognised two formidable sharks which threatened us. It was a couple of tintoreas, terrible creatures, with enormous tails and a dull glassy stare, the phosphorescent matter ejected from holes pierced around the muzzle. Monstrous brutes! which would crush a whole man in their iron jaws. I did not know whether Conseil stopped to classify them; for my part, I noticed their silver bellies, and their huge mouths bristling with teeth, from a very unscientific point of view, and more as a possible victim than as a naturalist.

Happily the voracious creatures do not see well. They passed without seeing us, brushing us with their brownish fins, and we escaped by a miracle from a danger certainly greater than meeting a tiger full-face in the forest. Half an hour after, guided by the electric light, we reached the *Nautilus*. The outside door had been left open, and Captain Nemo closed it as soon as we had entered the first cell. He then pressed a knob. I heard the pumps working in the midst of the vessel, I felt the water sinking from around me, and in a few moments the cell was entirely empty. The inside door then opened, and we entered the vestry.

There our diving-dress was taken off, not without some trouble; and, fairly worn out from want of food and sleep, I returned to my room, in great wonder at this surprising excursion at the bottom of the sea.

Chapter XVII

Four Thousand Leagues Under the Pacific

The next morning, the 18th of November, I had quite recovered from my fatigues of the day before, and I went up on to the platform, just as the second lieutenant was uttering his daily phrase.

I was admiring the magnificent aspect of the ocean when Captain Nemo appeared. He did not seem to be aware of my presence, and began a series of astronomical observations. Then, when he had finished, he went and leant on the cage of the watch-light, and gazed abstractedly on the ocean. In the meantime, a number of the sailors of the *Nautilus*, all strong and healthy men, had come up on to the platform. They came to draw up the nets that had been laid all night. These sailors were evidently of different nations, although the European type was visible in all of them. I recognised some unmistakable Irishmen, Frenchmen, some Sclaves, and a Greek or a Candiote. They were civil, and only used that odd language among themselves, the origin of which I could not guess, neither could I question them.

The nets were hauled in. They were a large kind of "chaluts," like those on the Normandy coasts, great pockets that the waves and a chain fixed in the smaller meshes, kept open. These pockets, drawn by iron poles, swept through the water, and gathered in everything in its way. That day they brought up curious specimens from these productive coasts,—fishing-frogs that, from their comical movements, have acquired the name of buffoons; black commersons, furnished with antennae; trigger-fish, encircled with red bands; orthragorisci, with very subtle venom; some olivecoloured lampreys; macrorhynci, covered with silvery scales; trichiuri, the electric power of which is equal to that of the gymnotus and cramp-fish; scaly notopteri, with transverse brown bands; greenish cod; several varieties of gobies, &c.; also some larger fish; a caranx with a prominent head a yard long; several fine bonitos, streaked with blue and silver; and three splendid tunnies, which, in spite of the swiftness of their motion, had not escaped the net.

I reckoned that the haul had brought in more than nine hundredweight of fish. It was a fine haul, but not to be wondered at. Indeed, the nets are let down for several hours, and enclose in their meshes an infinite variety. We had no lack of excellent food, and the rapidity of the *Nautilus* and the attraction of the electric light could always renew our supply. These several productions of the sea were immediately lowered through the panel to the steward's room, some to be eaten fresh, and others pickled.

The fishing ended, the provision of air renewed, I thought that the *Nautilus* was about to continue its submarine excursion, and was preparing to return to my room, when, without further preamble, the Captain turned to me, saying—

"Professor, is not this ocean gifted with real life. It has its tempers and its gentle moods. Yesterday it slept as we did, and now it has woke after a quiet night. Look!" he continued, "it wakes under the caresses of the sun. It is going to renew its diurnal existence. It is an interesting study to watch the play of its organisation. It has a pulse, arteries, spasms; and I agree with the learned Maury, who discovered in it a circulation as real as the circulation of blood in animals.

"Yes, the ocean has indeed circulation, and to promote it, the Creator has caused things to multiply in it—caloric, salt, and animalculae."

When Captain Nemo spoke thus, he seemed altogether changed, and aroused an extraordinary emotion in me.

"Also," he added, "true existence is there; and I can imagine the foundations of nautical towns, clusters of submarine houses, which, like the *Nautilus*, would ascend every morning to breathe at the surface of the water, free towns, independent cities. Yet who knows whether some despot"—

Captain Nemo finished his sentence with a violent gesture. Then, addressing me as if to chase away some sorrowful thought—

"M. Aronnax," he asked, "do you know the depth of the ocean?"

"I only know, Captain, what the principal soundings have taught us."

"Could you tell me them, so that I can suit them to my purpose?"

"These are some," I replied, "that I remember. If I am not mistaken, a depth of 8000 yards has been found in the North Atlantic, and 2500 yards in the Mediterannean. The most remarkable soundings have been made in the South Atlantic, near the 35th parallel, and they gave 12,000 yards, 14,000 yards, and 15,000 yards. So sum up all, it is reckoned that if the bottom of the sea were levelled, its mean depth would be about one and three quarter leagues."

"Well, Professor," replied the Captain, "we shall show you better than that I hope. As to the mean depth of this part of the Pacific, I tell you it is only 4000 yards."

Having said this, Captain Nemo went towards the panel, and disappeared down the ladder. I followed him, and went into the large drawing-room. The screw was immediately put in motion, and the log gave twenty miles an hour.

During the days and weeks that passed, Captain Nemo was very sparing of his visits. I seldom saw him. The lieutenant pricked the ship's course regularly on the chart, so I could always tell exactly the route of the *Nautilus*.

Nearly every day, for some time, the panels of the drawing-room were opened, and we were never tired of penetrating the mysteries of the submarine world.

The general direction of the *Nautilus* was south-east, and it kept between 100 and 150 yards of depth. One day, however, I do not know why, being drawn diagonally by means of the inclined planes, it touched the bed of the sea. The thermometer indicated a temperature of 4.25 (cent.); a temperature that at this depth seemed common to all latitudes.

At three o'clock in the morning of the 26th of November, the *Nautilus* crossed the tropic of Cancer at 172° longitude. On the 27th instant it sighted the Sandwich Islands, where Cook died, February 14, 1779. We had then gone 4860 leagues from our starting-point. In the morning, when I went on the platform, I saw, two miles to windward, Hawaii, the largest of the seven islands that form the group. I saw clearly the cultivated ranges, and the several mountain chains that run parallel with the side, and the volcanoes that overtop Mouna-Rea, which rise 5000 yards above the level of the sea. Besides other things the nets brought up, were several flabellariae and graceful polypi, that are peculiar to that part of the ocean. The direction of the *Nautilus* was still to the southeast. It crossed the equator December 1, in 142° longitude; and on the 4th of the same month, after crossing rapidly and without anything particular occurring, we sighted the Marquesas group. I saw, three miles off, at 8° 57' latitude south, and 139° 32' west longitude, Martin's peak in Nouka-Hiva, the largest of the group that belongs to France. I only saw the woody mountains against the horizon, because Captain Nemo did not wish to bring the ship to the wind. There the nets brought up beautiful specimens of fish; choryphenes, with azure fins and tails like gold, the flesh of which is unrivalled; hologymnoses, nearly destitute of scales, but of exquisite flavour; ostorhyncs, with bony jaws, and yellow-tinged thasards, as good as bonitos; all fish that would be of use to us. After leaving these charming islands protected by the French flag, from the 4th to the 11th of December the *Nautilus* sailed over about 2000 miles. This navigation was remarkable for the meeting with an immense shoal of calmars, near neighbours to the cuttle. The French fishermen call them *hornets:* they belong to the cephalopod class, and to the dibranchial family, that comprehends the cuttles and the argonauts. These animals were particularly studied by students of antiquity, and they furnished numerous metaphors to the popular orators, as well as excellent dishes for the tables of the rich citizens, if one can believe Athenaeus, a Greek doctor, who lived before Galen. It was during the night of the 9th or 10th of December that the *Nautilus* came across this shoal of molluscs, that are peculiarly nocturnal. One could count them by millions. The emigrate from the temperate to the warmer zones, following the track of herrings and sardines. We watched them through the thick crystal panes, swimming down the wind with great rapidity, moving by means of their locomotive tube, pursuing fish and molluscs, eating the little ones, eaten by the big ones, and tossing about in indescribable confusion the ten arms that nature has placed on their heads like a crest of pneumatic serpents. The *Nautilus*, in spite of its speed, sailed for several hours in the midst of these animals, and its nets brought in an enormous quantity, among which I recognised the nine species that D'Orbigny classed for the Pacific. One saw, while crossing, that the sea displays the most wonderful sights. They were in endless variety. The scene changed continually, and we were called upon not only to contemplate the works of the Creator in the midst of the liquid element, but to penetrate the awful mysteries of the ocean.

During the daytime of the 11th of December, I was busy reading in the large drawing-room. Ned Land and Conseil watched the luminous water through the half-open panels. The *Nautilus* was immovable. While its reservoirs were filled, it kept at a depth of 1000 yards, a region rarely visited in the ocean, and in which large fish were seldom seen.

I was then reading a charming book by Jean Macé, "The Slaves of the Stomach," and I was learning some valuable lessons from it, when Conseil interrupted me.

"Will master come here a moment?" he said, in a curious voice.

"What is the matter, Conseil?"

"I want master to look."

I rose, went and leaned on my elbows before the panes and watched.

In a full electric light, an enormous black mass, quite immovable, was suspended in the midst of the waters. I watched it attentively, seeking to find out the nature of this gigantic cetacean. But a sudden thought crossed my mind. "A vessel!" I said, half aloud.

"Yes," replied the Canadian, "a disabled ship that has sunk perpendicularly."

Ned Land was right; we were close to a vessel of which the tattered shrouds still hung from their chains. The keel seemed to be in good order, and it had been wrecked at most some few hours. Three stumps of masts, broken off about two feet above the bridge, showed that the vessel had had to sacrifice its masts. But, lying on its side, it had filled, and it was heeling over to port. This skeleton of what it had once been, was a sad spectacle as it lay lost under the waves, but sadder still was the sight of the bridge, where some corpses, bound with ropes, were still lying. I counted five;—four men, one of whom was standing at the helm, and a woman standing by the poop, holding an infant in her arms. She was quite young. I could distinguish her features, which the water had not decomposed, by the brilliant light from the *Nautilus*. In one despairing effort, she had raised her infant above her head, poor little thing! whose arms encircled its mother's neck. The attitude of the four sailors was frightful, distorted as they were by their convulsive movements, whilst making a last effort to free themselves from the cords that bound them to the vessel. The steersman alone, calm, with a grave, clear face, his grey hair glued to his forehead, and his hand clutching the wheel of the helm, seemed even then to be guiding the three broken masts through the depths of the ocean.

What a scene! We were dumb; our hearts beat fast before this shipwreck, taken as it were from life, and photographed in its last moments. And I saw already, coming towards it with hungry eyes, enormous sharks, attracted by the human flesh.

However the *Nautilus*, turning, went round the submerged vessel, and in one instant I read on the stern—"*The Florida, Sunderland.*"

Chapter XVIII
Vanikoro

This terrible spectacle was the forerunner of the series of maritime catastrophes that the *Nautilus* was destined to meet with in its route. As long as it went through more frequented waters, we often saw the hulls of shipwrecked vessels that were rotting in the depths, and deeper down, cannons, bullets, anchors, chains, and a thousand other iron materials eaten up by rust. However, on the 11th of December, we sighted the Pomotou Islands, the old "dangerous group" of Bougainville, that extend over a space of 500 leagues at E.S.E. to W.N.W., from the Island Ducie to that of Lazareff. This group covers an area of 370 square leagues, and it is formed of sixty groups of islands, among which the Gambier group is remarkable, over which France exercises sway. These are coral islands, slowly raised, but continuous, created by the daily work of polypi. Then this new island will be joined later on to the neighbouring groups, and a fifth continent will stretch from New Zealand and New Caledonia, and from thence to the Marquesas.

One day, when I was suggesting this theory to Captain Nemo, he replied coldly—

"The earth does not want new continents, but new men."

Chance had conducted the *Nautilus* towards the island of Clermont-Tonnere, one of the most curious of the group, that was discovered in 1822 by Captain Bell of the *Minerva*. I could study now the madreporal system, to which are due the islands in this ocean.

Madrepores (which must not be mistaken for corals) have a tissue lined with a calcareous crust, and the modifications of its structure have induced M. Milne Edwards, my worthy master, to class them into five sections. The animalculae that the marine polypus secretes live by millions at the bottom of their cells. Their calcareous deposits become rocks, reefs, and large and small islands. Here they form a ring, surrounding a little inland lake, that communicates with the sea by means of gaps. There they make barriers of reefs like those on the coasts of New Caledonia and the various Pomoton islands. In other places, like those at Reunion and at Maurice, they raise fringed reefs, high, straight walls, near which the depth of the ocean is considerable.

Some cable-lengths off the shores of the Island of Clermont, I admired the gigantic work accomplished by these microscopical workers. These walls are specially the work of those madrepores known as milleporas, porites, madrepores, and astraeas. These polypi are found particularly in the rough beds of the sea, near the surface; and consequently it is from the upper part that they begin their operations in which they bury themselves by degrees with the debris of the secretions that support them. Such is, at least, Darwin's theory, who thus explains the formation of the *atolls*, a superior theory (to my mind) to that given of the foundation of the madreporical works, summits of mountains or volcanoes, that are submerged some feet below the level of the sea.

I could observe closely these curious walls, for perpendicularly they were more than 300 yards deep, and our electric sheets lighted up this calcareous matter brilliantly. Replying to a question Conseil asked me as to the time these colossal barriers took to be raised, I astonished him much by telling him that learned men reckoned it about the eighth of an inch in a hundred years.

Towards evening Clermont-Tonnerre was lost in the distance, and the route of the *Nautilus* was sensibly changed. After having crossed the tropic of Capricorn in 135° longitude, it sailed W.N.W., making again for the tropical zone. Although the summer sun was very strong, we did not suffer from heat, for at fifteen or twenty fathoms below the surface, the temperature did not rise above from ten to twelve degrees.

On December 15, we left to the east the bewitching group of the Societies and the graceful Tahiti, queen of the Pacific. I saw in the morning, some miles to the windward, the elevated summits of the island. These waters furnished our table with excellent fish, mackerel, bonitos, and albicores, and some varieties of a sea-serpent called munirophis.

On the 25th of December the *Nautilus* sailed into the midst of the New Hebrides, discovered by Quiros in 1606, and that Bougainville explored in 1768, and to which Cook gave its present name in 1773. This group is composed principally of nine large islands, that form a band of 120 leagues N.N.S. to S.S.W., between 15° and 2° south latitude, and 164° and 168° longitude. We passed tolerably near to the Island of Aurou, that at noon looked like a mass of green woods, surmounted by a peak of great height.

That day being Christmas Day, Ned Land seemed to regret sorely the non-celebration of "Christmas," the family fête of which Protestants are so fond. I had not seen Captain Nemo for a week, when, on the morning of the 27th, he came into the large drawing-room, always seeming as if he had seen you five minutes before. I was busily tracing the route of the *Nautilus* on the planisphere. The Captain came up to me, put his finger on one spot on the chart, and said this single word—

"Vanikoro."

The effect was magical! it was the name of the islands on which La Perouse had been lost! I rose suddenly.

"The *Nautilus* has brought us to Vanikoro?" I asked.

"Yes, Professor," said the Captain.

"And I can visit the celebrated islands where the *Boussole* and the *Astrolabe* struck?"

"If you like, Professor."

"When shall we be there?"

"We are there now."

Followed by Captain Nemo, I went up on to the platform, and greedily scanned the horizon.

To the N.E. two volcanic islands emerged of unequal size, surrounded by a coral reef that measured forty miles in circumference. We were close to Vanikoro, really the one to which Dumont d'Urville gave the name of Isle de la Recherche, and exactly facing the little harbour of Vanou, situated in 16° 4' south latitude, and 164° 32' east longitude. The earth seemed covered with verdure from the shore to the summits in the interior, that were crowned by Mount Kapogo, 476 feet high. The *Nautilus*, having passed the outer belt of rocks by a narrow strait, found itself among breakers where the sea was from thirty to forty fathoms deep. Under the verdant shade of some mangroves I perceived some savages, who appeared greatly surprised at our approach. In the long black body, moving between wind and water, did they not see some formidable cetacean that they regarded with suspicion?

Just then Captain Nemo asked me what I knew about the wreck of La Perouse.

"Only what every one knows, Captain," I replied.

"And could you tell me what every one knows about it?" he inquired, ironically.

"Easily."

I related to him all that the last works of Dumont d'Urville had made known—works from which the following is a brief account.

La Perouse, and his second, Captain de Langle, were sent by Louis XVI., in 1785, on a voyage of circumnavigation. They embarked in the corvettes the *Boussole* and the *Astrolabe*, neither of which were again heard of. In 1791, the French Government, justly uneasy as to the fate of these two sloops, manned two large merchantmen, the *Recherche* and the *Esperance*, which left Brest the 28th of September, under the command of Bruni d'Entrecasteaux.

Two months after, they learned from Bowen, commander of the *Albemarle*, that the debris of shipwrecked vessels had been seen on the coasts of New Georgia. But D'Entrecasteaux, ignoring this communication—rather uncertain, besides—directed his course towards the Admiralty Isles, mentioned in a report of Captain Hunter's as being the place where La Perouse was wrecked.

They sought in vain. The *Esperance* and the *Recherche* passed before Vanikoro without stopping there, and in fact, this voyage was most disastrous, as it cost D'Entrecasteaux his life, and those of two of his lieutenants, besides several of his crew.

Captain Dillon, a shrewd old Pacific sailor, was the first to find unmistakable traces of the wrecks. On the 15th of May 1824, his vessel, the *St Patrick*, passed close to Tikopia, one of the New Hebrides. There a Lascar came alongside in a canoe, sold him the handle of a sword in silver, that bore the print of characters engraved on the hilt. The Lascar pretended that six years before, during a stay at Vanikoro, he had seen two Europeans that belonged to some vessels that had run aground on the reefs some years ago.

Dillon guessed that he meant La Perouse, whose disappearance had troubled the whole world. He tried to get on to Vanikoro, where, according to the Lascar, he would find numerous debris of the wreck, but winds and tide prevented him.

Dillon returned to Calcutta. There he interested the Asiatic Society and the Indian Company in his discovery. A vessel, to which was given the name of the *Recherche*, was put at his disposal, and he set out, January 23, 1827, accompanied by a French agent.

The *Recherche*, after touching at several points in the Pacific, cast anchor before Vanikoro, July 7, 1827, in that same harbour of Vanou where the *Nautilus* was at this time.

There it collected numerous relics of the wreck—iron utensils, anchors, pulley-strops, swivel-guns, an 18lb.-shot, fragments of astronomical instruments, a piece of crown-work, and a bronze clock, bearing this inscription—"*Bazin m'a fait*," the mark of the foundry of the arsenal at Brest about 1785. There could be no further doubt.

Dillon, having made all inquiries, stayed in the unlucky place till October. Then he quitted Vanikoro, and directed his course towards

New Zealand; put into Calcutta, April 7, 1828, and returned to France, where he was warmly welcomed by Charles X.

But at the same time, without knowing Dillon's movements, Dumont d'Urville had already set out to find the scene of the wreck. And they had learned from a whaler that some medals and a cross of St Louis had been found in the hands of some savages of Louisiade and New Caledonia. Dumont d'Urville, commander of the *Astrolabe*, had then sailed, and two months after Dillon had left Vanikoro, he put into Hobart Town. There he learned the results of Dillon's inquiries, and found that a certain James Hobbs, second lieutenant of the *Union* of Calcutta, after landing on an island situated 8° 18' south latitude, and 156° 30' east longitude, had seen some iron bars and red stuffs used by the natives of these parts. Dumont d'Urville, much perplexed, and not knowing how to credit the reports of low-class journals, decided to follow Dillon's track.

On the 10th of February 1828, the *Astrolabe* appeared off Tikopia, and took as guide and interpreter a deserter found on the island; made his way to Vanikoro, sighted it on the 12th inst., lay among the reefs until the 14th, and not until the 20th did he cast anchor within the barrier in the harbour of Vanou.

On the 23rd, several officers went round the island, and brought back some unimportant trifles. The natives, adopting a system of denials and evasions, refused to take them to the unlucky place. This ambiguous conduct led them to believe that the natives had ill-treated the castaways, and indeed they seemed to fear that Dumont d'Urville had come to avenge La Perouse and his unfortunate crew.

However, on the 26th, appeased by some presents, and understanding that they had no reprisals to fear, they lead M. Jacquireot to the scene of the wreck.

There, in three or four fathoms of water, between the reefs of Pacou and Vanou, lay anchors, cannons, pigs of lead and iron, embedded in the limy concretions. The large boat and the whaler belonging to the *Astrolabe* were sent to this place, and, not without some difficulty, their crews hauled up an anchor weighing 1800 lbs., a brass gun, some pigs of iron, and two copper swivel-guns.

Dumont d'Urville, questioning the natives, learned, too, that La Perouse, after losing both his vessels on the reefs of this island, had constructed a smaller boat, only to be lost a second time. Where?—no one knew.

But the French Government, fearing that Dumont d'Urville was not acquainted with Dillon's movements, had sent the sloop *Bayonnaise*, commanded by Legoarant de Tromelin, to Vanikoro, which had been stationed on the west coast of America. The *Bayonnaise* cast her anchor before Vanikoro some months after the departure of the *Astrolabe*, but found no new document; but stated that the savages had respected the monument to La Perouse. That is the substance of what I told to Captain Nemo.

"So," he said, "no one knows now where the third vessel perished that was constructed by the castaways on the island of Vanikoro?"

"No one knows."

Captain Nemo said nothing, but signed to me to follow him into the large saloon. The *Nautilus* sank several yards below the waves, and the panels were opened.

I hastened to the aperture, and under the crustations of coral, covered with fungi, syphonules, alcyons, madrepores, through myriads of charming fish—girelles, glyphisidri, pompherides, diacopes, and holocentres—I recognised certain debris that the drags had not been able to tear up—iron stirrups, anchors, cannons, bullets, capstan fittings, the stem of a ship, all objects clearly proving the wreck of some vessel, and now carpeted with living flowers. While I was looking on this desolate scene, Captain Nemo said, in a sad voice—

"Commander La Perouse set out December 7, 1785, with his vessels *La Bousolle* and the *Astrolabe*. He first cast anchor at Botany Bay, visited the Friendly Isles, New Caledonia, then directed his course towards Santa Cruz, and put into Namouka, one of the Hapai group. Then his vessels struck on the unknown reefs of Vanikoro. The *Bousolle*, which went first, ran aground on the southerly coast. The *Astrolabe* went to its help, and ran aground too. The first vessel was destroyed almost immediately. The second, stranded under the wind, resisted some days. The natives made the castaways welcome. They installed them-selves in the island, and constructed a smaller boat with the debris of the two large ones. Some sailors stayed willingly at Vanikoro; the oth-ers, weak and ill, set out with La Perouse. They directed their course towards the Solomon Isles, and there perished, with everything, on the westerly coast of the chief island of the group, between Capes Deception and Satisfaction."

"How do you know that?"

"By this, that I found on the spot where was the last wreck."

Captain Nemo showed me a tin-plate box, stamped with the French arms, and corroded by the salt water. He opened it, and I saw a bundle of papers, yellow but still readable.

They were the instructions of the naval minister to Commander La Perouse, annotated in the margin in Louis XVI.'s handwriting.

"Ah! it is a fine death for a sailor!" said Captain Nemo, at last. "A coral tomb makes a quiet grave; and I trust that I and my comrades will find no other."

Chapter XIX

Torres Straits

During the night of the 27th or 28th of December, the *Nautilus* left the shores of Vanikoro with great speed. Her course was south-westerly, and in three days she had gone over the 750 leagues that separated it from La Perouse's group and the south-east point of Papua.

Early on the 1st of January 1863, Conseil joined me on the platform.

"Master, will you permit me to wish you a happy new year?"

"What! Conseil; exactly as if I was at Paris in my study at the Jardin des Plantes? Well, I accept your good wishes, and thank you for them. Only, I will ask you what you mean by a 'Happy new year,' under our circumstances? Do you mean the year that will bring us to the end of our imprisonment, or the year that sees us continue this strange voyage?"

"Really, I do not know how to answer, master. We are sure to see curious things, and for the last two months we have not had time for ennui. The last marvel is always the most astonishing; and if we continue this progression, I do not know how it will end. It is my opinion that we shall never again see the like. I think, then, with no offence to master, that a happy year would be one in which we could see everything."

On January 2, we had made 11,340 miles, or 5250 French leagues, since our starting-point in the Japan Seas. Before the ship's head stretched the dangerous shores of the coral sea, on the north-east coast of Australia. Our boat lay along some miles from the redoubtable bank on which Cook's vessel was lost, June 10, 1770. The boat in which Cook was struck on a rock, and if it did not sink, it was owing to a piece of the coral that was broken by the shock, and fixed itself in the broken keel.

I had wished to visit the reef, 360 leagues long, against which the sea, always rough, broke with great violence, with a noise like thunder. But just then the inclined planes drew the *Nautilus* down to a great depth, and I could see nothing of the high coral walls. I had to content myself with the different specimens of fish brought up by the nets. I remarked, among others, some germons, a species of mackerel as large as a tunny, with bluish sides, and striped with transverse bands, that disappear with the animal's life. These fish followed us in shoals, and furnished us with very delicate food. We took also a large number of giltheads, about one and a half inches long, tasting like dorys; and flying pyrapeds like submarine swallows, which, in dark nights, light alternately the air and water with their phosphorescent light. Among the molluscs and zoophytes, I found in the meshes of the net several species of alcyonarians, echini, hammers, spurs, dials, cerites, and hyalleae. The flora was represented by beautiful floating sea-weeds, laminariae, and macrocystes, impregnated with the mucilage that transnudes through their pores; and among which I gathered an admirable *Nemastoma Geliniarois*, that was classed among the natural curiosities of the museum.

Two days after crossing the coral sea, January 4, we sighted the Papuan coasts. On this occasion, Captain Nemo informed me that his intention was to get into the Indian Ocean by the Strait of Torres. His communication ended there.

The Torres Straits are nearly thirty-four leagues wide; but they are obstructed by an innumerable quantity of islands, islets, breakers, and rocks, that make its navigation almost impracticable; so that Captain Nemo took all needful precautions to cross them. The *Nautilus*, floating betwixt wind and water, went at a moderate pace. Her screw, like a cetacean's tail, beat the waves slowly.

Profiting by this, I and my two companions went up on to the deserted platform. Before us was the steersman's cage, and I expected that Captain Nemo was there directing the course of the *Nautilus*. I had before me the excellent charts of the Strait of Torres made out by the hydrographical engineer Vincendon Dumoulin. These and Captain King's are the best charts that clear the intricacies of this strait, and I consulted them attentively. Round the *Nautilus* the sea dashed furiously. The course of the waves, that went from south-east to north-west at the rate of two and a half miles, broke on the coral that showed itself here and there.

"This is a bad sea!" remarked Ned Land.

"Detestable indeed, and one that does not suit a boat like the *Nautilus*."

"The captain must be very sure of his route, for I see there pieces of coral that would do for its keel if it only touched them slightly."

Indeed the situation was dangerous, but the *Nautilus* seemed to slide like magic off these rocks. It did not follow the routes of the *Astrolabe* and the *Zélée* exactly, for they proved fatal to Dumont d'Urville. It bore more northwards, coasted the Island of Murray, and came back to the south-west towards Cumberland Passage. I thought it was going to pass it by, when, going back to north-west, it went through a large quantity of islands and islets little known, towards the Island Sound and Canal Mauvais.

I wondered if Captain Nemo, foolishly imprudent, would steer his vessel into that pass where Dumont d'Urville's two corvettes touched; when, swerving again, and cutting straight through to the west, he steered for the Island of Gilboa.

It was then three in the afternoon. The tide began to recede, being quite full. The *Nautilus* approached the island, that I still saw, with its remarkable border of screw-pines. He stood off it at about two miles distant. Suddenly a shock overthrew me. The *Nautilus* just touched a rock, and stayed immovable, laying lightly to port side.

When I rose, I perceived Captain Nemo and his lieutenant on the platform. They were examining the situation of the vessel, and exchanging words in their incomprehensible dialect.

She was situated thus:—Two miles, on the starboard side, appeared Gilboa, stretching from north to west like an immense arm. Towards the south and east some coral showed itself, left by the ebb. We had run aground, and in one of those seas where the tides are middling,—a sorry matter for the floating of the *Nautilus*. However, the vessel had not suffered, for her keel was solidly joined. But if she could neither glide off nor move, she ran the risk of being for ever fastened to these rocks, and then Captain Nemo's submarine vessel would be done for.

I was reflecting thus, when the Captain, cool and calm, always master of himself, approached me.

"An accident?" I asked.

"No; an incident."

"But an incident that will oblige you perhaps to become an inhabitant of this land from which you flee?"

Captain Nemo looked at me curiously, and made a negative gesture, as much as to say that nothing would force him to set foot on *terra firma* again. Then he said—

"Besides, M. Aronnax, the *Nautilus* is not lost; it will carry you yet into the midst of the marvels of the ocean. Our voyage is only begun, and I do not wish to be deprived so soon of the honour of your company."

"However, Captain Nemo," I replied, without noticing the ironical turn of his phrase, "the *Nautilus* ran aground in open sea. Now the tides are not strong in the Pacific; and if you cannot lighten the *Nautilus*, I do not see how it be reinflated."

"The tides are not strong in the Pacific: you are right there, Professor; but in Torres Straits, one finds still a difference of a yard and a half between the level of high and low seas. To-day is January 4, and in five days the moon will be full. Now, I shall be very much astonished if that complaisant satellite does not raise these masses of water sufficiently, and render me a service that I should be indebted to her for."

Having said this, Captain Nemo, followed by his lieutenant, re-descended to the interior of the *Nautilus*. As to the vessel, it moved not, and was immovable, as if the coralline polypi had already walled it up with their indestructible cement.

"Well, sir?" said Ned Land, who came up to me after the departure of the Captain.

"Well, friend Ned, we will wait patiently for the tide on the 9th instant; for it appears that the moon will have the goodness to put it off again."

"Really?"

"Really."

"And this Captain is not going to cast anchor at all, since the tide will suffice?" said Conseil, simply.

The Canadian looked at Conseil, then shrugged his shoulders.

"Sir, you may believe me when I tell you that this piece of iron will navigate neither on nor under the sea again; it is only fit to be sold for its weight. I think, therefore, that the time has come to part company with Captain Nemo."

"Friend Ned, I do not despair of this stout *Nautilus*, as you do; and in four days we shall know what to hold to on the Pacific tides. Besides, flight might be possible if we were in sight of the English or Provencal coasts; but on the Papuan shores, it is another thing; and it will be time enough to come to that extremity if the *Nautilus* does not recover itself again, which I look upon as a grave event."

"But do they know, at least, how to act circumspectly? There is an island; on that island there are trees; under those trees, terrestrial animals, bearers of cutlets and roast-beef, to which I would willingly give a trial."

"In this, friend Ned is right," said Conseil, "and I agree with him. Could not master obtain permission from his friend Captain Nemo to put us on land, if only so as not to lose the habit of treading on the solid parts of our planet?"

"I can ask him, but he will refuse."

"Will master risk it?" asked Conseil, "and we shall know how to rely upon the Captain's amiability."

To my great surprise Captain Nemo gave me the permission I asked for, and he gave it very agreeably, without even exacting from me a promise to return to the vessel; but flight across New Guinea might be very perilous, and I should not have counselled Ned Land to attempt it. Better to be a prisoner on board the *Nautilus* then to fall into the hands of the natives.

At eight o'clock, armed with guns and hatchets, we got off the *Nautilus*. The sea was pretty calm; a slight breeze blew on land. Conseil and I rowing, we sped along quickly, and Ned steered in the straight passage that the breakers left between them. The boat was well handled, and moved rapidly.

Ned Land could not restrain his joy. He was like a prisoner that had escaped from prison, and knew not that it was necessary to re-enter it.

"Meat! We are going to eat some meat; and what meat!" he replied. "Real game! no, bread, indeed."

"I do not say that fish is not good; we must not abuse it; but a piece of fresh venison, grilled on live coals, will agreeably vary our ordinary course."

"Gourmand!" said Conseil, "he makes my mouth water."

"It remains to be seen," I said, "if these forests are full of game, and if the game is not such as will hunt the hunter himself."

"Well said, M. Aronnax," replied the Canadian, whose teeth seemed sharpened like the edge of a hatchet; "but I will eat tiger—loin of tiger—if there is no other quadruped on this island."

"Friend Ned is uneasy about it," said Conseil.

"Whatever it may be," continued Ned Land, "every animal with four paws without feathers, or with two paws without feathers, will be saluted by my first shot."

"Very well! Master Land's imprudences are beginning."

"Never fear, M. Aronnax," replied the Canadian; "I do not want twenty-five minutes to offer you a dish of my sort."

At half-past eight the *Nautilus* boat ran softly aground, on a heavy sand, after having happily passed the coral reef that surrounds the Island of Gilboa.

Chapter XX

A Few Days on Land

I was much impressed on touching land. Ned Land tried the soil with his feet, as if to take possession of it. However, it was only two months before that we had become, according to Captain Nemo, "passengers on board the *Nautilus*," but in reality, prisoners of its commander.

In a few minutes we were within musketshot of the coast. The soil was almost entirely madreporical, but certain beds of dried-up torrents, strewn with debris of granite, showed that this island was of the primary formation. The whole horizon was hidden behind a beautiful curtain of forests. Enormous trees, the trunks of which attained a height of 200 feet, were tied to each other by garlands of bindweed, real natural hammocks, which a light breeze rocked. They were mimosas, ficuses, casuarinae, teks, hibisci, and palmtrees, mingled together in profusion; and under the shelter of their verdant vault grew orchids, leguminous plants, and ferns.

But without noticing all these beautiful specimens of Papuan flora, the Canadian abandoned the agreeable for the useful. He discovered a cocoa-tree, beat down some of the fruit, broke them, and we drunk the milk and ate the nut, with a satisfaction that protested against the ordinary food on the *Nautilus*.

"Excellent!" said Ned Land.

"Exquisite!" replied Conseil.

"And I do not think," said the Canadian, "that he would object to our introducing a cargo of cocoa-nuts on board."

"I do not think he would, but he would not taste them."

"So much the worse for him," said Conseil.

"And so much the better for us," replied Ned Land. "There will be more for us."

"One word only, Master Land," I said to the harpooner, who was beginning to ravage another cocoa-nut tree. "Cocoa-nuts are good things, but before filling the canoe with them, it would be wise to reconnoitre and see if the island does not produce some substance not less useful. Fresh vegetables would be welcome on board the *Nautilus*."

"Master is right," replied Conseil; "and I propose to reserve three places in our vessel, one for fruits, the other for vegetables, and the third for the venison, of which I have not yet seen the smallest specimen."

"Conseil, we must not despair," said the Canadian.

"Let us continue," I returned, "and lie in wait. Although the island seems uninhabited, it might still contain some individuals that would be less hard than we on the nature of game."

"Ho! ho!" said Ned Land, moving his jaws significantly.

"Well, Ned!" cried Conseil.

"My word!" returned the Canadian, "I begin to understand the charms of anthropophagy."

"Ned! Ned! what are you saying? You, a man-eater? I should not feel safe with you, especially as I share your cabin. I might perhaps wake one day to find myself half devoured."

"Friend Conseil, I like you much, but not enough to eat you unnecessarily."

"I would not trust you," replied Conseil. "But enough. We must absolutely bring down some game to satisfy this cannibal, or else one of these fine mornings, master will find only pieces of his servant to serve him."

While we were talking thus, we were penetrating the sombre arches of the forest, and for two hours we surveyed it in all directions.

Chance rewarded our search for eatable vegetables, and one of the most useful products of the tropical zones furnished us with precious food that we missed on board. I would speak of the bread fruit-tree, very abundant in the island of Gilboa; and I remarked chiefly the variety destitute of seeds, which bears in Malaya the name of "rima."

Ned Land knew these fruits well. He had already eaten many during his numerous voyages, and he knew how to prepare the eatable substance. Moreover, the sight of them excited him, and he could contain himself no longer.

"Master," he said, "I shall die if I do not taste a little of this breadfruit pie."

"Taste it, friend Ned—taste it as you want. We are here to make experiments—make them."

"It won't take long," said the Canadian.

And provided with a lentil, he lighted a fire of dead wood, that crackled joyously. During this time, Conseil and I chose the best fruits of the artocarpus. Some had not then attained a sufficient degree of maturity; and their thick skin covered a white but rather fibrous pulp. Others, the greater number yellow and gelatinous, waited only to be picked.

These fruits enclosed no kernel. Conseil brought a dozen to Ned Land, who placed them on a coal-fire, after having cut them in thick slices, and while doing this repeating—

"You will see, master, how good this bread is. More so when one has been deprived of it so long. It is not even bread," added he, "but a delicate pastry. You have eaten none, master?"

"No, Ned."

"Very well, prepare yourself for a juicy thing. If you do not come for more, I am no longer the king of harpooners."

After some minutes, the part of the fruits that was exposed to the fire was completely roasted. The interior looked like a white pasty, a sort of soft crumb, the flavour of which was like that of an artichoke.

It must be confessed this bread was excellent, and I ate of it with great relish.

"What time is it now?" asked the Canadian.

"Two o'clock at least," replied Conseil.

"How time flies on firm ground!" sighed Ned Land.

"Let us be off," replied Conseil.

We returned through the forest, and completed our collection by a raid upon the cabbage-palms, that we gathered from the tops of the trees, little beans that I recognised as the "abrou" of the Malays, and yams of a superior quality.

We were loaded when we reached the boat. But Ned Land did not find his provision sufficient. Fate, however, favoured us. Just as we were pushing off, he perceived several trees, from twenty-five to thirty feet high, a species of palm-tree. These trees, as valuable as the artocarpus, justly are reckoned among the most useful products of Malaya.

At last, at five o'clock in the evening, loaded with our riches, we quitted the shore, and half an hour after we hailed the *Nautilus*. No one appeared on our arrival. The enormous ironplated cylinder seemed deserted. The provisions embarked, I descended to my chamber, and after supper slept soundly.

The next day, January 6, nothing new on board. Not a sound inside, not a sign of life. The boat rested along the edge, in the same place in which we had left it. We resolved to return to the island. Ned Land hoped to be more fortunate than on the day before with regard to the hunt, and wished to visit another part of the forest.

At dawn we set off. The boat, carried on by the waves that flowed to shore, reached the island in a few minutes.

We landed, and thinking that it was better to give in to the Canadian, we followed Ned Land, whose long limbs threatened to distance us. He wound up the coast towards the west: then, fording some torrents, he gained the high plain that was bordered with admirable forests. Some kingfishers were rambling along the water-courses, but they would not let themselves be approached. Their circumspection proved to me that these birds knew what to expect from bipeds of our species, and I concluded that, if the island was not inhabited, at least human being occasionally frequented it.

After crossing a rather large prairie, we arrived at the skirts of a little wood that was enlivened by the songs and flight of a large number of birds.

"There are only birds," said Conseil.

"But they are eatable," replied the harpooner.

"I do not agree with you, friend Ned, for I see only parrots there."

"Friend Conseil," said Ned, gravely, "the parrot is like pheasant to those who have nothing else."

"And," I added, "this bird, suitably prepared, is worth knife and fork."

Indeed, under the thick foliage of this wood, a world of parrots were flying from branch to branch, only needing a careful education to speak the human language. For the moment, they were chattering with parrots of all colours, and grave cockatoos, who seemed to meditate upon some philosophical problem, whilst brilliant red lories passed like a piece of bunting carried away by the breeze; papuans, with the finest azure colours, and in all a variety of winged things most charming to behold, but few eatable.

However, a bird peculiar to these lands, and which has never passed the limits of the Arrow and Papuan islands, was wanting in this collection. But fortune reserved it for me before long.

After passing through a moderately thick copse, we found a plain obstructed with bushes. I saw then those magnificent birds, the disposition of whose long feathers obliges them to fly against the wind. Their undulating flight, graceful aerial curves, and the shading of their colours, attracted and charmed one's looks. I had no trouble in recognising them.

"Birds of Paradise!" I exclaimed.

The Malays, who carry on a great trade in these birds with the Chinese, have several means that we could not employ for taking them. Sometimes they put snares at the top of high trees that the birds of Paradise prefer to frequent. Sometimes they catch them with a viscous birdlime that paralyses their movements. They even go so far as to poison the fountains that the birds generally drink from. But we were obliged to fire at them during flight, which gave us few chances to bring them down; and indeed, we vainly exhausted one half of our ammunition.

About eleven o'clock in the morning, the first range of mountains that form the centre of the island was traversed, and we had killed nothing. Hunger drove us on. The hunters had relied on the products of the chase, and they were wrong. Happily Conseil, to his great surprise, made a double shot and secured breakfast. He brought down a white pigeon and a wood-pigeon, which, cleverly plucked and suspended from a skewer, was roasted before a red fire of dead wood. Whilst these interesting birds were cooking, Ned prepared the fruit of the artocarpus. Then the wood-pigeons were devoured to the bones, and declared excellent. The nutmeg, with which they are in the habit of stuffing their crops, flavours their flesh and renders it delicious eating.

"Now, Ned, what do you miss now?"

"Some four-footed game, M. Aronnax. All these pigeons are only side-dishes, and trifles; and until I have killed an animal with cutlets, I shall not be content."

"Nor I, Ned, if I do not catch a bird of Paradise."

"Let us continue hunting," replied Conseil. "Let us go towards the sea. We have arrived at the first declivities of the mountains, and I think we had better regain the region of forests."

That was sensible advice, and was followed out. After walking for one hour, we had attained a forest of sago-trees. Some inoffensive serpents glided away from us. The birds of Paradise fled at our approach, and truly I despaired of getting near one, when Conseil, who was walking in front, suddenly bent down, uttered a triumphal cry, and came back to me bringing a magnificent specimen.

"Ah! bravo, Conseil!"

"Master is very good."

"No, my boy; you have made an excellent stroke. Take one of these living birds, and carry it in your hand."

"If master will examine it, he will see that I have not deserved great merit."

"Why, Conseil?"

"Because this bird is as drunk as a quail."

"Drunk!"

"Yes, sir; drunk with the nutmegs that it devoured under the nutmeg-tree, under which I found it. See, friend Ned, see the monstrous effects of intemperance!"

"By jove!" exclaimed the Canadian, "because I have drunk gin for two months, you must needs reproach me!"

However, I examined the curious bird. Conseil was right. The bird, drunk with the juice, was quite powerless. It could not fly; it could hardly walk.

This bird belonged to the most beautiful of the eight species that are found in Papua and in the neighbouring islands. It was the "large emerald bird, the most rare kind." It measured three feet in length. Its head was comparatively small, its eyes placed near the opening of the beak, and also small. But the shades of colour were beautiful, having a yellow beak, brown feet and claws, nut-coloured wings with purple tips, pale yellow at the back of the neck and head, and emerald colour at the throat, chestnut on the breast and belly. Two horned downy nets rose from below the tail, that prolonged the long light feathers of admirable fineness, and they completed the whole of this marvellous bird, that the natives have poetically named the "bird of the sun."

But if my wishes were satisfied by the possession of the bird of paradise, the Canadian's were not yet. Happily about two o'clock Ned Land brought down a magnificent hog, from the brood of those the native call "bari-outang." The animal came in time for us to procure real quadruped meat, and he was well received. Ned Land was very proud of his shot. The hog, hit by the electric ball, fell stone dead. The Canadian skinned and cleaned it properly, after having taken half-a-dozen cutlets, destined to furnish us with a grilled repast in the evening. Then the hunt was resumed, which was still more marked by Ned and Conseil's exploits.

Indeed, the two friends, beating the bushes, roused a herd of kangaroos, that fled and bounded along on their elastic paws. But these animals did not take flight so rapidly but what the electric capsule could stop their course.

"Ah, Professor!" cried Ned Land, who was carried away by the delights of the chase, "what excellent game, and stewed too! What a supply for the *Nautilus!* two! three! five down! And to think that we shall eat that flesh, and that the idiots on board shall not have a crumb!"

I think that, in the excess of his joy, the Canadian, if he had not talked so much, would have killed them all. But he contented himself with a single dozen of these interesting marsupians. These animals were small. They were a species of those "kangaroo rabbits" that live habitually in the hollows of trees, and whose speed is extreme; but they are moderately fat, and furnish, at least, estimable food. We were very satisfied with the results of the hunt. Happy Ned proposed to return to this enchanting island the next day, for he wished to depopulate it of all the eatable quadrupeds. But he reckoned without his host.

At six o'clock in the evening we had regained the shore, our boat was moored to the usual place. The *Nautilus*, like a long rock, emerged from the waves two miles from the beach. Ned Land, without waiting, occupied himself about the important dinner business. He understood all about cooking well. The "barioutang," grilled on the coals, soon scented the air with a delicious odour.

Indeed, the dinner was excellent. Two wood-pigeons completed this extraordinary *menu*. The sago pasty, the artocarpus bread, some mangoes, half-a-dozen pine-apples, and the liquor fermented from some cocoa-nuts, overjoyed us. I even think that my worthy companions' ideas had not all the plainness desirable.

"Suppose we do not return to the *Nautilus* this evening?" said Conseil.

"Suppose we never return?" added Ned Land.

Just then a stone fell at our feet, and cut short the harpooner's porposition.

Chapter XXI

Captain Nemo's Thunderbolt

We looked at the edge of the forest without rising, my hand stopping in the action of putting it to my mouth, Ned Land's completing its office.

"Stones do not fall from the sky," remarked Conseil, "or they would merit the name of aerolites."

A second stone, carefully aimed, that made a savoury pigeon's leg fall from Conseil's hand, gave still more weight to his observation. We all three arose, shouldered our guns, and were ready to reply to any attack.

"Are they apes?" cried Ned Land.

"Very nearly—they are savages."

"To the boat!" I said, hurrying to the sea.

It was indeed necessary to beat a retreat, for about twenty natives armed with bows and slings, appeared on the skirts of a copse that masked the horizon to the right, hardly a hundred steps from us.

Our boat was moored about sixty feet from us. The savages approached us, not running, but making hostile demonstrations. Stones and arrows fell thickly.

Ned Land had not wished to leave his provisions; and, in spite of his imminent danger, his pig on one side, and kangaroos on the other, he went tolerably fast. In two minutes we were on the shore. To load the boat with provisions and arms, to push it out to sea, and ship the oars, was the work of an instant. We had not gone two cables' lengths, when a hundred savages, howling and gesticulating, entered the water up to their waists. I watched to see if their apparition would attract some men from the *Nautilus* on to the platform. But no. The enormous machine, lying off, was absolutely deserted.

Twenty minutes later we were on board. The panels were open. After making the boat fast, we entered into the interior of the *Nautilus*.

I descended to the drawing-room, from whence I heard some chords. Captain Nemo was there, being over his organ, and plunged in a musical ecstasy.

"Captain!"

He did not hear me.

"Captain!" I said again, touching his hand.

He shuddered, and turning round, said, "Ah! it is you, Professor? Well, have you had a good hunt, have you botanised successfully?"

"Yes, Captain; but we have unfortunately brought a troop of bipeds, whose vicinity troubles me."

"What bipeds?"

"Savages."

"Savages!" he echoed, ironically. "So you are astonished, Professor, at having set foot on a strange land and finding savages? Savages! where are there not any? Besides, are they worse than others, these whom you call savages?"

"But, Captain"—

"How many have you counted?"

"A hundred at least."

"M. Aronnax," replied Captain Nemo, placing his fingers on the organ stops, "when all the natives of Papua are assembled on this shore, the *Nautilus* will have nothing to fear from their attacks."

The Captain's fingers were then running over the keys of the instrument, and I remarked that he touched only the black keys, which gave to his melodies an essentially Scotch character. Soon he had forgotten my presence, and had plunged into a reverie that I did not disturb. I went up again on to the platform:—night had already fallen; for, in this low latitude, the sun sets rapidly and without twilight. I could only see the island indistinctly; but the numerous fires, lighted on the beach, showed that the natives did not think of leaving it. I was alone for several hours, sometimes thinking of the natives,—but without any dread of them, for the imperturbable confidence of the Captain was catching,—sometimes forgetting them to admire the splendours of the night in the tropics. My remembrances went to France, in the train of those zodiacal stars that would shine in some hours' time. The moon shone in the midst of the constellations of the zenith.

The night slipped away without any mischance, the islanders frightened no doubt at the sight of a monster aground in the bay. The panels were open, and would have offered an easy access to the interior of the *Nautilus*.

At six o'clock in the morning of the 8th January, I went up on to the platform. The dawn was breaking. The island soon showed itself through the dissipating fogs, first the shore, then the summits.

The natives were there, more numerous than on the day before—500 or 600 perhaps—some of them, profiting by the low water, had come on to the coral, at less than two cable-lengths from the *Nautilus*. I distinguished them easily; they were true Papuans, with athletic figures, men of good race, large high foreheads, large, but not broad and flat, and white teeth. Their woolly hair, with a reddish tinge, showed off on their black shining bodies like those of the Nubians. From the lobes of their ears, cut and distended, hung chaplets of bones. Most of these savages were naked. Amongst them, I remarked some women, dressed from the hips to knees in quite a crinoline of herbs, that sustained a vegetable waistband. Some chiefs had ornamented their necks with a crescent and collars of glass beads, red and white; nearly all were armed with bows, arrows, and shields, and carried on their shoulders a sort of net containing those round stones which they cast from their slings with great skill. One of these chiefs, rather near to the *Nautilus*, examined it attentively. He was, perhaps, a "mado" of high rank, for he was draped in a mast of banana leaves, notched round the edges, and set off with brilliant colours.

I could easily have knocked down this native, who was within a short length; but I thought that it was better to wait for real hostile demonstrations. Between Europeans and savages, it is proper for the Europeans to parry sharply, not to attack.

During low water the natives roamed about near the *Nautilus*, but were not troublesome; I heard them frequently repeat the word "Assai," and by their gestures I understood that they invited me to go on land, an invitation that I declined.

So that, on that day, the boat did not push off, to the great displeasure of Master Land, who could not complete his provisions.

This adroit Canadian employed his time in preparing the viands and meat that he had brought off the island. As for the savages, they returned to the shore about eleven o'clock in the morning, as soon as the coral tops began to disappear under the rising tide; but I saw their numbers had increased considerably on the shore. Probably they came from the neighbouring islands, or very likely from Papua. However, I had not seen a single native canoe. Having nothing better to do, I thought of dragging these beautiful limpid waters, under which I saw a profusion of shells, zoophytes, and marine plants. Moreover, it was the last day that the *Nautilus* would pass in these parts, if it float in open sea the next day, according to Captain Nemo's promise.

I therefore called Conseil, who brought me a little light drag, very like those for the oyster fishery. Now to work! For two hours we fished unceasingly, but without bringing up any rarities. The drag was filled with midas-ears, harps, melames, and particularly the most beautiful hammers I have ever seen. We also brought up some holothurias, pearl-oysters, and a dozen little turtles, that were reserved for the pantry on board.

But just when I expected it least, I put my hand on a wonder, I might say a natural deformity, very rarely met with. Conseil was just dragging, and his net came up filled with divers ordinary shells, when, all at once, he saw me plunge my arm quickly into the net, to draw out a shell, and heard me utter a conchological cry, that is to say, the most piercing cry that human throat can utter.

"What is the matter, sir?" he asked, in surprise; "has master been bitten?"

"No, my boy; but I would willingly have given a finger for my discovery."

"What discovery?"

"This shell," I said, holding up the object of my triumph.

"It is simply an olive porphyry, genus olive, order of the pectini-branchidae, class of gasteropods, sub-class of mollusca."

"Yes, Conseil; but instead of being rolled from right to left, this olive turns from left to right."

"Is it possible?"

"Yes, my boy; it is a left shell."

Shells are all right-handed with rare exceptions; and, when by chance their spiral is left, amateurs are ready to pay their weight in gold.

Conseil and I were absorbed in the contemplation of our treasure, and I was promising myself to enrich the museum with it, when a stone unfortunately thrown by a native, struck against, and broke the precious object in Conseil's hand. I uttered a cry of despair! Conseil took up his gun, and aimed at a savage who was poising his sling at ten yards from him. I would have stopped him, but his blow took effect, and broke the bracelet of amulets which encircled the arm of the savage.

"Conseil!" cried I "Conseil!"

"Well, sir! do you not see that the cannibal has commenced the attack."

"A shell is not worth the life of a man," said I.

"Ah! the scoundrel!" cried Conseil; "I would rather he had broken my shoulder!"

Conseil was in earnest, but I was not of his opinion. However the situation had changed some minutes before, and we were not perceived. A score of canoes surrounded the *Nautilus*. These canoes, scooped out of the trunk of a tree, long, narrow, well adapted for speed, were balanced by means of a long bamboo pole, which floated on the water. They were managed by skilful half-naked paddlers and I watched their advance with some uneasiness. It was evident that these Papuans had already had dealings with the Europeans, and knew their ships. But this long iron cylinder anchored in the bay, without masts or chimney, what could they think of it? Nothing good, for at first they kept at a respectful distance. However, seeing it motionless, by degrees they took courage, and sought to familiarise themselves with it. Now, this familiarity was precisely what it was necessary to avoid. Our arms, which were noiseless, could only produce a moderate effect on the savages, who have little respect for aught but blustering things. The thunderbolt without the reverberations of thunder would frighten man but little, though the danger lies in the lightning, not in the noise.

At this moment the canoes approached the *Nautilus*, and a shower of arrows alighted on her.

I went down to the saloon, but found no one there. I ventured to knock at the door that opened into the Captain's room. "Come in," was the answer.

I entered, and found Captain Nemo deep in algebraical calculations of x and other quantities.

"I am disturbing you," said I, for courtesy sake.

"That is true, M. Aronnax," replied the Captain; "but I think you have serious reasons for wishing to see me?"

"Very grave ones; the natives are surrounding us in their canoes, and in a few minutes we shall certainly be attacked by many hundreds of savages."

"Ah!" said Captain Nemo, quietly, "they are come with their canoes?"

"Yes, sir."

"Well, sir, we must close the hatches."

"Exactly, and I came to say to you"—

"Nothing can be more simple," said Captain Nemo. And pressing an electric button, he transmitted an order to the ship's crew.

"It is all done, sir," said he, after some moments. "The pinnace is ready, and the hatches are closed. You do not fear, I imagine, that these gentlemen could stave in walls on which the balls of your frigate have had no effect?"

"No, Captain; but a danger still exists."

"What is that, sir?"

"It is that to-morrow, at about this hour, we must open the hatches to renew the air of the *Nautilus*. Now, if, at this moment, the Papuans should occupy the platform, I do not see how you could prevent them from entering."

"Then, sir, you suppose that they will board us?"

"I am certain of it."

"Well, sir, let them come. I see no reason for hindering them. After all, these Papuans are poor creatures, and I am unwilling that my visit to the Island of Gueberoan should cost the life of a single one of these wretches."

Upon that I was going away; but Captain Nemo detained me, and asked me to sit down by him. He questioned me with interest about our excursions on shore, and our hunting; and seemed not to understand the craving for meat that possessed the Canadian. Then the conversation turned on various subjects, and without being more communicative, Captain Nemo showed himself more amiable.

Amongst other things, we happened to speak of the situation of the *Nautilus*, run aground in exactly the same spot in this strait where Dumont d'Urville was nearly lost. Apropos of this—

"This D'Urville was one of your great sailors," said the Captain, to me, "one of your most intelligent navigators. He is the Captain Cook of you Frenchmen. Unfortunate man of science, after having braved the icebergs of the south pole, the coral reefs of Oceania, the cannibals of the Pacific, to perish miserably in a railway train! If this energetic man could have reflected during the last moments of his life, what must have been uppermost in his last thoughts, do you suppose?"

So speaking, Captain Nemo seemed moved, and his emotion gave me a better opinion of him. Then, chart in hand, we reviewed the travels of the French navigator, his voyages of circumnavigation, his double detention at the south pole, which led to the discovery of Adelaide and Louis Philippe, and fixing the hydrographical bearings of the principal islands of Oceania.

"That which your D'Urville has done on the surface of the seas," said Captain Nemo, "that have I done under them, and more easily, more completely than he. The *Astrolabe* and the *Zelia*, incessantly tossed about by the hurricanes, could not be worth the *Nautilus*, quiet repository of labour that she is, truly motionless in the midst of the waters."

"To-morrow," added the Captain, rising, "to-morrow, at twenty minutes to three P.M., the *Nautilus* shall float, and leave the Strait of Torres uninjured."

Having curtly pronounced these words, Captain Nemo bowed slightly. This was to dismiss me, and I went back to my room.

There I found Conseil, who wished to know the result of my interview with the Captain.

"My boy," said I, "when I feigned to believe that his *Nautilus* was threatened by the natives of Papua, the Captain answered me very sarcastically. I have but one thing to say to you: Have confidence in him, and go to sleep in peace."

"Have you no need of my services, sir?"

"No, my friend. What is Ned Land doing?"

"If you will excuse me, sir," answered Conseil, "friend Ned is busy making a kangaroo-pie, which will be a marvel."

I remained alone, and went to bed, but slept indifferently. I heard the noise of the savages, who stamped on the platform uttering deafening cries. The night passed thus, without disturbing the ordinary repose of the crew. The presence of these cannibals affected them no more than the soldiers of a masked battery care for the ants that crawl over its front.

At six in the morning I rose. The hatches had not been opened. The inner air was not renewed, but the reservoirs, filled ready for any emergency, were now resorted to, and discharged several cubic feet of oxygen into the exhausted atmosphere of the *Nautilus*.

I worked in my room till noon, without having seen Captain Nemo, even for an instant. On board no preparations for departure were visible.

I waited still some time, then went into the large saloon. The clock marked half-past two. In ten minutes it would be high-tide: and, if Captain Nemo had not made a rash promise, the *Nautilus* would be immediately detached. If not, many months would pass ere she could leave her bed of coral.

However, some warning vibrations began to be felt in the vessel. I heard the keel grating against the rough calcareous bottom of the coral reef.

At five-and-twenty minutes to three, Captain Nemo appeared in the saloon.

"We are going to start," said he.

"Ah!" replied I.

"I have given the order to open the hatches."

"And the Papuans?"

"The Papuans?" answered Captain Nemo, slightly shrugging his shoulders.

"Will they not come inside the *Nautilus*?"

"How?"

"Only by leaping over the hatches you have opened."

"M. Aronnax," quietly answered Captain Nemo, "they will not enter the hatches of the *Nautilus* in that way, even if they were open."

I looked at the Captain.

"You do not understand?" said he.

"Hardly."

"Well, come and you will see."

I directed my steps towards the central staircase. There Ned Land and Conseil were slyly watching some of the ship's crew, who were opening the hatches, while cries of rage and fearful vociferations resounded outside.

The port lids were pulled down outside. Twenty horrible faces appeared. But the first native who placed his hand on the stair-rail, struck from behind by some invisible force, I know not what, fled, uttering the most fearful cries, and making the wildest contortions.

Ten of his companions followed him. They met with the same fate.

Conseil was in ecstasy. Ned Land, carried away by his violent instincts, rushed on to the staircase. But the moment he seized the rail with both hands, he, in his turn, was overthrown.

"I am struck by a thunderbolt," cried he, with an oath.

This explained all. It was no rail, but a metallic cable, charged with electricity from the deck, communicating with the platform. Whoever touched it felt a powerful shock—and this shock would have been mortal, if Captain Nemo had discharged into the conductor the whole force of the current. It might truly be said that between his assailants and himself he had stretched a network of electricity which none could pass with impunity.

Meanwhile, the exasperated Papuans had beaten a retreat, paralysed with terror. As for us, half laughing, we consoled and rubbed the unfortunate Ned Land, who swore like one possessed.

But, at this moment, the *Nautilus*, raised by the last waves of the tide, quitted her coral bed exactly at the fortieth minute fixed by the Captain. Her screw swept the waters slowly and majestically. Her speed increased gradually, and sailing on the surface of the ocean, she quitted safe and sound the dangerous passes of the Straits of Torres.

Chapter XXII
"Aegri Somnia"

The following day, 10th January, the *Nautilus* continued her course between two seas, but with such remarkable speed that I could not estimate it at less than thirty-five miles an hour. The rapidity of her screw was such that I could neither follow nor count its evolutions. When I reflected that this marvellous electric agent, after having afforded motion, heat, and light to the *Nautilus*, still protected her from outward attack, and transformed her into an ark of safety, which no profane hand might touch without being thunder-stricken, my admiration was unbounded, and from the structure it extended to the engineer who had called it into existence.

Our course was directed to the west, and on 11th January we doubled Cape Wessel, situated in 135° longitude, and 10° north latitude, which forms the east point of the Gulf of Carpentaria. The reefs were still numerous, but more equalised, and marked on the chart with extreme precision. The *Nautilus* easily avoided the breakers of Money to port, and the Victoria reefs to starboard, placed at 130° longitude, and on the tenth parallel which we strictly followed.

On the 13th January, Captain Nemo arrived in the Sea of Timor, and recognised the island of that name in 122° longitude.

From this point, the direction of the *Nautilus* inclined towards the south-west. Her head was set for the Indian Ocean. Where would the fancy of Captain Nemo carry us next? Would he return to the coast of Asia? or would he approach again the shores of Europe? Improbable conjectures both, for a man who fled from inhabited continents. Then, would he descend to the south? Was he going to double the Cape of Good Hope, then Cape Horn, and finally go as far as the antarctic pole? Would he come back at last to the Pacific, where his *Nautilus* could sail free and independently? Time would show.

After having skirted the sands of Cartier, of Hibernia, Seringapatam, and Scott, last efforts of the solid against the liquid element, on the 14th January we lost sight of land altogether. The speed of the *Nautilus* was considerably abated, and, with irregular course, she sometimes swam in the bosom of the waters, sometimes floated on their surface.

During this period of the voyage, Captain Nemo made some interesting experiments on the varied temperature of the sea, in different beds. Under ordinary conditions, these observations are made by means of rather complicated instruments, and with somewhat doubtful results, by means of thermometrical sounding-leads, the glasses often breaking under the pressure of the water, or an apparatus grounded on the variations of the resistance of metals to the electric currents. Results so obtained could not be correctly calculated. On the contrary, Captain Nemo went himself to test the temperature in the depths of the sea, and his thermometer, placed in communication with the different sheets of water, gave him the required degree immediately and accurately.

It was thus that, either by overloading her reservoirs, or by descending obliquely by means of her inclined planes, the *Nautilus* successively attained the depth of three, four, five, seven, nine, and ten thousand yards, and the definite result of this experience was, that the sea preserved an average temperature of four degrees and a half, at a depth of five thousand fathoms, under all latitudes.

On the 16th January, the *Nautilus* seemed becalmed, only a few yards beneath the surface of the waves. Her electric apparatus remained inactive, and her motionless screw left her to drift at the mercy of the currents. I supposed that the crew was occupied with interior repairs, rendered necessary by the violence of the mechanical movements of the machine.

My companions and I then witnessed a curious spectacle. The hatches of the saloon were open, and as the beacon-light of the *Nautilus* was not in action, a dim obscurity reigned in the midst of the waters.

I observed the state of the sea under these conditions, and the largest fish appeared to me no more than scarcely defined shadows, when the *Nautilus* found herself suddenly transported into full light. I thought at first that the beacon had been lighted, and was casting its electric radiance into the liquid mass. I was mistaken, and after a rapid survey, perceived my error.

The *Nautilus* floated in the midst of a phosphorescent bed, which, in this obscurity, became quite dazzling. It was produced by myriads of luminous animalculae, whose brilliancy was increased as they glided over the metallic hull of the vessel. I was surprised by lightning in the midst of these luminous sheets, as though they had been rivulets of lead melted in an ardent furnace, or metallic masses brought to a white heat, so that, by force of contrast, certain portions of light appeared to cast a shade in the midst of the general ignition, from which all shade seemed banished. No; this was not the calm irradiation of our ordinary lightning. There was unusual life and vigour; this was truly living light!

In reality, it was an infinite agglomeration of coloured infusoria, of veritable globules of diaphanous jelly, provided with a thread-like tentacle, and of which as many as twenty-five thousand have been counted in less than two cubic half-inches of water; and their light was increased by the glimmering peculiar to the medusae, starfish, aurelia, and other phosphorescent zoophytes, impregnated by the grease of the organic matter decomposed by the sea, and, perhaps, the mucus secreted by the fish.

During several hours the *Nautilus* floated in these brilliant waves, and our admiration increased as we watched the marine monsters disporting themselves like salamanders. I saw there, in the midst of this fire that burns not, the swift and elegant porpoise (the indefatigable clown of the ocean), and some swordfish, ten feet long, those prophetic heralds of the hurricane, whose formidable sword would now and then strike the glass of the saloon. Then appeared the smaller fish, the variegated balista, the leaping mackerel, wolf-thorntails, and a hundred others which striped the luminous atmosphere as they swam. This dazzling spectacle was enchanting! Perhaps some atmospheric condition increased the intensity of this phenomenon. Perhaps some storm agitated the surface of the waves. But, at this depth of some yards, the *Nautilus* was unmoved by its fury, and reposed peacefully in still water.

So we progressed, incessantly charmed by some new marvel. Conseil arranged and classed his zoophytes, his articulata, his molluscs, his fishes. The days passed rapidly away, and I took no account of them. Ned, according to habit, tried to vary the diet on board. Like snails, we were fixed to our shells, and I declare it is easy to lead a snail's life.

Thus, this life seemed easy and natural, and we thought no longer of the life we led on land; but something happened to recall us to the strangeness of our situation.

On the 18th of January, the *Nautilus* was in 105° longitude and 15° south latitude. The weather was threatening, the sea rough and rolling. There was a strong east wind. The barometer, which had been going down for some days, foreboded a coming storm. I went up on to the platform just as the second lieutenant was taking the measure of the horary angles, and waited, according to habit, till the daily phrase was said. But, on this day, it was exchanged for another phrase not less incomprehensible. Almost directly, I saw Captain Nemo appear, with a glass, looking towards the horizon.

For some minutes he was immovable, without taking his eye off the point of observation. Then he lowered his glass, and exchanged a few words with his lieutenant. The latter seemed to be a victim to some emotion that he tried in vain to repress. Captain Nemo, having more command over himself, was cool. He seemed, too, to be making some objections, to which the lieutenant replied by formal assurances. At least I concluded so by the difference of their tones and gestures. For myself, I had looked carefully in the direction indicated without seeing anything. The sky and water were lost in the clear line of the horizon.

However, Captain Nemo walked from one end of the platform to the other, without looking at me, perhaps without seeing me. His step was firm, but less regular than usual. He stopped sometimes, crossed his arms, and observed the sea. What could he be looking for on that immense expanse?

The *Nautilus* was then some hundreds of miles from the nearest coast.

The lieutenant had taken up the glass, and examined the horizon steadfastly, going and coming, stamping his foot and showing more nervous agitation than his superior officer. Besides, this mystery must necessarily be solved, and before long; for, upon an order from Captain Nemo, the engine increasing its propelling power, made the screw turn more rapidly.

Just then, the lieutenant drew the Captain's attention again. The latter stopped walking and directed his glass towards the place indicated. He looked long. I felt very much puzzled, and descended to the drawing-room, and took out an excellent telescope that I generally used. Then leaning on the cage of the watch-light, that jutted out from the front of the platform, set myself to look over all the line of the sky and sea.

But my eye was no sooner applied to the glass, than it was quickly snatched out of my hands.

I turned round. Captain Nemo was before me, but I did not know him. His face was transfigured. His eyes flashed sullenly, his teeth were set; his stiff body, clenched fists, and head shrunk between his shoulders, betrayed the violent agitation that pervaded his whole frame. He did not move. My glass, fallen from his hands, had rolled at his feet.

Had I unwittingly provoked this fit of anger? Did this incomprehensible person imagine that I had discovered some forbidden secret? No; I was not the object of this hatred, for he was not looking at me, his eye was steadily fixed upon the impenetrable point of the horizon. At last Captain Nemo recovered himself. His agitation subsided. He addressed some words in a foreign language to his lieutenant, then turned to me. "M. Aronnax," he said, in rather an imperious tone, "I require you to keep one of the conditions that bind you to me."

"What is it, Captain?"

"You must be confined, with your companions, until I think fit to release you."

"You are the master," I replied, looking steadily at him. "But may I ask you one question?"

"None, sir."

There was no resisting this imperious command, it would have been useless. I went down to the cabin occupied by Ned Land and Conseil, and told them the Captain's determination. You may judge how this communication was received by the Canadian.

But there was no time for altercation. Four of the crew waited at the door, and conducted us to that cell where we had passed our first night on board the *Nautilus*.

Ned Land would have remonstrated, but the door was shut upon him.

"Will master tell us what this means?" asked Conseil.

I told my companions what had passed. They were as much astonished as I, and equally at a loss how to account for it.

Meanwhile, I was absorbed in my own reflections, and could think of nothing but the strange fear depicted in the Captain's countenance. I was utterly at a loss to account for it, when my cogitations were disturbed by these words from Ned Land—

"Hallo! breakfast is ready."

And indeed the table was laid. Evidently Captain Nemo had given this order at the same time that he had hastened the speed of the *Nautilus*.

"Will master permit me to make a recommendation?" asked Conseil.

"Yes, my boy."

"Well, it is that master breakfasts. It is prudent, for we do not know what may happen."

"You are right, Conseil."

"Unfortunately," said Ned Land, "they have only given us the ship's fare."

"Friend Ned," asked Conseil, "what would you have said if the breakfast had been entirely forgotten?"

This argument cut short the harpooners recriminations.

We sat down to table. The meal was eaten in silence.

Just then, the luminous globe that lighted the cell went out, and left us in total darkness. Ned Land was soon asleep, and what astonished me was that Conseil went off into a heavy sleep. I was thinking what could have caused his irresistible drowsiness, when I felt my brain becoming stupefied. In spite of my efforts to keep my eyes open, they would close. A painful suspicion seized me. Evidently soporific substances had been mixed with the food we had just taken. Imprisonment was not enough to conceal Captain Nemo's projects from us, sleep was more necessary.

I then heard the panels shut. The undulations of the sea, which caused a slight rolling motion, ceased. Had the *Nautilus* quitted the surface of the ocean? Had it gone back to the motionless bed of water. I tried to resist sleep. It was impossible. My breathing grew weak. I felt a mortal cold freeze my stiffened and half-paralysed limbs. My eyelids, like leaden caps, fell over my eyes. I could not raise them; a morbid sleep, full of hallucinations, bereft me of my being. Then the visions disappeared, and left me in complete insensibility.

Chapter XXIII

The Coral Kingdom

The next day I woke with my head singularly clear. To my great surprise I was in my own room. My companions, no doubt, had been reinstated in their cabin, without having perceived it any more than I. Of what had passed during the night they were as ignorant as I was, and to penetrate this mystery I only reckoned upon the chances of the future.

I then thought of quitting my room. Was I free again or a prisoner? Quite free. I opened the door, went to the half-deck, went up the central stairs. The panels, shut the evening before, were open. I went on to the platform.

Ned Land and Conseil waited there for me. I questioned them; they knew nothing. Lost in a heavy sleep in which they had been totally unconscious, they had been astonished at finding themselves in their cabin.

As for the *Nautilus*, it seemed quiet and mysterious as ever. It floated on the surface of the waves at a moderate pace. Nothing seemed changed on board.

The second lieutenant then came on to the platform, and gave the usual order below.

As for Captain Nemo, he did not appear.

Of the people on board, I only saw the impassive steward, who served me with his usual dumb regularity.

About two o'clock, I was in the drawingroom, busied in arranging my notes, when the Captain opened the door and appeared. I bowed. He made a slight inclination in return, without speaking. I resumed my work, hoping that he would perhaps give me some explanation of the events of the preceding night. He made none. I looked at him. He seemed fatigued; his heavy eyes had not been refreshed by sleep; his face looked very sorrowful. He walked to and fro, sat down and got up again, took up a chance book, put it down, consulted his instruments without taking his habitual notes, and seemed restless and uneasy. At last, he came up to me, and said—

"Are you a doctor, M. Aronnax?"

I so little expected such a question, that I stared some time at him without answering.

"Are you a doctor?" he repeated. "Several of your colleagues have studied medicine."

"Well," said I, "I am a doctor and resident surgeon to the hospital. I practised several years before entering the museum."

"Very well, sir."

My answer had evidently satisfied the Captain. But not knowing what he would say next, I waited for other questions, reserving my answers according to circumstances.

"M. Aronnax, will you consent to prescribe for one of my men?" he asked.

"Is he ill?"

"Yes."

"I am ready to follow you."

"Come then."

I own my heart beat, I do not know why. I saw a certain connection between the illness of one of the crew and the events of the day before; and this mystery interested me at least as much as the sick man.

Captain Nemo conducted me to the poop of the *Nautilus*, and took me into a cabin situated near the sailors' quarters.

There, on a bed, lay a man about forty years of age, with a resolute expression of countenance, a true type of an Anglo-Saxon.

I leant over him. He was not only ill, he was wounded. His head, swathed in bandages covered with blood, lay on a pillow. I undid the bandages, and the wounded man looked at me with his large eyes and gave no sign of pain as I did it. It was a horrible wound. The skull, shattered by some deadly weapon, left the brain exposed, which was much injured. Clots of blood had formed in the bruised and broken mass, in colour like the dregs of wine.

There was both contusion and suffusion of the brain. His breathing was slow, and some spasmodic movements of the muscles agitated his face. I felt his pulse. It was intermittent. The extremities of the body were growing cold already, and I saw death must inevitably ensue. After dressing the unfortunate man's wounds, I readjusted the bandages on his head, and turned to Captain Nemo.

"What caused this wound?" I asked.

"What does it signify?" he replied, evasively. "A shock has broken one of the levers of the engine, which struck myself. But your opinion as to his state?"

I hesitated before giving it.

"You may speak," said the Captain. "This man does not understand French."

I gave a last look at the wounded man.

"He will be dead in two hours."

"Can nothing save him?"

"Nothing."

Captain Nemo's hand contracted, and some tears glistened in his eyes, which I thought incapable of shedding any.

For some moments I still watched the dying man, whose life ebbed slowly. His pallor increased under the electric light that was shed over his death-bed. I looked at his intelligent forehead, furrowed with premature wrinkles, produced probably by misfortune and sorrow. I tried to learn the secret of his life from the last words that escaped his lips.

"You can go now, M. Aronnax," said the Captain.

I left him in the dying man's cabin, and returned to my room much affected by this scene. During the whole day, I was haunted by uncomfortable suspicions, and at night I slept badly, and, between my broken dreams, I fancied I heard distant sighs like the notes of a funeral psalm. Were they the prayers of the dead; murmured in that language that I could not understand?

The next morning I went on to the bridge. Captain Nemo was there before me. As soon as he perceived me he came to me.

"Professor, will it be convenient to you to make a submarine excursion to-day?"

"With my companions?" I asked.

"If they like."

"We obey your orders, Captain."

"Will you be so good then as to put on your cork-jackets?"

It was not a question of dead or dying. I rejoined Ned Land and Conseil, and told them of Captain Nemo's proposition. Conseil hastened to accept it, and this time the Canadian seemed quite willing to follow our example.

It was eight o'clock in the morning. At half-past eight we were equipped for this new excursion, and provided with two contrivances for light and breathing. The double door was open; and accompanied by Captain Nemo, who was followed by a dozen of the crew, we set foot, at a depth of about thirty feet, on the solid bottom on which the *Nautilus* rested.

A slight declivity ended in an uneven bottom, at fifteen fathoms depth. This bottom differed entirely from the one I had visited on my first excursion under the waters of the Pacific Ocean. Here, there was no fine sand, no submarine prairies, no sea-forest. I immediately recognised that marvellous region in which, on that day, the Captain did the honours to us. It was the coral kingdom. In the zoophyte branch and in the alcyon class I noticed the gorgoneae, the isidiae, and the corollariae.

The light produced a thousand charming varieties, playing in the midst of the branches that were so vividly coloured. I seemed to see the membraneous and cylindrical tubes tremble beneath the undulation of the waters. I was tempted to gather their fresh petals, ornamented with delicate tentacules, some just blown, the others budding, while small fish, swimming swiftly, touched them slightly, like flights of birds. But if my hand approached these living flowers, these animated sensitive plants, the whole colony took alarm. The white petals re-entered their red cases, the flowers faded as I looked, and the bush changed into a block of stony knobs.

Chance had thrown me just by the most precious specimens of this zoophyte. This coral was more valuable than that found in the Mediterranean, on the coasts of France, Italy, and Barbary. Its tints justified the poetical names of "Flower of Blood," and "Froth of Blood," that trade has given to its most beautiful productions. Coral is sold for £20 per ounce; and in this place, the watery beds would make the fortunes of a company of coral-divers. This precious matter, often confused with other polypi, formed then the inextricable plots called "macciota," and on which I noticed several beautiful specimens of pink coral.

But soon the bushes contract, and the arborisations increase. Real petrified thickets, long joists of fantastic architecture, were disclosed before us. Captain Nemo placed himself under a dark gallery, where by a slight declivity we reached a depth of 100 yards. The light from our lamps produced sometimes magical effects, following the rough outlines of the natural arches, and pendants disposed like lustres, that were tipped with points of fire. Between the coralline shrubs I noticed other polypi not less curious, melites, and irises with articulated ramifications, also some tufts of coral, some green, others red, like seaweed incrusted in their calcareous salts, that naturalists, after long discussion, have definitely classed in the vegetable kingdom. But following the remark of a thinking man, "there is perhaps the real point where life rises obscurely from the sleep of a stone, without detaching itself from the rough point of departure."

At last, after walking two hours, we had attained a depth of about 300 yards, that is to say, the extreme limit on which coral begins to form. But there was no isolated bush, nor modest brushwood, at the bottom of lofty trees. It was an immense forest of large mineral vegetations, enormous petrified trees, united by garlands of elegant plumarias, seabindweed, all adorned with clouds and reflections. We passed freely under their high branches, lost in the shade of the waves, while at our feet, tubipores, meandrines, stars, fungi, and caryophyllidae formed a carpet of flowers sown with dazzling gems. What an indescribable spectacle!

Captain Nemo had stopped. I and my companions halted, and turning round, I saw his men were forming a semicircle round their chief. Watching attentively, I observed that four of them carried on their shoulders an object of an oblong shape.

We occupied, in this place, the centre of a vast glade surrounded by the lofty foliage of the submarine forest. Our lamps threw over this place a sort of clear twilight that singularly elongated the shadows on the ground. At the end of the glade the darkness increased, and was only relieved by little sparks reflected by the points of coral.

Ned Land and Conseil were near me. We watched, and I thought I was going to witness a strange scene. On observing the ground, I saw that it was raised in certain places by slight excrescences encrusted with limy deposits, and disposed with a regularity that betrayed the hand of man.

In the midst of the glade, on a pedestal of rocks roughly piled up, stood a cross of coral, that extended its long arms that one might have thought were made of petrified blood.

Upon a sign from Captain Nemo, one of the men advanced; and at some feet from the cross, he began to dig a hole with a pickaxe that he took from his belt. I understood all! This glade was a cemetery, this hole a tomb, this oblong object the body of the man who had died in the night! The Captain and his men had come to bury their companion in this general resting-place, at the bottom of this inaccessible ocean!

The grave was being dug slowly; the fish fled on all sides while their retreat was being thus disturbed; I heard the strokes of the pickaxe, which sparkled when it hit upon some flint lost at the bottom of the waters. The hole was soon large and deep enough to receive the body. Then the bearers approached; the body, enveloped in a tissue of white byssus, was lowered into the damp grave. Captain Nemo, with his arms crossed on his breast, and all the friends of him who had loved them, knelt in prayer.

The grave was then filled in with the rubbish taken from the ground, which formed a slight mound. When this was done, Captain Nemo and his men rose; then, approaching the grave, they knelt again, and all extended their hands in sign of a last adieu. Then the funeral procession returned to the *Nautilus*, passing under the arches of the forest, in the midst of thickets, along the coral bushes, and still on the ascent. At last the fires on board appeared, and their luminous track guided us to the *Nautilus*. At one o'clock we had returned.

As soon as I had changed my clothes, I went up on to the platform, and, a prey to conflicting emotions, I sat down near the binnacle. Captain Nemo joined me. I rose and said to him—

"So, as I said he would, this man died in the night?"

"Yes, M. Aronnax."

"And he rests now, near his companions, in the coral cemetery?"

"Yes, forgotten by all else, but not by us. We dug the grave, and the polypi undertake to seal our dead for eternity." And burying his face quickly in his hands, he tried in vain to suppress a sob. Then he added—"Our peaceful cemetery is there, some hundred feet below the surface of the waves."

"Your dead sleep quietly, at least, Captain, out of the reach of sharks."

"Yes, sir, of sharks and *men*," gravely replied the Captain.

PART 2

Chapter I
The Indian Ocean

We now come to the second part of our journey under the sea. The first ended with the moving scene in the coral cemetery, which left such a deep impression on my mind. Thus, in the midst of this great sea, Captain Nemo's life was passing even to his grave, which he had prepared in one of its deepest abysses. There, not one of the ocean's monsters could trouble the last sleep of the crew of the *Nautilus*, of those friends riveted to each other in death as in life. "Nor any man either," had added the Captain. Still the same fierce, implacable defiance towards human society!

I could no longer content myself with the hypothesis which satisfied Conseil.

That worthy fellow persisted in seeing in the Commander of the *Nautilus* one of those unknown savants who return mankind contempt for indifference. For him, he was a misunderstood genius, who, tired of earth's deceptions, had taken refuge in this inaccessible medium, where he might follow his instincts freely. To my mind, this hypothesis explained but one side of Captain Nemo's character.

Indeed, the mystery of that last night, during which we had been chained in prison, the sleep, and the precautions so violently taken by the Captain of snatching from my eyes the glass I had raised to sweep the horizon, the mortal wound of the man, due to an unaccountable shock of the *Nautilus*, all put me on a new track. No; Captain Nemo was not satisfied with shunning man. His formidable apparatus not only suited his instinct of freedom, but, perhaps, also the design of some terrible retaliation.

At this moment, nothing is clear to me; I catch but a glimpse of light amidst all the darkness, and I must confine myself to writing as events shall dictate.

That day, the 24th of January 1868, at noon, the second officer came to take the altitude of the sun. I mounted the platform, lit a cigar, and watched the operation. It seemed to me that the man did not understand French; for several times I made remarks in a loud voice, which must have drawn from him some involutary sign of attention, if he had understood them; but he remained undisturbed and dumb.

As he was taking observations with the sextant, one of the sailors of the *Nautilus* (the strong man who had accompanied us on our first submarine excursion to the Island of Crespo) came to clean the glasses of the lantern. I examined the fittings of the apparatus, the strength of which was increased a hundredfold by lenticular rings, placed similar to those in a lighthouse, and which projected their brilliance in a horizontal plane. The electric lamp was combined in such a way as to give its most powerful light. Indeed, it was produced in *vacuo*, which insured both its steadiness and its intensity. This vacuum economised the graphite points, between which the luminous arc was developed,—an important point of economy for Captain Nemo, who could not easily have replaced them; and under these conditions their waste was imperceptible. When the *Nautilus* was ready to continue its submarine journey, I went down to the saloon. The panels were closed, and the course marked direct west.

We were furrowing the waters of the Indian Ocean, a vast liquid plain, with a surface of 1,200,000,000 of acres, and whose waters are so clear and transparent, that any one leaning over them would turn giddy. The *Nautilus* usually floated between fifty and a hundred fathoms deep. We went on so for some days. To any one but myself, who had a great love for the sea, the hours would have seemed long and monotonous; but the daily walks on the platform, when I steeped myself in the reviving air of the ocean, the sight of the rich waters through the windows of the saloon, the books in the library, the compiling of my memoirs, took up all my time, and left me not a moment of ennui or weariness.

For some days we saw a great number of aquatic birds, seamews or gulls. Some were cleverly killed, and, prepared in a certain way, made very acceptable water-game. Amongst large winged birds, carried a long distance from all lands, and resting upon the waves from the fatigue of their flight, I saw some magnificent albatrosses, uttering discordant cries like the braying of an ass, and birds belonging to the family of the longipennates. The family of the totipalmates was represented by the sea-swallows, which caught the fish from the surface, and by numerous phaetons, or lepturi; amongst others, the phaeton with red lines, as large as a pigeon, whose white plumage, tinted with pink, shows off to advantage the blackness of its wings.

As to the fish, they always provoked our admiration when we surprised the secrets of their aquatic life through the open panels. I saw many kinds which I never before had a chance of observing.

I shall notice chiefly ostracions peculiar to the Red Sea, the Indian Ocean, and that part which washes the coast of tropical America. These fishes, like the tortoise, the armadillo, the sea hedgehog, and the crustacea, are protected by a breastplate which is neither chalky nor stony, but real bone. In some it takes the form of a solid triangle, in others of a solid quadrangle. Amongst the triangular I saw some an inch and a half in length, with wholesome flesh and a delicious flavour; they are brown at the tail, and yellow at the fins, and I recommend their introduction into fresh water, to which a certain number of sea-fish easily accustom themselves. I would also mention quadrangular ostracions, having on the back four large tubercles; some dotted over with white spots on the lower part of the body, and which may be tamed like birds; trigons provided with spikes formed by the lengthening of their bony shell, and which, from their strange gruntings, are called "sea-pigs;" also dromedaries with large humps in the shape of a cone, whose flesh is very tough and leathery.

I now borrow from the daily notes of Master Conseil. "Certain fish of the genus petrodon peculiar to those seas, with red backs and white chests, which are distinguished by three rows of longitudinal filaments; and some electrical, seven inches long, decked in the liveliest colours. Then, as specimens of other kinds, some ovoides, resembling an egg of a dark brown colour, marked with white bands, and without tails; diodons, real sea-porcupines, furnished with spikes, and capable of swelling in such a way as to look like cushions bristling with darts; hippocampi, common to every ocean; some pegasi with lengthened snouts, which their pectoral fins, being much elongated and formed in the shape of wings, allow, if not to fly, at least to shoot into the air; pigeon spatulae, with tails covered with many rings of shell; macrognathi with long jaws, an excellent fish, nine inches long, and bright with most agreeable colours; pale-coloured calliomores, with rugged heads; and plenty of chaetodons, with long and tubular muzzles, which kill insects by shooting them, as from an air-gun, with a single drop of water. These we may call the fly-catchers of the seas.

"In the eighty-ninth genus of fishes, classed by Lacépède, belonging to the second lower class of bony, characterised by opercules and bronchial membranes, I remarked the scorpaena, the head of which is furnished with spikes, and which has but one dorsal fin; these creatures are covered, or not, with little shells, according to the subclass to which they belong. The second subclass gives us specimens of didactyles fourteen or fifteen inches in length, with yellow rays, and heads of a most fantastic appearance. As to the first subclass, it gives several specimens of that singular-looking fish appropriately called a "sea-frog," with large head, sometimes pierced with holes, sometimes swollen with protuberances, bristling with spikes, and covered with tubercles; it has irregular and hideous horns; its body and tail are covered with callosities; its sting makes a dangerous wound; it is both repugnant and horrible to look at."

From the 21st to the 23rd of January the *Nautilus* went at the rate of two hundred and fifty leagues in twenty-four hours, being five hundred and forty miles, or twenty-two miles an hour. If we recognised so many different varieties of fish, it was because, attracted by the electric light, they tried to follow us; the greater part, however, were soon distanced by our speed, though some kept their place in the waters of the *Nautilus* for a time. The morning of the 24th, in 12° 5' south latitude, and 94° 33' longitude, we observed Keeling Island, a madrepore formation, planted with magnificent cocoas, and which had been visited by Mr Darwin and Captain Fitzroy. The *Nautilus* skirted the shores of this desert island for a little distance. Its nets brought up numerous specimens of polypi, and curious shells of mollusca. Some precious productions of the species of delphinulae enriched the treasures of Captain Nemo, to which I added an astraea punctifera, a kind of parasite polypus often found fixed to a shell. Soon Keeling Island disappeared from the horizon, and our course was directed to the northwest in the direction of the Indian Peninsula.

From Keeling Island our course was slower and more variable, often taking us into great depths. Several times they made use of the inclined planes, which certain internal levers placed obliquely to the waterline. In that way we went about two miles, but without ever obtaining the greatest depths of the Indian Sea, which soundings of seven thousand fathoms have never reached. As to the temperature of the lower strata, the thermometer invariably indicated 4° above zero. I only observed that, in the upper regions, the water was always colder in the high levels than at the surface of the sea.

On the 25th of January, the ocean was entirely deserted; the *Nautilus* passed the day on the surface, beating the waves with its powerful screw, and making them rebound to a great height. Who under such circumstances would not have taken it for a gigantic cetacean? Three parts of this day I spent on the platform. I watched the sea. Nothing on the horizon, till about four o'clock a steamer running west on our counter. Her masts were visible for an instant, but she could not see the *Nautilus*, being too low in the water. I fancied this steamboat belonged to the P.O. Company, which runs from Ceylon to Sydney, touching at King George's Point and Melbourne.

At five o'clock in the evening, before that fleeting twilight which binds night to day in tropical zones, Conseil and I were astonished by a curious spectacle.

It was a shoal of argonauts travelling along on the surface of the ocean. We could count several hundreds. They belonged to the tubercle kind which are peculiar to the Indian seas.

These graceful molluscs moved backwards by means of their locomotive tube, through which they propelled the water already drawn in. Of their eight tentacles, six were elongated, and stretched out floating on the water, whilst the other two, rolled up flat, were spread to the wind like a light sail. I saw their spiralshaped and fluted shells, which Cuvier justly compares to an elegant skiff. A boat indeed! It bears the creature which secretes it without its adhering to it.

For nearly an hour the *Nautilus* floated in the midst of this shoal of molluscs, then I know not what sudden fright they took. But as if at a signal every sail was furled, the arms folded, the body drawn in, the shells turned over, changing their centre of gravity, and the whole fleet disappeared under the waves. Never did the ships of a squadron manoeuvre with more unity.

At that moment night fell suddenly, and the reeds, scarcely raised by the breeze, lay peaceably under the sides of the *Nautilus*.

The next day, 26th of January, we cut the equator at the eighty-second meridian, and entered the northern hemisphere. During the day, a formidable troop of sharks accompanied us, terrible creatures, which multiply in these seas, and make them very dangerous. They were "cestracio philippi" sharks, with brown backs and whitish bellies, armed with eleven rows of teeth—eyed sharks—their throat being marked with a large black spot surrounded with white like an eye. There were also some Isabella sharks, with rounded snouts marked with dark spots. These powerful creatures often hurled themselves at the windows of the saloon with such violence as to make us feel very insecure. At such times Ned Land was no longer master of himself. He wanted to go to the surface and harpoon the monsters, particularly certain smooth-hound sharks, whose mouth is studded with teeth like a mosaic; and large tiger-sharks nearly six yards long, the last named of which seemed to excite him more particularly. But the *Nautilus*, accelerating her speed, easily left the most rapid of them behind.

The 27th of January, at the entrance of the vast Bay of Bengal, we met repeatedly a forbidding spectacle, dead bodies floating on the surface of the water. They were the dead of the Indian villages, carried by the Ganges to the level of the sea, and which the vultures, the only undertakers of the country, had not been able to devour. But the sharks did not fail to help them at their funereal work.

About seven o'clock in the evening, the *Nautilus*, half immersed, was sailing in a sea of milk. At first sight the ocean seemed lactified. Was it the effect of the lunar rays? No; for the moon, scarcely two days old, was still lying hidden under the horizon in the rays of the sun. The whole sky, though lit by the sidereal rays, seemed black by contrast with the whiteness of the waters.

Conseil could not believe his eyes, and questioned me as to the cause of this strange phenomenon. Happily I was able to answer him.

"It is called a milk sea," I explained, "a large extent of white wavelets often to be seen on the coasts of Amboyna, and in these parts of the sea."

"But, sir," said Conseil, "can you tell me what causes such an effect? for I suppose the water is not really turned into milk."

"No, my boy; and the whiteness which surprises you is caused only by the presence of myriads of infusoria, a sort of luminous little worm, gelatinous and without colour, of the thickness of a hair, and whose length is not more than the 7/1000 of an inch. These insects adhere to one another sometimes for several leagues."

"Several leagues!" exclaimed Conseil.

"Yes, my boy; and you need not try to compute the number of these infusoria. You will not be able; for, if I am not mistaken, ships have floated on these milk seas for more than forty miles."

Towards midnight the sea suddenly resumed its usual colour; but behind us, even to the limits of the horizon, the sky reflected the whitened waves, and for a long time seemed impregnated with the vague glimmerings of an aurora borealis.

Chapter II

A Novel Proposal of Captain Nemo's

On the 28th of February, when at noon the *Nautilus* came to the surface of the sea, in 9° 4' north latitude, there was land in sight about eight miles to westward. The first thing I noticed was a range of mountains about two thousand feet high, the shapes of which were most capricious. On taking the bearings, I knew that we were nearing the Island of Ceylon, the pearl which hangs from the lobe of the Indian Peninsula.

Captain Nemo and his second appeared at this moment. The Captain glanced at the map. Then, turning to me, said—

"The Island of Ceylon, noted for its pearl-fisheries. would you like to visit one of them, M. Aronnax?"

"Certainly, Captain."

"Well, the thing is easy. Though if we see the fisheries, we shall not see the fishermen. The annual exportation has not yet begun. Never mind, I will give orders to make for the Gulf of Manaar, where we shall arrive in the night."

The Captain said something to his second, who immediately went out. Soon the *Nautilus* returned to her native element, and the manometer showed that she was about thirty feet deep.

"Well, sir," said Captain Nemo, "you and your companions shall visit the Bank of Manaar, and if by chance some fisherman should be there, we shall see him at work."

"Agreed, Captain!"

"By the by, M. Aronnax, you are not afraid of sharks?"

"Sharks!" exclaimed I.

This question seemed a very hard one.

"Well?" continued Captain Nemo.

"I admit, Captain, that I am not yet very familiar with that kind of fish."

"*We* are accustomed to them," replied Captain Nemo, "and in time you will be too. However, we shall be armed, and on the road we may be able to hunt some of the tribe. It is interesting. So, till to-morrow, sir, and early."

This said in a careless tone, Captain Nemo left the saloon. Now, if you were invited to hunt the bear in the mountains of Switzerland, what would you say? "Very well! to-morrow we will go and hunt the bear." If you were asked to hunt the lion in the plains of Atlas, or the tiger in the Indian jungles, what would you say? "Ha! ha! it seems we are going to hunt the tiger or the lion!" But when you are invited to hunt the shark in its natural element, you would perhaps reflect before accepting the invitation. As for myself, I passed my hand over my forehead, on which stood large drops of cold perspiration. "Let us reflect," said I, "and take our time. Hunting otters in submarine forests, as we did in the Island of Crespo, will pass; but going up and down at the bottom of the sea, where one is almost certain to meet sharks, is quite another thing! I know well that in certain countries, particularly in the

Andaman Islands, the negroes never hesitate to attack them with a dagger in one hand and a running noose in the other; but I also know that few who affront those creatures ever return alive. However, I am not a negro, and, if I were, I think a little hesitation in this case would not be ill-timed."

At this moment, Conseil and the Canadian entered, quite composed, and even joyous. They knew not what awaited them.

"Faith, sir," said Ned Land, "your Captain Nemo—the devil take him!—has just made us a very pleasant offer."

"Ah!" said I, "you know?"

"If agreeable to you, sir," interrupted Conseil, "the Commander of the *Nautilus* has invited us to visit the magnificent Ceylon fisheries to-morrow, in your company; he did it kindly, and behaved like a real gentleman."

"He said nothing more?"

"Nothing more, sir, except that he had already spoken to you of this little walk."

"Sir," said Conseil, "would you give us some details of the pearl-fishery?"

"As to the fishing itself," I asked, "or the incidents, which?"

"On the fishing," replied the Canadian; "before entering upon the ground, it is as well to know something about it."

"Very well; sit down, my friends, and I will teach you."

Ned and Conseil seated themselves on an ottoman, and the first thing the Canadian asked was—

"Sir, what is a pearl?"

"My worthy Ned," I answered, "to the poet, a pearl is a tear of the sea; to the Orientals, it is a drop of dew solidified; to the ladies, it is a jewel of an oblong shape, of a brilliancy of mother-of-pearl substance, which they wear on their fingers, their necks, or their ears; for the chemist, it is a mixture of phosphate and carbonate of lime, with a little gelatine; and lastly, for naturalists, it is simply a morbid secretion of the organ that produces the mother-of-pearl amongst certain bivalves."

"Branch of mollusca," said Conseil, "class of acephali, order of testacea."

"Precisely so, my learned Conseil; and, amongst these testacea, the earshell, the tridacnae, the turbots, in a word, all those which secrete mother-of-pearl, that is, the blue, bluish, violet, or white substance which lines the interior of their shells, are capable of producing pearls."

"Mussels too?" asked the Canadian.

"Yes, mussels of certain waters in Scotland, Wales, Ireland, Saxony, Bohemia, and France."

"Good! For the future I shall pay attention," replied the Canadian.

"But," I continued, "the particular mollusc which secretes the pearl is the *pearl-oyster*, the *meleagrina margaritifera*, that precious pintadine. The pearl is nothing but a nacreous formation, deposited in a globular form, either adhering to the oyster-shell, or buried in the folds of the creature. On the shell it is fast; in the flesh it is loose; but always has for a kernel a small hard substance, may be a barren egg, may be a grain of sand, around which the pearly matter deposits itself year after year successively, and by thin concentric layers."

"Are many pearls found in the same oyster?" asked Conseil.

"Yes, my boy. There are some pintadines a perfect casket. One oyster has been mentioned, though I allow myself to doubt it, as having contained no less than a hundred and fifty sharks."

"A hundred and fifty sharks!" exclaimed Ned Land.

"Did I say sharks?" said I, hurriedly. "I meant to say a hundred and fifty pearls. Sharks would not be sense."

"Certainly not," said Conseil; "but will you tell us now by what means they extract these pearls?"

"They proceed in various ways. When they adhere to the shell, the fishermen often pull them off with pincers; but the most common way is to lay the pintadines on mats of the seaweed which covers the banks. Thus they die in the open air; and at the end of ten days they are in a forward state of decomposition. They are then plunged into large reservoirs of seawater; then they are opened and washed. Now begins the double work of the sorters. First they separate the layers of pearl, known in commerce by the name of bastard whites and bastard blacks, which are delivered in boxes of two hundred and fifty and three hundred pounds each. Then they take the parenchyma of the oyster, boil it, and pass it through a sieve in order to extract the very smallest pearls."

"The price of these pearls varies according to their size?" asked Conseil.

"Not only according to their size," I answered, "but also according to their shape, their *water* (that is, their colour), and their lustre; that is, that bright and diapered sparkle which makes them so charming to the eye. The most beautiful are called virgin pearls or paragons. They are formed alone in the tissue of the mollusc, are white, often opaque, and sometimes have the transparency of an opal; they are generally round or oval. The round are made into bracelets, the oval into pendants; and, being more precious, are sold singly. Those adhering to the shell of the oyster are more irregular in shape, and are sold by weight. Lastly, in a lower order are classed those small pearls known under the name of seed-pearls; they are sold by measure, and are especially used in embroidery for church ornaments."

"But," said Conseil, "is this pearl-fishery dangerous?"

"No," I answered, quickly; "particularly if certain precautions are taken."

"What does one risk in such a calling?" said Ned Land; "the swallowing of some mouthfuls of sea-water?"

"As you say, Ned. By the by," said I, trying to take Captain Nemo's careless tone, "are you afraid of sharks, brave Ned?"

"I!" replied the Canadian; "a harpooner by profession? It is my trade to make light of them."

"But," said I, "it is not a question of fishing for them with an iron swivel, hoisting them into the vessel, cutting off their tails with a blow of a chopper, ripping them up, and throwing their heart into the sea!"

"Then, it is a question of"—

"Precisely."

"In the water?"

"In the water"

"Faith, with a good harpoon! You know, sir, these sharks are ill-fashioned beasts. They must turn on their bellies to seize you, and in that time"—

Ned Land had a way of saying "seize," which made my blood run cold.

"Well, and you, Conseil, what do you think of sharks?"

"Me!" said Conseil. "I will be frank, sir."

"So much the better," thought I.

"If you, sir, mean to face the sharks, I do not see why your faithful servant should not face them with you."

Chapter III

A Pearl of Ten Millions

The next morning at four o'clock I was awakened by the steward, whom Captain Nemo had placed at my service. I rose hurriedly, dressed, and went into the saloon.

Captain Nemo was awaiting me.

"M. Aronnax," said he, "are you ready to start?"

"I am ready."

"Then, please to follow me."

"And my companions, Captain?"

"They have been told, and are waiting."

"Are we not to put on our diver's dresses?" asked I.

"Not yet. I have not allowed the *Nautilus* to come too near this coast, and we are some distance from the Manaar Bank; but the boat is ready, and will take us to the exact point of disembarking, which will save us a long way. It carries our diving apparatus, which we will put on when we begin our submarine journey."

Captain Nemo conducted me to the central staircase, which led on to the platform. Ned and Conseil were already there, delighted at the idea of the "pleasure party" which was preparing. Five sailors from the *Nautilus*, with their oars, waited in the boat, which had been made fast against the side.

The night was still dark. Layers of clouds covered the sky, allowing but few stars to be seen. I looked on the side where the land lay, and saw nothing but a dark line enclosing three parts of the horizon, from south-west to north-west. The *Nautilus*, having returned during the night up the western coast of Ceylon, was now west of the bay, or rather gulf, formed by the mainland and the island of Manaar. There, under the dark waters, stretched the pintadine bank, an inexhaustible field of pearls, the length of which is more than twenty miles.

Captain Nemo, Ned Land, Conseil, and I, took our places in the stern of the boat. The master went to the tiller; his four companions leaned on their oars, the painter was cast off, and we sheered off.

The boat went towards the south; the oarsmen did not hurry. I noticed that their strokes, strong in the water, only followed each other every ten seconds, according to the method generally adopted in the navy. Whilst the craft was running by its own velocity, the liquid drops struck the dark depths of the waves crisply like spats of melted lead. A little billow, spreading wide, gave a slight roll to the boat, and some samphire reeds flapped before it.

We were silent. What was Captain Nemo thinking of? Perhaps of the land he was approaching, and which he found too near to him, contrary to the Canadian's opinion, who thought it too far off. As to Conseil, he was merely there from curiosity.

About half-past five, the first tints on the horizon showed the upper line of coast more distinctly. Flat enough in the east, it rose a little to the south. Five miles still lay between us, and it was indistinct owing to the mist on the water. At six o'clock it became suddenly daylight, with that rapidity peculiar to tropical regions, which know neither dawn nor twilight. The solar rays pierced the curtain of clouds, piled up on the eastern horizon, and the radiant orb rose rapidly. I saw land distinctly, with a few trees scattered here and there. The boat neared Manaar Island, which was rounded to the south. Captain Nemo rose from his seat and watched the sea.

At a sign from him the anchor was dropped, but the chain scarcely ran, for it was little more than a yard deep, and this spot was one of the highest points of the bank of pintadines.

"Here we are, M. Aronnax," said Captain Nemo. "You see that enclosed bay? Here, in a month, will be assembled the numerous fishing-boats of the exporters, and these are the waters their divers will ransack so boldly. Happily, this bay is well situated for that kind of fishing. It is sheltered from the strongest winds; the sea is never very rough here, which makes it favourable for the diver's work. We will now put on our dresses, and begin our walk."

I did not answer, and while watching the suspected waves, began with the help of the sailors to put on my heavy sea-dress. Captain Nemo and my companions were also dressing. None of the *Nautilus* men were to accompany us on this new excursion.

Soon we were enveloped to the throat in india-rubber clothing; the air apparatus fixed to our backs by braces. As to the Ruhmkorff apparatus, there was no necessity for it. Before putting my head into the copper cap, I had asked the question of the Captain.

"They would be useless," he replied. "We are going to no great depth, and the solar rays will be enough to light our walk. Besides, it would not be prudent to carry the electric light in these waters; its brilliancy might attract some of the dangerous inhabitants of the coast most inopportunely."

As Captain Nemo pronounced these words, I turned to Conseil and Ned Land. But my two friends had already encased their heads in the metal cap, and they could neither hear nor answer.

One last question remained to ask of Captain Nemo.

"And our arms?" asked I; "our guns?"

"Guns! what for? Do not mountaineers attack the bear with a dagger in their hand, and is not steel surer than lead? Here is a strong blade; put it in your belt, and we start."

I looked at my companions; they were armed like us, and, more than that, Ned Land was brandishing an enormous harpoon, which he had placed in the boat before leaving the *Nautilus*.

Then, following the Captain's example, I allowed myself to be dressed in the heavy copper helmet, and our reservoirs of air were at once in activity. An instant after we were landed, one after the other, in about two yards of water upon an even sand. Captain Nemo made a sign with his hand, and we followed him by a gentle declivity till we disappeared under the waves.

Over our feet, like coveys of snipe in a bog, rose shoals of fish, of the genus monoptera, which have no other fins but their tail. I recognised the Javanese, a real serpent two and a half feet long, of a livid colour underneath, and which might easily be mistaken for a conger eel if it was not for the golden stripes on its sides. In the genus stromateus, whose bodies are very flat and oval, I saw some of the most brilliant colours, carrying their dorsal fin like a scythe; an excellent eating fish, which, dried and pickled, is known by the name of *Karawade;* then some tranquebars, belonging to the genus apsiphoroides, whose body is covered with a shell cuirass of eight longitudinal plates.

The heightening sun lit the mass of waters more and more. The soil changed by degrees. To the fine sand succeeded a perfect causeway of boulders, covered with a carpet of molluscs and zoophytes. Amongst the specimens of these branches I noticed some placenae, with thin unequal shells, a kind of ostracion peculiar to the Red Sea and the Indian Ocean; some orange lucinae with rounded shells;

rockfish three feet and a half long, which raised themselves under the waves like hands ready to seize one. There were also some panopyres, slightly luminous; and lastly, some oculines, like magnificent fans, forming one of the richest vegetations of these seas.

In the midst of these living plants, and under the arbours of the hydrophytes, were layers of clumsy articulates, particularly some raninae, whose carapace formed a slightly rounded triangle; and some horrible looking parthenopes.

At about seven o'clock we found ourselves at last surveying the oyster-banks, on which the pearl-oysters are reproduced by millions.

Captain Nemo pointed with his hand to the enormous heap of oysters; and I could well understand that this mine was inexhaustible, for Nature's creative power is far beyond man's instinct of destruction. Ned Land, faithful to his instinct, hastened to fill a net which he carried by his side with some of the finest specimens. But we could not stop. We must follow the Captain, who seemed to guide himself by paths known only to himself. The ground was sensibly rising, and sometimes, on holding up my arm, it was above the surface of the sea. Then the level of the bank would sink capriciously. Often we rounded high rocks scarped into pyramids. In their dark fractures huge crustacea, perched upon their high claws like some war-machine, watched us with fixed eyes, and under our feet crawled various kinds of annelides.

At this moment there opened before us a large grotto, dug in a picturesque heap of rocks, and carpeted with all the thick warp of the submarine flora. At first it seemed very dark to me. The solar rays seemed to be extinguished by successive gradations, until its vague transparency became nothing more than drowned light. Captain Nemo entered; we followed. My eyes soon accustomed themselves to this relative state of darkness. I could distinguish the arches springing capriciously from natural pillars, standing broad upon their granite base, like the heavy columns of Tuscan architecture. Why had our incomprehensible guide led us to the bottom of this submarine

crypt? I was soon to know. After descending a rather sharp declivity, our feet trod the bottom of a kind of circular pit. There Captain
Nemo stopped, and with his hand indicated an object I had not yet
perceived. It was an oyster of extraordinary dimensions, a gigantic
tridacne, a goblet which could have contained a whole lake of holy
water, a basin the breadth of which was more than two yards and a
half, and consequently larger than that ornamenting the saloon of the
Nautilus. I approached this extraordinary mollusc. It adhered by its
byssus to a table of granite, and there, isolated, it developed itself in
the calm waters of the grotto. I estimated the weight of this tridacne
at 600 pounds. Such an oyster would contain thirty pounds of meat;
and one must have the stomach of a Gargantua, to demolish some
dozens of them.

Captain Nemo was evidently acquainted with the existence of this
bivalve, and seemed to have a particular motive in verifying the actual
state of this tridacne. The shells were a little open; the Captain came
near and put his dagger between to prevent them from closing; then
with his hand he raised the membrane with its fringed edges, which
formed a cloak for the creature. There, between the folded plaits, I
saw a loose pearl, whose size equalled that of a cocoa-nut. Its globular
shape, perfect clearness, and admirable lustre made it altogether a
jewel of inestimable value. Carried away by my curiosity I stretched
out my hand to seize it, weight it, and touch it; but the Captain stopped
me, made a sign of refusal, and quickly withdrew his dagger, and the
two shells closed suddenly. I then understood Captain Nemo's intention. In leaving this pearl hidden in the mantle of the tridacne, he
was allowing it to grow slowly. Each year the secretions of the mollusc
would add new concentric circles. I estimated its value at £500,000
at least.

After ten minutes Captain Nemo stopped suddenly. I thought he
had halted previously to returning. No; by a gesture he bade us crouch
beside him in a deep fracture of the rock, his hand pointed to one part
of the liquid mass, which I watched attentively.

About five yards from me a shadow appeared, and sank to the ground. The disquieting idea of sharks shot through my mind, but I was mistaken; and once again it was not a monster of the ocean that we had anything to do with.

It was a man, a living man, an Indian, a fisherman, a poor devil who, I suppose, had come to glean before the harvest. I could see the bottom of his canoe anchored some feet above his head. He dived and went up successively. A stone held between his feet, cut in the shape of a sugar loaf, whilst a rope fastened him to his boat, helped him to descend more rapidly. This was all his apparatus. Reaching the bottom about five yards deep, he went on his knees and filled his bag with oysters picked up at random. Then he went up, emptied it, pulled up his stone, and began the operation once more, which lasted thirty seconds.

The diver did not see us. The shadow of the rock hid us from sight. And how should this poor Indian ever dream that men, beings like himself, should be there under the water watching his movements, and losing no detail of the fishing? Several times he went up in this way, and dived again. He did not carry away more than ten at each plunge, for he was obliged to pull them from the bank to which they adhered by means of their strong byssus. And how many of those oysters for which he risked his life had no pearl in them! I watched him closely, his manoeuvres were regular; and, for the space of half an hour, no danger appeared to threaten him.

I was beginning to accustom myself to the sight of this interesting fishing, when suddenly, as the Indian was on the ground, I saw him make a gesture of terror, rise, and make a spring to return to the surface of the sea.

I understood his dread. A gigantic shadow appeared just above the unfortunate diver. It was a shark of enormous size advancing diagonally, his eyes on fire, and his jaws open. I was mute with horror, and unable to move.

The voracious creature shot towards the Indian, who threw himself on one side in order to avoid the shark's fins; but not its tail, for it struck his chest, and stretched him on the ground.

This scene lasted but a few seconds: the shark returned, and, turning on his back, prepared himself for cutting the Indian in two, when I saw Captain Nemo rise suddenly, and then, dagger in hand, walk straight to the monster, ready to fight face to face with him. The very moment the shark was going to snap the unhappy fisherman in two, he perceived his new adversary, and turning over, made straight towards him.

I can still see Captain Nemo's position. Holding himself well together, he waited for the shark with admirable coolness; and, when it rushed at him, threw himself on one side with wonderful quickness, avoiding the shock, and burying his dagger deep into its side. But it was not all over. A terrible combat ensued.

The shark had seemed to roar, if I might say so. The blood rushed in torrents from its wound. The sea was dyed red, and through the opaque liquid I could distinguish nothing more. Nothing more until the moment when, like lightning, I saw the undaunted Captain hanging on to one of the creature's fins, struggling, as it were, hand to hand with the monster, and dealing successive blows at his enemy, yet still unable to give a decisive one.

The shark's struggles agitated the water with such fury that the rocking threatened to upset me.

I wanted to go to the Captain's assistance, but, nailed to the spot with horror, I could not stir.

I saw the haggard eye; I saw the different phases of the fight. The Captain fell to the earth, upset by the enormous mass which leant upon him. The shark's jaws opened wide, like a pair of factory shears, and it would have been all over with the Captain; but, quick as thought, harpoon in hand, Ned Land rushed towards the shark and struck it with its sharp point.

The waves were impregnated with a mass of blood. They rocked under the shark's movements, which beat them with indescribable fury. Ned Land had not missed his aim. It was the monster's death-rattle. Struck to the heart, it struggled in dreadful convulsions, the shock of which overthrew Conseil.

But Ned Land had disentangled the Captain, who, getting up without any wound, went straight to the Indian, quickly cut the cord which held him to his stone, took him in his arms, and, with a sharp blow of his heel, mounted to the surface.

We all three followed in a few seconds, saved by a miracle, and reached the fisherman's boat.

Captain Nemo's first care was to recall the unfortunate man to life again. I did not think he could succeed. I hoped so, for the poor creature's immersion was not long; but the blow from the shark's tail might have been his death-blow.

Happily, with the Captain's and Conseil's sharp friction, I saw consciousness return by degrees. He opened his eyes. What was his surprise, his terror even, at seeing four great copper heads leaning over him! And, above all, what must he have thought when Captain Nemo, drawing from the pocket of his dress a bag of pearls, placed it in his hand! This munificent charity from the man of the waters to the poor Cingalese was accepted with a trembling hand. His wondering eyes showed that he knew not to what superhuman beings he owed both fortune and life.

At a sign from the Captain we regained the bank, and following the road already traversed, came in about half an hour to the anchor which held the canoe of the *Nautilus* to the earth.

Once on board, we each, with the help of the sailors, got rid of the heavy copper helmet.

Captain Nemo's first word was to the Canadian.

"Thank you, Master Land," said he.

"It was in revenge, Captain," replied Ned Land. "I owed you that."

A ghastly smile passed across the Captain's lips, and that was all.

"To the *Nautilus*," said he.

The boat flew over the waves. Some minutes after, we met the shark's dead body floating. By the black marking of the extremity of its fins, I recognised the terrible melanopteron of the Indian Seas, of the species of shark properly so called. It was more than twenty-five feet long; its enormous mouth occupied one-third of its body. It was an adult, as was known by its six rows of teeth placed in an isosceles triangle in the upper jaw.

Conseil looked at it with scientific interest, and I am sure that he placed it, and not without reason, in the cartilaginous class, of the chondropterygian order, with fixed gills, of the selacian family, in the genus of the sharks.

Whilst I was contemplating this inert mass, a dozen of these voracious beasts appeared round the boat; and, without noticing us, threw themselves upon the dead body and fought with one another for the pieces.

At half-past eight we were again on board the *Nautilus*. There I reflected on the incidents which had taken place in our excursion to the Manaar Bank.

Two conclusions I must inevitably draw from it—one bearing upon the unparalleled courage of Captain Nemo, the other upon his devotion to a human being, a representative of that race from which he fled beneath the sea. Whatever he might say, this strange man had not yet succeeded in entirely crushing his heart.

When I made this observation to him, he answered in a slightly moved tone—

"That Indian sir, is an inhabitant of an oppressed country; and I am still, and shall be, to my last breath, one of them!"

Chapter IV
The Red Sea

In the course of the day of the 29th of January, the Island of Ceylon disappeared under the horizon, and the *Nautilus*, at a speed of twenty miles an hour, slid into the labyrinth of canals which separate the Maldives from the Laccadives. It coasted even the Island of Kiltan, a land originally madreporic, discovered by Vasco de Gama in 1499, and one of the nineteen principal islands of the Laccadive Archipelago, situated between 10° and 14° 30' north latitude, and 69° 50' 72" east longitude.

We had made 16,220 miles, or 7500 (French) leagues from our starting-point in the Japanese Seas.

The next day (30th January), when the *Nautilus* went to the surface of the ocean, there was no land in sight. Its course was N.N.E., in the direction of the Sea of Oman, between Arabia and the Indian Peninsula, which serves as an outlet to the Persian Gulf. It was evidently a block without any possible egress. Where was Captain Nemo taking us to? I could not say. This, however, did not satisfy the Canadian, who that day came to me asking where we were going.

"We are going where our Captain's fancy takes us, Master Ned."

"His fancy cannot take us far, then," said the Canadian. "The Persian Gulf has no outlet: and if we do go in, it will not be long before we are out again."

"Very well, then, we will come out again, Master Land; and if, after the Persian Gulf, the *Nautilus* would like to visit the Red Sea, the Straits of Bab-el-mandeb are there to give us entrance."

"I need not tell you, sir," said Ned Land, "that the Red Sea is as much closed as the Gulf, as the Isthmus of Suez is not yet cut; and if it was, a boat as mysterious as ours would not risk itself in a canal cut with sluices. And again, the Red Sea is not the road to take us back to Europe."

"But I never said we were going back to Europe."

"What do you suppose, then?"

"I suppose that, after visiting the curious coasts of Arabia and Egypt, the *Nautilus* will go down the Indian Ocean again, perhaps cross the Channel of Mozambique, perhaps off the Mascarenhas, so as to gain the Cape of Good Hope."

"And once at the Cape of Good Hope?" asked the Canadian, with peculiar emphasis.

"Well, we shall penetrate into that Atlantic which we do not yet know. Ah! friend Ned, you are getting tired of this journey under the sea; you are surfeited with the incessantly varying spectacle of submarine wonders. For my part, I shall be sorry to see the end of a voyage which it is given to so few men to make."

For four days, till the 3rd of February, the *Nautilus* scoured the Sea of Oman, at various speeds and at various depths. It seemed to go at random, as if hesitating as to which road it should follow, but we never passed the Tropic of Cancer.

In quitting this sea we sighted Muscat for an instant, one of the most important towns of the country of Oman. I admired its strange aspect, surrounded by black rocks upon which its white houses and forts stood in relief. I saw the rounded domes of its mosques, the elegant points of its minarets, its fresh and verdant terraces. But it was only a vision! the *Nautilus* soon sank under the waves of that part of the sea.

We passed along the Arabian coast of Mahrah and Hadramaut, for a distance of six miles, its undulating line of mountains being occasionally relieved by some ancient ruin. The 5th of February we at last entered the Gulf of Aden, a perfect funnel introduced into the neck of Bab-el-mandeb, through which the Indian waters entered the Red Sea.

The 6th of February, the *Nautilus* floated in sight of Aden, perched upon a promontory which a narrow isthmus joins to the mainland, a kind of inaccessible Gibraltar, the fortifications of which were rebuilt by the English after taking possession in 1839. I caught a glimpse of the octagon minarets of this town, which was at one time, according to the historian Edrisi, the richest commercial magazine on the coast.

I certainly thought that Captain Nemo, arrived at this point, would back out again; but I was mistaken, for he did no such thing, much to my surprise.

The next day, the 7th of February, we entered the Straits of Bab-el-mandeb, the name of which, in the Arab tongue, means "The gate of tears."

To twenty miles in breadth, it is only thirty-two in length. And for the *Nautilus*, starting at full-speed, the crossing was scarcely the work of an hour. But I saw nothing, not even the Island of Perim, with which the British Government has fortified the position of Aden. There were too many English or French steamers of the line of Suez to Bombay, Calcutta to Melbourne, and from Bourbon to the Mauritius, furrowing this narrow passage, for the *Nautilus* to venture to show itself. So it remained prudently below. At last, about noon, we were in the waters of the Red Sea.

I would not even seek to understand the caprice which had decided Captain Nemo upon entering the gulf. But I quite approved of the *Nautilus* entering it. Its speed was lessened: sometimes it kept on the surface, sometimes it dived to avoid a vessel, and thus I was able to observe the upper and lower parts of this curious sea.

The 8th of February, from the first dawn of day, Mocha came in sight, now a ruined town, whose walls would fall at a gun-shot, yet which shelters here and there some verdant datetrees; once an important city, containing six public markets, and twenty-six mosques, and whose walls, defended by fourteen forts, formed a girdle of two miles in circumference.

The *Nautilus* then approached the African shore, where the depth of the sea was greater. There, between two waters clear as crystal, through the open panels we were allowed to contemplate the beautiful bushes of brilliant coral, and large blocks of rock clothed with a

splendid fur of green algae and fuci. What an indescribable spectacle, and what variety of sites and landscapes along these sandbanks
and volcanic islands which bound the Lybian coast! But where these
shrubs appeared in all their beauty was on the eastern coast, which the
Nautilus soon gained. It was on the coast of Tehama, for there not only
did this display of zoophytes flourish beneath the level of the sea, but
they also formed picturesque interlacings which unfolded themselves
about sixty feet above the surface, more capricious but less highly coloured than those whose freshness was kept up by the vital power of
the waters.

What charming hours I passed thus at the window of the saloon!
What new specimens of submarine flora and fauna did I admire under
the brightness of our electric lantern!

There grew sponges of all shapes, pediculated, foliated, globular, and digital. They certainly justified the names of baskets, cups,
distaffs, elk's-horns, lion's-feet, peacock'stails, and Neptune's-gloves,
which have been given to them by the fishermen, greater poets than
the savants.

Other zoophytes which multiply near the sponges consist principally of medusae of a most elegant kind. The molluscs were represented by varieties of the calmar (which, according to Orbigny, are
peculiar to the Red Sea); and reptiles by the virgata turtle, of the
genus of cheloniae, which furnished a wholesome and delicate food
for our table.

As to the fish, they were abundant, and often remarkable. The following are those which the nets of the *Nautilus* brought more frequently
on board:—

Rays of a red-brick colour, with bodies marked with blue spots,
and easily recognisable by their double spikes; some superb caranxes,
marked with seven transverse bands of jet-black, blue and yellow fins,
and gold and silver scales; mullets with yellow heads; gobies, and
a thousand other species, common to the ocean which we had just
traversed.

The 9th of February, the *Nautilus* floated in the broadest part of the Red Sea, which is comprised between Souakin, on the west coast, and Koomfidah, on the east coast, with a diameter of ninety miles.

That day at noon, after the bearings were taken, Captain Nemo mounted the platform, where I happened to be, and I was determined not to let him go down again without at least pressing him regarding his ulterior projects. As soon as he saw me he approached, and graciously offered me a cigar.

"Well, sir, does this Red Sea please you? Have you sufficiently observed the wonders it covers, its fishes, its zoophytes, its parterres of sponges, and its forests of coral? Did you catch a glimpse of the towns on its borders."

"Yes, Captain Nemo," I replied; "and the *Nautilus* is wonderfully fitted for such a study. Ah! it is an intelligent boat!"

"Yes, sir, intelligent and invulnerable. It fears neither the terrible tempests of the Red Sea, nor its currents, nor its sandbanks."

"Certainly," said I, "this sea is quoted as one of the worst, and in the time of the ancients, if I am not mistaken, its reputation was detestable."

"Detestable, M. Aronnax. The Greek and Latin historians do not speak favourably of it, and Strabo says it is very dangerous during the Etesian winds, and in the rainy season. The Arabian Edrisi portrays it under the name of the Gulf of Colzoum, and relates that vessels perished there in great numbers on the sandbanks, and that no one would risk sailing in the night. It is, he pretends, a sea-subject to fearful hurricanes, strewn with inhospitable islands, and 'which offers nothing good either on its surface or in its depths.' Such, too, is the opinion of Arrian, Agatharcides, and Artemidorus."

"One may see," I replied, "that these historians never sailed on board the *Nautilus*."

"Just so," replied the Captain, smiling; "and in that respect moderns are not more advanced than the ancients. It required many ages to find out the mechanical power of steam. Who knows if, in another hundred years, we may not see a second *Nautilus?* Progress is slow, M. Aronnax."

"It is true," I answered; "your boat is at least a century before its time, perhaps an era. What a misfortune that the secret of such an invention should die with its inventor!"

Captain Nemo did not reply. After some minutes' silence he continued—

"You were speaking of the opinions of ancient historians upon the dangerous navigation of the Red Sea."

"It is true," said I; "but were not their fears exaggerated?"

"Yes and no, M. Aronnax," replied Captain Nemo, who seemed to know the Red Sea by heart. "That which is no longer dangerous for a modern vessel, well rigged, strongly built, and master of its own course, thanks to obedient steam, offered all sorts of perils to the ships of the ancients. Picture to yourself those first navigators venturing in ships made of planks sown with the cords of the palm-tree, saturated with the grease of the sea-dog, and covered with powdered resin! They had not even instruments wherewith to take their bearings, and they went by guess amongst currents of which they scarcely knew anything. Under such conditions shipwrecks were, and must have been, numerous. But in our time, steamers running between Suez and the South Seas have nothing more to fear from the fury of this gulf, in spite of contrary tradewinds. The captain and passengers do not prepare for their departure by offering propitiatory sacrifices: and, on their return, they no longer go ornamented with wreaths and gilt fillets to thank the gods in the neighbouring temple."

"I agree with you," said I; "and steam seems to have killed all gratitude in the hearts of sailors. But, Captain, since you seem to have especially studied this sea, can you tell me the origin of its name?"

"There exist several explanations on the subject, M. Aronnax. Would you like to know the opinion of a chronicler of the fourteenth century?"

"Willingly."

"This fanciful writer pretends that its name was given to it after the passage of the Israelites, when Pharaoh perished in the waves which closed at the voice of Moses."

"A poet's explanation, Captain Nemo," I replied; "but I cannot content myself with that. I ask you for your personal opinion."

"Here it is, M. Aronnax. According to my idea, we must see in this appellation of the Red Sea a translation of the Hebrew word 'Edom'; and if the ancients gave it that name, it was on account of the particular colour of its waters."

"But up to this time I have seen nothing but transparent waves and without any particular colour."

"Very likely; but as we advance to the bottom of the gulf, you will see this singular appearance. I remember seeing the Bay of Tor entirely red, like a sea of blood."

"And you attribute this colour to the presence of a microscopic seaweed?"

"Yes; it is a mucilaginous purple matter, produced by the restless little plants known by the name of trichodesmia, and of which it requires 40,000 to occupy the space of a square .04 of an inch. Perhaps we shall meet some when we get to Tor."

"So, Captain Nemo, it is not the first time you have overrun the Red Sea on board the *Nautilus?*"

"No, sir."

"As you spoke a while ago of the passage of the Israelites, and of the catastrophe to the Egyptians, I will ask whether you have met with traces under the water of this great historical fact?"

"No, sir; and for a very good reason."

"What is it?"

"It is, that the spot where Moses and his people passed is now so blocked up with sand, that the camels can barely bathe their legs there. You can well understand that there would not be water enough for my *Nautilus.*"

"And the spot?" I asked.

"The spot is situated a little above the Isthmus of Suez, in the arm which formerly made a deep estuary, when the Red Sea extended to the Salt Lakes. Now, whether this passage were miraculous or not, the Israelites, nevertheless, crossed there to reach the Promised Land, and Pharaoh's army perished precisely on that spot; and I think that excavations made in the middle of the sand would bring to light a large number of arms and instruments of Egyptian origin."

"That is evident," I replied; "and for the sake of archaeologists let us hope that these excavations will be made sooner or later, when new towns are established on the isthmus, after the construction of the Suez Canal; a canal, however, very useless to a vessel like the *Nautilus*."

"Very likely; but useful to the whole world," said Captain Nemo. "The ancients well understood the utility of a communication between the Red Sea and the Mediterranean for their commercial affairs: but they did not think of digging a canal direct, and took the Nile as an intermediate. Very probably the canal which united the Nile to the Red Sea was began by Sesostris, if we may believe tradition. One thing is certain, that in the year 615 before Jesus Christ, Necos undertook the works of an alimentary canal to the waters of the Nile, across the plain of Egypt, looking towards Arabia. It took four days to go up this canal, and it was so wide that two triremes could go abreast. It was carried on by Darius, the son of Hystaspes, and probably finished by Ptolemy II. Strabo saw it navigated; but its decline from the point of departure, near Bubastes, to the Red Sea was so slight, that it was only navigable for a few months in the year. This canal answered all commercial purposes to the age of Antoninus, when it was abandoned and blocked up with sand. Restored by order of the Caliph Omar, it was definitively destroyed in 761 or 762 by Caliph Al-Mansor, who wished to prevent the arrival of provisions to Mohammed-ben-Abdallah, who had revolted against him. During the expedition into Egypt, your General Bonaparte discovered traces of the works in the Desert of Suez; and surprised by the tide, he nearly perished before regaining Hadjaroth, at the very place where Moses had encamped three thousand years before him."

"Well, Captain, what the ancients dared not undertake, this junction between the two seas, which will shorten the road from Cadiz to India, M. Lesseps has succeeded in doing; and before long he will have changed Africa into an immense island."

"Yes, M. Aronnax; you have the right to be proud of your countryman. Such a man brings more honour to a nation than great captains. He began, like so many others, with disgust and rebuffs; but he has triumphed, for he has the genius of will. And it is sad to think that a work like that, which ought to have been an international work, and which would have sufficed to make a reign illustrious, should have succeeded by the energy of one man. All honour to M. Lesseps!"

"Yes, honour to the great citizen!" I replied, surprised by the manner in which Captain Nemo had just spoken.

"Unfortunately," he continued, "I cannot take you through the Suez Canal; but you will be able to see the long jetty of Port Said after to-morrow, when we shall be in the Mediterranean."

"The Mediterranean!" I exclaimed.

"Yes, sir; does that astonish you?"

"What astonishes me is to think that we shall be there the day after to-morrow."

"Indeed?"

"Yes, Captain, although by this time I ought to have accustomed myself to be surprised at nothing since I have been on board your boat."

"But the cause of this surprise?"

"Well! it is the fearful speed you will have to put on the *Nautilus*, if the day after to-morrow she is to be in the Mediterranean, having made the round of Africa, and doubled the Cape of Good Hope!"

"Who told you that she would make the round of Africa, and double the Cape of Good Hope, sir?"

"Well, unless the *Nautilus* sails on dry land, and passes above the isthmus"—

"Or beneath it, M. Aronnax."

"Beneath it?"

"Certainly," replied Captain Nemo, quietly. "A long time ago Nature made under this tongue of land what man has this day made on its surface."

"What! such a passage exists?"

"Yes; a subterranean passage, which I have named the Arabian Tunnel. It takes us beneath Suez, and opens into the Gulf of Pelusium."

"But this isthmus is composed of nothing but quicksands?"

"To a certain depth. But at fifty-five yards only, there is a solid layer of rock."

"Did you discover this passage by chance?" I asked, more and more surprised.

"Chance and reasoning, sir; and by reasoning even more than by chance. Not only does this passage exist, but I have profited by it several times. Without that I should not have ventured this day into the impassable Red Sea. I noticed that in the Red Sea and in the Mediterranean there existed a certain number of fishes of a kind perfectly identical—ophidia, fiatoles, girelles, and exocoeti. Certain of that fact, I asked myself was it possible that there was no communication between the two seas? If there was, the subterranean current must necessarily run from the Red Sea to the Mediterranean, from the sole cause of difference of level. I caught a large number of fishes in the neighbourhood of Suez. I passed a copper ring through their tails, and threw them back into the sea. Some months later, on the coast of Syria, I caught some of my fish ornamented with the ring. Thus the communication between the two was proved. I then sought for it with my *Nautilus;* I discovered it, ventured into it, and before long, sir, you too will have passed through my Arabian tunnel!"

Chapter V
The Arabian Tunnel

That same evening, in 21° 30' north latitude, the *Nautilus* floated on the surface of the sea, approaching the Arabian coast. I saw Djeddah, the most important counting-house of Egypt, Syria, Turkey, and India. I distinguished clearly enough its buildings, the vessels anchored at the quays, and those whose draught of water obliged them to anchor in the roads. The sun, rather low on the horizon, struck full on the houses of the town, bringing out their whiteness. Outside, some wooden cabins, and some made of reeds, showed the quarter inhabited by the Bedouins. Soon Djeddah was shut out from view by the shadows of night, and the *Nautilus* found herself under water slightly phosphorescent.

The next day, the 10th of February, we sighted several ships running to windward. The *Nautilus* returned to its submarine navigation; but at noon, when her bearings were taken, the sea being deserted, she rose again to her waterline.

Accompanied by Ned and Conseil, I seated myself on the platform. The coast on the eastern side looked like a mass faintly printed upon a damp fog.

We were leaning on the sides of the pinnace, talking of one thing and another, when Ned Land, stretching out his hand towards a spot on the sea, said—

"Do you see anything there, sir?"

"No, Ned," I replied; "but I have not your eyes, you know."

"Look well," said Ned, "there, on the starboard beam, about the height of the lantern! Do you not see a mass which seems to move?"

"Certainly," said I, after close attention; "I see something like a long black body on the top of the water."

And certainly before long the black object was not more than a mile from us. It looked like a great sandbank deposited in the open sea. It was a gigantic dugong!

Ned Land looked eagerly. His eyes shone with covetousness at the sight of the animal. His hand seemed ready to harpoon it. One would have thought he was awaiting the moment to throw himself into the sea, and attack it in its element.

At this instant Captain Nemo appeared on the platform. He saw the dugong, understood the Canadian's attitude, and addressing him, said—

"If you held a harpoon just now, Master Land, would it not burn your hand?"

"Just so, sir."

"And you would not be sorry to go back, for one day, to your trade of a fisherman, and to add this cetacean to the list of those you have already killed?"

"I should not, sir,"

"Well, you can try."

"Thank you, sir," said Ned Land, his eyes flaming.

"Only," continued the Captain, "I advise you for your own sake not to miss the creature."

"Is the dugong dangerous to attack?" I asked, in spite of the Canadian's shrug of the shoulders.

"Yes," replied the Captain; "sometimes the animal turns upon its assailants and overturns their boat. But for Master Land, this danger is not to be feared. His eye is prompt, his arm sure."

At this moment seven men of the crew, mute and immovable as ever, mounted the platform. One carried a harpoon and a line similar to those employed in catching whales. The pinnace was lifted from the bridge, pulled from its socket, and let down into the sea. Six oarsmen took their seats, and the coxswain went to the tiller. Ned, Conseil, and I went to the back of the boat.

"You are not coming, Captain?" I asked.

"No, sir; but I wish you good sport."

The boat put off, and lifted by the six rowers, drew rapidly towards the dugong, which floated about two miles from the *Nautilus*.

Arrived some cables' length from cetacean, the speed slackened, and the oars dipped noiselessly into the quiet waters. Ned Land, harpoon in hand, stood in the fore part of the boat. The harpoon used for striking the whale is generally attached to a very long cord, which runs out rapidly as the wounded creature draws it after him. But here the cord was not more than ten fathoms long, and the extremity was attached to a small barrel, which, by floating, was to show the course the dugong took under the water.

I stood, and carefully watched the Canadian's adversary. This dugong, which also bears the name of the halicore, closely resembles the manatee; its oblong body terminated in a lengthened tail, and its lateral fins in perfect fingers. Its difference from the manatee consisted in its upper jaw, which was armed with two long and pointed teeth, which formed on each side diverging tusks.

This dugong, which Ned Land was preparing to attack, was of colossal dimensions; it was more than seven yards long. It did not move, and seemed to be sleeping on the waves, which circumstance made it easier to capture.

The boat approached within six yards of the animal. The oars rested on the rowlocks. I half rose. Ned Land, his body thrown a little back, brandished the harpoon in his experienced hand.

Suddenly a hissing noise was heard, and the dugong disappeared. The harpoon, although thrown with great force, had apparently only struck the water.

"Curse it!" exclaimed the Canadian, furiously; "I have missed it!"

"No," said I; "the creature is wounded—look at the blood; but your weapon has not stuck in his body."

"My harpoon! my harpoon!" cried Ned Land.

The sailors rowed on, and the coxswain made for the floating barrel. The harpoon regained, we followed in pursuit of the animal.

The latter came now and then to the surface to breathe. Its wound had not weakened it, for it shot onwards with great rapidity.

The boat, rowed by strong arms, flew on its track. Several times it approached within some few yards, and the Canadian was ready to strike, but the dugong made off with a sudden plunge, and it was impossible to reach it.

Imagine the passion which excited impatient Ned Land! He hurled at the unfortunate creature the most energetic expletives in the English tongue. For my part, I was only vexed to see the dugong escape all our attacks.

We pursued it without relaxation for an hour, and I began to think it would prove difficult to capture, when the animal, possessed with the perverse idea of vengeance, of which he had cause to repent, turned upon the pinnace and assailed us in its turn.

This manoeuvre did not escape the Canadian.

"Look out!" he cried.

The coxswain said some words in his outlandish tongue, doubtless warning the men to keep on their guard.

The dugong came within twenty feet of the boat, stopped, sniffed the air briskly with its large nostrils (not pierced at the extremity, but in the upper part of its muzzle). Then taking a spring he threw himself upon us.

The pinnace could not avoid the shock, and half upset, shipped at least two tons of water, which had to be emptied; but thanks to the coxswain, we caught it sideways, not full front, so we were not quite overturned. While Ned Land, clinging to the bows, belaboured the gigantic animal with blows from his harpoon, the creature's teeth were buried in the gunwhale, and it lifted the whole thing out of the water, as a lion does a roebuck. We were upset over one another, and I know not how the adventure would have ended, if the Canadian, still enraged with the beast, had not struck it to the heart.

I heard its teeth grind on the iron plate, and the dugong disappeared, carrying the harpoon with him. But the barrel soon returned to the surface, and shortly after the body of the animal, turned on its back. The boat came up with it, took it in tow, and made straight for the *Nautilus*.

It required tackle of enormous strength to hoist the dugong on to the platform. It weighed 10,000 lbs.

The next day, February 11th, the larder of the *Nautilus* was enriched by some more delicate game. A flight of sea-swallows rested on the *Nautilus*. It was a species of the Sterna nilotica, peculiar to Egypt; its beak is black, head grey and pointed, the eye surrounded by white spots, the back, wings, and tail of a greyish colour, the belly and throat white, and claws red. They also took some dozen of Nile ducks, a wild bird of high flavour, its throat and upper part of the head white with black spots.

About five o'clock in the evening we sighted to the north the Cape of Ras-Mohammed. This cape forms the extremity of Arabia Petraea, comprised between the Gulf of Suez and the Gulf of Acabah.

The *Nautilus* penetrated into the Straits of Jubal, which leads to the Gulf of Suez. I distinctly saw a high mountain, towering between the two gulfs of Ras-Mohammed. It was Mount Horeb, that Sinai at the top of which Moses saw God face to face.

At six o'clock the *Nautilus*, sometimes floating, sometimes immersed, passed some distance from Tor, situated at the end of the bay, the waters of which seemed tinted with red, an observation already made by Captain Nemo. Then night fell in the midst of a heavy silence, sometimes broken by the cries of the pelican and other night-birds, and the noise of the waves breaking upon the shore, chafing against the rocks, or the panting of some far-off steamer beating the waters of the Gulf with its noisy paddles.

From eight to nine o'clock the *Nautilus* remained some fathoms under the water. According to my calculation we must have been very near Suez. Through the panel of the saloon I saw the bottom of the rocks brilliantly lit up by our electric lamp. We seemed to be leaving the Straits behind us more and more.

At a quarter-past nine, the vessel having returned to the surface, I mounted the platform. Most impatient to pass through Captain Nemo's tunnel, I could not stay in one place, so came to breathe the fresh night-air.

Soon in the shadow I saw a pale light, half discoloured by the fog, shining about a mile from us.

"A floating lighthouse!" said some one near me.

I turned, and saw the Captain.

"It is the floating light of Suez," he continued. "It will not be long before we gain the entrance of the tunnel."

"The entrance cannot be easy?"

"No, sir; and for that reason I am accustomed to go into the steersman's cage, and myself direct our course. And now if you will go down, M. Aronnax, the *Nautilus* is going under the waves, and will not return to the surface until we have passed through the Arabian Tunnel."

Captain Nemo led me towards the central staircase; half-way down he opened a door, traversed the upper deck, and landed in the pilot's cage, which it may be remembered rose at the extremity of the platform. It was a cabin measuring six feet square, very much like that occupied by the pilot on the steamboats of the Mississippi or Hudson. In the midst worked a wheel, placed vertically, and caught to the tiller-rope, which ran to the back of the *Nautilus*. Four light-ports with lenticular glasses, let in a groove in the partition of the cabin, allowed the man at the wheel to see in all directions.

This cabin was dark; but soon my eyes accustomed themselves to the obscurity, and I perceived the pilot, a strong man, with his hands resting on the spokes of the wheel. Outside, the sea appeared vividly lit up by the lantern, which shed its rays from the back of the cabin to the other extremity of the platform.

"Now," said Captain Nemo, "let us try to make our passage."

Electric wires connected the pilot's cage with the machinery room, and from there the Captain could communicate simultaneously to his *Nautilus* the direction and the speed. He pressed a metal knob, and at once the speed of the screw diminished.

187

I looked in silence at the high straight wall we were running by at this moment, the immovable base of a massive sandy coast. We followed it thus for an hour only some few yards off.

Captain Nemo did not take his eye from the knob, suspended by its two concentric circles in the cabin. At a simple gesture, the pilot modified the course of the *Nautilus* every instant.

I had placed myself at the port-scuttle, and saw some magnificent substructures of coral, zoophytes, seaweed, and fucus, agitating their enormous claws, which stretched out from the fissures of the rock.

At a quarter-past ten, the Captain himself took the helm. A large gallery, black and deep, opened before us. The *Nautilus* went boldly into it. A strange roaring was heard round its sides. It was the waters of the Red Sea, which the incline of the tunnel precipitated violently towards the Mediterranean. The *Nautilus* went with the torrent, rapid as an arrow, in spite of the efforts of the machinery, which, in order to offer more effective resistance, beat the waves with reversed screw.

On the walls of the narrow passage I could see nothing but brilliant rays, straight lines, furrows of fire, traced by the great speed, under the brilliant electric light. My heart beat fast.

At thirty-five minutes past ten, Captain Nemo quitted the helm; and, turning to me, said—

"The Mediterranean!"

In less than twenty minutes, the *Nautilus*, carried along by the torrent, had passed through the Isthmus of Suez.

Chapter VI
The Grecian Archipelago

The next day, the 12th of February, at the dawn of day, the *Nautilus* rose to the surface. I hastened on to the platform. Three miles to the south the dim outline of Pelusium was to be seen. A torrent had carried us from one sea to the other. About seven o'clock Ned and Conseil joined me.

"Well, Sir Naturalist," said the Canadian, in a slightly jovial tone, "and the Mediterranean?"

"We are floating on its surface, friend Ned."

"What!" said Conseil, "this very night."

"Yes, this very night; in a few minutes we have passed this impassable isthmus."

"I do not believe it," replied the Canadian.

"Then you are wrong, Master Land," I continued; "this low coast which rounds off to the south is the Egyptian coast. And you, who have such good eyes, Ned, you can see the jetty of Port Said stretching into the sea."

The Canadian looked attentively.

"Certainly you are right, sir, and your Captain is a first-rate man. We are in the Mediterranean. Good! Now, if you please, let us talk of our own little affair, but so that no one hears us."

I saw what the Canadian wanted, and, in any case, I thought it better to let him talk, as he wished it; so we all three went and sat down near the lantern, where we were less exposed to the spray of the blades.

"Now, Ned, we listen; what have you to tell us?"

"What I have to tell you is very simple. We are in Europe; and before Captain Nemo's caprices drag us once more to the bottom of the Polar Seas, or lead us into Oceania, I ask to leave the *Nautilus*."

I wished in no way to shackle the liberty of my companion, but I certainly felt no desire to leave Captain Nemo.

Thanks to him, and thanks to his apparatus, I was each day nearer the completion of my submarine studies; and I was re-writing my book of submarine depths in its very element. Should I ever again have such an opportunity of observing the wonders of the ocean? No, certainly not! And I could not bring myself to the idea of abandoning the *Nautilus* before the cycle of investigation was accomplished.

"Friend Ned, answer me frankly, are you tired of being on board? Are you sorry that destiny has thrown us into Captain Nemo's hands?"

The Canadian remained some moments without answering. Then crossing his arms, he said—

"Frankly, I do not regret this journey under the seas. I shall be glad to have made it; but now that it is made, let us have done with it. That is my idea."

"It will come to an end, Ned."

"Where and when?"

"Where I do not know—when I cannot say; or rather, I suppose it will end when these seas have nothing more to teach us."

"Then what do you hope for?" demanded the Canadian.

"That circumstances may occur as well six months hence as now by which we may and ought to profit."

"Oh!" said Ned Land, "and where shall we be in six months, if you please, Sir Naturalist?"

"Perhaps in China; you know the *Nautilus* is a rapid traveller. It goes through water as swallows through the air, or as an express on the land. It does not fear frequented seas; who can say that it may not beat the coasts of France, England, or America, on which flight may be attempted as advantageously as here."

"M. Aronnax," replied the Canadian, "your arguments are rotten at the foundation. You speak in the future, 'We shall be there! we shall be here!' I speak in the present, 'We are here, and we must profit by it.'"

Ned Land's logic pressed me hard, and I felt myself beaten on that ground. I knew not what argument would now tell in my favour.

"Sir," continued Ned, "let us suppose an impossibility; if Captain Nemo should this day offer you your liberty, would you accept it?"

"I do not know," I answered.

"And if," he added, "the offer he made you this day was never to be renewed, would you accept it?"

"Friend Ned, this is my answer. Your reasoning is against me. We must not rely on Captain Nemo's good-will. Common prudence forbids him to set us at liberty. On the other side, prudence bids us profit by the first opportunity to leave the *Nautilus*."

"Well, M. Aronnax, that is wisely said."

"Only one observation—just one. The occasion must be serious, and our first attempt must succeed; if it fails, we shall never find another, and Captain Nemo will never forgive us."

"All that is true," replied the Canadian. "But your observation applies equally to all attempts at flight, whether in two years' time, or in two days. But the question is still this: If a favourable opportunity presents itself, it must be seized."

"Agreed! and now, Ned, will you tell me what you mean by a favourable opportunity?"

"It will be that which, on a dark night, will bring the *Nautilus* a short distance from some European coast."

"And you will try and save yourself by swimming?"

"Yes, if we were near enough to the bank, and if the vessel was floating at the time. Not if the bank was far away, and the boat was under the water."

"And in that case?"

"In that case, I should seek to make myself master of the pinnace. I know how it is worked. We must get inside, and the bolts once drawn, we shall come to the surface of the water, without even the pilot, who is in the bows, perceiving our flight."

"Well, Ned, watch for the opportunity; but do not forget that a hitch will ruin us."

"I will not forget, sir."

"And now, Ned, would you like to know what I think of your project?"

"Certainly, M. Aronnax."

"Well, I think—I do not say I hope—I think that this favourable opportunity will never present itself."

"Why not?"

"Because Captain Nemo cannot hide from himself that we have not given up all hope of regaining our liberty, and he will be on his guard, above all, in the seas, and in the sight of European coasts."

"We shall see," replied Ned Land, shaking his head determinedly.

"And now, Ned Land," I added, "let us stop here. Not another word on the subject. The day that you are ready, come and let us know, and we will follow you. I rely entirely upon you."

Thus ended a conversation which, at no very distant time, led to such grave results. I must say here that facts seemed to confirm my foresight, to the Canadian's great despair. Did Captain Nemo distrust us in these frequented seas? or did he only wish to hide himself from the numerous vessels, of all nations, which ploughed the Mediterranean? I could not tell; but we were oftener between waters, and far from the coast. Or, if the *Nautilus* did emerge, nothing was to be seen but the pilot's cage; and sometimes it went to great depths, for, between the Grecian Archipelago and Asia Minor, we could not touch the bottom by more than a thousand fathoms.

Thus I only knew we were near the Island of Carpathos, one of the Sporades, by Captain Nemo reciting these lines from Virgil—

"Est in Carpathio Neptuni gurgite vates, Caeruleus Proteus,"

as he pointed to a spot on the planisphere.

It was indeed the ancient abode of Proteus, the old shepherd of Neptune's flocks, now the Island of Scarpanto, situated between Rhodes and Crete. I saw nothing but the granite base through the glass panels of the saloon.

The next day, the 14th of February, I resolved to employ some hours in studying the fishes of the Archipelago; but for some reason or other, the panels remained hermetically sealed. Upon taking the course of the *Nautilus* I found that we were going towards Candia, the ancient Isle of Crete. At the time I embarked on the *Abraham Lincoln*, the whole of this island had risen in insurrection against the despotism of the Turks. But how the insurgents had fared since that time I was absolutely ignorant, and it was not Captain Nemo, deprived of all land communications, who could tell me.

I made no allusion to this event when that night I found myself alone with him in the saloon. Besides, he seemed to be taciturn and preoccupied. Then, contrary to his custom, he ordered both panels to be opened, and going from one to the other, observed the mass of waters attentively. To what end I could not guess; so, on my side, I employed my time in studying the fish passing before my eyes.

Amongst others, I remarked some gobies, mentioned by Aristotle, and commonly known by the name of sea-braches, which are more particularly met with in the salt waters lying near the Delta of the Nile. Near them rolled some sea-bream, half phosphorescent, a kind of sparus, which the Egyptians ranked amongst their sacred animals, whose arrival in the waters of their river announced a fertile overflow, and was celebrated by religious ceremonies. I also noticed some cheilines about nine inches long, a bony fish with transparent shell, whose livid colour is mixed with red spots; they are great eaters of marine vegetation, which gives them an exquisite flavour. These cheilines were much sought after by the epicures of ancient Rome; the inside, dressed with the soft roe of the lamprey, peacocks' brains, and tongues of the phenicoptera, composed that divine dish of which Vitellius was sno enamoured.

Another inhabitant of these seas drew my attention, and led my mind back to recollections of antiquity. It was the remora, that fastens on to the shark's belly. This little fish, according to the ancients, hooking on to the ship's bottom, could stop its movements; and one of them, by keeping back Antony's ship during the battle of Actium, helped Augusta to gain the victory. On how little hangs the destiny of nations! I observed some fine anthiae, which belong to the order of lutjans, a fish held sacred by the Greeks, who attributed to them the power of hunting the marine monsters from waters they frequented. Their name signifies *flower*, and they justify their appellation by their shaded colours, their shades comprising the whole gamut of reds, from the paleness of the rose to the brightness of the ruby, and the fugitive tints that clouded their dorsal fin. My eyes could not leave these wonders of the sea, when they were suddenly struck by an unexpected apparition.

In the midst of the waters a man appeared, a diver, carrying at his belt a leathern purse. It was not a body abandoned to the waves; it was a living man, swimming with a strong hand, disappearing occasionally to take breath at the surface.

I turned towards Captain Nemo, and in an agitated voice exclaimed—

"A man shipwrecked! He must be saved at any price!"

The Captain did not answer me, but came and leaned against the panel.

The man had approached, and with his face flattened against the glass, was looking at us.

To my great amazement, Captain Nemo signed to him. The diver answered with his hand, mounted immediately to the surface of the water, and did not appear again.

"Do not be uncomfortable," said Captain Nemo. "It is Nicholas of Cape Matapan, surnamed Pesca. He is well-known in all the Cyclades. A bold diver! water is his element, and he lives more in it than on land, going continually from one island to another, even as far as Crete."

"You know him, Captain?"

"Why not, M. Aronnax?"

Saying which, Captain Nemo went towards a piece of furniture standing near the left panel of the saloon. Near this piece of furniture, I saw a chest bound with iron, on the cover of which was a copper plate, bearing the cypher of the *Nautilus* with its device.

At that moment, the Captain, without noticing my presence, opened the piece of furniture, a sort of strong box, which held a great many ingots.

They were ingots of gold. From whence came this precious metal, which represented an enormous sum? Where did the Captain gather this gold from? and what was he going to do with it?

I did not say one word. I looked. Captain Nemo took the ingots one by one, and arranged them methodically in the chest, which he filled entirely. I estimated the contents at more than 4000 lbs. weight of gold, that is to say, nearly £200,000.

The chest was securely fastened, and the Captain wrote an address on the lid, in characters which must have belonged to Modern Greece.

This done, Captain Nemo pressed a knob, the wire of which communicated with the quarters of the crew. Four men appeared, and, not without some trouble, pushed the chest out of the saloon. Then I heard them hoisting it up the iron staircase by means of pulleys.

At that moment, Captain Nemo turned to me.

"And you were saying, sir?" said he.

"I was saying nothing, Captain."

"The, sir, if you will allow me, I will wish you good-night."

Whereupon he turned and left the saloon.

I returned to my room much troubled, as one may believe. I vainly tried to sleep,—I sought the connecting link between the apparition of the diver and the chest filled with gold. Soon, I felt by certain movements of pitching and tossing, that the *Nautilus* was leaving the depths and returning to the surface.

Then I heard steps upon the platform; and I knew they were unfastening the pinnace, and launching it upon the waves. For one instant it struck the side of the *Nautilus*, then all noise ceased.

Two hours after, the same noise, the same going and coming was renewed; the boat was hoisted on board, replaced in its socket, and the *Nautilus* again plunged under the waves.

So these millions had been transported to their address. To what point of the Continent? Who was Captain Nemo's correspondent?

The next day, I related to Conseil and the Canadian the events of the night, which had excited by curiosity to the highest degree. My companions were not less surprised than myself.

"But where does he take his millions to?" asked Ned Land.

To that there was no possible answer. I returned to the saloon after having breakfast, and set to work. Till five o'clock in the evening, I employed myself in arranging my notes. At that moment—(ought I to attribute it to some peculiar idiosyncrasy),—I felt so great a heat that I was obliged to take off my coat of byssus! It was strange, for we were not under low latitudes; and even then, the *Nautilus*, submerged as it was, ought to experience no change of temperature. I looked at the manometer; it showed a depth of sixty feet, to which atmospheric heat could never attain.

I continued my work, but the temperature rose to such a pitch as to be intolerable.

"Could there be fire on board?" I asked myself.

I was leaving the saloon, when Captain Nemo entered; he approached the thermometer, consulted it, and turning to me, said—

"Forty-two degrees."

"I have noticed it, Captain," I replied; "and if it gets much hotter we cannot bear it."

"Oh! sir, it will not get hotter if we do not wish it."

"You can reduce it as you please, then?"

"No; but I can go further from the stove which produces it."

"It is outward then!"

"Certainly; we are floating in a current of boiling water."

"Is it possible!" I exclaimed.

"Look."

The panels opened, and I saw the sea entirely white all round. A sulphurous smoke was curling amid the waves, which boiled like water in a copper. I placed my hand on one of the panes of glass, but the heat was so great that I quickly took it off again.

"Where are we?" I asked.

"Near the Island of Santorin, sir," replied the Captain, "and just in the canal which separates Nea Kamenni from Pali Kamenni. I wished to give you a sight of the curious spectacle of a submarine eruption."

"I thought," said I, "that the formation of these new islands was ended."

"Nothing is ever ended in the volcanic parts of the sea," replied Captain Nemo; "and the globe is always being worked by subterranean fires. Already, in the nineteenth year of our era, according to Cassiodorus and Pliny, a new island, Theia (the divine), appeared in the very place where these islets have recently been formed. They they sank under the waves, to rise again in the year 69, when they again subsided. Since that time to our days, the Plutonian work has been suspended. But, on the 3rd of February 1866, a new island, which they named George Island, emerged from the midst of the sulphurous vapour near Nea Kamenni, and settled again the 6th of the same month. Seven days after, the 13th of February, the Island of Aphroessa appeared, leaving between Nea Kamenni and itself a canal ten yards broad. I was in these seas when the phenomenon occurred, and I was able therefore to observe all the different phases. The Island of Aphroessa, of round form, measured 300 feet in diameter, and thirty feet in height. It was composed of black and vitreous lava, mixed with fragments of felspar. And lastly, on the 10th of March, a smaller island, called Reka, showed itself near Nea Kamenni, and since then, these three have joined together, forming but one and the same island."

"And the canal in which we are at this moment?" I asked.

"Here it is," replied Captain Nemo, showing me a map of the Archipelago. "You see I have marked the new islands."

I returned to the glass. The *Nautilus* was no longer moving, the heat was becoming unbearable. The sea, which till now had been white, was red, owing to the presence of salts of iron. In spite of the ship's being hermetically sealed, an insupportable smell of sulphur filled the saloon, and the brilliancy of the electricity was entirely extinguished by bright scarlet flames. I was in a bath, I was choking, I was broiled.

"We can remain no longer in this boiling water," said I to the Captain.

"It would not be prudent," replied the impassive Captain Nemo.

An order was given; the *Nautilus* tacked about and left the furnace it could not brave with impunity. A quarter of an hour after we were breathing fresh air on the surface. The thought then struck me that, if Ned Land had chosen this part of the sea for our flight, we should never have come alive out of this sea of fire.

The next day, the 16th of February, we left the basin which, between Rhodes and Alexandria, is reckoned about 1500 fathoms in depth, and the *Nautilus,* passing some distance from Cerigo, quitted the Grecian Archipelago, after having doubled Cape Matapan.

Chapter VII

The Mediterranean in Forty-Eight Hours

The Mediterranean, the blue sea *par excellence,* "the great sea" of the Hebrews, "the sea" of the Greeks, the "mare nostrum" of the Romans, bordered by orange-trees, aloes, cacti, and sea-pines; embalmed with the perfume of the myrtle, surrounded by rude mountains, saturated with pure and transparent air, but incessantly worked by underground fires, a perfect battlefield in which Neptune and Pluto still dispute the empire of the world!

It is upon these banks, and on these waters, says Michelet, that man is renewed in one of the most powerful climates of the globe. But, beautiful as it was, I could only take a rapid glance at the basin whose superficial area is two million of square yards. Even Captain Nemo's knowledge was lost to me, for this enigmatical person did not appear once during our passage at full speed. I estimated the course which the *Nautilus* took under the waves of the sea at about six hundred leagues, and it was accomplished in forty-eight hours. Starting on the morning of the 16th of February from the shores of Greece, we had crossed the Straits of Gibraltar by sunrise on the 18th.

It was plain to me that this Mediterranean, enclosed in the midst of those countries which he wished to avoid, was distasteful to Captain Nemo. Those waves and those breezes brought back too many remembrances, if not too many regrets. Here he had no longer that independence and that liberty of gait which he had when in the open seas, and his *Nautilus* felt itself cramped between the close shores of Africa and Europe.

Our speed was now twenty-five miles an hour. It may be well understood that Ned Land, to his great disgust, was obliged to renounce his intended flight. He could not launch the pinnace, going at the rate of twelve or thirteen yards every second. To quit the *Nautilus* under such conditions would be as bad as jumping from a train going at full speed—an imprudent thing, to say the least of it. Besides, our vessel only mounted to the surface of the waves at night to renew its stock of air; it was steered entirely by the compass and the log.

I saw no more of the interior of this Mediterranean than a traveller by express train perceives of the landscape which flies before his eyes; that is to say, the distant horizon, and not the nearer objects which pass like a flash of lightning.

In the midst of the mass of waters brightly lit up by the electric light, glided some of those lampreys, more than a yard long, common to almost every climate. Some of the oxyrhynchi, a kind of ray five feet broad, with white belly and grey spotted back, spread out like a large shawl carried along by the current. Other rays passed so quickly that I could not see if they deserved the name of eagles which was given to them by the ancient Greeks, or the qualification of rats, toads, and bats, with which modern fishermen have loaded them. A few milander sharks, twelve feet long, and much feared by divers, struggled amongst them. Sea-foxes eight feet long, endowed with wonderful fineness of scent, appeared like large blue shadows. Some dorades of the shark kind, some of which measured seven feet and a half, showed themselves in their dress of blue and silver, encircled by small bands which struck sharply against the sombre tints of their fins, a fish consecrated to Venus, the eyes of which are encased in a socket of gold, a precious species, friend of all waters, fresh or salt, an inhabitant of rivers, lakes, and oceans, living in all climates, and bearing all temperatures; a race belonging to the geological era of the earth, and which has preserved all the beauty of its first days. Magnificent sturgeons, nine or ten yards long, creatures of great speed, striking the panes of glass with their strong tails, displayed their bluish backs with small brown spots; the resembled the sharks, but are not equal to them in strength, and are to be met with in all seas. But of all the diverse inhabitants of the Mediterranean, those I observed to the greatest advantage, when the *Nautilus* approached the surface, belonged to the sixty-third genus of bony fish. They were a kind of tunny, with bluish black backs, and silvery breastplates, whose dorsal fins threw out sparkles of gold. They are said to follow in the wake of vessels whose refreshing shade they seek from the fire of a tropical sky, and they did not belie the saying, for they accompanied the *Nautilus* as they did in former times the vessel of La Perouse. For many a long hour they struggled to keep up with our vessel. I was never tired of admiring these creatures really built for speed,—their small heads, their bodies lithe and cigar-shaped, which in some were more than three yards long, their pectoral fins and forked tail endowed with remarkable strength. They swam in a triangle, like certain flocks of birds, whose rapidity they equalled, and of which the ancients used to say that they understood geometry and strategy. But still they do not escape the pursuit of the Provencals, who esteem them as highly as the inhabitants of the Propontis and of Italy used to do; and these precious, but blind and foolhardy creatures, perish by millions in the nets of the Marseillaise.

With regard to the species of fish common to the Atlantic and the Mediterranean, the giddy speed of the *Nautilus* prevented me from observing them with any degree of accuracy.

As to marine mammals, I thought, in passing the entrance of the Adriatic, that I saw two or three cachalots, furnished with one dorsal fin, of the genus physetera, some dolphins of the genus globicephali, peculiar to the Mediterranean, the back part of the head being marked like a zebra with small lines; also, a dozen of seals, with white bellies and black hair, known by the name of *monks*, and which really have the air of a Dominican; they are about three yards in length.

As to zoophytes, for some instants I was able to admire a beautiful orange galeolaria, which had fastened itself to the port panel; it held on by a long filament, and was divided into an infinity of branches, terminated by the finest lace which could ever have been woven by the rivals of Arachne herself. Unfortunately, I could not take this admirable specimen; and doubtless no other Mediterranean zoophyte would have offered itself to my observation, if, on the night of the 16th, the *Nautilus* had not, singularly enough, slackened its speed, under the following circumstances.

We were then passing between Sicily and the coast of Tunis. In the narrow space between Cape Bon and the Straits of Messina, the bottom of the sea rose almost suddenly. There was a perfect bank, on which there was not more than nine fathoms of water, whilst on either side the depth was ninety fathoms.

The *Nautilus* had to manoeuvre very carefully so as not to strike against this submarine barrier.

I showed Conseil, on the map of the Mediterranean, the spot occupied by this reef.

"But if you please, sir," observed Conseil, "it is like a real isthmus joining Europe to Africa."

"Yes, my boy, it forms a perfect bar to the Straits of Lybia, and the soundings of Smith have proved that in former times the continents between Cape Boco and Cape Furina were joined."

"I can well believe it," said Conseil.

"I will add," I continued, "that a similar barrier exists between Gibraltar and Ceuta, which in geological times formed the entire Mediterranean."

"What if some volcanic burst should one day raise these two barriers above the waves?"

"It is not probable, Conseil."

"Well, but allow me to finish, please, sir; if this phenomenon should take place, it will be troublesome for M. Lesseps, who has taken so much pains to pierce the isthmus."

"I agree with you; but I repeat, Conseil, this phenomenon will never happen. The violence of subterranean force is ever diminishing. Volcanoes, so plentiful in the first days of the world, are being extinguished by degrees; the internal heat is weakened, the temperature of the lower strata of the globe is lowered by a perceptible quantity every century to the detriment of our globe, for its heat is its life."

"But the sun?"

"The sun is not sufficient, Conseil. Can it give heat to a dead body?"

"Not that I know of."

"Well, my friend, this earth will one day be that cold corpse; it will become uninhabitable and uninhabited like the moon, which has long since lost all its vital heat."

"In how many centuries?"

"In some hundreds of thousands of years, my boy."

"Then," said Conseil, "we shall have time to finish our journey, that is, if Ned Land does not interfere with it."

And Conseil, reassured, returned to the study of the bank, which the *Nautilus* was skirting at a moderate speed.

There, beneath the rocky and volcanic bottom, lay outspread a living flora of sponges and reddish cydippes, which emitted a slight phosphorescent light, commonly known by the name of sea-cucumbers; and walking comatulae more than a yard long, the purple of which completely coloured the water around.

The *Nautilus* having now passed the high bank in the Lybian Straits, returned to the deep waters and its accustomed speed.

From that time no more molluscs, no more articulates, no more zoophytes; barely a few large fish passing like shadows.

During the night of the 16th and 17th February, we had entered the second Mediterranean basin, the greatest depth of which was 1450 fathoms. The *Nautilus*, by the action of its screw, slid down the inclined planes, and buried itself in the lowest depths of the sea.

On the 18th of February, about three o'clock in the morning, we were at the entrance of the Straits of Gibraltar. There once existed two currents: an upper one, long since recognised, which conveys the waters of the ocean into the basin of the Mediterranean; and a lower counter-current, which reasoning has now shown to exist. Indeed, the volume of water in the Mediterranean, incessantly added to by the waves of the Atlantic, and by rivers falling into it, would each year raise the level of this sea, for its evaporation is not sufficient to restore the equilibrium. As it is not so, we must necessarily admit the existence of an under-current, which empties into the basin of the Atlantic, through the Straits of Gibraltar, the surplus waters of the Mediterranean. A fact, indeed; and it was this counter-current by which the *Nautilus* profited. It advanced rapidly by the narrow pass. For one instant I caught a glimpse of the beautiful ruins of the temple of Hercules, buried in the ground, according to Pliny, and with the low island which supports it; and a few minutes later we were floating on the Atlantic.

Chapter VIII
Vigo Bay

The Atlantic! a vast sheet of water, whose superficial area covers twenty-five millions of square miles, the length of which is nine thousand miles, with a mean breadth of two thousand seven hundred,—an ocean whose parallel winding shores embrace an immense circumference, watered by the largest rivers of the world, the St Lawrence, the Mississippi, the Amazon, the Plata, the Orinoco, the Niger, the Senegal, the Elbe, the Loire, and the Rhine, which carry water from the most civilised, as well as from the most savage countries! Magnificent field of water, incessantly ploughed by vessels of every nation, sheltered by the flags of every nation, and which terminates in those two terrible points so dreaded by mariners, Cape Horn, and the Cape of Tempests!

The *Nautilus* was piercing the water with its sharp spur, after having accomplished nearly ten thousand leagues in three months and a half, a distance greater than the great circle of the earth. Where were we going now? and what was reserved for the future? The *Nautilus*, leaving the Straits of Gibraltar, had gone far out. It returned to the surface of the waves, and our daily walks on the platform were restored to us.

I mounted at once, accompanied by Ned Land and Conseil. At a distance of about twelve miles, Cape St Vincent was dimly to be seen, forming the south-western point of the Spanish peninsula. A strong southerly gale was blowing. The sea was swollen and billowy; it made the *Nautilus* rock violently. It was almost impossible to keep one's footing on the platform, which the heavy rolls of the sea beat over every instant. So we descended after inhaling some mouthfuls of fresh air.

I returned to my roon, Conseil to his cabin; but the Canadian, with a preoccupied air, followed me. Our rapid passage across the Mediterranean had not allowed him to put his project into execution, and he could not help showing his disappointment. When the door of my room was shut, he sat down and looked at me silently.

"Friend Ned," said I, "I understand you; but you cannot reproach yourself. To have attempted to leave the *Nautilus* under the circumstances would have been folly."

Ned Land did not answer; his compressed lips, and frowning brow, showed with him the violent possession this fixed idea had taken of his mind.

"Let us see," I continued; "we need not despair yet. We are going up the coast of Portugal again; France and England are not far off, where we can easily find refuge. Now, if the *Nautilus*, on leaving the Straits of Gibraltar, had gone to the south, if it had carried us towards regions where there were no continents, I should share your uneasiness. But we know now that Captain Nemo does not fly from civilised seas, and in some days I think you can act with security."

Ned Land still looked at me fixedly; at length his fixed lips parted, and he said, "It is for to-night."

I drew myself up suddenly. I was, I admit, little prepared for this communication. I wanted to answer the Canadian, but words would not come.

"We agreed to wait for an opportunity," continued Ned Land, "and the opportunity has arrived. This night we shall be but a few miles from the Spanish coast. It is cloudy. The wind blows freely. I have your word, M. Aronnax, and I rely upon you."

As I was still silent, the Canadian approached me.

"To-night, at nine o'clock," said he. "I have warned Conseil. At that moment, Captain Nemo will be shut up in his room, probably in bed. Neither the engineers nor the ship's crew can see us. Conseil and I will gain the central staircase, and you, M. Arronax, will remain in the library, two steps from us, waiting my signal. The oars, the mast, and the sail, are in the canoe. I have even succeeded in getting in some provisions. I have procured an English wrench, to unfasten the bolts which attach it to the shell of the *Nautilus*. So all is ready, till to-night."

"The sea is bad."

"That I allow," replied the Canadian; "but we must risk that. Liberty is worth paying for; besides, the boat is strong, and a few miles with a fair wind to carry us, is no great thing. Who knows but by to-morrow we may be a hundred leagues away? Let circumstances only favour us, and by ten or eleven o'clock we shall have landed on some spot of *terra firma*, alive or dead. But adieu now till to-night."

With these words the Canadian withdrew, leaving me almost dumb. I had imagined that, the chance gone, I should have time to reflect and discuss the matter. My obstinate companion had given me no time; and, after all, what could I have said to him? Ned Land was perfectly right. There was almost the opportunity to profit by. Could I retract my word, and take upon myself the responsibility of compromising the future of my companions? Tomorrow Captain Nemo might take us far from all land.

At that moment a rather loud hissing told me that the reservoirs were filling, and that the *Nautilus* was sinking under the waves of the Atlantic.

A sad day I passed, between the desire of regaining my liberty of action, and of abandoning the wonderful *Nautilus*, and leaving my submarine studies incomplete.

What dreadful hours I passed thus! sometimes seeing myself and companions safely landed, sometimes wishing, in spite of my reason, that some unforeseen circumstances would prevent the realisation of Ned Land's project.

Twice I went to the saloon. I wished to consult the compass. I wished to see if the direction the *Nautilus* was taking was bringing us nearer or taking us farther from the coast. But no; the *Nautilus* kept in Portuguese waters.

I must therefore take my part, and prepare for flight. My luggage was not heavy; my notes nothing more.

As to Captain Nemo, I asked myself what he would think of our escape; what trouble, what wrong it might cause him, and what he might do in case of its discovery or failure. Certainly I had no cause to complain of him; on the contrary, never was hospitality freer than his. In leaving him I could not be taxed with ingratitude. No oath bound us to him. It was on the strength of circumstances he relied, and not upon our word, to fix us for ever.

I had not seen the Captain since our visit to the Island of Santorin. Would chance bring me to his presence before our departure? I wished it, and I feared it at the same time. I listened if I could hear him walking in the room contiguous to mine. No sound reached my ear. I felt an unbearable uneasiness. This day of waiting seemed eternal. Hours struck too slowly to keep pace with my impatience.

My dinner was served in my roon as usual. I ate but little, I was too preoccupied. I left the table at seven o'clock. A hundred and twenty minutes (I counted them) still separated me from the moment in which I was to join Ned Land. My agitation redoubled. My pulse beat violently. I could not remain quiet. I went and came, hoping to calm my troubled spirit by constant movement. The idea of failure in our bold enterprise was the least painful of my anxieties; but the thought of seeing our project discovered before leaving the *Nautilus*, of being brought before Captain Nemo, irritated, or (what was worse) saddened at my desertion, made my heart beat.

I wanted to see the saloon for the last time. I descended the stairs, and arrived in the museum where I had passed so many useful and agreeable hours. I looked at all its riches, all its treasures, like a man on the eve of an eternal exile, who was leaving never to return. These wonders of Nature, these masterpieces of Art, amongst which, for so many days, my life had been concentrated, I was going to abandon them for ever! I should like to have taken a last look through the windows of the saloon into the waters of the Atlantic: but the panels were hermetically closed, and a cloak of steel separated me from that ocean which I had not yet explored.

In passing through the saloon, I came near the door, let into the angle, which opened into the Captain's room. To my great surprise, this door was ajar. I drew back, involuntarily. If Captain Nemo should be in his room, he could see me. But, hearing no noise, I drew nearer. The room was deserted. I pushed open the door, and took some steps forward. Still the same monk-like severity of aspect.

Suddenly the clock struck eight. The first beat of the hammer on the bell awoke me from my dreams. I trembled as if an invisible eye had plunged into my most secret thoughts, and I hurried from the room.

There my eye fell upon the compass. Our course was still north. The log indicated moderate speed, the manometer a depth of about sixty feet.

I returned to my room, clothed myself warmly—sea boots, an otter-skin cap, a great coat of byssus, lined with sealskin; I was ready, I was waiting. The vibration of the screw alone broke the deep silence which reigned on board. I listened attentively. Would no loud voice suddenly inform me that Ned Land had been surprised in his projected flight? A mortal dread hung over me, and I vainly tried to regain my accustomed coolness.

At a few minutes to nine, I put my ear to the Captain's door. No noise. I left my room and returned to the saloon, which was half in obscurity, but deserted.

I opened the door communicating with the library. The same insufficient light, the same solitude. I placed myself near the door leading to the central staircase, and there waited for Ned Land's signal.

At that moment the trembling of the screw sensibly diminished, then it stopped entirely. The silence was now only disturbed by the beatings of my own heart. Suddenly a slight shock was felt; and I knew that the *Nautilus* had stopped at the bottom of the ocean. My uneasiness increased. The Canadian's signal did not come. I felt inclined to join Ned Land and beg of him to put off his attempt. I felt that we were not sailing under our usual conditions.

At this moment the door of the large saloon opened, and Captain Nemo appeared. He saw me, and, without further preamble, began in an amiable tone of voice—

"Ah, sir! I have been looking for you. Do you know the history of Spain?"

Now, one might know the history of one's own country by heart; but in the condition I was at the time, with troubled mind and head quite lost, I could not have said a word of it.

"Well," continued Captain Nemo, "you heard by question? Do you know the history of Spain?"

"Very slightly," I answered.

"Well, here are learned men having to learn," said the captain. "Come, sit down, and I will tell you a curious episode in this history.—Sir, listen well," said he; "this history will interest you on one side, for it will answer a question which doubtless you have not been able to solve."

"I listen, Captain," said I, not knowing what my interlocutor was driving at, and asking myself if this incident was bearing on our projected flight.

"Sir, if you have no objection, we will go back to 1702. You cannot be ignorant that your king, Louis XIV., thinking that the gesture of a potentate was sufficient to bring the Pyrenees under his yoke, had imposed the Duke of Anjou, his grandson, on the Spaniards. This prince reigned more or less badly under the name of Philip V., and had a strong party against him abroad. Indeed, the preceding year, the royal houses of Holland, Austria, and England, had concluded a treaty of alliance at the Hague, with the intention of plucking the crown of Spain from the head of Philip V., and placing it on that of an archduke to whom they prematurely gave the title of Charles III.

"Spain must resist this coalition; but she was almost entirely unprovided with either soldiers or sailors. However, money would not fail them, provided that their galleons, laden with gold and silver from America, once entered their ports. And about the end of 1702 they expected a rich convoy which France was escorting with a fleet of twenty-three vessels, commanded by Admiral Château-Renaud, for the ships of the coalition were already beating the Atlantic. This convoy was to go to Cadiz, but the Admiral, hearing that an English fleet was cruising in those waters, resolved to make for a French port.

"The Spanish commanders of the convoy objected to this decision. They wanted to be taken to a Spanish port, and if not to Cadiz, into Vigo Bay, situated on the north-West coast of Spain, and which was not blocked.

"Admiral Château-Renaud had the rashness to obey this injunction, and the galleons entered Vigo Bay.

"Unfortunately, it formed an open road which could not be defended in any way. They must therefore hasten to unload the galleons before the arrival of the combined fleet; and time would not have failed them had not a miserable question of rivalry suddenly arisen.

"You are following the chain of events?" asked Captain Nemo.

"Perfectly," said I, not knowing the end proposed by this historical lesson.

"I will continue. This is what passed. The merchants of Cadiz had a privilege by which they had the right of receiving all merchandise coming from the West Indies. Now, to disembark these ingots at the port of Vigo, was depriving them of their rights. They complained at Madrid, and obtained the consent of the weak-minded Philip that the convoy, without discharging its cargo, should remain sequestered in the roads of Vigo until the enemy had disappeared.

"But whilst coming to this decision, on the 22nd of October 1702, the English vessels arrived in Vigo Bay, when Admiral Château-Renaud, in spite of inferior forces, fought bravely. But seeing that the treasure must fall into the enemy's hands, he burnt and scuttled every galleon, which went to the bottom with their immense riches."

Captain Nemo stopped. I admit I could not yet see why this history should interest me.

"Well?" I asked.

"Well, M. Aronnax," replied Captain Nemo, "we are in that Vigo Bay; and it rests with yourself whether you will penetrate its mysteries."

The captain rose, telling me to follow him. I had had time to recover. I obeyed. The saloon was dark, but through the transparent glass the waves were sparkling. I looked.

For half a mile around the *Nautilus*, the waters seemed bathed in electric light. The sandy bottom was clean and bright. Some of the ship's crew in their diving dresses were clearing away half rotten barrels and empty cases from the midst of the blackened wrecks. From these cases and from these barrels escaped ingots of gold and silver, cascades of piastres and jewels. The sand was heaped up with them. Laden with their precious booty the men returned to the *Nautilus*, disposed of their burden, and went back to this inexhaustible fishery of gold and silver.

I understood now. This was the scene of the battle of the 22nd of October 1702. Here on this very spot the galleons laden for the Spanish Government had sunk. Here Captain Nemo came, according to his wants, to pack up those millions with which he burdened the *Nautilus*. It was for him and him alone America had given up her precious metals. He was heir direct, without any one to share, in those treasures torn from the Incas and from the conquered of Ferdinand Cortez.

"Did you know, sir," he asked, smiling, "that the sea contained such riches?"

"I knew," I answered, "that they value the money held in suspension in these waters at two millions."

"Doubtless; but to extract this money the expense would be greater than the profit. Here, on the contrary, I have but to pick up what man has lost,—and not only in Vigo Bay, but in a thousand other spots where shipwrecks have happened, and which are marked on my submarine map. Can you understand now the source of the millions I am worth?"

"I understand, Captain. But allow me to tell you that in exploring Vigo Bay you have only been beforehand with a rival society."

"And which?"

"A society which has received from the Spanish Government the privilege of seeking these buried galleons. The shareholders are led on by the allurement of an enormous bounty, for they value these rich shipwrecks at five hundred millions."

"Five hundred millions they were," answered Captain Nemo, "but they are so no longer."

"Just so," said I; "and a warning to those shareholders would be an act of charity. But who knows if it would be well received? What gamblers usually regret above all is less the loss of their money, than of their foolish hopes. After all, I pity them less than the thousands of unfortunates to whom so much riches well-distributed would have been profitable, whilst for them they will be for ever barren."

I had no sooner expressed this regret, than I felt that it must have wounded Captain Nemo.

"Barren!" he exclaimed, with animation. "Do you think then, sir, that these riches are lost because I gather them? Is it for myself alone, according to your idea, that I take the trouble to collect these treasures? Who told you that I did not make a good use of it? Do you think I am ignorant that there are suffering beings and oppressed races on this earth, miserable creatures to console, victims to avenge? Do you not understand?"

Captain Nemo stopped at these last words, regretting perhaps that he had spoken so much. But I had guessed that whatever the motive which had forced him to seek independence under the sea, it had left him still a man, that his heart still beat for the sufferings of humanity, and that his immense charity was for oppressed races as well as

individuals. And I then understood for whom those millions were destined, which were forwarded by Captain Nemo when the *Nautilus* was
cruising in the waters of Crete.

Chapter IX

A Vanished Continent

The next morning, the 19th of February, I saw the Canadian enter my
room. I expected this visit. He looked very disappointed.

"Well, sir?" said he.

"Well, Ned, fortune was against us yesterday."

"Yes; that Captain must needs stop exactly at the hour we intended
leaving his vessel."

"Yes, Ned, he had business at his bankers."

"His bankers!"

"Or rather his banking-house; by that I mean the ocean, where his
riches are safer than in the chests of the State."

I then related to the Canadian the incidents of the preceding night,
hoping to bring him back to the idea of not abandoning the Captain;
but my recital had no other result than an energetically expressed
regret from Ned, that he had not been able to take a walk on the battlefield of Vigo on his own account.

"However," said he, "all is not ended. It is only a blow of the harpoon
lost. Another time we must succeed; and to-night, if necessary"—

"In what direction is the *Nautilus* going?" I asked.

"I do not know," replied Ned.

"Well, at noon we shall see the point."

The Canadian returned to Conseil. As soon as I was dressed, I went into the saloon. The compass was not reassuring. The course of the *Nautilus* was S.S.W. We were turning our backs on Europe.

I waited with some impatience till the ship's place was pricked on the chart. At about half-past eleven the reservoirs were emptied, and our vessel rose to the surface of the ocean. I rushed towards the platform. Ned Land had preceded me. No more land in sight. Nothing but an immense sea. Some sails on the horizon, doubtless those going to San Roque in search of favourable winds for doubling the Cape of Good Hope. The weather was cloudy. A gale of wind was preparing. Ned raved, and tried to pierce the cloudy horizon. He still hoped that behind all that fog stretched the land he so longed for.

At noon the sun showed itself for an instant. The second profited by this brightness to take its height. Then the sea becoming more billowy, we descended, and the panel closed.

An hour after, upon consulting the chart, I saw the position of the *Nautilus* was marked at 16° 17' longitude, and 33° 22' latitude, at 150 leagues from the nearest coast. There was no means of flight, and I leave you to imagine the rage of the Canadian, when I informed him of our situation.

For myself, I was not particularly sorry. I felt lightened of the load which had oppressed me, and was able to return with some degree of calmness to my accustomed work.

That night, about eleven o'clock, I received a most unexpected visit from Captain Nemo. He asked me very graciously if I felt fatigued from my watch of the preceding night. I answered in the negative.

"Then, M. Aronnax, I propose a curious excursion."

"Propose, Captain?"

"You have hitherto only visited the submarine depths by daylight, under the brightness of the sun. Would it suit you to see them in the darkness of the night?"

"Most willingly."

"I warn you, the way will be tiring. We shall have far to walk, and must climb a mountain. The roads are not well kept."

"What you say, Captain, only heightens my curiosity; I am ready to follow you."

"Come then, sir, we will put on our diving dresses."

Arrived at the robing-room, I saw that neither of my companions nor any of the ship's crew were to follow us on this excursion. Captain Nemo had not even proposed my taking with me either Ned or Conseil.

In a few moments we had put on our diving dresses; they placed on our backs the reservoirs, abundantly filled with air, but no electric lamps were prepared. I called the Captain's attention to the fact.

"They will be useless," he replied.

I thought I had not heard aright, but I could not repeat my observation, for the Captain's head had already disappeared in its metal case. I finished harnessing myself, I felt them put an iron-pointed stick into my hand, and some minutes later, after going through the usual form, we set foot on the bottom of the Atlantic, at a depth of 150 fathoms. Midnight was near. The waters were profoundly dark, but Captain Nemo pointed out in the distance a reddish spot, a sort of large light shining brilliantly, about two miles from the *Nautilus*. What this fire might be, what could feed it, why and how it lit up the liquid mass, I could not say. In any case, it did light our way, vaguely, it is true, but I soon accustomed myself to the peculiar darkness, and I understood, under such circumstances, the uselessness of the Rumhkorff apparatus.

As we advanced, I heard a kind of pattering above my head. The noise redoubling, sometimes producing a continual shower, I soon understood the cause. It was rain falling violently, and crisping the surface of the waves. Instinctively the thought flashed across my mind that I should be wet through! By the water! in the midst of the water! I could not help laughing at the odd idea. But indeed, in the thick diving dress, the liquid element is no longer felt, and one only seems to be in an atmosphere somewhat denser than the terrestrial atmosphere. Nothing more.

After half an hour's walk the soil became stony. Medusae, microscopic crustacea, and pennatules lit it slightly with their phosophorescent gleam. I caught a glimpse of pieces of stone covered with millions of zoophytes, and masses of seaweed. My feet often slipped upon this viscous carpet of seaweed, and without my iron-tipped stick I should have fallen more than once. In turning round, I could still see the whitish lantern of the *Nautilus* beginning to pale in the distance.

But the rosy light which guided us increased and lit up the horizon. The presence of this fire under water puzzled me in the highest degree. Was it some electric effulgence? Was I going towards a natural phenomenon as yet unknown to the savants of the earth? Or even (for this thought crossed my brain) had the hand of man aught to do with this conflagration? Had he fanned this flame? Was I to meet in these depths companions and friends of Captain Nemo whom he was going to visit, and who, like him, led this strange existence? Should I find down there a whole colony of exiles, who, weary of the miseries of this earth, had sought and found independence in the deep ocean? All these foolish and unreasonable ideas pursued me. And in this condition of mind, over-excited by the succession of wonders continually passing before my eyes, I should not have been surprised to meet at the bottom of the sea one of those submarine towns of which Captain Nemo dreamed.

Our road grew lighter and lighter. The white glimmer came in rays from the summit of a mountain about 800 feet high. But what I saw was simply a reflection, developed by the clearness of the waters. The source of this inexplicable light was a fire on the opposite side of the mountain.

In the midst of this stony maze, furrowing the bottom of the Atlantic, Captain Nemo advanced without hesitation. He knew this dreary road. Doubtless he had often travelled over it, and could not lose himself. I followed him with unshaken confidence. He seemed to me like a genie of the sea; and, as he walked before me, I could not help admiring his stature, which was outlined in black on the luminous horizon.

It was one in the morning when we arrived at the first slopes of the mountain; but to gain access to them we must venture through the difficult paths of a vast copse.

Yes; a copse of dead trees, without leaves, without sap, trees petrified by the action of the water, and here and there overtopped by gigantic pines. It was like a coal pit, still standing, holding by the roots to the broken soil, and whose branches, like fine black paper cuttings, showed distinctly on the watery ceiling. Picture to yourself a forest in the Hartz, hanging on to the sides of the mountain, but a forest swallowed up. The paths were encumbered with seaweed and fucus, between which grovelled a whole world of crustacea. I went along, climbing the rocks, striding over extended trunks, breaking the sea bind-weed, which hung from one tree to the other; and frightening the fishes, which flew from branch to branch. Pressing onward, I felt no fatigue. I followed my guide, who was never tired. What a spectacle! how can I express it? how paint the aspect of those woods and rocks in this medium,—their under parts dark and wild, the upper coloured with red tints, by that light which the reflecting powers of the waters doubled? We climbed rocks, which fell directly after with gigantic bounds, and the low growling of an avalanche. To right and left ran long, dark galleries, where sight was lost. Here opened vast glades which the hand of man seemed to have worked; and I sometimes asked myself if some inhabitant of these submarine regions would not suddenly appear to me.

But Captain Nemo was still mounting. I could not stay behind. I followed boldly. My stick gave me good help. A false step would have been dangerous on the narrow passes sloping down to the sides of the gulfs; but I walked with firm step, without feeling any giddiness. Now I jumped a crevice the depth of which would have made me hesitate had it been among the glaciers on the land; now I ventured on the unsteady trunk of a tree, thrown across from one abyss to the other, without looking under my feet, having only eyes to admire the wild sites of this region.

There, monumental rocks, leaning on their regularly cut bases, seemed to defy all laws of equilibrium. From between their stony knees, trees sprang, like a jet under heavy pressure, and upheld others which upheld them. Natural towers, large scarps, cut perpendicularly, like a "curtain," inclined at an angle which the laws of gravitation could never have tolerated in terrestrial regions.

Two hours after quitting the *Nautilus*, we had crossed the lines of trees, and a hundred feet above our heads rose the top of the mountain, which cast a shadow on the brilliant irradiation of the opposite slope. Some petrified shrubs ran fantastically here and there. Fishes got up under our feet like birds in the long grass. The massive rocks were rent with impenetrable fractures, deep grottos, and unfathomable holes, at the bottom of which formidable creatures might be heard moving. My blood curdled when I saw enormous antennae blocking my road, or some frightful claw closing with a noise in the shadow of some cavity. Millions of luminous spots shone brightly in the midst of the darkness. They were the eyes of giant crustacea crouched in their holes; giant lobsters setting themselves up like halberdiers, and moving their claws with the clicking sound of pincers; titanic crabs, pointed like a gun on its carriage; and frightful looking poulps, interweaving their tentacles like a living nest of serpents.

We had now arrived on the first platform, where other surprises awaited me. Before us lay some picturesque ruins, which betrayed the hand of man, and not that of the Creator. There were vast heaps of stone, amongst which might be traced the vague and shadowy forms of castles and temples, clothed with a world of blossoming zoophytes, and over which, instead of ivy, sea-weed and fucus threw a thick vegetable mantle. But what was this portion of the globe which had been swallowed by cataclysms? Who had placed those rocks and stones like cromlechs of pre-historic times? Where was I? Whither had Captain Nemo's fancy hurried me?

I would fain have asked him; not being able to, I stopped him—I seized his arm. But shaking his head, and pointing to the highest point of the mountain, he seemed to say—

"Come, come along; come hither!"

I followed, and in a few minutes I had climbed to the top, which for a cricle of ten yards commanded the whole mass of rock.

I looked down the side we had just climbed. The mountain did not rise more than seven or eight hundred feet above the level of the plain; but on the opposite side it commanded from twice that height the depths of this part of the Atlantic. My eyes ranged far over a large space lit by a violent fulguration. In fact, the mountain was a volcano.

At fifty feet above the peak, in the midst of a rain of stones and scoriae, a large crater was vomiting forth torrents of lava which fell in a cascade of fire into the bosom of the liquid mass. Thus situated, this volcano lit the lower plain like an immense torch, even to the extreme limits of the horizon. I said that the submarine crater threw up lava, but no flames. Flames require the oxygen of the air to feed upon, and cannot be developed under water; but streams of lava, having in themselves the principles of their incandescence, can attain a white heat, fight vigorously against the liquid element, and turn it to vapour by contact.

Rapid currents bearing all these gases in diffusion, and torrents of lava, slid to the bottom of the mountain like an eruption of Vesuvius on another Terra del Greco.

There, indeed, under my eyes, ruined, destroyed, lay a town,—its roofs open to the sky, its temples fallen, its arches dislocated, its columns lying on the ground, from which one could still recognise the massive character of Tuscan architecture. Further on, some remains of a gigantic aqueduct; here the high base of an Acropolis, with the floating outline of a Parthenon; there traces of a quay, as if an ancient port had formerly abutted on the borders of the ocean, and disappeared with its merchant vessels and its war-galleys. Further on again, long lines of sunken walls and broad deserted streets—a perfect Pompeii escaped beneath the waters. Such was the sight that Captain Nemo brought before my eyes!

Where was I? Where was I? I must know, at any cost. I tried to speak, but Captain Nemo stopped me by a gesture, and picking up a piece of chalk stone, advanced to a rock of black basalt, and traced the one word—

Atlantis

What a light shot through my mind! Atlantis, the ancient Meropis of Theopompus, the Atlantis of Plato, that continent denied by Origen, Jamblichus, D'Anville, Malte-Brun, and Humboldt, who placed its disappearance amongst the legendary tales admitted by Posidonius, Pliny, Ammianus Marcellinus, Tertullian, Engel, Buffon, and D'Avezac. I had it there now before my eyes, bearing upon it the unexceptionable testimony of its catastrophe. The region thus engulfed was beyond Europe, Asia, and Lybia, beyond the columns of Hercules, where those powerful people, the Atlantides, lived, against whom the first wars of ancient Greece were waged.

Thus, led by the strangest destiny, I was treading under foot the mountains of this continent, touching with my hand those ruins a thousand generations old, and contemporary with the geological epochs. I was walking on the very spot where the contemporaries of the first man had walked.

Whilst I was trying to fix in my mind every detail of this grand landscape, Captain Nemo remained motionless, as if petrified in mute ecstasy, leaning on a mossy stone. Was he dreaming of those generations long since disappeared? Was he asking them the secret of human destiny? Was it here this strange man came to steep himself in historical recollections, and live again this ancient life,—he who wanted no modern one? What would I not have given to know his thoughts, to share them, to understand them! We remained for an hour at this place, contemplating the vast plain under the brightness of the lava, which was sometimes wonderfully intense. Rapid tremblings ran along the mountain caused by internal bubblings, deep noises distinctly transmitted through the liquid medium were echoed with majestic grandeur. At this moment the moon appeared through the mass of waters, and threw her pale rays on the buried continent. It was but a gleam, but what an indescribable effect! The Captain rose, cast one last look on the immense plain, and then bade me follow him.

We descended the mountain rapidly, and the mineral forest once passed, I saw the lantern of the *Nautilus* shining like a star. The Captain walked straight to it, and we got on board as the first rays of light whitened the surface of the ocean.

Chapter X

The Submarine Coal Mines

The next day, the 20th of February, I awoke very late: the fatigues of the previous night had prolonged my sleep until eleven o'clock. I dressed quickly, and hastened to find the course the *Nautilus* was taking. The instruments showed it to be still towards the south, with a speed of twenty miles an hour, and a depth of fifty fathoms.

The species of fishes here did not differ much from those already noticed. There were rays of giant size, five yards long, and endowed with great muscular strength, which enabled them to shoot above the waves; sharks of many kinds, amongst others, a glaucus of fifteen feet long, with triangular sharp teeth, and whose transparency rendered it almost invisible in the water; brown sagrae; humantins, prism-shaped, and clad with a tuberculous hide; sturgeons, resembling their congeners of the Mediterranean; trumpet syngnathes, a foot and a half long, furnished with greyish bladders, without teeth or tongue, and as supple as snakes.

Amongst bony fish, Conseil noticed some blackish makairas, about three yards long, armed at the upper jaw with a piercing sword; other bright coloured creatures, known in the time of Aristotle by the name of the sea-dragon, which are dangerous to capture on account of the spikes on their back; also some coryphaenes, with brown backs marked with little blue stripes, and surrounded with a gold border; some beautiful dorades; and swordfish four-and-twenty feet long, swimming in troops, fierce animals, but rather herbivorous than carnivorous.

About four o'clock, the soil, generally composed of a thick mud mixed with petrified wood, changed by degrees, and it became more stony, and seemed strewn with conglomerate and pieces of basalt, with a sprinkling of lava and sulphurous obsidian. I thought that a mountainous region was succeeding the long plains; and accordingly, after a few evolutions of the *Nautilus*, I saw the southerly horizon blocked by a high wall which seemed to close all exit. Its summit evidently passed the level of the ocean. It must be a continent, or at least an island,—one of the Canaries, or of the Cape Verd Islands. The bearings not being yet taken, perhaps designedly, I was ignorant of our exact position. In any case, such a wall seemed to me to mark the limits of that Atlantis, of which we had in reality passed over only the smallest part.

Much longer should I have remained at the window, admiring the beauties of sea and sky, but the panels closed. At this moment the *Nautilus* arrived at the side of this high perpendicular wall. What it would do, I could not guess. I returned to my room; it no longer moved. I laid myself down with the full intention of waking after a few hours' sleep; but it was eight o'clock the next day when I entered the saloon. I looked at the manometer. It told me that the *Nautilus* was floating on the surface of the ocean. Besides, I heard steps on the platform. I went to the panel. It was open; but, instead of broad daylight, as I expected, I was surrounded by profound darkness. Where were we? Was I mistaken? Was it still night? No; not a star was shining, and night has not that utter darkness.

I knew not what to think, when a voice near me said—

"Is that you, Professor?"

"Ah! Captain," I answered, "where are we?"

"Under ground, sir."

"Under ground!" I exclaimed. "And the *Nautilus* floating still?"

"It always floats."

"But I do not understand."

"Wait a few minutes, our lantern will be lit, and if you like light places, you will be satisfied."

I stood on the platform and waited. The darkness was so complete that I could not even see Captain Nemo; but looking to the zenith, exactly above my head, I seemed to catch an undecided gleam, a kind of twilight filling a circular hole. At this instant the lantern was lit, and its vividness dispelled the faint light. I closed my dazzled eyes for an instant, and then looked again. The *Nautilus* was stationary, floating near a mountain which formed a sort of quay. The lake then supporting it was a lake imprisoned by a circle of walls, measuring two miles in diameter, and six in circumference. Its level (the manometer showed) could only be the same as the outside level, for there must necessarily be a communication between the lake and the sea. The high partitions, leaning forward on their base, grew into a vaulted roof bearing the shape of an immense funnel turned upside down, the height being about five or six hundred yards. At the summit was a circular orifice, by which I had caught the slight gleam of light, evidently daylight.

"Where are we?" I asked.

"In the very heart of an extinct volcano, the interior of which has been invaded by the sea, after some great convulsion of the earth. Whilst you were sleeping, Professor, the *Nautilus* penetrated to this lagoon by a natural canal, which opens about ten yards beneath the surface of the ocean. This is its harbour of refuge, a sure, commodious, and mysterious one, sheltered from all gales. Show me, if you can, on the coasts of any of your continents or islands, a road which can give such perfect refuge from all storms."

"Certainly," I replied, "you are in safety here, Captain Nemo. Who could reach you in the heart of a volcano? But did I not see an opening at its summit?"

"Yes; its crater, formerly filled with lava, vapour, and flames, and which now gives entrance to the life-giving air we breathe."

"But what is this volcanic mountain?"

"It belongs to one of the numerous islands with which this sea is strewn,—to vessels a simple sandbank,—to us an immense cavern. Chance led me to discover it, and chance served me well."

"But of what us is this refuge, Captain? The *Nautilus* wants no port."

"No, sir; but it wants electricity to make it move, and the where-withal to make the electricity—sodium to feed the elements, coal from which to get the sodium, and a coal-mine to supply the coal. And exactly on this spot the sea covers entire forests embedded during the geological periods, now mineralised, and transformed into coal; for me they are an inexhaustible mine."

"Your men follow the trade of miners here, then, Captain?"

"Exactly so. These mines extend under the waves like the mines of Newcastle. Here, in their diving dresses, pickaxe and shovel in hand, my men extract the coal, which I do not even ask from the mines of the earth. When I burn this combustible for the manufacture of sodium, the smoke, escaping from the crater of the mountain, gives it the appearance of a still active volcano."

"And we shall see your companion at work?"

"No; not this time at least; for I am in a hurry to continue our sub-marine tour of the earth. So I shall content myself with drawing from the reserve of sodium I already possess. The time for loading is one day only, and we continue our voyage. So if you wish to go over the cavern, and make the round of the lagoon, you must take advantage of to-day, M. Aronnax."

I thanked the Captain, and went to look for my companions, who had not yet left their cabin. I invited them to follow me without saying where we were. They mounted the platform. Conseil, who was astonished at nothing, seemed to look upon it as quite natural that he should wake under a mountain, after having fallen asleep under the waves. But Ned Land thought of nothing but finding whether the cavern had any exit. After breakfast, about ten o'clock, we went down on to the mountain.

"Here we are, once more on land," said Conseil.

"I do not call this land," said the Canadian. "And besides, we are not on it, but beneath it."

Between the walls of the mountain and the waters of the lake lay a sandy shore, which, at its greatest breadth, measured five hundred feet. On this soil one might easily make the tour of the lake. But the base of the high partitions was stony ground, with volcanic blocks and enormous pumice stones lying in picturesque heaps. All these detached masses, covered with enamel, polished by the action of the subterraneous fires, shone resplendent by the light of our electric lantern. The mica dust from the shore, rising under our feet, flew like a cloud of sparks. The bottom now rose sensibly, and we soon arrived at long circuitous slopes, or inclined planes, which took us higher by degrees; but we were obliged to walk carefully among these conglomerates, bound by no cement, the feet slipping on the glassy trachyte, composed of crystal, felspar, and quartz.

The volcanic nature of this enormous excavation was confirmed on all sides, and I pointed it out to my companions.

"Picture to yourselves," said I, "what this crater must have been when filled with boiling lava, and when the level of the incandescent liquid rose to the orifice of the mountain, as though melted on the top of a hot plate."

"I can picture it perfectly," said Conseil. "But, sir, will you tell me why the Great Architect has suspended operations, and how it is that the furnace is replaced by the quiet waters of the lake?"

"Most probably, Conseil, because some convulsion beneath the ocean produced that very opening which has served as a passage for the *Nautilus*. Then the waters of the Atlantic rushed into the interior of the mountain. There must have been a terrible struggle between the two elements, a struggle which ended in the victory of Neptune. But many ages have run out since then, and the submerged volcano is now a peaceable grotto."

"Very well," replied Ned Land; "I accept the explanation, sir; but, in our own interests, I regret that the opening of which you speak was not made above the level of the sea."

"But, friend Ned," said Conseil, "if the passage had not been under the sea, the *Nautilus* could not have gone through it."

We continued ascending. The steps became more and more perpendicular and narrow. Deep excavations, which we were obliged to cross, cut them here and there; sloping masses had to be turned. We slid upon our knees and crawled along. But Conseil's dexterity and the Canadian's strength surmounted all obstacles. At a height of about thirty-one feet, the nature of the ground changed without becoming more practicable. To the conglomerate and trachyte succeeded black basalt, the first dispread in layers full of bubbles, the latter forming regular prisms, placed like a colonnade supporting the spring of the immense vault, an admirable specimen of natural architecture. Between the blocks of basalt wound long streams of lava, long since grown cold, encrusted with bituminous rays; and in some places there were spread large carpets of sulphur. A more powerful light shone through the upper crater, shedding a vague glimmer over these volcanic depressions for ever buried in the bosom of this extinguished mountain. But our upward march was soon stopped at a height of about two hundred and fifty feet by impassable obstacles. There was a complete vaulted arch overhanging us, and our ascent was changed to a circular walk. At the last change vegetable life began to struggle with the mineral. Some shrubs, and even some trees, grew from the fractures of the walls. I recognised some euphorbias, with the caustic sugar coming from them; heliotropes, quite incapable of justifying their name, sadly drooped their clusters of flowers, both their colour and perfume half gone. Here and there some chrysanthemums grew timidly at the foot of an aloe with long sickly-looking leaves. But between the streams of lava, I saw some little violets still slightly perfumed, and I admit that I smelt them with delight. Perfume is the soul of the flower, and sea-flowers, those splendid hydrophytes, have no soul.

We had arrived at the foot of some sturdy dragon-trees, which had pushed aside the rocks with their strong roots, when Ned Land exclaimed—

"Ah! sir, a hive! a hive!"

"A hive!" I replied, with a gesture of incredulity.

"Yes, a hive," repeated the Canadian, "and bees humming round it."

I approached, and was bound to believe my own eyes. There, at a hole bored in one of the dragon-trees, were some thousands of these ingenious insects, so common in all the Canaries, and whose produce is so much esteemed. Naturally enough, the Canadian wished to gather the honey, and I could not well oppose his wish. A quantity of dry leaves, mixed with sulphur, he lit with a spark from his flint, and he began to smoke out the bees. The humming ceased by degrees, and the hive eventually yielded several pounds of the sweetest honey, with which Ned Land filled his haversack.

"When I have mixed this honey with the paste of the artocarpus," said he, "I shall be able to offer you a succulent cake."

"Upon my word," said Conseil, "it will be gingerbread."

"Never mind the gingerbread," said I; "let us continue our interesting walk."

At every turn of the path we were following, the lake appeared in all its length and breadth. The lantern lit up the whole of its peaceable surface which knew neither ripple nor wave. The *Nautilus* remained perfectly immovable. On the platform, and on the mountain, the ship's crew were working like black shadows clearly carved against the luminous atmosphere. We were now going round the highest crest of the first layers of rock which upheld the roof. I then saw that bees were not the only representatives of the animal kingdom in the interior of this volcano. Birds of prey hovered here and there in the shadows, or fled from their nests on the top of the rocks. There were sparrow-hawks with white breasts, and kestrels, and down the slopes scampered, with their long legs, several fine fat bustards. I leave any one to imagine the covetousness of the Canadian at the sight of this savoury game, and whether he did not regret having no gun. But he did his best to replace the lead by stones, and after several fruitless attempts, he succeeded in wounding a magnificent bird. To say that he risked his life twenty times before reaching it, is but the truth; but he managed so well, that the creature joined the honeycakes in his bag. We were now obliged to descend towards the shore, the crest becoming impracticable. Above us the crater seemed to gape like the mouth of a well. From this place the sky could be clearly seen, and clouds, dissipated by the west wind, leaving behind them, even on the summit of the mountain, their misty remnants—certain proof that they were only moderately high, for the volcano did not rise more than eight hundred feet above the level of the ocean. Half an hour after the Canadian's last exploit we had regained the inner shore. Here the flora was represented by large carpets of marine crystal, a little umbelliferous plant very good to pickle, which also bears the name of pierce-stone, and sea-fennel. Conseil gathered some bundles of it. As to the fauna, it might be counted by thousands of crustacea of all sorts, lobsters, crabs, palaemons, spider crabs, chameleon shrimps, and a large number of shells, rockfish and limpets. Three-quarters of an hour later, we had finished our circuitous walk, and were on board. The crew had just finished loading the sodium, and the *Nautilus* could have left that instant. But Captain Nemo gave no order. Did he wish to wait until night, and leave the submarine passage secretly? Perhaps so. Whatever it might be, the next day, the *Nautilus*, having left its port, steered clear of all land at a few yards beneath the waves of the Atlantic.

Chapter XI

The Sargasso Sea

That day the *Nautilus* crossed a singular part of the Atlantic Ocean. No one can be ignorant of the existence of a current of warm water, known by the name of the Gulf Stream. After leaving the Gulf of

Florida, we went in the direction of Spitzbergen. But before entering the Gulf of Mexico, about the forty-fifth degree of north latitude, this current divides into two arms, the principal one going towards the coast of Ireland and Norway, whilst the second bends to the south about the height of the Azores; then, touching the African shore, and describing a lengthened oval, returns to the Antilles. This second arm—it is rather a collar than an arm—surround with its circles of warm water that portion of the cold, quiet, immovable ocean called the Sargasso Sea, a perfect lake in the open Atlantic: it takes no less than three years for the great current to pass round it. Such was the region the *Nautilus* was now visiting, a perfect meadow, a close carpet of seaweed, fucus, and tropical berries, so thick and so compact, that the stem of a vessel could hardly tear its way through it. And Captain Nemo, not wishing to entangle his screw in this herbaceous mass, kept some yards beneath the surface of the waves. The name Sargasso comes from the Spanish word "sargazzo," which signified kelp. This kelp or varech, or berry-plant, is the principal formation of this immense bank. And this is the reason, according to the learned Maury, the author of "The Physical Geography of the Globe," why these hydrophytes unite in the peaceful basin of the Atlantic. The only explanation which can be given, he says, seems to me to result from the experience known to all the world. Place in a vase some fragments of cork or other floating body, and give to the water in the vase a circular movement, the scattered fragments will unite in a group in the centre of the liquid surface, that is to say, in the part least agitated. In the phenomenon we are considering, the Atlantic is the vase, the Gulf Stream the circular current, and the Sargasso Sea the central point at which the floating bodies unite.

I share Maury's opinion, and I was able to study the phenomenon in the very midst, where vessels rarely penetrate. Above us floated products of all kinds, heaped up among these brownish plants; trunks of trees torn from the Andes or the Rocky Mountains, and floated by the Amazon or the Mississippi; numerous wrecks, remains of keels, or ships' bottoms, side planks stove in, and so weighted with shells and barnacles, that they could not again rise to the surface. And time will one day justify Maury's other opinion, that these substances thus accumulated for ages, will become petrified by the action of the water, and will then form inexhaustible coal-mines—a precious reserve prepared by far-seeing Nature for the moment when men shall have exhausted the mines of continents.

In the midst of this inextricable mass of plants and seaweed, I noticed some charming pink halcyons and actiniae, with their long tentacles trailing after them; medusae, green, red, and blue, and the great rhyostoms of Cuvier, the large umbrella of which was bordered and festooned with violet.

All the day of the 22nd of February we passed in the Sargasso Sea, where such fish as are partial to marine plants and fuci find abundant nourishment. The next, the ocean had returned to its accustomed aspect. From this time for nineteen days, from the 23rd of February to the 12th of March, the *Nautilus* kept in the middle of the Atlantic, carrying us at a constant speed of a hundred leagues in twenty-four hours. Captain Nemo evidently intended accomplishing his submarine programme, and I imagined that he intended, after doubling Cape Horn, to return to the Australian seas of the Pacific. Ned Land had cause for fear. In these large seas, void of islands, we could not attempt to leave the boat. Nor had we any means of opposing Captain Nemo's will. Our only course was to submit; but what we could neither gain by force nor cunning, I liked to think might be obtained by persuasion. This voyage ended, would he not consent to restore our liberty, under an oath never to reveal his existence?—an oath of honour which we should have religiously kept. But we must consider that delicate question with the Captain. But was I free to claim this liberty? Had he not himself said from the beginning, in the firmest manner, that the secret of his life exacted from him our lasting imprisonment on board the *Nautilus*? And would not my four months' silence appear to him a tacit acceptance of our situation? And would not a return to the subject result in raising suspicions which might be hurtful to our projects, if at some future time a favourable opportunity offered to return to them?

During the nineteen days mentioned above, no incident of any note happened to signalise our voyage. I saw little of the Captain; he was at work. In the library I often found his books left open, especially those on Natural History. My work on submarine depths, conned over by him, was covered with marginal notes, often contradicting my theories and systems; but the Captain contented himself with thus purging my work; it was very rare for him to discuss it with me. Sometimes I heard the melancholy tones of his organ; but only at night, in the midst of the deepest obscurity, when the *Nautilus* slept upon the deserted ocean. During this part of our voyage we sailed whole days on the surface of the waves. The sea seemed abandoned. A few sailingvessels, on the road to India, were making for the Cape of Good Hope. One day we were followed by the boats of a whaler, who, no doubt, took us for some enormous whale of great price; but Captain Nemo did not wish the worthy fellows to lose their time and trouble, so ended the chase by plunging under the water. Our navigation continued until the 13th of March; that day the *Nautilus* was employed in taking soundings, which greatly interested me. We had then made about 13,000 leagues since our departure from the high seas of the Pacific. The bearings gave us 45° 37' south latitude, and 37° 53' west longitude. It was the same water in which Captain Denham of the *Herald* sounded 7000 fathoms without finding the bottom. There, too, Lieutenant Parker, of the American frigate *Congress*, could not touch the bottom with 15,140 fathoms. Captain Nemo intended seeking the bottom of the ocean by a diagonal sufficiently lengthened by means of lateral planes placed at an angle of forty-five degrees with the water-line of the *Nautilus*. Then the screw set to work at its maximum speed, its four blades beating the waves with indescribable force. Under this powerful pressure the hull of the *Nautilus* quivered like a sonorous chord, and sank regularly under the water.

At 7000 fathoms I saw some blackish tops rising from the midst of the waters; but these summits might belong to high mountains like the Himalayas or Mount Blanc, even higher; and the depth of the abyss remained incalculable. The *Nautilus* descended still lower, in spite of the great pressure. I felt the steel plates tremble at the fastenings of the bolts; its bars bent, its partitions groaned; the windows of the saloon seemed to curve under the pressure of the waters. And this firm structure would doubtless have yielded, if, as its Captain had said, it had not been capable of resistance like a solid block. In skirting the declivity of these rocks, lost under the water, I still saw some shells, some serpulae and spinorbes, still living, and some specimens of asteriads. But soon this last representative of animal life disappeared; and at the depth of more than three leagues, the *Nautilus* had passed the limits of submarine existence, even as a balloon does when it rises above the respirable atmosphere. We had attained a depth of 16,000 yards (four leagues), and the sides of the *Nautilus* then bore a pressure of 1600 atmospheres, that is to say, 3200 pounds to each square two-fifths of an inch of its surface.

"What a situation to be in!" I exclaimed. "To overrun these deep regions where man has never trod! Look, Captain, look at these magnificent rocks, these uninhabited grottoes, these lowest receptacles of the globe, where life is no longer possible! What unknown sights are here! Why should we be unable to preserve a remembrance of them?"

"Would you like to carry away more than the remembrance?" said Captain Nemo.

"What do you mean by those words?"

"I mean to say that nothing is easier than to take a photographic view of this submarine region."

I had not time to express my surprise at this new proposition, when, at Captain Nemo's call, an objective was brought into the saloon. Through the widely opened panel, the liquid mass was bright with electricity, which was distributed with such uniformity, that not a shadow, not a gradation, was to be seen in our manufactured light. The *Nautilus* remained motionless, the force of its screw subdued by the inclination of its planes: the instrument was propped on the bottom of the oceanic site, and in a few seconds we had obtained a perfect negative. I here give the positive, from which may be seen those primitive rocks, which have never looked upon the light of heaven; that lowest granite which forms the foundation of the globe; those deep grottoes, woven in the stony mass whose outlines were of such sharpness, and the border lines of which is marked in black, as if done by the brush of some Flemish artist. Beyond that again a horizon of mountains, an admirable undulating line, forming the prospective of the landscape. I cannot describe the effect of these smooth, black, polished rocks, without moss, without a spot, and of strange forms, standing solidly on the sandy carpet, which sparkled under the jets of our electric light.

But the operation being over, Captain Nemo said, "Let us go up; we must not abuse our position, nor expose the *Nautilus* too long to such great pressure."

"Go up again!" I exclaimed.

"Hold well on."

I had not time to understand why the Captain cautioned me thus, when I was thrown forward on to the carpet. At a signal from the Captain, its screw was shipped, and its blades raised vertically; the *Nautilus* shot into the air like a balloon, rising with stunning rapidity, and cutting the mass of waters with a sonorous agitation. Nothing was visible; and in four minutes it had shot through the four leagues which separated it from the ocean, and after emerging like a flying-fish, fell, making the waves rebound to an enormous height.

Chapter XII
Cachalots and Whales

During the nights of the 13th and 14th of March, the *Nautilus* returned to its southerly course. I fancied that, when on a level with Cape Horn, he would turn the helm westward, in order to beat the Pacific seas, and so complete the tour of the world. He did nothing of the kind, but continued on his way to the southern regions. Where was he going to? To the pole? It was madness! I began to think that the Captain's temerity justified Ned Land's fears. For some time past the Canadian had not spoken to me of his projects of flight; he was less communicative, almost silent. I could see that this lengthened imprisonment was weighing upon him, and I felt that rage was burning within him. When he met the Captain, his eyes lit up with suppressed anger; and I feared that his natural violence would lead him into some extreme. That day, the 14th of March, Conseil and he came to me in my room. I inquired the cause of their visit.

"A simple question to ask you, sir," replied the Canadian.

"Speak, Ned."

"How many men are there on board the *Nautilus*, do you think?"

"I cannot tell, my friend."

"I should say that its working does not require a large crew."

"Certainly, under existing conditions, ten men, at the most, ought to be enough."

"Well, why should there be any more?"

"Why?" I replied, looking fixedly at Ned Land, whose meaning was easy to guess. "Because," I added, "if my surmises are correct, and if I have well understood the Captain's existence, the *Nautilus* is not only a vessel: it is also a place of refuge for those who, like its commander, have broken every tie upon earth."

"Perhaps so," said Conseil; "but, in any case, the *Nautilus* can only contain a certain number of men. Could not you, sir, estimate their maximum?"

"How, Conseil?"

"By calculation; given the size of the vessel, which you know, sir, and consequently the quantity of air it contains, knowing also how much each man expends at a breath, and comparing these results with the fact that the *Nautilus* is obliged to go to the surface every twenty-four hours."

Conseil had not finished the sentence before I saw what he was driving at.

"I understand," said I; "but that calculation, though simple enough, can give but a very uncertain result."

"Never mind," said Ned Land, urgently.

"Here it is, then," said I. "In one hour each man consumes the oxygen contained in twenty gallons of air; and in twenty-four, that contained in 480 gallons. We must, therefore, find how many times 480 gallons of air the *Nautilus* contains."

"Just so," said Conseil.

"Or," I continued, "the size of the *Nautilus* being 1500 tons; and one ton holding 200 gallons, it contains 300,000 gallons of air, which, divided by 480, gives a quotient of 625. Which means to say, strictly speaking, that the air contained in the *Nautilus* would suffice for 625 men for twenty-four hours."

"Six hundred and twenty-five!" repeated Ned.

"But remember, that all of us, passengers, sailors, and officers included, would not form a tenth part of that number."

"Still too many for three men," murmured Conseil.

The Canadian shook his head, passed his hand across his forehead, and left the room without answering.

"Will you allow me to make one observation, sir?" said Conseil. "Poor Ned is longing for everything that he cannot have. His past life is always present to him; everything that we are forbidden he regrets.

His head is full of old recollections. And we must understand him. What has he to do here? Nothing; he is not learned like you, sir; and has not the same taste for the beauties of the sea that we have. He would risk everything to be able to go once more into a tavern in his own country."

Certainly the monotony on board must seem intolerable to the Canadian, accustomed as he was to a life of liberty and activity. Events were rare which could arouse him to any show of spirit; but that day an event did happen which recalled the bright days of the harpooner. About eleven in the morning, being on the surface of the ocean, the *Nautilus* fell in with a troop of whales—an encounter which did not astonish me, knowing that these creatures, hunted to the death, had taken refuge in high latitudes.

We were seated on the platform, with a quiet sea. The month of October in those latitudes gave us some lovely autumnal days. It was the Canadian—he could not be mistaken —who signalled a whale on the eastern horizon. Looking attentively one might see its black back rise and fall with the waves five miles from the *Nautilus*.

"Ah!" exclaimed Ned Land, "if I was on board a whaler now such a meeting would give me pleasure. It is one of large size. See with what strength its blow-holes throw up columns of air and steam! Confound it, why am I bound to these steel plates?"

"What, Ned," said I, "you have not forgotten your old ideas of fishing?"

"Can a whale-fisher ever forget his old trade, sir? Can he ever tire of the emotions caused by such a chase?"

"You have never fished in these seas, Ned?"

"Never, sir; in the northern only, and as much in Behring as in Davis Straits."

"Then the southern whale is still unknown to you. It is the Greenland whale you have hunted up to this time, and that would not risk passing through the warm waters of the equator. Whales are localised, according to their kinds, in certain seas which they never leave. And if one of these creatures went from Behring to Davis Straits, it must be simply because there is a passage from one sea to the other, either on the American or the Asiatic side."

"In that case, as I have never fished in these seas, I do not know the kind of whale frequenting them."

"I have told you, Ned."

"A greater reason for making their acqaintance," said Conseil.

"Look! look!" exclaimed the Canadian, "they approach; they aggravate me; they know that I cannot get at them!"

Ned stamped his feet. His hand trembled, as he grasped an imaginary harpoon.

"Are these cetacea as large as those of the northern seas?" asked he.

"Very nearly, Ned."

"Because I have seen large whales, sir, whales measuring a hundred feet. I have even been told that those of Hullamoch and Umgallick, of the Aleutian Islands, are sometimes a hundred and fifty feet long."

"That seems to me exaggeration. These creatures are only balaenopterons, provided with dorsal fins; and, like the cachalots, are generally much smaller than the Greenland whale."

"Ah!" exclaimed the Canadian, whose eyes had never left the ocean, "they are coming nearer; they are in the same water as the *Nautilus!*"

Then returning to the conversation, he said—

"You spoke of the cachalot as a small creature. I have heard of gigantic ones. They are intelligent cetacea. It is said of some that they cover themselves with seaweed and fucus, and then are taken for islands. People encamp upon them, and settle there; light a fire,"—

"And build houses," said Conseil.

"Yes, joker," said Ned Land. "And one fine day the creature plunges, carrying with it all the inhabitants to the bottom of the sea."

"Something like the travels of Sinbad the Sailor," I replied, laughing.

"Ah!" suddenly exclaimed Ned Land, "it is not one whale; there are ten,—there are twenty,—it is a whole troop! And I not able to do anything! hand and feet tied!"

"But, friend Ned," said Conseil, "why do you not ask Captain Nemo's permission to chase them?"

Conseil had not finished his sentence when Ned Land had lowered himself through the panel to seek the Captain. A few minutes afterwards the two appeared together on the platform.

Captain Nemo watched the troop of cetacea playing on the waters about a mile from the *Nautilus*.

"They are southern whales," said he; "there goes the fortune of a whole fleet of whalers."

"Well, sir," asked the Canadian, "can I not chase them, if only to remind me of my old trade of harpooner?"

"And to what purpose?" replied Captain Nemo; "only to destroy! We have nothing to do with whale-oil on board."

"But, sir," continued the Canadian, "in the Red Sea you allowed us to follow the dugong."

"Then it was to procure fresh meat for my crew. Here it would be killing for killing's sake. I know that is a privilege reserved for man, but I do not approve of such murderous pastime. In destroying the southern whale (like the Greenland whale, an inoffensive creature), your traders do a culpable action, Master Land. They have already depopulated the whole of Baffin's Bay, and are annihilating a class of useful animals. Leave the unfortunate cetacea alone. They have plenty of natural enemies, cachalots, swordfish, and sawfish, without *your* troubling them."

The Captain was right. The barbarous and inconsiderate greed of these fishermen will one day cause the disappearance of the last whale in the ocean. Ned Land whistled "Yankeedoodle" between his teeth, thrust his hands into his pockets, and turned his back upon us. But Captain Nemo watched the troop of cetacea, and addressing me, said—

"I was right in saying that whales had natural enemies enough, without counting man. These will have plenty to do before long. Do you see, M. Aronnax, about eight miles to leeward, those blackish moving points?"

"Yes, Captain," I replied.

"Those are cachalots,—terrible animals, which I have sometimes met in troops of two or three hundred. As to *those*, they are cruel mischievous creatures; they would be right in exterminating them."

The Canadian turned quickly at the last words.

"Well, Captain," said he, "it is still time, in the interest of the whales."

"It is useless to expose one's self, Professor. The *Nautilus* will disperse them. It is armed with a steel spur as good as Master Land's harpoon, I imagine."

The Canadian did not put himself out enough to shrug his shoulders. Attack cetacea with blows of a spur! Who had ever heard of such a thing?

"Wait, M. Aronnax," said Captain Nemo. "We will show you something you have never yet seen. We have no pity for these ferocious creatures. They are nothing but mouth and teeth."

Mouth and teeth! No one could better describe the macrocephalous cachalot, which is sometimes more than seventy-five feet long. Its enormous head occupies one-third of its entire body. Better armed than the whale, whose upper jaw is furnished only with whalebone, it is supplied with twenty-five large tusks, about eight inches long, cylindrical and conical at the top, each weighing two pounds. It is in the upper part of this enormous head, in great cavities divided by cartilages, that is to be found from six to eight hundred pounds of that precious oil called spermaceti. The cachalot is a disagreeable creature, more tadpole than fish, according to Fredol's description. It is badly formed, the whole of its left side being (if we may say it), a "failure," and being only able to see with its right eye. But the formidable troop was nearing us. They had seen the whales and were preparing to attack them. One could judge beforehand that the cachalots would be victorious, not only because they were better built for attack than their inoffensive adversaries, but also because they could remain longer under water without coming to the surface. There was only just time to go to the help of the whales. The *Nautilus* went under water. Conseil, Ned Land, and I took our places before the window in the saloon, and Captain Nemo joined the pilot in his cage to work his apparatus as an engine of destruction. Soon I felt the beatings of the screw quicken, and our speed increased. The battle between the cachalots and the whales had already begun when the *Nautilus* arrived. They did not at first show any fear at the sight of this new monster joining in the conflict. But they soon had to guard against its blows. What a battle! The *Nautilus* was nothing but a formidable harpoon, brandished by the hand of its captain. It hurled itself against the fleshy mass, passing through from one part to the other, leaving behind it two quivering halves of the animal. It could not feel the formidable blows from their tails upon its sides, nor the shock which it produced itself, much more. One cachalot killed, it ran at the next, tacked on the spot that it might not miss its prey, going forwards and backwards, answering to its helm, plunging when the cetacean dived into the deep waters, coming up with it when it returned to the surface, striking it front or sideways, cutting or tearing in all directions, and at any pace, piercing it with its terrible spur. What carnage! What a noise on the surface of the waves! What sharp hissing, and what snorting peculiar to these enraged animals! In the midst of these waters, generally so peaceful, their tails made perfect billows. For one hour this wholesale massacre continued, from which the cachalots could not escape. Several times ten or twelve united tried to crush the *Nautilus* by their weight. From the window we could see their enormous mouths studded with tusks, and their formidable eyes. Ned Land could not contain himself, he threatened and swore at them. We could feel them clinging to our vessel like dogs worrying a wild boar in a copse. But the *Nautilus*, working its screw, carried them here and there, or to the upper levels of the ocean, without caring for their enormous weight, nor the powerful strain on the vessel. At length, the mass of cachalots broke up, the waves became quiet, and I felt that we were rising to the surface. The panel opened, and we hurried on to the platform. The sea was covered with mutilated bodies. A formidable explosion would not have divided and torn this fleshy mass with more violence. We were floating amid gigantic bodies, bluish on the back and white underneath, covered with enormous protuberances. Some terrified cachalots were flying towards the horizon. The waves were dyed red for several miles, and the *Nautilus* floated in a sea of blood. Captain Nemo joined us.

"Well, Master Land?" said he.

"Well, sir," replied the Canadian, whose enthusiasm had somewhat calmed; "it is a terrible spectacle, certainly. But I am not a butcher. I am a hunter, and I call this a butchery."

"It is a massacre of mischievous creatures," replied the Captain; "and the *Nautilus* is not a butcher's knife."

"I like my harpoon better," said the Canadian.

"Every one to his own," answered the Captain, looking fixedly at Ned Land.

I feared he would commit some act of violence, which would end in sad consequences. But his anger was turned by the sight of a whale which the *Nautilus* had just come up with. The creature had not quite escaped from the cachalot's teeth. I recognised the southern whale by its flat head, which is entirely black. Anatomically, it is distinguished from the white whale and the North Cape whale by the seven cervical vertebrae, and it has two more ribs than its congeners. The unfortunate cetacean was lying on its side, riddled with holes from the bites, and quite dead. From its mutilated fin still hung a young whale which it could not save from the massacre. Its open mouth let the water flow in and out, murmuring like the waves breaking on the shore. Captain Nemo steered close to the corpse of the creature. Two of his men mounted its side, and I saw, not without surprise, that they were drawing from its breasts all the milk which they contained, that is to say, about two or three tons. The Captain offered me a cup of the milk, which was still warm. I could not help showing my repugnance to the drink; but he assured me that it was excellent, and not to be distinguished from cow's milk. I tasted it, and was of his opinion. It was a useful reserve to us, for in the shape of salt butter or cheese it would form an agreeable variety from our ordinary food. From that day I noticed with uneasiness that Ned Land's ill-will towards Captain Nemo increased, and I resolved to watch the Canadian's gestures closely.

Chapter XIII
The Iceberg

The *Nautilus* was steadily pursuing its southerly course, following the fiftieth meridian with considerable speed. Did he wish to reach the pole? I did not think so, for every attempt to reach that point had hitherto failed. Again the season was far advanced, for in the antarctic regions, the 13th of March corresponds with the 13th of September of northern regions which begin at the equinoctial season. On the 14th of March I saw floating ice in latitude 55°, merely pale bits of debris from twenty to twenty-five feet long, forming banks over which the sea curled. The *Nautilus* remained on the surface of the ocean. Ned Land, who had fished in the arctic seas, was familiar with its icebergs; but Conseil and I admired them for the first time. In the atmosphere towards the southern horizon stretched a white dazzling band. English whalers have given it the name of "ice blink." However thick the clouds may be, it is always visible, and announces the presence of an ice pack or bank. Accordingly, larger blocks soon appeared, whose brilliancy changed with the caprices of the fog. Some of these masses showed green veins, as if long undulating lines had been traced with sulphate of copper; others resembled enormous amethysts with the light shining through them. Some reflected the light of day upon a thousand crystal facets. Others shaded with vivid calcareous reflections resembled a perfect town of marble. The more we neared the south, the more these floating islands increased both in number and importance.

At the sixtieth degree of latitude, every pass had disappeared. But seeking carefully, Captain Nemo soon found a narrow opening, through which he boldly slipped, knowing, however, that it would close behind him. Thus, guided by this clever hand, the *Nautilus* passed through all the ice with a precision which quite charmed Conseil; icebergs or mountains, icefields or smooth plains, seeming to have no limits, drift ice or floating ice packs, or plains broken up, called *Palchs* when they are circular, and streams when they are made up of long strips. The temperature was very low; the thermometer exposed to the air marked two or three degrees below zero, but we were warmly clad with fur, at the expense of the sea-bear and seal. The interior of the *Nautilus*, warmed regularly by its electric apparatus, defied the most intense cold. Besides, it would only have been necessary to go some yards beneath the waves to find a more bearable temperature. Two months earlier we should have had perpetual daylight in these latitudes; but already we had three or four hours night, and by and by there would be six months of darkness in these circumpolar regions. On the 15th of March we were in the latitude of New Shetland and South Orkney. The Captain told me that formerly numerous tribes of seal inhabited them; but that English and American whalers, in their rage for destruction, massacred both old and young; thus where there was once life and animation, they had left silence and death.

About eight o'clock on the morning of the 16th of March, the *Nautilus*, following the fifty-fifth meridian, cut the antarctic polar circle. Ice surrounded us on all sides, and closed the horizon. But Captain Nemo went from one opening to another, still going higher. I cannot express my astonishment at the beauties of these new regions. The ice took most surprising forms. Here the grouping formed an oriental town, with innumerable mosques and minarets; there a fallen city thrown to the earth, as it were, by some convulsion of nature. The whole aspect was constantly changed by the oblique rays of the sun, or lost in the greyish fog amidst hurricanes of snow. Detonations and falls were heard on all sides, great overthrows of icebergs, which altered the whole landscape like a diorama. Often seeing no exit, I thought we were definitively prisoners; but instinct guiding him at the slightest indication, Captain Nemo would discover a new pass. He was never mistaken when he saw the thin threads of bluish water trickling along the ice-fields; and I had no doubt that he had already ventured into the midst of these antarctic seas before. On the 16th of March, however, the ice-fields absolutely blocked our road. It was not the iceberg itself, as yet, but vast fields cemented by the cold. But this obstacle could not stop Captain Nemo: he hurled himself against it with frightful violence. The *Nautilus* entered the brittle mass like a wedge, and split it with frightful crackings. It was the battering ram of the ancients hurled by infinite strength. The ice, thrown high in the air, fell like hail around us. By its own power of impulsion our apparatus made a canal for itself; sometimes carried away by its own impetus it lodged on the ice-field, crushing it with its weight, and sometimes buried beneath it, dividing it by a simple pitching movement, producing large rents in it. Violent gales assailed us at this time, accompanied by thick fogs, through which, from one end of the platform to the other, we could see nothing. The wind blew sharply from all points of the compass, and the snow lay in such hard heaps that we had to break it with blows of a pickaxe. The temperature was always at five degrees below zero; every outward part of the *Nautilus* was covered with ice. A rigged vessel could never have worked its way there, for all the rigging would have been entangled in the blocked-up gorges. A vessel without sails, with electricity for its motive power, and wanting no coal, could alone brave such high latitudes. At length, on the 18th of March, after many useless assaults, the *Nautilus* was positively blocked. It was no longer either streams, packs, or ice-fields, but an interminable and immovable barrier, formed by mountains soldered together.

"An iceberg!" said the Canadian to me.

I knew that to Ned Land, as well as to all other navigators who had preceded us, this was an inevitable obstacle. The sun appearing for an instant at noon, Captain Nemo took an observation as near as possible, which gave our situation at 51° 30' longitude and 67° 39' of south latitude. We had advanced one degree more in this antarctic region. Of the liquid surface of the sea there was no longer a glimpse. Under the spur of the *Nautilus* lay stretched a vast plain, entangled with confused blocks. Here and there sharp points, and slender needles rising to a height of 200 feet; further on a steep shore, hewn as it were with an axe, and clothed with greyish tints; huge mirrors, reflecting a few rays of sunshine, half drowned in the fog. And over this desolate face of Nature a stern silence reigned, scarcely broken by the flapping of the wings of petrels and puffins. Everything was frozen—even the noise. The *Nautilus* was then obliged to stop in its adventurous course amid these fields of ice. In spite of our efforts, in spite of the powerful means employed to break up the ice, the *Nautilus* remained immovable. Generally, when we can proceed no further, we have return still open to us; but here return was as impossible as advance, for every pass had closed behind us; and for the few moments when we were stationary, we were likely to be entirely blocked, which did, indeed, happen about two o'clock in the afternoon, the fresh ice forming around its sides with astonishing rapidity. I was obliged to admit that Captain Nemo was more than imprudent. I was on the platform at that moment. The Captain had been observing our situation for some time past, when he said to me—

"Well, sir, what do you think of this?"

"I think that we are caught, Captain."

"So, M. Aronnax, you really think that the *Nautilus* cannot disengage itself?"

"With difficulty, Captain; for the season is already too far advanced for you to reckon on the breaking up of the ice."

"Ah! sir," said Captain Nemo, in an ironical tone, "you will always be the same. You see nothing but difficulties and obstacles. I affirm that not only can the *Nautilus* disengage itself, but also that it can go further still."

"Further to the south?" I asked, looking at the Captain.

"Yes, sir; it shall go to the pole."

"To the pole!" I exclaimed, unable to repress a gesture of incredulity.

"Yes," replied the Captain, coldly, "to the antarctic pole,—to that unknown point from whence springs every meridian of the globe. *You* know whether I can do as I please with the *Nautilus!*"

Yes, I knew that. I knew that this man was bold, even to rashness. But to conquer those obstacles which bristled round the south pole, rendering it more inaccessible than the north, which had not yet been reached by the boldest navigators,—was it not a mad enterprise, one which only a maniac would have conceived? It then came into my head to ask Captain Nemo if he had ever discovered that pole which had never yet been trodden by a human creature?

"No, sir," he replied; "but we will discover it together. Where others have failed, *I* will not fail. I have never yet led my *Nautilus* so far into southern seas; but, I repeat, it shall go further yet."

"I can well believe you, Captain," said I, in a slightly ironical tone. "I believe you! Let us go ahead! There are no obstacles for us! Let us smash this iceberg! Let us blow it up; and if it resists, let us give the *Nautilus* wings to fly over it!"

"Over it, sir!" said Captain Nemo, quietly; "no, not *over* it, but *under* it!"

"Under it!" I exclaimed, a sudden idea of the Captain's projects flashing upon my mind. I understood; the wonderful qualities of the *Nautilus* were going to serve us in this super-human enterprise.

"I see we are beginning to understand one another, sir," said the Captain, half smiling. "You begin to see the possibility—I should say the success—of this attempt. That which is impossible for an ordinary vessel, is easy to the *Nautilus*. If a continent lies before the pole, it must stop before the continent; but if, on the contrary, the pole is washed by open sea, it will go even to the pole."

"Certainly," said I, carried away by the Captain's reasoning; "if the surface of the sea is solidified by the ice, the lower depths are free by the providential law which has placed the maximum of density of the waters of the ocean one degree higher than freezing point; and, if I am not mistaken, the portion of this iceberg which is above the water, is as four to one to that which is below."

"Very nearly, sir; for one foot of iceberg above the sea there are three below it. If these ice mountains are not more than 300 feet above the surface, they are not more than 900 beneath. And what are 900 feet to the *Nautilus*?"

"Nothing, sir."

"It could even seek at greater depths that uniform temperature of sea-water, and there brave with impunity the thirty or forty degrees of surface cold."

"Just so, sir—just so," I replied, getting animated.

"The only difficulty," continued Captain Nemo, "is that of remaining several days without renewing our provision of air."

"Is that all? The *Nautilus* has vast reservoirs; we can fill them, and they will supply us with all the oxygen we want."

"Well thought of, M. Aronnax," replied the Captain, smiling. "But not wishing you to accuse me of rashness, I will first give you all my objections."

"Have you any more to make?"

"Only one. It is possible, if the sea exists at the south pole, that it may be covered; and, consequently, we shall be unable to come to the surface."

"Good, sir! but do you forget that the *Nautilus* is armed with a powerful spur, and could we not send it diagonally against these fields of ice, which would open at the shock."

"Ah! sir, you are full of ideas to-day."

"Besides, Captain," I added, enthusiastically, "why should we not find the sea open at the south pole as well as at the north? The frozen poles and the poles of the earth do not coincide, either in the southern or in the northern regions; and, until it is proved to the contrary, we may suppose either a continent or an ocean free from ice at these two points of the globe."

"I think so too, M. Aronnax," replied Captain Nemo. "I only wish you to observe that, after having made so many objections to my project, you are now crushing me with arguments in its favour!"

The preparations for this audacious attempt now began. The powerful pumps of the *Nautilus* were working air into the reservoirs and storing it at high pressure. About four o'clock, Captain Nemo announced the closing of the panels on the platform. I threw one last look at the massive iceberg which we were going to cross. The weather was clear, the atmosphere pure enough, the cold very great, being twelve degrees below zero; but the wind having gone down, this temperature was not so unbearable. About ten men mounted the sides of the *Nautilus*, armed with pickaxes to break the ice around the vessel, which was soon free. The operation was quickly performed, for the fresh ice was still very thin. We all went below. The usual reservoirs were filled with the newly liberated water, and the *Nautilus* soon descended. I had taken my place with Conseil in the saloon; through the open window we could see the lower beds of the Southern Ocean. The thermometer went up, the needle of the compass deviated on the dial. At about 900 feet, as Captain Nemo had foreseen, we were floating beneath the undulating bottom of the iceberg. But the *Nautilus* went lower still—it went to the depth of four hundred fathoms. The temperature of the water at the surface showed twelve degrees, it was now only eleven; we had gained two. I need not say the temperature of the *Nautilus* was raised by its heating apparatus to a much higher degree; every manoeuvre was accomplished with wonderful precision.

"We shall pass it, if you please, sir," said Conseil.

"I believe we shall," I said, in a tone of firm conviction.

In this open sea, the *Nautilus* had taken its course direct to the pole, without leaving the fifty-second meridian. From 67° 30' to 90°, twenty-two degrees and a half of latitude remained to travel; that is, about five hundred leagues. The *Nautilus* kept up a mean speed of twenty-six miles an hour—the speed of an express train. If that was kept up, in forty hours we should reach the pole.

For a part of the night the novelty of the situation kept us at the window. The sea was lit with the electric lantern; but it was deserted; fishes did not sojourn in these imprisoned waters; they only found there a passage to take them from the antarctic ocean to the open polar sea. Our pace was rapid; we could feel it by the quivering of the long steel body. About two in the morning, I took some hours' repose, and Conseil did the same. In crossing the waist I did not meet Captain Nemo: I supposed him to be in the pilot's cage. The next morning, the 19th of March, I took my post once more in the saloon. The electric log told me that the speed of the *Nautilus* had been slackened. It was then going towards the surface; but prudently emptying its reservoirs very slowly. My heart beat fast. Were we going to emerge and regain the open polar atmosphere? No! A shock told me that the *Nautilus* had struck the bottom of the iceberg, still very thick, judging from the deadened sound. We had indeed "struck," to use a sea expression, but in an inverse sense, and at a thousand feet deep. This would give three thousand feet of ice above us; one thousand being above the water-mark. The iceberg was then higher than at its borders—not a very reassuring fact. Several times that day the *Nautilus* tried again, and every time it struck the wall which lay like a ceiling above it. Sometimes it met with but 900 yards, only 200 of which rose above the surface. It was twice the height it was when the *Nautilus* had gone under the waves. I carefully noted the different depths, and thus obtained a submarine profile of the cabin as it was developed under the water. That night no change had taken place in our situation. Still ice between four and five hundred yards in depth! It was evidently diminishing, but still what a thickness between us and the surface of the ocean! It was then eight. According to the daily custom on board the *Nautilus*, its air should have been renewed four hours ago; but I did not suffer much, although Captain Nemo had not yet made any demand upon his reserve of oxygen. My sleep was painful that night; hope and fear besieged me by turns: I rose several times. The groping of the *Nautilus* continued. About three in the morning, I noticed that the lower surface of the iceberg was only about fifty feet deep. One hundred and fifty feet now separated us from the surface of the waters. The iceberg was by degrees becoming an ice-field, the mountains a plain. My eyes never left the manometer. We were still rising diagonally to the surface, which sparkled under the electric rays. The iceberg was stretching both above and beneath into lengthening slopes; mile after mile it was getting thinner. At length, at six in the morning of that memorable day, the 19th of March, the door of the saloon opened, and Captain Nemo appeared.

"The sea is open!" was all he said.

Chapter XIV
The South Pole

I rushed on to the platform. Yes! the open sea, with but a few scattered pieces of ice and moving icebergs;—a long stretch of sea; a world of birds in the air, and myriads of fishes under those waters, which varied from intense blue to olive green, according to the bottom. The thermometer marked three degrees centigrade above zero. It was comparatively spring, shut up as we were behind this iceberg, whose lengthened mass was dimly seen on our northern horizon.

"Are we at the pole?" I asked the Captain, with a beating heart.

"I do not know," he replied. "At noon I will take our bearings."

"But will the sun show himself through this fog?" said I, looking at the leaden sky.

"However little it shows, it will be enough," replied the Captain.

About ten miles south, a solitary island rose to a height of one hundred and four yards. We made for it, but carefully, for the sea might be strewn with banks. One hour afterwards we had reached it, two hours later we had made the round of it. It measured four or five miles in circumference. A narrow canal separated it from a considerable stretch of land, perhaps a continent, for we could not see its limits. The existence of this land seemed to give some colour to Maury's hypothesis. The ingenious American has remarked, that between the south pole and the sixtieth parallel, the sea is covered with floating ice of enormous size, which is never met with in the North Atlantic. From this fact he has drawn the conclusion that the antarctic circle encloses considerable continents, as icebergs cannot form in open sea, but only on the coasts. According to these calculations, the mass of ice surrounding the southern pole forms a vast cap, the circumference of which must be, at least, 2500 miles. But the *Nautilus*, for fear of running aground, had stopped about three cables' length from a strand over which reared a superb heap of rocks. The boat was launched; the Captain, two of his men bearing instruments, Conseil, and myself, were in it. It was ten in the morning. I had not seen Ned Land. Doubtless the Canadian did not wish to admit the presence of the south pole. A few strokes of the oar brought us to the sand, where we ran ashore. Conseil was going to jump on to the land, when I held him back.

"Sir," said I to Captain Nemo, "to you belongs the honour of first setting foot on this land."

"Yes, sir," said the Captain; "and if I do not hesitate to tread this south pole, it is because, up to this time, no human being has left a trace there."

Saying this, he jumped lightly on to the sand. His heart beat with emotion. He climbed a rock, sloping to a little promontory, and there, with his arms crossed, mute and motionless, and with an eager look, he seemed to take possession of these southern regions. After five minutes passed in this ecstasy, he turned to us.

"When you like, sir."

I landed, followed by Conseil, leaving the two men in the boat. For a long way the soil was composed of a reddish, sandy stone, something like crushed brick, scoriae, streams of lava, and pumice stones. One could not mistake its volcanic origin. In some parts, slight curls of smoke emitted a sulphurous smell, proving that the internal fires had lost nothing of their expansive powers, though, having climbed a high acclivity, I could see no volcano for a radius of several miles. We know that in those antarctic countries, James Ross found two craters, the Erebus and Terror, in full activity, on the 167th meridian, latitude 77° 32'. The vegetation of this desolate continent seemed to me much restricted. Some lichens of the species unsnea melanoxantha lay upon the black rocks; some microscopic plants, rudimentary diatomas, a kind of cells, placed between two quartz shells; long purple and scarlet fucus, supported on little swimming bladders, which the breaking of the waves brought to the shore. These constituted the meagre flora of this region. The shore was strewn with molluscs, little mussels, limpets, smooth bucards in the shape of a heart, and particularly some clios, with oblong membraneous bodies, the head of which was formed of two rounded lobes. I also saw myriads of northern clios, one and a quarter inches long, of which a whale would swallow a whole world at a mouthful; and some charming pretopods, perfect sea-butterflies, animating the waters on the skirts of the shore.

Amongst other zoophytes, there appeared on the high bottoms some coral shrubs, of that kind which, according to James Ross, live in the antarctic seas to the depth of more than 1000 yards. Then there were little kingfishers, belonging to the species procellaria pelagica, as well as a large number of asteriads, peculiar to these climates, and starfish studding the soil. But where life abounded most was in the air. There thousands of birds fluttered and flew of all kinds, deafening us with their cries; others crowded the rocks, looking at us as we passed by without fear, and pressing familiarly close by our feet. There were penguins, so agile in the water, that they have been taken for the rapid bonitos, heavy and awkward as they are on the ground; they were uttering harsh cries, a large assembly, sober in gesture, but extravagant in clamour. Amongst the birds I noticed the chionis, of the long-legged family, as large as pigeons, white, with a short conical beak, and the eye framed in a red circle. Conseil laid in a stock of them, for these winged creatures, properly prepared, make an agreeable meat. Albatrosses passed in the air (the expanse of their wings being at least four yards and a half), and justly called the vultures of the ocean; some gigantic petrels, and some damiers, a kind of small duck, the under part of whose body is black and white; then there were a whole series of petrels, some whitish, with brown-bordered wings, others blue, peculiar to the antarctic seas, and so oily, as I told Conseil, that the inhabitants of the Ferroe Islands had nothing to do before lighting them, but to put a wick in.

"A little more," said Conseil, "and they would be perfect lamps! After that, we cannot expect Nature to have previously furnished them with wicks!"

About half a mile further on, the soil was riddled with ruff's nests, a sort of laying ground, out of which many birds were issuing. Captain Nemo had some hundreds hunted. They uttered a cry like the braying of an ass, were about the size of a goose, slate colour on the body, white beneath, with a yellow line round their throats; they allowed themselves to be killed with a stone, never trying to escape. But the fog did not lift, and at eleven the sun had not yet shown itself. Its absence made me uneasy. Without it no observations were possible. How then could we decide whether we had reached the pole? When I rejoined Captain Nemo, I found him leaning on a piece of rock, silently watching the sky. He seemed impatient and vexed. But what was to be done? This rash and powerful man could not command the sun as he did the sea. Noon arrived without the orb of day showing itself for an instant. We could not even tell its position behind the curtain of fog; and soon the fog turned to snow.

"Till to-morrow," said the Captain, quietly, and we returned to the *Nautilus* amid these atmospheric disturbances.

The tempest of snow continued till the next day. It was impossible to remain on the platform. From the saloon, where I was taking notes of incidents happening during this excursion to the polar continent, I could hear the cries of petrels and albatrosses sporting in the midst of this violent storm. The *Nautilus* did not remain motionless, but skirted the coast, advancing ten miles more to the south in the half light left by the sun as it skirted the edge of the horizon. The next day, the 20th of March, the snow had ceased. The cold was a little greater, the thermometer showing two degrees below zero. The fog was rising, and I hoped that that day our observation might be taken. Captain Nemo not having yet appeared, the boat took Conseil and myself to land. The soil was still of the same volcanic nature; everywhere were traces of lava, scoriae, and basalt; but the crater which had vomited them I could not see. Here, as lower down, this continent was alive with myriads of birds. But their rule was now divided with large troops of sea-mammals, looking at us with their soft eyes. There were several kinds of seals, some stretched on the earth, some on flakes of ice, many going in and out of the sea. They did not flee at our approach, never having had anything to do with man; and I reckoned that there were provisions there for hundreds of vessels.

"Sir," said Conseil, "will you tell me the names of these creatures?"

"They are seals and morses."

It was now eight in the morning. Four hours remained to us before the sun could be observed with advantage. I directed our steps towards a vast bay cut in the steep granite shore. There, I can aver that earth and ice were lost to sight by the numbers of sea-mammals covering them, and I involuntarily sought for old Proteus, the mythological shepherd who watched these immense flocks of Neptune. There were more seals than anything else, forming distinct groups, male and female, the father watching over his family, the mother suckling her little ones, some already strong enough to go a few steps. When they wished to change their place, they took little jumps, made by the contraction of their bodies, and helped awkwardly enough by their imperfect fin, which, as with the lamantin, their congener, forms a perfect forearm. I should say that, in the water, which is their element—the spine of these creatures is flexible—with smooth and close skin, and webbed feet, they swim admirably. In resting on the earth they take the most graceful attitudes. Thus the ancients, observing their soft and expressive looks, which cannot be surpassed by the most beautiful look a woman can give, their clear voluptuous eyes, their charming positions, and the poetry of their manners, metamorphosed them, the male into a triton and the female into a mermaid. I made Conseil notice the considerable development of the lobes of the brain in these interesting cetaceans. No mammal, except man, has such a quantity of cerebral matter; they are also capable of receiving a certain amount of education, are easily domesticated, and I think, with other naturalists, that, if properly taught, they would be of great service as fishing-dogs. The greater part of them slept on the rocks or on the sand. Amongst these seals, properly so called, which have no external ears (in which they differ from the otter, whose ears are prominent), I noticed several varieties of stenorhynchi about three yards long, with a white coat, bulldog heads, armed with teeth in both jaws, four incisors at the top and four at the bottom, and two large canine teeth in the shape of a "fleur de lis." Amongst them glided sea-elephants, a kind of seal, with short flexible trunks. The giants of this species measured twenty feet round, and ten yards and a half in length; but they did not move as we approached.

"These creatures are not dangerous?" asked Conseil.

"No; not unless you attack them. When they have to defend their young, their rage is terrible, and it is not uncommon for them to break the fishing-boats to pieces."

"They are quite right," said Conseil.

"I do not say they are not."

Two miles further on we were stopped by the promontory which shelters the bay from the southerly winds. Beyond it we heard loud bellowings such as a troop of ruminants would produce.

"Good!" said Conseil; "a concert of bulls!"

"No; a concert of morses."

"They are fighting!"

"They are either fighting or playing."

We now began to climb the blackish rocks, amid unforeseen stumbles, and over stones which the ice made slippery. More than once I rolled over at the expense of my loins. Conseil, more prudent or more steady, did not stumble, and helped me up, saying—

"If, sir, you would have the kindness to take wider steps, you would preserve your equilibrium better."

Arrived at the upper ridge of the promontory, I saw a vast white plain covered with morses. They were playing amongst themselves, and what we heard were bellowings of pleasure, not of anger.

As I passed near these curious animals, I could examine them leisurely, for they did not move. Their skins were thick and rugged, of a yellowish tint, approaching to red; their hair was short and scant.

Some of them were four yards and a quarter long. Quieter, and less timid than their congeners of the north, they did not, like them, place sentinels round the outskirts of their encampment. After examining this city of morses, I began to think of returning. It was eleven o'clock, and if Captain Nemo found the conditions favourable for observations, I wished to be present at the operation. We followed a narrow pathway running along the summit of the steep shore. At half-past eleven we had reached the place where we landed. The boat had run aground bringing the Captain. I saw him standing on a block of basalt, his instruments near him, his eyes fixed on the northern horizon, near which the sun was then describing a lengthened curve. I took my place beside him, and waited without speaking. Noon arrived, and, as before, the sun did not appear. It was a fatality. Observations were still want-ing. If not accomplished tomorrow, we must give up all idea of taking any. We were indeed exactly at the 20th of March. To-morrow, the 21st, would be the equinox; the sun would disappear behind the horizon for six months, and with its disappearance the long polar night would begin. Since the September equinox it had emerged from the north-ern horizon, rising by lengthened spirals up to the 21st of December. At this period, the summer solstice of the northern regions, it had begun to descend; and to-morrow was to shed its last rays upon them. I communicated my fears and observations to Captain Nemo.

"You are right, M. Aronnax," said he; "if to-morrow I cannot take the altitude of the sun, I shall not be able to do it for six months. But pre-cisely because chance has led me into these seas on the 21st of March, my bearings will be easy to take, if at twelve we can see the sun."

"Why, Captain?"

"Because then the orb of day describes such lengthened curves, that it is difficult to measure exactly its height above the horizon, and grave errors may be made with instruments."

"What will you do then?"

"I shall only use my chronometer," replied Captain Nemo. "If to-morrow, the 21st of March, the disc of the sun, allowing for refraction, is exactly cut by the northern horizon, it will show that I am at the south pole."

"Just so," said I. "But this statement is not mathematically correct, because the equinox does not necessarily begin at noon."

"Very likely, sir; but the error will not be a hundred yards, and we do not want more. Till to-morrow then!"

Captain Nemo returned on board. Conseil and I remained to survey the shore, observing and studying until five o'clock. Then I went to bed, not, however, without invoking, like the Indian, the favour of the radiant orb. The next day, the 21st of March, at five in the morning, I mounted the platform. I found Captain Nemo there.

"The weather is lightening a little," said he. "I have some hope. After breakfast we will go on shore, and choose a post for observation."

That point settled, I sought Ned Land. I wanted to take him with me. But the obstinate Canadian refused, and I saw that his taciturnity and his bad humour grew day by day. After all I was not sorry for his obstinacy under the circumstances. Indeed, there were too many seals on shore, and we ought not to lay such temptation in this unreflecting fisherman's way. Breakfast over, we went on shore. The *Nautilus* had gone some miles further up in the night. It was a whole league from the coast, above which reared a sharp peak about five hundred yards high. The boat took with me Captain Nemo, two men of the crew, and the instruments, which consisted of a chronometer, a telescope, and a barometer. While crossing, I saw numerous whales belonging to the three kinds peculiar to the southern seas; the whale, or the English "right whale," which has no dorsal fin; the "humpback," or balaeno-pteron, with reeved chest, and large whitish fins, which, in spite of its name, do not form wings; and the fin-back, of a yellowish brown, the liveliest of all the cetacea. This powerful creature is heard a long way off when he throws to a great height columns of air and vapour, which look like whirlwinds of smoke. These different mammals were disporting themselves in troops in the quiet waters; and I could see that this basin of the antarctic pole served as a place of refuge to the cetacea too closely tracked by the hunters. I also noticed long whitish lines of salpae, a kind of gregarious mollusc, and large medusae float-ing between the reeds.

At nine we landed; the sky was brightening, the clouds were fly-ing to the south, and the fog seemed to be leaving the cold surface of the waters. Captain Nemo went towards the peak, which he doubtless meant to be his observatory. It was a painful ascent over the sharp lava and the pumice stones, in an atmosphere often impregnated with a sulphurous smell from the smoking cracks. For a man unaccustomed to walk on land, the Captain climbed the steep slopes with an agility I never saw equalled, and which a hunter would have envied. We were two hours getting to the summit of this peak, which was half por-phyry and half basalt. From thence we looked upon a vast sea, which, towards the north, distinctly traced its boundary line upon the sky. At our feet lay fields of dazzling whiteness. Over our heads a pale azure, free from fog. To the north the disc of the sun seemed like a ball of fire, already horned by the cutting of the horizon. From the bosom of the water rose sheaves of liquid jets by hundreds. In the distance lay the *Nautilus* like a cetacean asleep on the water. Behind us, to the south and east, an immense country, and a chaotic heap of rocks and ice, the limits of which were not visible. On arriving at the summit, Captain Nemo carefully took the mean height of the barometer, for he would have to consider that in taking his observations. At a quarter to twelve, the sun, then seen only by refraction, looked like a golden disc shedding its last rays upon this deserted continent, and seas which never man had yet ploughed. Captain Nemo, furnished with a len-ticular glass, which, by means of a mirror, corrected the refraction, watched the orb sinking below the horizon by degrees, following a lengthened diagonal. I held the chronometer. My heart beat fast. If the disappearance of the half-disc of the sun coincided with twelve o'clock on the chronometer, we were at the pole itself.

"Twelve!" I exclaimed.

"The South Pole!" replied Captain Nemo, in a grave voice, hand-ing me the glass, which showed the orb cut in exactly equal parts by the horizon.

I looked at the last rays crowning the peak, and the shadows mounting by degrees up its slopes. At that moment Captain Nemo, resting with his hand on my shoulder, said—

"I, Captain Nemo, on this 21st day of March 1868, have reached the south pole on the ninetieth degree; and I take possession of this part of the globe, equal to one-sixth of the known continents."

"In whose name, Captain?"

"In my own, sir!"

Saying which, Captain Nemo unfurled a black banner, bearing an N in gold quartered on its bunting. Then turning towards the orb of day, whose last rays lapped the horizon of the sea, he exlaimed—

"Adieu, sun! Disappear, thou radiant orb! rest beneath this open sea, and let a night of six months spread its shadows over my new domains!"

Chapter XV

Accident or Incident?

The next day, the 22nd of March, at six in the morning, preparations for departure were begun. The last gleams of twilight were melting into night. The cold was great; the constellations shone with wonderful intensity. In the zenith glittered that wondrous Southern Cross— the polar bear of antarctic regions. The thermometer showed twelve degrees below zero, and when the wind freshened, it was most biting. Flakes of ice increased on the open water. The sea seemed everywhere alike. Numerous blackish patches spread on the surface, showing the formation of fresh ice. Evidently the southern basin, frozen during the six winter months, was absolutely inaccessible. What became of the whales in that time? Doubtless they went beneath the icebergs, seeking more practicable seas. As to the seals and morses, accustomed to live in a hard climate, they remained on these icy shores. These creatures have the instinct to break holes in the ice-fields, and to keep them open. To these holes they come for breath; when the birds, driven away by the cold, have emigrated to the north, these sea mammals remain sole masters of the polar continent. But the reservoirs were filling with water, and the *Nautilus* was slowly descending. At 1000 feet deep it stopped; its screw beat the waves, and it advanced straight towards the north, at a speed of fifteen miles an hour. Towards night it was already floating under the immense body of the iceberg. At three in the morning I was awakened by a violent shock. I sat up in my bed and listened in the darkness, when I was thrown into the middle of the room. The *Nautilus*, after having struck, had rebounded violently. I groped along the partition, and by the staircase to the saloon, which was lit by the luminous ceiling. The furniture was upset. Fortunately the windows were firmly set, and had held fast. The pictures on the starboard-side, from being no longer vertical, were clinging to the paper, whilst those of the port-side were hanging at least a foot from the wall. The *Nautilus* was lying on its starboard side perfectly motionless. I heard footsteps, and a confusion of voices; but Captain Nemo did not appear. As I was leaving the saloon, Ned Land and Conseil entered.

"What is the matter?" said I, at once.

"I came to ask you, sir," replied Conseil.

"Confound it!" exclaimed the Canadian, "I know well enough! The *Nautilus* has struck; and judging by the way she lies, I do not think she will right herself as she did the first time in Torres Straits."

"But," I asked, "has she at least come to the surface of the sea?"

"We do not know," said Conseil.

"It is easy to decide," I answered. I consulted the manometer. To my great surprise it showed a depth of more than 180 fathoms. "What does that mean?" I exclaimed.

"We must ask Captain Nemo," said Conseil.

"But where shall we find him?" said Ned Land.

"Follow me," said I, to my companions.

We left the saloon. There was no one in the library. At the centre staircase, by the berths of the ship's crew, there was no one. I thought that Captain Nemo must be in the pilot's cage. It was best to wait. We all returned to the saloon. For twenty minutes we remained thus, trying to hear the slightest noise which might be made on board the *Nautilus*, when Captain Nemo entered. He seemed not to see us; his face, generally so impassive, showed signs of uneasiness. He watched the compass silently, then the manometer; and going to the planisphere, placed his finger on a spot representing the southern seas. I would not interrupt him; but, some minutes later, when he turned towards me, I said, using one of his own expressions in the Torres Straits—

"An incident, Captain?"

"No, sir; an accident this time."

"Serious?"

"Perhaps."

"Is the danger immediate?"

"No."

"The *Nautilus* has stranded?"

"Yes."

"And this has happened—how?"

"From a caprice of nature, not from the ignorance of man. Not a mistake has been made in the working. But we cannot prevent equilibrium from producing its effects. We may brave human laws, but we cannot resist natural ones."

Captain Nemo had chosen a strange moment for uttering this philosophical reflection. On the whole, his answer helped me little.

"May I ask, sir, the cause of this accident?"

"An enormous block of ice, a whole mountain, has turned over," he replied. "When icebergs are undermined at their base by warmer water or reiterated shocks, their centre of gravity rises, and the whole thing turns over. This is what has happened; one of these blocks, as it fell, struck the *Nautilus*, then, gliding under its hull, raised it with irresistible force, bringing it into beds which are no so thick, where it is lying on its side."

"But can we not get the *Nautilus* off by emptying its reservoirs, that it may regain its equilibrium?"

"That, sir, is being done at this moment. You can hear the pump working. Look at the needle of the manometer; it shows that the *Nautilus* is rising, but the block of ice is rising with it; and, until some obstacle stops its ascending motion, our position cannot be altered."

Indeed, the *Nautilus* still held the same position to starboard; doubtless it would right itself when the block stopped. But at this moment who knows if we may not strike the upper part of the iceberg, and if we may not be frightfully crushed between the two glassy surfaces? I reflected on all the consequences of our position. Captain Nemo never took his eyes off the manometer. Since the fall of the iceberg, the *Nautilus* had risen about a hundred and fifty feet, but it still made the same angle with the perpendicular. Suddenly a slight movement was felt in the hold. Evidently it was righting a little. Things hanging in the saloon were sensibly returning to their normal position. The partitions were nearing the upright. No one spoke. With beating hearts we watched and felt the straightening. The boards became horizontal under our feet. Ten minutes passed.

"At last we have righted!" I exclaimed.

"Yes," said Captain Nemo, going to the door of the saloon.

"But are we floating?" I asked.

"Certainly," he replied; "since the reservoirs are not empty; and, when empty, the *Nautilus* must rise to the surface of the sea."

We were in open sea; but at a distance of about ten yards, on either side of the *Nautilus*, rose a dazzling wall of ice. Above and beneath the same wall. Above, because the lower surface of the iceberg stretched over us like an immense ceiling. Beneath, because the overturned block, having slid by degrees, had found a resting-place on the lateral

walls, which kept it in that position. The *Nautilus* was really imprisoned in a perfect tunnel of ice more than twenty yards in breadth,
filled with quiet water. It was easy to get out of it by going either
forward or backward, and then make a free passage under the iceberg, some hundreds of yards deeper. The luminous ceiling had been
extinguished, but the saloon was still resplendent with intense light.
It was the powerful reflection from the glass partition sent violently
back to the sheets of the lantern. I cannot describe the effect of the
voltaic rays upon the great blocks so capriciously cut; upon every
angle, every ridge, every facet was thrown a different light, according
to the nature of the veins running through the ice; a dazzling mine
of gems, particularly of sapphires, their blue rays crossing with the
green of the emerald. Here and there were opal shades of wonderful softness, running through bright spots like diamonds of fire, the
brilliancy of which the eye could not bear. The power of the lantern
seemed increased a hundredfold, like a lamp through the lenticular
plates of a first-class lighthouse.

"How beautiful! how beautiful!" cried Conseil.

"Yes," I said, "it is a wonderful sight. Is it not, Ned?"

"Yes, confound it! Yes," answered Ned Land, "it is superb! I am
mad at being obliged to admit it. No one has ever seen anything like
it; but the sight may cost us dear. And if I must say all, I think we are
seeing here things which God never intended man to see."

Ned was right, it was too beautiful. Suddenly a cry from Conseil
made me turn.

"What is it?" I asked.

"Shut your eyes, sir! do not look, sir!" Saying which, Conseil clapped
his hands over his eyes.

"But what is the matter, my boy?"

"I am dazzled, blinded."

My eyes turned involuntarily towards the glass, but I could not
stand the fire which seemed to devour them. I understood what had
happened. The *Nautilus* had put on full speed. All the quiet lustre of

the ice-walls was at once changed into flashes of lightning. The fire from these myriads of diamonds was blinding. It required some time to calm our troubled looks. At last the hands were taken down.

"Faith, I should never have believed it," said Conseil.

It was then five in the morning; and at that moment a shock was felt at the bows of the *Nautilus*. I knew that its spur had struck a block of ice. It must have been a false manoeuvre, for this submarine tunnel, obstructed by blocks, was not very easy navigation. I thought that Captain Nemo, by changing his course, would either turn these obstacles, or else follow the windings of the tunnel. In any case, the road before us could not be entirely blocked. But, contrary to my expectations, the *Nautilus* took a decided retrograde motion.

"We are going backwards?" said Conseil.

"Yes," I replied. "This end of the tunnel can have no egress."

"And then?"

"Then," said I, "the working is easy. We must go back again, and go out at the southern opening. That is all."

In speaking thus, I wished to appear more confident than I really was. But the retrograde motion of the *Nautilus* was increasing; and, reversing the screw, it carried us at great speed.

"It will be a hindrance," said Ned.

"What does it matter, some hours more or less, provided we get out at last?"

"Yes," repeated Ned Land, "provided we do get out at last!"

For a short time I walked from the saloon to the library. My companions were silent. I soon threw myself on an ottoman, and took a book, which my eyes overran mechanically. A quarter of an hour after, Conseil, approaching me, said, "Is what you are reading very interesting, sir?"

"Very interesting!" I replied.

"I should think so, sir. It is your own book you are reading."

"My book?"

And indeed I was holding in my hand the work on the "Great Submarine Depths." I did not even dream of it. I closed the book, and returned to my walk. Ned and Conseil rose to go.

"Stay here, my friends," said I, detaining them. "Let us remain together until we are out of this block."

"As you please, sir," Conseil replied.

Some hours passed. I often looked at the instruments hanging from the partition. The manometer showed that the *Nautilus* kept at a constant depth of more than three hundred yards; the compass still pointed to the south; the log indicated a speed of twenty miles an hour, which, in such a cramped space, was very great. But Captain Nemo knew that he could not hasten too much, and that minutes were worth ages to us. At twenty-five minutes past eight a second shock took place, this time from behind. I turned pale. My companions were close by my side. I seized Conseil's hand. Our looks expressed our feelings better than words. At this moment the Captain entered the saloon. I went up to him.

"Our couse is barred southward?" I asked.

"Yes, sir. The iceberg has shifted, and closed every outlet."

"We are blocked up, then?"

"Yes."

Chapter XVI
Want of Air

Thus, around the *Nautilus*, above and below, was an impenetrable wall of ice. We were prisoners to the iceberg. I watched the Captain. His countenance had resumed its habitual imperturbability.

"Gentlemen," he said, Calmly, "there are two ways of dying in the circumstances in which we are placed." (This inexplicable person had the air of a mathematical professor lecturing to his pupils.) "The first is to be crushed; the second is to die of suffocation. I do not speak of the possibility of dying of hunger, for the supply of provisions in the *Nautilus* will certainly last longer than we shall. Let us then calculate our chances."

"As to suffocation, Captain," I replied, "that is not to be feared, because our reservoirs are full."

"Just so; but they will only yield two days' supply of air. Now, for thirty-six hours we have been hidden under the water, and already the heavy atmospheres of the *Nautilus* requires renewal. In forty-eight hours our reserve will be exhausted."

"Well, Captain, can we be delivered before forty-eight hours?"

"We will attempt it, at least, by piercing the wall that surrounds us."

"On which side?"

"Sound will tell us. I am going to run the *Nautilus* aground on the lower bank, and my men will attack the iceberg on the side that is least thick."

Captain Nemo went out. Soon I discovered by a hissing noise that the water was entering the reservoirs. The *Nautilus* sank slowly, and rested on the ice at a depth of 350 yards, the depth at which the lower bank was immersed.

"My friends," I said, "our situation is serious, but I rely on your courage and energy."

"Sir," replied the Canadian, "I am ready to do anything for the general safety."

"Good! Ned," and I held out my hand to the Canadian.

"I will add," he continued, "that being as handy with the pickaxe as with the harpoon, if I can be useful to the Captain, he can command my services."

"He will not refuse your help. Come, Ned!"

I led him to the room where the crew of the *Nautilus* were putting on their cork-jackets. I told the Captain of Ned's proposal, which he accepted. The Canadian put on his seacostume, and was ready as soon as his companions. When Ned was dressed, I re-entered the drawing-room, where the panes of glass were open, and, posted near Conseil, I examined the ambient beds that supported the *Nautilus*. Some instants after, we saw a dozen of the crew set foot on the bank of ice, and among them Ned Land, easily known by his stature. Captain Nemo was with them. Before proceeding to dig the walls, he took the soundings, to be sure of working in the right direction. Long sounding lines were sunk in the side walls, but after fifteen yards they were again stopped by the thick wall. It was useless to attack it on the ceiling-like surface, since the iceberg itself measured more than 400 yards in height. Captain Nemo then sounded the lower surface. There ten yards of wall separated us from the water, so great was the thickness of the ice-field. It was necessary, therefore, to cut from it a piece equal in extent to the waterline of the *Nautilus*. There were about 6000 cubic yards to detach, so as to dig a hole by which we could descend to the ice-field. The work was begun immediately, and carried on with indefatigable energy. Instead of digging round the *Nautilus*, which would have involved greater difficulty, Captain Nemo had an immense trench made at eight yards from the port quarter. Then the men set to work simultaneously with their screws, on several points of its circumference. Presently the pickaxe attacked this compact matter vigorously, and large blocks were detached from the mass. By a curious effect of specific gravity, these blocks, lighter than water, fled, so to speak, to the vault of the tunnel, that increased in thickness at the top in proportion as it diminished at the base. But that mattered little, so long as the lower part grew thinner. After two hours' hard work, Ned Land came in exhausted. He and his comrades were replaced by new workers, whom Conseil and I joined. The second lieutenant of the *Nautilus* superintended us. The water seemed singularly cold, but I soon got warm handling the pickaxe. My movements were free enough, although they were made under a pressure of thirty atmospheres. When I re-entered, after working two hours, to take some food and rest, I found a perceptible difference between the pure fluid with which the Rouquayrol engine supplied me, and the atmosphere of the *Nautilus*, already changed with carbonic acid. The air had not been renewed for forty-eight hours, and its vivifying qualities were considerably enfeebled. However, after a lapse of twelve hours, we had only raised a block of ice one yard thick, on the marked surface, which was about 600 cubic yards! Reckoning that it took twelve hours to accomplish this much, it would take five nights and four days to bring this enterprise to a satisfactory conclusion. Five nights and four days! And we have only air enough for two days in the reservoirs! "Without taking into account," said Ned, "that, even if we get out of this infernal prison, we shall also be imprisoned under the iceberg, shut out from all possible communication with the atmosphere." True enough! Who could then foresee the minimum of time necessary for our deliverance? We might be suffocated before the *Nautilus* could regain the surface of the waves? Was it destined to perish in this ice-tomb, with all those it enclosed? The situation was terrible. But every one had looked the danger in the face, and each was determined to do his duty to the last.

As I expected, during the night a new block a yard square was carried away, and still further sank the immense hollow. But in the morning when, dressed in my cork-jacket, I traversed the slushy mass at a temperature of six or seven degrees below zero, I remarked that the side walls were gradually closing in. The beds of water farthest from the trench, that were not warmed by the men's mere work, showed a tendency to solidification. In presence of this new and imminent danger, what would become of our chances of safety, and how hinder the solidification of this liquid medium, that would burst the partitions of the *Nautilus* like glass?

I did not tell my companions of this new danger. What was the good of damping the energy they displayed in the painful work of escape? But when I went on board again, I told Captain Nemo of this grave complication.

"I know it," he said, in that calm tone which could counteract the most terrible apprehensions. "It is one danger more; but I see no way of escaping it; the only chance of safety is to go quicker than solidification. We must be beforehand with it, that is all."

On this day for several hours I used my pickaxe vigorously. The work kept me up. Besides, to work was to quit the *Nautilus*, and breathe directly the pure air drawn from the reservoirs, and supplied by our apparatus, and to quit the impoverished and vitiated atmosphere. Towards evening the trench was dug one yard deeper. When I returned on board, I was nearly suffocated by the carbonic acid with which the air was filled—ah! if we had only the chemical means to drive away this deleterious gas. We had plenty of oxygen; all this water contained a considerable quantity, and by dissolving it with our powerful piles, it would restore the vivifying fluid. I had thought well over it; but of what good was that, since the carbonic acid produced by our respiration had invaded every part of the vessel? To absorb it, it was necessary to fill some jars with caustic potash, and to shake them incessantly. Now this substance was wanting on board, and nothing could replace it. On that evening, Captain Nemo ought to open the taps of his reservoirs, and let some pure air into the interior of the *Nautilus;* without this precaution, we could not get rid of the sense of suffocation. The next day, March 26th, I resumed my miner's work in beginning the fifth yard. The side walls and the lower surface of the iceberg thickened visibly. It was evident that they would meet before the *Nautilus* was able to disengage itself. Despair seized me for an instant, my pickaxe nearly fell from my hands. What was the good of digging if I must be suffocated, crushed by the water that was turning into stone?—a punishment that the ferocity of the savages even would not have invented! Just then Captain Nemo passed near me. I touched his hand and showed him the walls of our prison. The wall to port had advanced to at least four yards from the hull of the *Nautilus*. The Captain understood me, and signed to me to follow him. We went on board. I took off my cork-jacket, and accompanied him into the drawing-room.

"M. Aronnax, we must attempt some desperate means, or we shall be sealed up in this solidified water as in cement."

"Yes; but what is to be done?"

"Ah! if my *Nautilus* were strong enough to bear this pressure without being crushed!"

"Well?" I asked, not catching the Captain's idea.

"Do you not understand," he replied, "that this congelation of water will help us? Do you not see that, by its solidification, it would burst through this field of ice that imprisons us, as, when it freezes, it bursts the hardest stones? Do you not perceive that it would be an agent of safety instead of destruction?"

"Yes, Captain, perhaps. But whatever resistance to crushing the *Nautilus* possesses, it could not support this terrible pressure, and would be flattened like an iron plate."

"I know it, sir. Therefore we must not reckon on the aid of nature, but on our own exertions. We must stop this solidification. Not only will the side walls be pressed together; but there is not ten feet of water before or behind the *Nautilus*. The congelation gains on us on all sides."

"How long will the air in the reservoirs last for us to breathe on board?"

The Captain looked in my face. "After to-morrow they will be empty!"

A cold sweat came over me. However, ought I to have been astonished at the answer? On March 22nd, the *Nautilus* was in the open polar seas. We were at 26°. For five days we had lived on the reserve on board.

And what was left of the respirable air must be kept for the workers. Even now, as I write, my recollection is still so vivid, that an involuntary terror seizes me, and my lungs seem to be without air. Meanwhile, Captain Nemo reflected silently, and evidently an idea had struck him; but he seemed to reject it. At last, these words escaped his lips—

"Boiling water!" he muttered.

"Boiling water?" I cried.

"Yes, sir. We are enclosed in a space that is relatively confined. Would not jets of boiling water, constantly injected by the pumps, raise the temperature in this part, and stay the congelation?"

"Let us try it," I said, resolutely.

"Let us try, Professor."

The thermometer then stood at seven degrees outside. Captain Nemo took me to the galleys, where the vast distillatory machines stood that furnished the drinkable water by evaporation. They filled these with water, and all the electric heat from the piles were thrown through the worms bathed in the liquid. In a few minutes this water reached a hundred degrees. It was directed towards the pumps, while fresh water replaced it in proportion. The heat developed by the troughs was such that cold water, drawn up from the sea, after only having gone through the machines, came boiling into the body of the pump. The injection was begun, and three hours after the thermometer marked six degrees below zero outside. One degree was gained. Two hours later, the thermometer only marked four degrees.

"We shall succeed," I said to the Captain, after having anxiously watched the result of the operation.

"I think," he answered, "that we shall not be crushed. We have no more suffocation to fear."

During the night the temperature of the water rose to one degree below zero. The injections could not carry it to a higher point. But as the congelation of the sea-water produces at least two degrees, I was at last reassured against the dangers of solidification.

The next day, March 27th, six yards of ice had been cleared, four yards only remaining to be cleared away. There was yet forty-eight hours' work. The air could not be renewed in the interior of the *Nautilus*. And this day would make it worse. An intolerable weight oppressed me. Towards three o'clock in the evening, this feeling rose to a violent degree. Yawns dislocated my jaws. My lungs panted as they inhaled this burning fluid, which became rarified more and more. A moral torpor took hold of me. I was powerless, almost unconscious. My brave Conseil, though exhibiting the same symptoms and suffering in the same manner, never left me. He took my hand and encouraged me, and I heard him murmur, "Oh! if I could only not breathe, so as to leave more air for my master!"

Tears came into my eyes on hearing him speak thus. If our situation to all was intolerable in the interior, with what haste and gladness would we put on our cork-jackets to work in our turn! Pickaxes sounded on the frozen ice-beds. Our arms ached, the skin was torn off our hands. But what were these fatigues, what did the wounds matter? Vital air came to the lungs! we breathed! we breathed!

All this time, no one prolonged his voluntary task beyond the prescribed time. His task accomplished, each one handed in turn to his panting companions the apparatus that supplied him with life. Captain Nemo set the example, and submitted first to this severe discipline. When the time came, he gave up his apparatus to another, and returned to the vitiated air on board, calm, unflinching unmurmuring.

On that day the ordinary work was accomplished with unusual vigour. Only two yards remained to be raised from the surface. Two yards only separated us from the open sea. But the reservoirs were nearly emptied of air. The little that remained ought to be kept for the workers; not a particle for the *Nautilus*. When I went back on board, I was half suffocated. What a night! I know not how to describe it. The next day my breathing was oppressed. Dizziness accompanied the pain in my head, and made me like a drunken man. My companions showed the same symptoms. Some of the crew had rattling in the throat.

On that day, the sixth of our imprisonment, Captain Nemo, finding the pickaxes work too slowly, resolved to crush the ice-bed that still separated us from the liquid sheet. This man's coolness and energy never forsook him. He subdued his physical pains by moral force.

By his orders the vessel was lightened, that is to say, raised from the ice-bed by a change of specific gravity. When it floated they towed it so as to bring it above the immense trench made on the level of the water-line, then filling his reservoirs of water, he descended and shut himself up in the hole.

Just then all the crew came on board, and the double door of communication was shut. The *Nautilus* then rested on the bed of ice, which was not one yard thick, and which the sounding leads had perforated in a thousand places. The taps of the reservoirs were then opened, and a hundred cubic yards of water was let in, increasing the weight of the *Nautilus* to 1800 tons. We waited, we listened, forgetting our sufferings in hope. Our safety depended on this last chance. Notwithstanding the buzzing in my head, I soon heard the humming sound under the hull of the *Nautilus*. The ice cracked with a singular noise, like tearing paper, and the *Nautilus* sank.

"We are off!" murmured Conseil in my ear.

I could not answer him. I seized his hand, and pressed it convulsively. All at once, carried away by its frightful overcharge, the *Nautilus* sank like a bullet under the waters, that is to say, it fell as if it was in a vacuum. Then all the electric force was put on the pumps, that soon began to let the water out of the reservoirs. After some minutes, our fall was stopped. Soon, too, the manometer indicated an ascending movement. The screw, going at full speed, made the iron hull tremble to its very bolts, and drew us towards the north. But if this floating under the iceberg is to last another day before we reach the open sea, I shall be dead first.

Half stretched upon a divan in the library, I was suffocating. My face was purple, my lips blue, my faculties suspended. I neither saw nor heard. All notion of time had gone from my mind. My muscles could not contract. I do not know how many hours passed thus, but

I was conscious of the agony that was coming over me. I felt as if I was going to die. Suddenly I came to. Some breaths of air penetrated my lungs. Had we risen to the surface of the waves? Were we free of the iceberg? No; Ned and Conseil, my two brave friends, were sacrificing themselves to save me. Some particles of air still remained at the bottom of one apparatus. Instead of using it, they had kept it for me, and while they were being suffocated, they gave me life drop by drop. I wanted to push back the thing; they held my hands, and for some moments I breathed freely. I looked at the clock; it was eleven in the morning. It ought to be the 28th of March. The *Nautilus* went at a frightful pace, forty miles an hour. It literally tore through the water. Where was Captain Nemo? Had he succumbed? Were his companions dead with him? At the moment, the manometer indicated that we were not more than twenty feet from the surface. A mere plate of ice separated us from the atmosphere, could we not break it? Perhaps. In any case the *Nautilus* was going to attempt it. I felt that it was in an oblique position, lowering the stern, and raising the bows. The introduction of water had been the means of disturbing its equilibrium. Then, impelled by its powerful screw, it attacked the ice-field from beneath like a formidable battering-ram. It broke it by backing and then rushing forward against the field, which gradually gave way; and at last, dashing suddenly against it, shot forwards on the icy field, that crushed beneath its weight. The panels was opened—one might say torn off—and the pure air came in in abundance to all parts of the *Nautilus*.

Chapter XVII

From Cape Horn to the Amazon

How I got on to the platform, I have no idea; perhaps the Canadian had carried me there. But I breathed, I inhaled the vivifying sea-air. My two companions were getting drunk with the fresh particles. The other unhappy men had been so long without food, that they could not with impunity indulge in the simplest aliments that were given them. We, on the contrary, had no need to restrain ourselves; we could draw this air freely into our lungs, and it was the breeze, the breeze alone, that filled us with this keen enjoyment.

"Ah!" said Conseil, "how delightful this oxygen is! Master need not fear to breathe it. There is enough for everybody."

Ned Land did not speak, but he opened his jaws wide enough to frighten a shark. Our strength soon returned, and when I looked round me, I saw we were alone on the platform. The foreign seamen in the *Nautilus* were contented with the air that circulated in the interior; none of them had come to drink in the open air.

The first words I spoke were words of gratitude and thankfulness to my two companions. Ned and Conseil had prolonged my life during the last hours of this long agony. All my gratitude could not repay such devotion.

"My friends," said I, "we are bound one to the other for ever, and I am under infinite obligations to you."

"Which I shall take advantage of," exclaimed the Canadian.

"What do you mean?" said Conseil.

"I mean that I shall take you with me when I leave this infernal *Nautilus*."

"Well," said Conseil, "after all this, are we going right?"

"Yes," I replied, "for we are going the way of the sun, and here the sun is in the north."

"No doubt," said Ned Land; "but it remains to be seen whether he will bring the ship into the Pacific or the Atlantic Ocean, that is, into frequented or deserted seas."

I could not answer that question, and I feared that Captain Nemo would rather take us to the vast ocean that touches the coasts of Asia and America at the same time. He would thus complete the tour round the submarine world, and return to those waters in which the *Nautilus* could sail freely. We ought, before long, to settle this important point. The *Nautilus* went at a rapid pace. The polar circle was soon passed, and the course shaped for Cape Horn. We were off the American point, March 31, at seven o'clock in the evening. Then all our past sufferings were forgotten. The remembrance of that imprisonment in the ice was effaced from our minds. We only thought of the future. Captain Nemo did not appear again either in the drawing-room or on the platform. The point shown each day on the planisphere, and marked by the lieutenant, showed me the exact direction of the *Nautilus*. Now, on that evening, it was evident, to my great satisfaction, that we were going back to the north by the Atlantic. The next day, April 1st, when the *Nautilus* ascended to the surface, some minutes before noon, we sighted land to the west. It was Terra del Fuego, which the first navigators named thus from seeing the quantity of smoke that rose from the natives' huts. The coast seemed low to me, but in the distance rose high mountains. I even thought I had a glimpse of Mount Sarmiento, that rises 2070 yards above the level of the sea, with a very pointed summit, which, according as it is misty or clear, is a sign of fine or of wet weather. At this moment, the peak was clearly defined against the sky. The *Nautilus*, diving again under the water, approached the coast, which was only some few miles off. From the glass windows in the drawing-room, I saw long seaweeds, and gigantic fuci, and varech, of which the open polar sea contains so many specimens, with their sharp polished filaments; they measured about 300 yards in length,—real real cables, thicker than one's thumb; and having great tenacity, they are often used as ropes for vessels. Another weed known as velp, with leaves four feet long, buried in the coral concretions, hung at the bottom. It served as nest and food for myriads of crustacea and molluscs, crabs and cuttlefish. There seals and otters had splendid repasts, eating the flesh of fish with sea-vegetables, according to the English fashion. Over this fertile and luxuriant ground the *Nautilus* passed with great rapidity. Towards evening, it approached the Falkland group, the rough summits of which I recognised the following day. The depth of the sea was moderate. On the shores, our nets brought in beautiful specimens of seaweed, and particularly a certain fucus, the roots of which were filled with the best mussels in the world. Geese and ducks fell by dozens on the platform, and soon took their places in the pantry on board. With regard to fish, I observed especially specimens of the goby species, some two feet long, all over white and yellow spots. I admired also numerous medusae, and the finest of the sort, the crysaora, peculiar to the sea about the Falkland Isles. I should have liked to preserve some specimens of these delicate zoophytes: but they are only like clouds, shadows, apparitions, that sink and evaporate, when out of their native element.

When the last heights of the Falklands had disappeared from the horizon, the *Nautilus* sank to between twenty and twenty-five yards, and followed the American coast. Captain Nemo did not show himself. Until the 3rd of April we did not quit the shores of Patagonia, sometimes under the ocean, sometimes at the surface. The *Nautilus* passed beyond the large estuary formed by the mouth of the Plata, and was, on the 4th of April, fifty-six miles off Uraguay. Its direction was northwards, and followed the long windings of the coast of South America. We had then made 1600 miles since our embarkation in the seas of Japan. About eleven o'clock in the morning the Tropic of Capricorn was crossed on the thirty-seventh meridian, and we passed Cape Frio standing out to sea. Captain Nemo, to Ned Land's great displeasure, did not like the neighbourhood of the inhabited coasts of Brazil, for we went at a giddy speed. Not a fish, not a bird of the swiftest kind could follow us, and the natural curiosities of these seas escaped all observation.

This speed was kept up for several days, and in the evening of the 9th of April we sighted the most westerly point of South America that forms Cape San Roque. But then the *Nautilus* swerved again, and sought the lowest depth of a submarine valley which is between this cape and Sierra Leone on the African coast. This valley bifurcates to the parallel of the Antilles, and terminates at the north by the enormous depression of 9000 yards. In this place, the geological basin of the ocean forms, as far as the Lesser Antilles, a cliff of three and a half miles perpendicular in height, and at the parallel of the Cape Verd Islands, another wall not less considerable, that encloses thus all the sunk continent of the Atlantic. The bottom of this immense valley is dotted with some mountains, that give to these submarine places a picturesque aspect. I speak, moreover, from the manuscript charts that were in the library of the *Nautilus*—charts evidently due to Captain Nemo's hand, and made after his personal observations. For two days the desert and deep waters were visited by means of the inclined planes. The *Nautilus* was furnished with long diagonal broadsides which carried it to all elevations. But, on the 11th of April, it rose suddenly, and land appeared at the mouth of the Amazon River, a vast estuary, the embouchure of which is so considerable that it freshens the sea-water for the distance of several leagues.

The equator was crossed. Twenty miles to the west were the Guianas, a French territory, on which we could have found an easy refuge; but a stiff breeze was blowing, and the furious waves would not have allowed a single boat to face them. Ned Land understood that, no doubt, for he spoke not a word about it. For my part, I made no allusion to his schemes of flight, for I would not urge him to make an attempt that must inevitably fail. I made the time pass pleasantly by interesting studies. During the days of April 11th and 12th, the *Nautilus* did not leave the surface of the sea, and the net brought in a marvellous haul of zoophytes, fish and reptiles. Some zoophytes had been fished up by the chain of the nets; they were for the most part beautiful phyctallines, belonging to the actinidian family, and among other species the phyctalis protexta, peculiar to that part of the ocean, with a little cylindrical trunk, ornamented with vertical lines, speckled with red dots, crowning a marvellous blossoming of tentacles. As to the molluscs, they consisted of some I had already observed—turritellas, olive porphyras, with regular lines intercrossed, with red spots standing out plainly against the flesh; odd pteroceras, like petrified scorpions; translucid hyaleas, argonauts, cuttle-fish (excellent eating), and certain species of calmars that naturalists of antiquity have classed amongst the flying-fish, and that serve principally for bait for cod-fishing. I had not an opportunity of studying several species of fish on these shores. Amongst the cartilaginous ones, petromyzons-pricka, a sort of eel, fifteen inches long, with a greenish head, violet fins, grey-blue back, brown belly, silvered and sown with bright spots, the pupil of the eye encircled with gold—a curious animal, that the current of the Amazon had drawn to the sea, for they inhabit fresh waters—tuberculated streaks, with pointed snouts, and a long loose tail, armed with a long jagged sting; little sharks, a yard long, grey and whitish skin, and several rows of teeth, bent back, that are generally known by the name of pantouffles; vespertilios, a kind of red isosceles triangle, half a yard long, to which pectorals are attached by fleshy prolongations that make them look like bats, but that their horny appendage, situated near the nostrils, has given them the name of sea-unicorns; lastly, some species of balistae, the curassavian, whose spots were of a brilliant gold colour, and the capriscus of clear violet, and with varying shades like a pigeon's throat.

I end here this catalogue, which is somewhat dry perhaps, but very exact, with a series of bony fish that I observed in passing belonging to the apteronotes, and whose snout is white as snow, the body of a beautiful black, marked with a very long loose fleshy strip; odontognathes, armed with spikes; sardines, nine inches long, glittering with a bright silver light; a species of mackerel provided with two anal fins; centronotes of a blackish tint, that are fished for with torches, long fish, two yards in length, with fat flesh, white and firm, which, when they are fresh, taste like eel, and when dry, like smoked salmon; labres, half red, covered with scales only at the bottom of the dorsal and anal fins; chrysoptera, on which gold and silver blend their brightness with that of the ruby and topaz; golden-tailed spares, the flesh of which is extremely delicate, and whose phosphorescent properties betray them in the midst of the waters; orange-coloured spares with a long tongue; maigres, with gold caudal fins, dark thorn-tails, anableps of Surinam, &c.

Notwithstanding this "etcetera," I must not omit to mention fish that Conseil will long remember, and with good reason. One of our nets had hauled up a sort of very flat rayfish, which, with the tail cut off, formed a perfect disc, and weighed twenty ounces. It was white underneath, red above, with large round spots of dark blue encircled with black, very glossy skin, terminating in a bilobed fin. Laid out on the platform, it struggled, tried to turn itself by convulsive movements, and made so many efforts, that one last turn had nearly sent it into the sea. But Conseil, not wishing to let the fish go, rushed to it, and, before I could prevent him, had seized it with both hands. In a moment he was overthrown, his legs in the air, and half his body paralysed, crying—

"Oh! master, master! come to me!"

It was the first time the poor boy had not spoken to me in the third person. The Canadian and I took him up, and rubbed his contracted arms till he became sensible. The unfortunate Conseil had attacked a crampfish of the most dangerous kind, the cumana. This odd animal, in a medium conductor like water, strikes fish at several yards' distance, so great is the power of its electric organ, the two principal surfaces of which do not measure less than twenty-seven square feet. The next day, April 12th, the *Nautilus* approached the Dutch coast, near the mouth of the Maroni. There several groups of sea-cows herded together; they were manatees, that, like the dugong and the stellera, belong to the sirenian order. These beautiful animals, peaceable and inoffensive, from eighteen to twenty-one feet in length, weigh at least sixteen hundredweight. I told Ned Land and

Conseil that provident nature had assigned an important *rôle* to these mammalia. Indeed, they, like the seals, are designed to graze on the submarine prairies, and thus destroy the accumulation of weed that obstructs the tropical rivers.

"And do you know," I added, "what has been the result since men have almost entirely annihilated this useful race? That the putrified weeds have poisoned the air, and the poisoned air causes the yellow fever, that desolates these beautiful countries. Enormous vegetations are multiplied under the torrid seas, and the evil is irresistibly developed from the mouth of the Rio de la Plata to Florida. If we are to believe Toussenel, this plague is nothing to what it would be if the seas were cleared of whales and seals. Then, infested with poulps, medusae, and cuttle-fish, they would become immense centres of infection, since their waves would not possess 'these vast stomachs that God had charged to infest the surface of the seas.'"

However, without disputing these theories, the crew of the *Nautilus* took possession of half a dozen manatees. They provisioned the larders with excellent flesh, superior to beef and veal. This sport was not interesting. The manatees allowed themselves to be hit without defending themselves. Several thousand pounds of meat were stored up on board to be dried. On this day, a successful haul of fish increased the stores of the *Nautilus*, so full of game were these seas. They were echeneides belonging to the third family of the malacopterygiens; their flattened discs were composed of transverse movable cartilaginous plates, by which the animal was enabled to create a vacuum, and so to adhere to any object like a cupping-glass. The remora that I had observed in the Mediterranean belongs to this species. But the one of which we are speaking was the echeneis osteochera, peculiar to this sea.

The fishing over, the *Nautilus* neared the coast. About here a number of sea-turtles were sleeping on the surface of the water. It would have been difficult to capture these precious reptiles, for the least noise awakens them, and their solid skull is proof against the harpoon. But the echeneis effects their capture with extraordinary precision and certainty. This animal is, indeed, a living fishhook, which would make the fortune of an inexperienced fisherman. The crew of the *Nautilus* tied a ring to the tail of these fish, so large as not to encumber their movements, and to this ring a long cord, lashed to the ship's side by the other end. The echeneids, thrown into the sea, directly began their game, and fixed themselves to the breastplate of the turtles. Their tenacity was such, that they were torn rather than let go their hold. The men hauled them on board, and with them the turtles to which they adhered. They took also several cacouannes a yard long, which weighed 400 lbs. Their carapace covered with large horny plates, thin, transparent, brown, with white and yellow spots, fetch a good price in the market. Besides, they were excellent in an edible point of view, as well as the fresh turtles, which have an exquisite flavour. This day's fishing brought to a close our stay on the shores of the Amazon, and by nightfall the *Nautilus had regained the high seas.*

Chapter XVIII
The Poulps

For several days the *Nautilus* kept off from the American coast. Evidently it did not wish to risk the tides of the Gulf of Mexico, or of the sea of the Antilles. April 16th, we sighted Martinique and Guadaloupe from a distance of about thirty miles. I saw their tall peaks for an instant. The Canadian, who counted on carrying out his projects in the Gulf, by either landing, or hailing one of the numerous boats that coast from one island to another, was quite disheartened. Flight would have been quite practicable, if Ned Land had been able to take possession of the boat without the Captain's knowledge. But in the open sea it could not be thought of. The Canadian, Conseil, and I, had a long conversation on this subject. For six months we had been prisoners on board the *Nautilus*. We had travelled 17,000 leagues; and, as Ned Land said, there was no reason why it should not come to an end. We could hope nothing from the Captain of the *Nautilus*, but only from ourselves. Besides, for some time past he had become graver, more retired, less sociable. He seemed to shun me. I met him rarely. Formerly, he was pleased to explain the submarine marvels to me; now, he left me to my studies, and came no more to the saloon. What change had come over him? For what cause? For my part, I did not wish to bury with me my curious and novel studies. I had now the power to write the true book of the sea; and this book, sooner or later, I wished to see daylight. Then again, in the water by the Antilles, ten yards below the surface of the waters, by the open panels, what interesting products I had to enter on my daily notes! There were, among other zoophytes, those known under the name of physalis pelagica, a sort of large oblong bladder, with mother-of-pearl rays, holding our their membranes to the wind, and letting their blue tentacles float like threads of silk; charming medusae to the eye, real nettles to the touch, that distil a corrosive fluid. There were also annelides, a yard and a half long, furnished with a pink horn, and with 1700 locomotive organs, that wind through the waters, and throw out in passing all the light of the solar spectrum. There were, in the fish category, some Malabar rays, enormous gristly things, ten feet long, weighing 600 pounds, the pectoral fin triangular in the midst of a slightly humped back, the eyes fixed in the extremities of the face, beyond the head, and which floated like weft, and looked sometimes like an opaque shutter on our glass window. There were American balistae, which nature has only dressed in black and white; gobies, with yellow fins and prominent jaw; mackerel sixteen feet long, with short-pointed teeth, covered with small scales, belonging to the albicore species. Then, in swarms, appeared grey mullet, covered with stripes of gold from the head to the tail, beating their resplendent fins, like masterpieces of jewellery, consecrated formerly to Diana, particularly sought after by rich Romans, and of which the proverb says, "Whoever takes them does not eat them." Lastly, pomacanthe dorees, ornamented with emerald bands, dressed in velvet and silk, passed before our eyes like Veronese lords; spurred spari passed with their pectoral fins; clupanodons fifteen inches long, enveloped in their phosphorescent light; mullet beat the sea with their large jagged tail; red vendaces seemed to mow the waves with their showy pectoral fins; and silvery selenes, worthy of their name, rose on the horizon of the waters like so many moons with whitish rays. April 20th, we had risen to a mean height of 1500 yards. The land nearest us then was the archipelago of the Bahamas. There rose high submarine cliffs covered with large weeds, giant laminariae and fuci, a perfect espalier of hydrophytes worthy of a Titan world. It was about eleven o'clock when Ned Land drew my attention to a formidable pricking, like the sting of an ant, which was produced by means of large seaweeds.

"Well," I said, "these are proper caverns for poulps, and I should not be astonished to see some of these monsters."

"What!" said Conseil; "cuttle-fish, real cuttle-fish, of the cephalopod class?"

"No," I said; "poulps of huge dimensions."

"I will never believe that such animals exist," said Ned.

"Well," said Conseil, with the most serious air in the world; "I remember perfectly to have seen a large vessel drawn under the waves by a cephalopod's arm."

"You saw that?" said the Canadian.

"Yes, Ned."

"With your own eyes?"

"With my own eyes."

"Where, pray, might that be?"

"At St Malo," answered Conseil.

"In the port?" said Ned, ironically.

"No; in a church," replied Conseil.

"In a church!" cried the Canadian.

"Yes; friend Ned. In a picture representing the poulp in question."

"Good!" said Ned Land, bursting out laughing.

"He is quite right," I said. "I have heard of this picture; but the subject represented is taken from a legend, and you know what to think of legends in the matter of natural history. Besides, when it is a question of monsters, the imagination is apt to run wild. Not only is it supposed that these poulps can draw down vessels, but a certain Olaüs Magnus speaks of a cephalopod a mile long, that is more like an island than an animal. It is also said that the Bishop of Nidros was building an altar on an immense rock. Mass finished, the rock began to walk, and returned to the sea. The rock was a poulp. Another bishop, Pontoppidan, speaks also of a poulp on which a regiment of cavalry could manoeuvre. Lastly, the ancient naturalists speak of monsters whose mouths were like gulfs, and which were too large to pass through the Straits of Gibraltar."

"But how much is true of these stories?" asked Conseil.

"Nothing, my friends; at least of that which passes the limit of truth to get to fable or legend. Nevertheless, there must be some ground for the imagination of the story-tellers. One cannot deny that poulps and cuttle-fish exist of a large species, inferior, however, to the cetaceans. Aristotle has stated the dimensions of a cuttle-fish as five cubits, or nine feet two inches. Our fishermen frequently see some that are more than four feet long. Some skeletons of poulps are preserved in the museums of Trieste and Montpelier, that measure two yards in length. Besides, according to the calculations of some naturalists, one of these animals, only six feet long, would have tentacles twenty-seven feet long. That would suffice to make a formidable monster."

"Do they fish for them in these days?" asked Ned.

"If they do not fish for them, sailors see them at least. One of my friends, Captain Paul Bos of Havre, has often affirmed that he met one of these monsters, of colossal dimensions, in the Indian seas. But the most astonishing fact, and which does not permit of the denial of the existence of these gigantic animals, happened some years ago, in 1861."

"What is the fact?" asked Ned Land.

"This is it. In 1861, to the north-east of Teneriffe, very nearly in the same latitude we are in now, the crew of the despatch-boat *Alector* perceived a monstrous cuttle-fish swimming in the waters. Captain Bouguer went near to the animal, and attacked it with harpoons and guns, without much success, for balls and harpoons glided over the soft flesh. After several fruitless attempts, the crew tried to pass a slip-knot round the body of the mollusc. The noose slipped as far as the caudal fins, and there stopped. They tried then to haul it on board, but its weight was so considerable that the tightness of the cord separated the tail from the body, and, deprived of this ornament, he disappeared under the water."

"Indeed! is that a fact?"

"An indisputable fact, my good Ned. They proposed to name this poulp 'Bouguer's cuttle-fish.' "

"What length was it?" asked the Canadian.

"Did it not measure about six yards?" said Conseil, who, posted at the window, was examining again the irregular windings of the cliff.

"Precisely," I replied.

"Its head," rejoined Conseil, "was it not crowned with eight tentacles, that beat the water like a nest of serpents?"

"Precisely."

"Had not its eyes, placed at the back of its head, considerable development?"

"Yes, Conseil."

"And was not its mouth like a parrot's beak?"

"Exactly, Conseil."

"Very well! no offence to master," he replied, quietly; "if this is not bouguer's cuttle-fish, it is, at least, one of its brothers."

I looked at Conseil. Ned Land hurried to the window.

"What a horrible beast!" he cried.

I looked in my turn, and could not repress a gesture of disgust. Before my eyes was a horrible monster, worthy to figure in the legends of the marvellous. It was an immense cuttle-fish, being eight yards long. It swam crossways in the direction of the *Nautilus* with great speed, watching us with its enormous staring green eyes. Its eight arms, or rather feet, fixed to its head, that have given the name of cephalopod to these animals, were twice as long as its body, and were twisted like the furies' hair. One could see the 250 air-holes on the inner side of the tentacles. The monster's mouth, a horned beak like a parrot's, opened and shut vertically. Its tongue, a horned substance, furnished with several rows of pointed teeth, came out quivering from this veritable pair of shears. What a freak of nature, a bird's beak on a mollusc! Its spindle-like body formed a fleshy mass that might weigh 4000 to 5000 lbs.; the varying colour changing with great rapidity, according to the irritation of the animal, passed successively from livid grey to reddish brown. What irritated this mollusc? No doubt the presence of the *Nautilus*, more formidable than itself, and on which its suckers or its jaws had no hold. Yet, what monsters these poulps are! what vitality the Creator has given them! what vigour in their movements! and they possess three hearts! Chance had brought us in presence of this cuttle-fish, and I did not wish to lose the opportunity of carefully studying this specimen of cephalopods. I overcame the horror that inspired me; and, taking a pencil, began to draw it.

"Perhaps this is the same which the *Alecto* saw," said Conseil.

"No," replied the Canadian; "for this is whole, and the other had lost its tail."

"That is no reason," I replied. "The arms and tails of these animals are reformed by redintegration; and, in seven years, the tail of Bouguer's cuttle-fish has no doubt had time to grow."

By this time other poulps appeared at the port light. I counted seven. They formed a procession after the *Nautilus*, and I heard their beaks gnashing against the iron hull. I continued my work. These monsters kept in the water with such precision, that they seemed immovable. Suddenly the *Nautilus* stopped. A shock made it tremble in every plate.

"Have we struck anything?" I asked.

"In any case," replied the Canadian, "we shall be free, for we are floating."

The *Nautilus* was floating, no doubt, but it did not move. A minute passed. Captain Nemo, followed by his lieutenant, entered the drawing-room. I had not seen him for some time. He seemed dull. Without noticing or speaking to us, he went to the panel, looked at the poulps, and said something to his lieutenant. The latter went out. Soon the panels were shut. The ceiling was lighted. I went towards the Captain.

"A curious collection of poulps?" I said.

"Yes, indeed, Mr Naturalist," he replied; "and we are going to fight them, man to beast."

I looked at him. I thought I had not heard aright.

"Man to beast?" I repeated.

"Yes, sir. The screw is stopped. I think that the horny jaws of one of the cuttle-fish is entangled in the blades. That is what prevents our moving."

"What are you going to do?"

"Rise to the surface, and slaughter this vermin."

"A difficult enterprise."

"Yes, indeed. The electric bullets are powerless against the soft flesh, where they do not find resistance enough to go off. But we shall attack them with the hatchet."

"And the harpoon, sir," said the Canadian, "if you do not refuse my help."

"I will accept it, Master Land."

"We will follow you," I said, and following Captain Nemo, we went towards the central staircase.

There, about ten men with boarding hatchers were ready for the attack. Conseil and I took two hatchets; Ned Land seized a harpoon. The *Nautilus* had then risen to the surface. One of the sailors, posted on the top ladder-step, unscrewed the bolts of the panels. But hardly were the screws loosed, when the panel rose with great violence, evidently drawn by the suckers of a poulp's arm. Immediately one of these arms slid like a serpent down the opening, and twenty others were above. With one blow of the axe, Captain Nemo cut this formidable tentacle, that slid wriggling down the ladder. Just as we were pressing one on the other to reach the platform, two other arms, lashing the air, came down on the seaman placed before Captain Nemo, and lifted him up with irresistible power. Captain Nemo uttered a cry, and rushed out. We hurried after him.

What a scene! The unhappy man, seized by the tentacle, and fixed to the suckers, was balanced in the air at the caprice of this enormous trunk. He rattled in his throat, he was stifled, he cried, "Help! help!" These words, *spoken in French*, startled me! I had a fellow-countryman on board, perhaps several! That heart-rending cry! I shall hear it all my life. The unfortunate man was lost. Who could rescue him from that powerful pressure? However, Captain Nemo had rushed to the poulp, and with one blow of the axe had cut through one arm. His lieutenant struggled furiously against other monsters that crept on the flanks of the *Nautilus*. The crew fought with their axes. The Canadian, Conseil, and I, buried our weapons in the fleshy masses; a strong smell of musk penetrated the atmosphere. It was horrible!

For one instant, I thought the unhappy man, entangled with the poulp, would be torn from its powerful suction. Seven of the eight arms had been cut off. One only wriggled in the air, brandishing the victim like a feather. But just as Captain Nemo and his lieutenant threw themselves on it, the animal ejected a stream of black liquid. We were blinded with it. When the cloud dispersed, the cuttle-fish had disappeared, and my unfortunate countryman with it. Ten or twelve poulps now invaded the platform and sides of the *Nautilus*. We rolled pell-mell into the midst of this nest of serpents, that wriggled on the platform in the waves of blood and ink. It seemed as though these slimy tentacles sprang up like the hydra's heads. Ned Land's harpoon, at each stroke, was plunged into the staring eyes of the cuttlefish. But my bold companion was suddenly overturned by the tentacles of a monster he had not been able to avoid.

Ah! how my heart beat with emotion and horror! The formidable beak of a cuttle-fish was open over Ned Land. The unhappy man would be cut in two. I rushed to his succour. But Captain Nemo was before me; his axe disappeared between the two enormous jaws, and miraculously saved the Canadian, rising, plunged his harpoon deep into the triple heart of the poulp.

"I owed myself this revenge!" said the Captain to the Canadian.

Ned bowed without replying. The combat had lasted a quarter of an hour. The monsters, vanquished and mutilated, left us at last, and disappeared under the waves. Captain Nemo, covered with blood, nearly exhausted, gazed upon the sea that had swallowed up one of his companions, and great tears gathered in his eyes.

Chapter XIX

The Gulf Stream

This terrible scene of the 20th of April none of us can ever forget. I have written it under the influence of violent emotion. Since then I have revised the recital; I have read it to Conseil and to the Canadian. They found it exact as to facts, but insufficient as to effect. To paint such pictures, one must have the pen of the most illustrious of our poets, the author of "The Toilers of the Deep."

I have said that Captain Nemo wept while watching the waves; his grief was great. It was the second companion he had lost since our arrival on board, and what a death! That friend, crushed, stifled, bruised by the dreadful arms of a poulp, pounded by his iron jaws, would not rest with his comrades in the peaceful coral cemetery! In the midst of the struggle, it was the despairing cry uttered by the unfortunate man that had torn my heart. The poor Frenchman, forgetting his conventional language, had taken to his own mother tongue, to utter a last appeal! Amongst the crew of the *Nautilus*, associated with the body and soul of the Captain, recoiling like him from all contact with men, I had a fellow countryman. Did he alone represent France in this mysterious association, evidently composed of individuals of divers nationalities? It was one of these insoluble problems that rose up unceasingly before my mind!

Captain Nemo entered his room, and I saw him no more for some time. But that he was sad and irresolute I could see by the vessel, of which he was the soul, and which received all his impressions. The *Nautilus* did not keep on in its settled course; it floated about like a corpse at the will of the waves. It went at random. He could not tear himself away from the scene of the last struggle, from this sea that had devoured one of his men. Ten days passed thus. It was not till the 1st of May that the *Nautilus* resumed its northerly course, after having sighted the Bahamas at the mouth of the Bahama Canal. We were then following the current from the largest river to the sea, that has its banks, its fish, and its proper temperatures. I mean the gulf Stream. It is really a river, that flows freely to the middle of the Atlantic, and whose waters do not mix with the ocean waters. It is a salt river, salter than the surrounding sea. Its mean depth is 1500 fathoms, its mean breadth ten miles. In certain places the current flows with the speed of two miles and a half an hour. The body of its waters is more considerable than that of all the rivers in the globe. It was on this ocean river that the *Nautilus* then sailed.

This current carried with it all kinds of living things. Argonauts, so common in the Mediterranean, were there in quantities. Of the gristly sort, the most remarkable were the turbot, whose slender tails form nearly the third part of the body, and that looked like large lozenges twenty-five feet long; also, small sharks a yard long, with large heads, short rounded muzzles, pointed teeth in several rows, and whose bodies seemed covered with scales. Among the bony fish I noticed some grey gobies, peculiar to these waters; black giltheads, whose iris shone like fire; sirenes a yard long, with large snouts thickly set with little teeth, that uttered little cries; blue coryphaenes, in gold and silver; parrots, like the rainbows of the ocean, that could rival in colour the most beautiful tropical birds; blennies with triangular heads; bluish rhombs destitute of scales; batrachoides covered with yellow transversal bands like a Greek *r*; heaps of little gobies spotted with yellow; dipterodons with silvery heads and yellow tails; several specimens of salmon, mugilomores slender in shape, shining with a soft light that Lacépède consecrated to the service of his wife; and lastly, a beautiful fish, the American-knight, that, decorated with all the orders and ribbons, frequents the shores of this great nation, that esteems orders and ribbons so little.

I must add that, during the night, the phosphorescent waters of the Gulf Stream rivalled the electric power of our watch-light, especially in the stormy weather that threatened us so frequently. May 8th, we were still crossing Cape Hatteras, at the height of the North Caroline. The width of the Gulf Stream there is seventy-five miles, and its depth 210 yards. The *Nautilus* still went at random; all supervision seemed abandoned. I thought that, under these circumstances, escape would be possible. Indeed, the inhabited shores offered anywhere an easy refuge. The sea was incessantly ploughed by the steamers that ply between New York or Boston and the Gulf of Mexico, and overrun day and night by the little schooners coasting about the several parts of the American coast. We could hope to be picked up. It was a favourable opportunity, notwithstanding the thirty miles that separated the *Nautilus* from the coasts of the Union. One unfortunate circumstance thwarted the Canadian's plans. The weather was very bad. We were nearing these shores where tempests are so frequent, that country of waterspouts and cyclones actually engendered by the current of the Gulf Stream. To tempt the sea in a frail boat was certain destruction. Ned Land owned this himself. He fretted, seized with nostalgia that flight only could cure.

"Master," he said that day to me, "this must come to an end. I must make a clean breast of it. This Nemo is leaving land and going up to the north. But I declare to you, I have had enough of the South Pole, and I will not follow him to the North."

"What is to be done, Ned, since flight is impracticable just now?"

"We must speak to the Captain," said he; "you said nothing when we were in your native seas. I will speak, now we are in mine. When I think that before long the *Nautilus* will be by Nova Scotia, and that there near Newfoundland is a large bay, and into that bay the St Lawrence empties itself, and that the St Lawrence is my river, the river by Quebec my native town,—when I think of this, I feel furious, it makes my hair stand on end. Sir, I would rather throw myself into the sea! I will not stay here! I am stifled!"

The Canadian was evidently losing all patience. His vigorous nature could not stand this prolonged imprisonment. His face altered daily; his temper became more surly. I knew what he must suffer, for I was seized with nostalgia myself. Nearly seven months had passed without our having had any news from land; Captain Nemo's isolation, his altered spirits, especially since the fight with the poulps, his taciturnity, all made me view things in a different light.

"Well, sir?" said Ned, seeing I did not reply.

"Well, Ned! do you wish me to ask Captain Nemo his intentions concerning us?"

"Yes, sir."

"Although he has already made them known?"

"Yes; I wish it settled finally. Speak for me, in my name only, if you like."

"But I so seldom meet him. He avoids me."

"That is all the more reason for you to go to see him."

I went to my room. From thence I meant to go to Captain Nemo's. It would not do to let this opportunity of meeting him slip. I knocked at the door. No answer. I knocked again, then turned the handle. The door opened, I went in. The Captain was there. Bending over his work-table, he had not heard me. Resolved not to go without having spoken, I approached him. He raised his head quickly, frowned, and said roughly, "You here! What do you want?"

"To speak to you, Captain."

"But I am busy, sir; I am working. I leave you at liberty to shut yourself up; cannot I be allowed the same?"

This reception was not encouraging; but I was determined to hear and answer everything.

"Sir," I said, coldly, "I have to speak to you on a matter that admits of no delay."

"What is that, sir?" he replied, ironically. "Have you discovered something that has escaped me, or has the sea delivered up any new secrets?"

We were at cross-purposes. But before I could reply, he showed me an open manuscript on his table, and said, in a more serious tone, "Here, M. Aronnax, is a manuscript written in several languages. It contains the sum of my studies of the sea; and, if it please God, it shall not perish with me. This manuscript, signed with my name, completed with the history of my life, will be shut up in a little insubmersible case. The last survivor of all of us on board the *Nautilus* will throw this case into the sea, and it will go whither it is borne by the waves."

This man's name! his history written by himself! His mystery would then be revealed some day.

"Captain," I said, "I can but approve of the idea that makes you act thus. The result of your studies must not be lost. But the means you employ seem to me to be primitive. Who knows where the winds will carry this case, and in whose hands it will fall? Could you not use some other means? Could not you, or one of yours"—

"Never, sir!" he said, hastily interrupting me.

"But I and my companions are ready to keep this manuscript in store; and, if you will put us at liberty"—

"At liberty?" said the Captain, rising.

"Yes, sir; that is the subject on which I wish to question you. For seven months we have been here on board, and I ask you to-day, in the name of my companions, and in my own, if your intention is to keep us here always?"

"M. Aronnax, I will answer you to-day as I did seven months ago: Whoever enters the *Nautilus* must never quit it."

"You impose actual slavery on us!"

"Give it what name you please."

"But everywhere the slave has the right to regain his liberty."

"Who denies you this right? Have I ever tried to chain you with an oath?"

He looked at me with his arms crossed.

"Sir," I said, "to return a second time to this subject will be neither to your nor to my taste; but, as we have entered upon it, let us go through with it. I repeat, it is not only myself whom it concerns. Study is to me a relief, a diversion, a passion that could make me forget everything. Like you, I am willing to live obscure, in the frail hope of bequeathing one day, to future time, the result of my labours. But it is otherwise with Ned Land. Every man, worthy of the name, deserves some considera-tion. Have you thought that love of liberty, hatred of slavery, can give rise to schemes of revenge in a nature like the Canadian's; that he could think, attempt, and try"—

I was silenced; Captain Nemo rose.

"Whatever Ned Land thinks of, attempts, or tries, what does it mat-ter to me? I did not seek him! It is not for my pleasure that I keep him on board! As for you, M. Aronnax, you are one of those who can under-stand everything, even silence. I have nothing more to say to you. Let this first time you have come to treat of this subject be the last; for a second time I will not listen to you."

I retired. Our situation was critical. I related my conversation to my two companions.

"We know now," said Ned, "that we can expect nothing from this man. The *Nautilus* is nearing Long Island. We will escape, whatever the weather may be."

But the sky became more and more threatening. Symptoms of a hurricane became manifest. The atmosphere was becoming white and misty. On the horizon fine streaks of cirrhous clouds were succeeded by masses of cumuli. Other low clouds passed swiftly by. The swollen sea rose in huge billows. The birds disappeared, with the exception of the petrels, those friends of the storm. The barometer fell sensibly, and indicated an extreme tension of the vapours. The mixture of the storm glass was decomposed under the influence of the electricity that pervaded the atmosphere. The tempest burst on the 18th of May, just as the *Nautilus* was floating off Long Island, some miles from the port of New York. I can describe this strife of the elements! for, instead of fleeing to the depths of the sea, Captain Nemo, by an unaccountable caprice, would brave it at the surface. The wind blew from the south-west at first. Captain Nemo, during the squalls, had taken his place on the platform. He had made himself fast, to prevent being washed overboard by the monstrous waves. I had hoisted myself up, and made myself fast also, dividing my admiration between the tempest and this extraordinary man who was coping with it. The raging sea was swept by huge cloud-drifts, which were actually saturated with the waves. The *Nautilus*, sometimes lying on its side, sometimes standing up like a mast, rolled and pitched terribly. About five o'clock a torrent of rain fell, that lulled neither sea nor wind. The hurricane blew nearly forty leagues an hour. It is under these conditions that it overturns houses, breaks iron gates, displaces twenty-four pounders. However, the *Nautilus*, in the midst of the tempest, confirmed the words of a clever engineer, "There is no well-constructed hull that cannot defy the sea." This was not a resisting rock; it was a steel spindle, obedient and movable, without rigging or masts, that braved its fury and impunity. However, I watched these raging waves attentively. They measured fifteen feet in height, and 150 to 175 yards long, and their speed of propagation was thirty feet per second. Their bulk and power increased with the depth of the water. Such waves as these, at the Hebrides, have displaced a mass weighing 8400 lbs. They are they which, in the tempest of December 23, 1864, after destroying the town of Yeddo, in Japan, broke the same day on the shores of America. The intensity of the tempest increased with the night. The barometer, as in 1860 at Reunion during a cyclone, fell seven-tenths at the close of day. I saw a large vessel pass the horizon struggling painfully. She was trying to lie to under half-steam, to keep up above the waves. It was probably one of the steamers of the line from New York to Liverpool, or Havre. It soon disappeared in the gloom. At ten o'clock in the evening the sky was on fire. The atmosphere was streaked with vivid lightning. I could not bear the brightness of it; while the Captain, looking at it, seemed to envy the spirit of the tempest. A terrible noise filled the air, a complex noise, made up of the howls of the crushed waves, the roaring of the wind, and the claps of thunder. The wind veered suddenly to all points of the horizon; and the cyclone, rising in the east, returned after passing by the north, west, and south, in the inverse course pursued by the circular storms of the southern hemisphere. Ah, that Gulf Stream! It deserves its name of the King of Tempests. It is that which causes those formidable cyclones, by the difference of temperature between its air and its currents. A shower of fire had succeeded the rain. The drops of water were changed to sharp spikes. One would have thought that Captain Nemo was courting a death worthy of himself, a death by lightning. As the *Nautilus*, pitching dreadfully, raised its steel spur in the air, it seemed to act as a conductor, and I saw long sparks burst from it. Crushed and without strength, I crawled to the panel, opened it, and descended to the saloon. The storm was then at its height. It was impossible to stand upright in the interior of the *Nautilus*. Captain Nemo came down about twelve. I heard the reservoirs filling by degrees, and the *Nautilus* sank slowly beneath the waves. Through the open windows in the saloon I saw large fish terrified, passing like phantoms in the water. Some were struck before my eyes. The *Nautilus* was still descending. I thought that at about eight fathoms deep we should find a calm. But no! the upper beds were too violently agitated for that. We had to seek repose at more than twenty-five fathoms in the bowels of the deep. But there, what quiet, what silence, what peace! Who could have told that such a hurricane had been let loose on the surface of that ocean?

Chapter XX

From Latitude 47° 24', to Longitude 17° 28'

In consequence of the storm, we had been thrown eastward once more. All hope of escape on the shores of New York or St Lawrence had faded away; and poor Ned, in despair, had isolated himself like Captain Nemo. Conseil and I, however, never left each other. I said that the *Nautilus* had gone aside to the east. I should have said (to be more exact), the north-east. For some days, it wandered first on the surface, and then beneath it, amid these fogs so dreaded by sailors. What accidents are due to these thick fogs! What shocks upon these reefs when the wind drowns the breaking of the waves! What collisions between vessels, in spite of their warning lights, whistles, and alarm bells! And the bottoms of these seas look like a field of battle, where still lie all the conquered of the ocean; some old and already encrusted, others fresh and reflecting from their iron bands and copperplates the brilliancy of our lantern.

On the 15th of May we were at the extreme south of the Bank of Newfoundland. This bank consists of alluvia, or large heaps of organic matter, brought either from the Equator by the Gulf Stream, or from the North Pole by the counter current of cold water which skirts the American coast. There also are heaped up those erratic blocks which are carried along by the broken ice; and close by, a vast charnel-house of molluscs or zoophytes, which perish here by millions. The depth of the sea is not great at Newfoundland —not more than some hundreds of fathoms; but towards the south is a depression of 1500 fathoms. There the Gulf Stream widens. It loses some of its speed and some of its temperature, but it becomes a sea.

It was on the 17th of May, about 500 miles from Heart's Content, at a depth of more than 1400 fathoms, that I saw the electric cable lying on the bottom. Conseil, to whom I had not mentioned it, thought at first that it was a gigantic sea-serpent. But I undeceived the worthy fellow, and by way of consolation related several particulars in the laying of this cable. The first one was laid in the years 1857 and 1858; but, after transmitting about 400 telegrams, would not act any longer. In 1863, the engineers constructed another one, measuring 2000 miles in length, and weighing 4500 tons, which was embarked on the *Great Eastern*. This attempt also failed.

On the 25th of May the *Nautilus*, being at a depth of more than 1918 fathoms, was on the precise spot where the rupture occurred which ruined the enterprise. It was within 638 miles of the coast of Ireland; and at half-past two in the afternoon, they discovered that communication with Europe had ceased. The electricians on board resolved to cut the cable before fishing it up, and at eleven o'clock at night they had recovered the damaged part. They made another point and spliced it, and it was once more submerged. But some days after it broke again, and in the depths of the ocean could not be recaptured. The Americans, however, were not discouraged. Cyrus Field, the bold promoter of the enterprise, as he had sunk all his own fortune, set a new subscription on foot, which was at once answered, and another cable was constructed on better principles. The bundles of conducting wires were each enveloped in gutta-percha, and protected by a wadding of hemp, contained in a metallic covering. The *Great Eastern* sailed on the 13th of July 1866. The operation worked well. But one incident occurred. Several times in unrolling the cable they observed that nails had been recently forced into it, evidently with the motive of destroying it. Captain Anderson, the officers, and engineers, consulted together, and had it posted up that if the offender was surprised on board, he would be thrown without further trial into the sea. From that time the criminal attempt was never repeated.

On the 23rd of July the *Great Eastern* was not more than 500 miles from Newfoundland, when they telegraphed from Ireland news of the armistice concluded between Prussia and Austria after Sadowa. On the 27th, in the midst of heavy fogs, they reached the port of Heart's Content. The enterprise was successfully terminated; and for its first despatch, young America addressed old Europe in these words of wisdom so rarely understood— "Glory to God in the highest, and on earth peace, goodwill towards men."

I did not expect to find the electric cable in its primitive state, such as it was on leaving the manufactory. The long serpent, covered with the remains of shells, bristling with foraminiferae, was encrusted with a strong coating which served as a protection against all boring molluscs. It lay quietly sheltered from the motions of the sea, and under a favourable pressure for the transmission of the electric spark which passes from Europe to America in .32 of a second. Doubtless this cable will last for a great length of time, for they find that the gutta-percha covering is improved by the sea-water. Besides, on this level, so well chosen, the cable is never so deeply submerged as to cause it to break. The *Nautilus* followed it to the lowest depth, which was more than 2212 fathoms, and there it lay without any anchorage; and then we reached the spot where the accident had taken place in 1863. The bottom of the ocean then formed a valley about 100 miles broad, in which Mont-Blanc might have been placed without its summit appearing above the waves. This valley is closed at the east by a perpendicular wall more than 2000 yards high. We arrived there on the 28th of May, and the *Nautilus* was then not more than 120 miles from Ireland.

Was Captain Nemo going to land on the British Isles? No. To my great surprise he made for the south, once more coming back towards European seas. In rounding the Emerald Isle, for one instant I caught sight of Cape Clear, and the light which guides the thousands of vessels leaving Glasgow or Liverpool. An important question then arose in my mind. Did the *Nautilus* dare entangle itself in the Mauch? Ned Land, who had reappeared since we had been nearing land, did not cease to question me. How could I answer? Captain Nemo remained invisible. After having shown the Canadian a glimpse of American shores, was he going to show me the coast of France?

But the *Nautilus* was still going southward. On the 30th of May, it passed in sight of the Land's End, between the extreme point of England and the Scilly Isles, which were left to starboard. If he wished to enter the Mauch he must go straight to the east. He did not do so.

During the whole of the 31st of May, the *Nautilus* described a series of circles on the water, which greatly interested me. It seemed to be seeking a spot it had some trouble in finding. At noon, Captain Nemo himself came to work the ship's log. He spoke no word to me, but seemed gloomier than ever. What could sadden him thus? Was it his proximity to European shores? Had he some recollections of his abandoned country? If not, what did he feel? Remorse or regret? For a long while this thought haunted my mind, and I had a kind of presentiment that before long chance would betray the Captain's secrets.

The next day, the 31st of June, the *Nautilus* continued the same process. It was evidently seeking some particular spot in the ocean. Captain Nemo took the sun's altitude as he had done the day before. The sea was beautiful, the sky clear. About eight miles to the east, a large steam vessel could be discerned on the horizon. No flag fluttered from its mast, and I could not discover its nationality. Some minutes before the sun passed the meridian, Captain Nemo took his sextant, and watched with great attention. The perfect rest of the water greatly helped the operation. The *Nautilus* was motionless; it neither rolled nor pitched.

I was on the platform when the altitude was taken, and the Captain pronounced these words—"It is here."

He turned and went below. Had he seen the vessel which was changing its course and seemed to be nearing us? I could not tell. I returned to the saloon. The panels closed, I heard the hissing of the water in the reservoirs. The *Nautilus* began to sink, following a vertical line, for its screw communicated no motion to it. Some minutes later it stopped at a depth of more than 420 fathoms, resting on the ground. The luminous ceiling was darkened, then the panels were opened, and through the glass I saw the sea brilliantly illuminated by the rays of our lantern for at least half a mile round us.

I looked to the port side, and saw nothing but an immensity of quiet waters. But to starboard, on the bottom appeared a large protuberance, which at once attracted my attention. One would have thought it a ruin buried under a coating of white shells, much resembling a covering of snow. Upon examining the mass attentively, I could recognise the ever thickening form of a vessel bare of its masts, which must have sunk. It certainly belonged to past times. This wreck, to be thus encrusted with the lime of the water, must already be able to count many years passed at the bottom of the ocean.

What was this vessel? Why did the *Nautilus* visit its tomb? Could it have been aught but a shipwreck which had drawn it under the water? I knew not what to think, when near me in a slow voice I heard Captain Nemo say—

"At one time this ship was called the *Marseillais*. It carried seventy-four guns, and was launched in 1762. In 1778, the 13th of August, commanded by La Poype-Vertrieux, it fought boldly against the *Preston*. In 1779, on the 4th of July, it was at the taking of Grenada, with the squadron of Admiral Estaing. In 1781, on the 5th of September, it took part in the battle of Comte de Grasse, in Chesapeake Bay. In 1794, the French Republic changed its name. On the 16th of April, in the same year, it joined the squadron of Villaret Joyeuse, at Brest, being entrusted with the escort of a cargo of corn coming from America, under the command of Admiral Van Stabel. On the 11th and 12th Prairal of the second year, this squadron fell in with an English vessel. Sir, to-day is the 13th Prairal, the 1st of June 1868. It is now seventy-four years ago, day for day on this very spot, in latitude 47° 24', longitude 17° 28', that this vessel, after fighting heroically, losing its three masts, with the water in its hold, and the third of its crew disabled, preferred sinking with its 356 sailors or surrendering; and nailing its colours to the poop, disappeared under the waves to the cry of 'Long live the Republic!' "

"The *Avenger!*" I exclaimed.

"Yes, sir, the *Avenger!* A good name!" muttered Captain Nemo, crossing his arms.

Chapter XXI

A Hecatomb

The way of describing this unlooked-for scene, the history of the patriot ship, told at first so coldly, and the emotion with which this strange man pronounced the last words, the name of the *Avenger*, the significance of which could not escape me, all impressed itself deeply on my mind. My eyes did not leave the Captain; who, with his hand stretched out to sea, was watching with a glowing eye the glorious wreck. Perhaps I was never to know who he was, from whence he came, or where he was going to, but I saw the man move, and apart from the savant. It was no common misanthropy which had shut Captain Nemo and his companions within the *Nautilus*, but a hatred, either monstrous or sublime, which time could never weaken. Did this hatred still seek for vengeance? The future would soon teach me that. But the *Nautilus* was rising slowly to the surface of the sea, and the form of the *Avenger* disappeared by degrees from my sight. Soon a slight rolling told me that we were in the open air. At that moment a dull boom was heard. I looked at the Captain. He did not move.

"Captain?" said I.

He did not answer. I left him and mounted the platform. Conseil and the Canadian were already there.

"Where did that sound come from?" I asked.

"It was a gunshot," replied Ned Land.

I looked in the direction of the vessel I had already seen. It was nearing the *Nautilus*, and we could see that it was putting on steam. It was within six miles of us.

"What is that ship, Ned?"

"By its rigging, and the height of its lower masts," said the Canadian, "I bet she is a ship of war. May it reach us; and, if necessary, sink this cursed *Nautilus*."

"Friend Ned," replied Conseil, "what harm can it do to the *Nautilus*? Can it attack it beneath the waves? Can it cannonade us at the bottom of the sea?"

"Tell me, Ned," said I, "can you recognise what country she belongs to?"

The Canadian knitted his eyebrows, dropped his eyelids, and screwed up the corners of his eyes, and for a few moments fixed a piercing look upon the vessel.

"No, sir," he replied; "I cannot tell what nation she belongs to, for she shows no colours. But I can declare she is a man-of-war, for a long pennant flutters from her mainmast."

For a quarter of an hour we watched the ship which was steaming towards us. I could not, however, believe that she could see the *Nautilus* from that distance; and still less, that she could know what this submarine engine was. Soon the Canadian informed me that she was a large armoured two-decker ram. A thick black smoke was pouring from her two funnels. Her closely-furled sails were stopped to her yards. She hoisted no flag at her mizenpeak. The distance prevented us from distinguishing the colours of her pennant, which floated like a thin ribbon. She advanced rapidly. If Captain Nemo allowed her to approach, there was a chance of salvation for us.

"Sir," said Ned Land, "if that vessel passes within a mile of us I shall throw myself into the sea, and I should advise you to do the same."

I did not reply to the Canadian's suggestion, but continued watching the ship. Whether English, French, American, or Russian, she would be sure to take us in if we could only reach her. Presently a white smoke burst from the fore part of the vessel; some second after the water, agitated by the fall of a heavy body, splashed the stern of the *Nautilus*, and shortly afterwards a loud explosion struck my ear.

"What! they are firing at us!" I exclaimed.

"So please you, sir," said Ned, "they have recognised the unicorn, and they are firing at us."

"But," I exclaimed, "surely they can see that there are men in the case?"

"It is, perhaps, because of that," replied Ned Land, looking at me.

A whole flood of light burst upon my mind. Doubtless they knew now how to believe the stories of the pretended monster. No doubt, on board the *Abraham Lincoln*, when the Canadian struck it with the harpoon, Commander Farragut had recognised in the supposed narwhal a submarine vessel, more dangerous than a supernatural cetacean. Yes, it must have been so; and on every sea they were now seeking this engine of destruction. Terrible indeed! if, as we supposed, Captain Nemo employed the *Nautilus* in works of vengeance. On the night when we were imprisoned in that cell, in the midst of the Indian Ocean, had he not attacked some vessel? The man buried in the coral cemetery, had he not been a victim to the shock caused by the *Nautilus?* Yes, I repeat it, it must be so. One part of the mysterious existence of Captain Nemo had been unveiled; and, if his identity had not been recognised, at least, the nations united against him were no longer hunting a chimerical creature, but a man who had vowed a deadly hatred against them. All the formidable past rose before me. Instead of meeting friends on board the approaching ship, we could only expect pitiless enemies. But the shot rattled about us. Some of them struck the sea and ricochetted, losing themselves in the distance. But none touched the *Nautilus*. The vessel was not more than three miles from us. In spite of the serious connonade, Captain Nemo did not appear on the platform; but, if one of the conical projectiles had struck the shell of the *Nautilus*, it would have been fatal. The Canadian then said, "Sir, we must do all we can to get out of this dilemma. Let us signal them. They will then, perhaps, understand that we are honest folks."

Ned Land took his handkerchief to wave in the air; but he had scarcely displayed it, when he was struck down by an iron hand, and fell, in spite of his great strength, upon the deck.

"Fool!" exclaimed the Captain, "do you wish to be pierced by the spur of the *Nautilus* before it is hurled at this vessel?"

Captain Nemo was terrible to hear; he was still more terrible to see. His face was deadly pale, with a spasm at his heart. For an instant it must have ceased to beat. His pupils were fearfully contracted. He did not *speak*, he *roared*, as, with his body thrown forward, he wrung the Canadian's shoulders. Then, leaving him, and turning to the ship of war, whose shot was still raining around him, he exclaimed, with a powerful voice, "Ah, ship of an accursed nation, you know who I am! I do not want your colours to know you by! Look! and I will show you mine!"

And on the fore part of the platform Captain Nemo unfurled a black flag, similar to the one he had placed at the south-pole. At that moment a shot struck the shell of the *Nautilus* obliquely, without piercing it; and, rebounding near the Captain, was lost in the sea. He shrugged his shoulders; and addressing me, said shortly, "Go down, you and your companions, go down!"

"Sir," I exclaimed, "are you going to attack this vessel?"

"Sir, I am going to sink it."

"You will not do that?"

"I shall do it," he replied, coldly. "And I advise you not to judge me, sir. Fate has shown you what you ought not have seen. The attack has begun; go down."

"What is this vessel?"

"You do not know? Very well! so much the better! its nationality to you, at least, will be a secret. Go down!"

We could but obey. About fifteen of the sailors surrounded the Captain, looking with implacable hatred at the vessel nearing them. One could feel that the same desire of vengeance animated every soul. I went down at the moment another projectile struck the *Nautilus*, and I heard the Captain exclaim—

"Strike, mad vessel! Shower your useless shot! And then, you will not escape the spur of the *Nautilus*. But it is not here that you shall perish! I would not have your ruins mingle with those of the *Avenger!*"

I reached my room. The Captain and his second had remained on the platform. The screw was set in motion, and the *Nautilus*, moving with speed, was soon beyond the reach of the ship's guns. But the pursuit continued, and Captain Nemo contented himself with keeping his distance.

About four in the afternoon, being no longer able to contain my impatience, I went to the central staircase. The panel was open, and I ventured on to the platform. The Captain was still walking up and down with an agitated step. He was looking at the ship, which was five or six miles to leeward.

He was going round it like a wild beast, and drawing it eastward, he allowed them to pursue. But he did not attack. Perhaps he still hesitated? I wished to mediate once more. But I had scarcely spoken, when Captain Nemo imposed silence, saying—

"I am the law, and I am the judge! I am the oppressed, and there is the oppressor! Through him I have lost all that I loved, cherished, and venerated,—country, wife, children, father, and mother. I saw all perish! All that I hate is there! Say no more!"

I cast a last look at the man-of-war, which was putting on steam, and rejoined Ned and Conseil.

"We will fly!" I exclaimed.

"God!" said Ned. "What is this vessel?"

"I do not know; but whatever it is, it will be sunk before night. In any case, it is better to perish with it, than be made accomplices in a retaliation, the justice of which we cannot judge."

"That is my opinion too," said Ned Land, coolly. "Let us wait for night."

Night arrived. Deep silence reigned on board. The compass showed that the *Nautilus* had not altered its course. It was on the surface, rolling slightly. My companions and I resolved to fly when the vessel should be near enough either to hear us or to see us; for the moon, which would be full in two or three days, shone brightly. Once on board the ship, if we could not prevent the blow which threatened it, we could, at least we would, do all that circumstances would allow. Several times

I thought the *Nautilus* was preparing for attack; but Captain Nemo contented himself with allowing his adversary to approach, and then fled once more before it.

Part of the night passed without any incident. We watched the opportunity for action. We spoke little, for we were too much moved. Ned Land would have thrown himself into the sea, but I forced him to wait. According to my idea, the *Nautilus* would attack the ship at her waterline, and then it would not only be possible, but easy to fly.

At three in the morning, full of uneasiness, I mounted the platform. Captain Nemo had not left it. He was standing at the forepart near his flag, which a slight breeze displayed above his head. He did not take his eyes from the vessel. The intensity of his look seemed to attract, and fascinate, and draw it onward more purely than if he had been towing it. The moon was then passing the meridian. Jupiter was rising in the east. Amid this peaceful scene of nature, sky and ocean rivalled each other in tranquillity, the sea offering to the orbs of night the finest mirror they could ever have in which to reflect their image. As I thought of the deep calm of these elements, compared with all those passions brooding imperceptably within the *Nautilus*, I shuddered.

The vessel was within two miles of us. It was ever nearing that phosphorescent light which showed the presence of the *Nautilus*. I could see its green and red lights, and its white lantern hanging from the large mizenmast. An indistinct vibration quivered through its rigging, showing that the furnaces were heated to the uttermost. Sheaves of sparks and red ashes flew from the funnels, shining in the atmosphere like stars.

I remained thus until six in the morning, without Captain Nemo noticing me. The ship stood about a mile and a half from us, and with the first dawn of day the firing began afresh. The moment could not be far off when, the *Nautilus* attacking its adversary, my companions and myself should for ever leave this man. I was preparing to go down to remind them, when the second mounted the platform, accompanied by several sailors. Captain Nemo either did not, or would not, see them. Some steps were taken which might be called the signal for action. They were very simple. The iron balustrade around the plat-form was lowered, and the lantern and pilot cages were pushed within the shell until they were flush with the deck. The long surface of the steel cigar no longer offered a single point to check its manoeuvres. I returned to the saloon. The *Nautilus* still floated; some streaks of light were filtering through the liquid beds. With the undulations of the waves the windows were brightened by the red streaks of the rising sun, and this dreadful day of the 2nd of June had dawned.

At five o'clock, the log showed that the speed of the *Nautilus* was slackening, and I knew that it was allowing them to draw nearer. Besides, the reports were heard more distinctly, and the projectiles, labouring through the ambient water, were extinguished with a strange hissing noise.

"My friends," said I, "the moment is come. One grasp of the hand, and may God protect us!"

Ned Land was resolute, Conseil calm, myself so nervous that I knew not how to contain myself. We all passed into the library; but the moment I pushed the door opening on to the central staircase, I heard the upper panel close sharply. The Canadian rushed on to the stairs, but I stopped him. A well-known hissing noise told me that the water was running into the reservoirs, and in a few minutes the *Nautilus* was some yards beneath the surface of the waves. I understood the manoeuvre. It was too late to act. The *Nautilus* did not wish to strike at the impenetrable cuirass, but below the waterline, where the metallic covering no longer protected it.

We were again imprisoned, unwilling witnesses of the dreadful drama that was preparing. We had scarcely time to reflect; taking ref-uge in my room, we looked at each other without speaking. A deep stu-por had taken hold of my mind: thought seemed to stand still. I was in that painful state of expectation preceding a dreadful report. I waited, I listened, every sense was merged in that of hearing! The speed of the *Nautilus* was accelerated. It was preparing to rush. The whole ship trembled. Suddenly I screamed. I felt the shock, but comparatively light. I felt the penetrating power of the steel spur. I heard rattlings and scrapings. But the *Nautilus*, carried along by its propelling power, passed through the mass of the vessel, like a needle through sailcloth!

I could stand it no longer. Mad, out of my mind, I rushed from my room into the saloon. Captain Nemo was there, mute, gloomy, implacable; he was looking through the port panel. A large mass cast a shadow on the water; and that it might lose nothing of her agony, the *Nautilus* was going down into the abyss with her. Ten yards from me I saw the open shell through which the water was rushing with the noise of thunder, then the double line of guns and the netting. The bridge was covered with black agitated shadows.

The water was rising. The poor creatures were crowding the ratlings, clinging to the masts, struggling under the water. It was a human ant-heap overtaken by the sea. Paralysed, stiffened with anguish, my hair standing on end, with eyes wide open, panting, without breath, and without voice, I too was watching! An irresistible attraction glued me to the glass! Suddenly an explosion took place. The compressed air blew up her decks, as if the magazines had caught fire. Then the unfortunate vessel sunk more rapidly. Her topmast, laden with victims, now appeared; then her spars, bending under the weight of men; and last of all, the top of her mainmast. Then the dark mass disappeared, and with it the dead crew, drawn down by the strong eddy.

I turned to Captain Nemo. That terrible avenger, a perfect archangel of hatred, was still looking. When all was over, he turned to his room, opened the door, and entered. I followed him with my eyes. On the end wall beneath his heroes, I saw the portrait of a woman still young, and two little children. Captain Nemo looked at them for some moments, stretched his arms towards them, and kneeling down burst into deep sobs.

Chapter XXII
The Last Words of Captain Nemo

The panels had closed on this dreadful vision, but light had not returned to the saloon: all was silence and darkness within the *Nautilus*. At wonderful speed, a hundred feet beneath the water, it was leaving this desolate spot. Whither was it going? To the north or south? Where was the man flying to after such dreadful retaliation? I had returned to my room, where Ned and Conseil had remained silent enough. I felt an insurmountable horror for Captain Nemo. Whatever he had suffered at the hands of these men, he had no right to punish thus. He had made me, if not an accomplice, at least a witness of his vengeance. At eleven the electric light reappeared. I passed into the saloon. It was deserted. I consulted the different instruments. The *Nautilus* was flying northward at the rate of twenty-five miles an hour, now on the surface, and now thirty feet below it. On taking the bearings by the chart, I saw that we were passing the mouth of the Manche, and that our course was hurrying us towards the northern seas at a frightful speed. That night we had crossed two hundred leagues of the Atlantic. The shadows fell, and the sea was covered with darkness until the rising of the moon. I went to my room, but could not sleep. I was troubled with dreadful nightmare. The horrible scene of destruction was continually before my eyes. From that day, who could tell into what part of the North Atlantic basin the *Nautilus* would take us? Still, with unaccountable speed. Still in the midst of these northern fogs. Would it touch at Spitzbergen, or on the shores of Nova Zembla? Should we explore those unknown seas, the White Sea, the Sea of Kara, the gulf of Obi, the Archipelago of Liarrov, and the unknown coast of

Asia? I could not say. I could no longer judge of the time that was passing. The clocks had been stopped on board. It seemed, as in polar countries, that night and day no longer followed their regular course. I felt myself being drawn into that strange region where the foundered imagination of Edgar Poe roamed at will. Like the fabulous Gordon Pym, at every moment I expected to see "That veiled human figure, of larger proportions than those of any inhabitant of the earth, thrown across the cataract which defends the approach to the pole." I estimated (though, perhaps, I may be mistaken),— I estimated this adventurous course of the *Nautilus* to have lasted fifteen or twenty days. And I know not how much longer it might have lasted, had it not been for the catastrophe which ended this voyage. Of Captain Nemo I saw nothing whatever now, nor of his second. Not a man of the crew was visible for an instant. The *Nautilus* was almost incessantly under water. When we came to the surface to renew the air, the panels opened and shut mechanically. There were no more marks on the planisphere. I knew not where we were. And the Canadian, too, his strength and patience at an end, appeared no more. Conseil could not draw a word from him; and fearing that, in a dreadful fit of madness, he might kill himself, watched him with constant devotion. One morning (what date it was I could not say), I had fallen into a heavy sleep towards the early hours, a sleep both painful and unhealthy, when I suddenly awoke. Ned Land was leaning over me, saying, in a low voice, "We are going to fly."

I sat up.

"When shall we go?" I asked.

"To-morrow night. All inspection on board the *Nautilus* seems to have ceased. All appear to be stupified. You will be ready, sir?"

"Yes; where are we?"

"In sight of land. I took the reckoning this morning in the fog,— twenty miles to the east."

"What country is it?"

"I do not know; but whatever it is, we will take refuge there."

"Yes, Ned, yes. We will fly to-night, even if the sea should swallow us up."

"The sea is bad, the wind violent, but twenty miles in that light boat of the *Nautilus* does not frighten me. Unknown to the crew, I have been able to procure food and some bottles of water."

"I will follow you."

"But," continued the Canadian, "if I am surprised, I will defend myself; I will force them to kill me."

"We will die together, friend Ned."

I had made up my mind to all. The Canadian left me. I reached the platform, on which I could with difficulty support myself against the shock of the waves. The sky was threatening; but, as land was in those thick brown shadows, we must fly. I returned to the saloon, fearing and yet hoping to see Captain Nemo, wishing and yet not wishing to see him. What could I have said to him? Could I hide the involuntary horror with which he inspired me? No. It was better that I should not meet him face to face; better to forget him. And yet—. How long seemed that day, the last that I should pass in the *Nautilus*. I remained alone. Ned Land and Conseil avoided speaking, for fear of betraying themselves. At six I dined, but I was not hungry; I forced myself to eat in spite of my disgust, that I might not weaken myself. At half-past six Ned Land came to my room, saying, "We shall not see each other again before our departure. At ten the moon will not be risen. We will profit by the darkness. Come to the boat; Conseil and I will wait for you."

The Canadian went out without giving me time to answer. Wishing to verify the course of the *Nautilus*, I went to the saloon. We were running N.N.E. at frightful speed, and more than fifty yards deep. I cast a last look on these wonders of nature, on the riches of art heaped up in this museum, upon the unrivalled collection destined to perish at the bottom of the sea, with him who had formed it. I wished to fix an indelible impression of it in my mind. I remained an hour thus, bathed in the light of that luminous ceiling, and passing in review those treasures shining under their glasses. Then I returned to my room.

I dressed myself in strong sea clothing. I collected my notes, placing them carefully about me. My heart beat loudly. I could not check its pulsations. Certainly my trouble and agitation would have betrayed me to Captain Nemo's eyes. What was he doing at this moment? I listened at the door of his room. I heard steps. Captain Nemo was there. He had not gone to rest. At every moment I expected to see him appear, and ask me why I wished to fly. I was constantly on the alert. My imagination magnified everything. The impression became at last so poignant, that I asked myself if it would not be better to go to the Captain's room, see him face to face, and brave him with look and gesture.

It was the inspiration of a madman; fortunately I resisted the desire, and stretched myself on my bed to quiet by bodily agitation. My nerves were somewhat calmer, but in my excited brain I saw over again all my existence on board the *Nautilus*; every incident, either happy or unfortunate, which had happened since my disappearance from the *Abraham Lincoln*;—the submarine hunt, the Torres Straits, the savages of Papua, the running ashore, the coral cemetery, the passage of Suez, the island of Santorin, the Cretan diver, Vigo Bay, Atlants, the iceberg, the south pole, the imprisonment in the ice, the fight among the poulps, the storm in the Gulf Stream, the *Avenger*, and the horrible scene of the vessel sunk with all her crew. All these events passed before my eyes like scenes in a drama. Then Captain Nemo seemed to grown enormously, his features to assume superhuman proportions. He was no longer my equal, but a man of the waters, the genie of the sea.

It was then half-past nine. I held my head between my hands to keep it from bursting. I closed my eyes, I would not think any longer. There was another half hour to wait, another half hour of a nightmare, which might drive me mad.

At that moment I heard the distant strains of the organ, a sad harmony to an undefinable chaunt, the wail of a soul longing to break these earthly bonds. I listened with every sense, scarcely breathing; plunged, like Captain Nemo, in that musical ecstacy, which was drawing him in spirit to the end of life.

Then a sudden thought terrified me. Captain Nemo had left his room. He was in the saloon, which I must cross to fly. There I should meet him for the last time. He would see me, perhaps speak to me. A gesture of his might destroy me, a single word chain me on board.

But ten was about to strike. The moment had come for me to leave my room, and join my companions.

I must not hesitate, even if Captain Nemo himself should rise before me. I opened my door carefully; and even then, as it turned on its hinges, it seemed to me to make a dreadful noise. Perhaps it only existed in my own imagination.

I crept along the dark stairs of the *Nautilus*, stopping at each step to check the beating of my heart. I reached the door of the saloon, and opened it gently. It was plunged in profound darkness. The strains of the organ sounded faintly. Captain Nemo was there. He did not see me. In the full light I do not think he would have noticed me, so entirely was he absorbed in the ecstacy.

I crept along the carpet, avoiding the slightest sound which might betray my presence. I was at least five minutes reaching the door, at the opposite side, opening into the library.

I was going to open it, when a sigh from Captain Nemo nailed me to the spot. I knew that he was rising. I could even see him, for the light from the library came through to the saloon. He came towards me silently, with his arms crossed, gliding like a spectre rather than walking. His breast was swelling with sobs; and I heard him murmur these words (the last which ever struck my ear)—

"Almighty God! enough! enough!"

Was it a confession of remorse which thus escaped from this man's conscience?

In desperation I rushed through the library, mounted the central staircase, and following the upper flight reached the boat. I crept through the opening, which had already admitted my two companions.

"Let us go! let us go!" I exclaimed.

"Directly!" replied the Canadian.

The orifice in the plates of the *Nautilus* was first closed, and fastened down by means of a false key, with which Ned Land had provided himself; the opening in the boat was also closed. The Canadian began to loosen the bolts which still held us to the submarine boat.

Suddenly a noise within was heard. Voices were answering each other loudly. What was the matter? Had they discovered our flight? I felt Ned Land slipping a dagger into my hand.

"Yes," I murmured, "we know how to die!"

The Canadian had stopped in his work. But one word many times repeated, a dreadful word, revealed the cause of the agitation spreading on board the *Nautilus*. It was not we the crew were looking after!

"The maëlstrom! the maëlstrom!" I exclaimed.

The maëlstrom! Could a more dreadful word in a more dreadful situation have sounded in our ears! We were then upon the dangerous coast of Norway. Was the *Nautilus* being drawn into the gulf at the moment our boat was going to leave its sides? We knew that at the tide the pent-up waters between the islands of Ferroe and Loffoden rush with irresistible violence, forming a whirlpool from which no vessel ever escapes. From every point of the horizon enormous waves were meeting, forming a gulf justly called the "Navel of the Ocean," whose power of attraction extends to a distance of twelve miles. There, not only vessels, but whales are sacrificed, as well as white bears from the northern regions.

It is thither that the *Nautilus*, voluntarily or involuntarily, had been run by the Captain.

It was describing a spiral, the circumference of which was lessening by degrees, and the boat, which was still fastened to its side, was carried along with giddy speed. I felt that sickly giddiness which arises from long-continued whirling round.

We were in dread. Our horror was at its height, circulation had stopped, all nervous influence was annihilated, and we were covered with cold sweat, like a sweat of agony! And what noise around our frail bark! What roarings repeated by the echo miles away! What an uproar was that of the waters broken on the sharp rocks at the bottom, where the hardest bodies are crushed, and trees worn away, "with all the fur rubbed off," according to the Norwegian phrase!

What a situation to be in! We rocked frightfully. The *Nautilus* defended itself like a human being. Its steel muscles cracked. Sometimes it seemed to stand upright, and we with it!

"We must hold on," said Ned, "and look after the bolts. We may still be saved if we stick to the *Nautilus*"—

He had not finished the words, when we heard a crashing noise, the bolts gave way, and the boat, torn from its groove, was hurled like a stone from a sling into the midst of the whirlpool.

My head struck on a piece of iron, and with the violent shock I lost all consciousness.

Chapter XXIII
Conclusion

Thus ends the voyage under the seas. What passed during that night— how the boat escaped from the eddies of the maëlstrom— how Ned Land, Conseil, and myself ever came out of the gulf, I cannot tell.

But when I returned to consciousness, I was lying in a fisherman's hut, on the Loffoden Isles. My two companions, safe and sound, were near me holding my hands. We embraced each other heartily.

At that moment we could not think of returning to France. The means of communication between the north of Norway and the south are rare. And I am therefore obliged to wait for the steamboat running monthly from Cape North.

And among the worthy people who have so kindly received us, I revise my record of these adventures once more. Not a fact has been omitted, not a detail exaggerated. It is a faithful narrative of this incredible expedition in an element inaccessible to man, but to which Progress will one day open a road.

Shall I be believed? I do not know. And it matters little, after all. What I now affirm is, that I have a right to speak of these seas, under which, in less than ten months, I have crossed 20,000 leagues in that submarine tour of the world, which has revealed so many wonders.

But what has become of the *Nautilus*? Did it resist the pressure of the maëlstrom? Does Captain Nemo still live? And does he still follow under the ocean those frightful retaliations? Or, did he stop after that last hecatomb?

Will the waves one day carry to him this manuscript containing the history of his life? Shall I ever know the name of this man? Will the missing vessel tell us by its nationality that of Captain Nemo?

I hope so. And I also hope that this powerful vessel has conquered the sea at its most terrible gulf, and that the *Nautilus* has survived where so many other vessels have been lost! If it be so—if Captain Nemo still inhabits the ocean, his adopted country, may hatred be appeased in that savage heart! May the contemplation of so many wonders extinguish for ever the spirit of vengeance! May the judge disappear, and the philosopher continue the peaceful exploration of the sea! If his destiny be strange, it is also sublime. Have I not understood it myself? Have I not lived ten months of this unnatural life? And to the question asked by Ecclesiastes 3000 years ago, "That which is far off and exceeding deep, who can find it out?" two men alone of all now living have the right to give an answer—

CAPTAIN NEMO AND MYSELF.

A Winter in the Ice

Chapter I
The Black Flag

The curé of the ancient church of Dunkirk rose at five o'clock on the 12th of May, 18—, to perform, according to his custom, low mass for the benefit of a few pious sinners.

Attired in his priestly robes, he was about to proceed to the altar, when a man entered the sacristy, at once joyous and frightened. He was a sailor of some sixty years, but still vigorous and sturdy, with an open, honest countenance.

"Monsieur the curé," said he, "stop a moment, if you please."

"What do you want so early in the morning, Jean Cornbutte?" asked the curé.

"What do I want? Why, to embrace you in my arms, i' faith!"

"Well, after the mass at which you are going to be present—"

"The mass?" returned the old sailor, laughing. "Do you think you are going to say your mass now, and that I will let you do so?"

"And why should I not say my mass?" asked the curé. "Explain yourself. The third bell has sounded—"

"Whether it has or not," replied Jean Cornbutte, "it will sound many more to-day, monsieur the curé, for you have promised me that you will bless, with your own hands, the marriage of my son Louis and my niece Marie!"

"He has arrived, then," said the curé, joyfully.

"About the same thing," replied Cornbutte, rubbing his hands. "Our brig was signalled from the lookout at sunrise,—our brig, which you yourself christened by the good name of the 'Jeune-Hardie'!"

"I congratulate you with all my heart, my old Cornbutte," said the curé, taking off his chasuble and stole. "I remember our agreement.

319

The vicar will take my place, and I will put myself at your disposition against your dear son's arrival."

"And I promise you that he will not make you fast long," replied the sailor. "You have already published the banns, and you will only have to absolve him from the sins he may have committed between sky and water, in the Northern Ocean. I had a famous idea, that the marriage should be celebrated the very day he arrived, and that my son Louis should leave his ship to repair at once to the church."

"Go, then, and arrange everything, Cornbutte."

"I fly, monsieur the curé. Good morning!"

The sailor hastened with rapid steps to his house, which stood on the quays, whence could be seen the Northern Ocean, of which he seemed so proud.

Jean Cornbutte had amassed a cosey fortune at his calling. After having long commanded the vessels of a rich ship-owner of Havre, he had settled down in his native town, where he had caused the brig "Jeune-Hardie" to be constructed at his own expense. Several successful voyages had been made in the North, and the ship always found a good sale for its cargoes of wood, iron, and tar. Jean Cornbutte then gave up the command of her to his son Louis, a fine sailor of thirty, who, according to all the coasting captains, was the boldest mariner in Dunkirk.

Louis Cornbutte had gone away deeply attached to Marie, his father's niece, who found the time of his absence very long and weary. Marie was scarcely twenty. She was a pretty Flemish girl, with some Dutch blood in her veins. Her mother, on dying, had confided her to her brother, Jean Cornbutte. The brave old sailor loved her as a daughter, and saw in her proposed union with Louis a source of real and durable happiness.

The arrival of the ship, already signalled off the coast, completed an important business operation, from which Jean Cornbutte expected large profits. The "Jeune-Hardie," which had left three months before, came last from Bodoi, on the west coast of Norway, and had made a quick voyage thence.

On returning home, Jean Cornbutte found the whole house alive. Marie, with radiant face, had assumed her wedding-dress.

"I hope the ship will not arrive before us!" she said.

"Hurry, little one," replied Jean Cornbutte, "for the wind is north, and she sails well, you know."

"Have our friends been notified, uncle?" asked Marie.

"They have."

"The notary, and the curé?"

"Rest easy. You alone are keeping us waiting."

At this moment Clerbaut, an old crony, came in.

"Well, my old Cornbutte," cried he, "here's luck! Your ship has arrived at the very moment that the government has decided to purchase a large quantity of wood for refitting the navy!"

"What is that to me?" replied Jean Cornbutte. "What care I for the government?"

"You see, Monsieur Clerbaut," said Marie, "but one thing absorbs us,—Louis's return."

"I don't dispute that," replied Clerbaut. "But—in short—these purchases of wood—"

"And you shall be at the wedding," replied Jean Cornbutte, interrupting the merchant, and shaking his hand as if he would crush it.

"These purchases of wood—"

"And with all our friends, landsmen and seamen, Clerbaut. I have already notified everybody, and I shall invite the whole crew of the ship"

"And shall we go and await them on the barricade?" asked Marie.

"We will, indeed," replied Jean Cornbutte. "We will defile, two by two, with the violins at the head."

Jean Cornbutte's invited guests soon arrived. Though it was very early, not a single one failed to appear. All congratulated the honest old sailor whom they loved. Meanwhile Marie, kneeling down, changed her prayers to God into thanks. She soon returned, lovely and decked out, to the company; and all the women kissed her on the check, while the men vigorously grasped her by the hand. Then Jean Cornbutte gave the signal of departure.

It was a curious sight to see this joyous group taking its way, at sunrise, towards the sea The news of the ship's arrival had spread through the port, and many heads, in nightcaps, appeared at the windows and at the half-opened doors. Sincere compliments and pleasant nods came from every side.

The party reached the barricade in the midst of a concert of praise and blessings. The weather was magnificent, and the sun seemed to take part in the festivity. A fresh north-wind made the waves foam; and some fishing-smacks, trimmed for leaving port, streaked the sea with their rapid tracks between the barricades.

The two piers of Dunkirk stretch far out into the sea. The wedding-party occupied the whole width of the northern pier, and soon reached a small house situated at its extremity, inhabited by the master of the port. The wind freshened, and the "Jeune-Hardie" ran swiftly under her topsails, mizzen, brigantine,? gallant, and royal. There was evidently rejoicing on board as well as on land. Jean Cornbutte, spy-glass in hand, responded merrily to the questions of his friends.

"See my fine ship!" he cried; "clean and steady as if she had been rigged at Dunkirk! Not a damage,—not a rope wanting!"

"Do you see your son, the captain?" asked one.

"No, not yet. Ah, he's at his business!"

"Why does n't he run up his flag?" asked Clerbaut.

"I scarcely know, old friend. He has a reason for it, no doubt."

"Your spy-glass, uncle?" said Marie, taking it from him. "I wish to be the first to perceive him."

"But he is my son, mademoiselle!"

"He has been your son for thirty years," answered the young girl, laughing, "and he has only been my betrothed for two!"

The "Jeune-Hardie" was now entirely visible. Already the crew was preparing to cast anchor. The upper sails had been brailed. The sailors who were among the rigging might be recognized. But neither Marie nor Jean Cornbutte had yet been able to wave their hands at the captain of the ship.

"Faith! there's the second mate, André Vasling," cried Clerbaut.

"And there's Fidèle Misonne, the carpenter," said another.

"And our friend Penellan," said a third, saluting the sailor named

The "Jeune-Hardie" was only three cables' lengths from the shore, when a black flag ascended to the gaff of the brigantine. There was mourning on board!

A shudder of terror seized the party and the heart of the young girl.

The ship sadly swayed into port, and an icy silence reigned on its deck. Soon it had passed the end of the barricade. Marie, Jean Cornbutte, and all their friends hurried towards the quay at which she was to anchor, and m a moment found themselves on board.

"My son!" said Jean Cornbutte, who could only articulate these words.

The sailors, with uncovered heads, pointed to the mourning flag.

Marie uttered a cry of anguish, and fell into old Cornbutte's arms.

André Vasling had brought back the "Jeune-Hardie," but Louis Cornbutte, Marie's betrothed, was not on board.

Chapter II

Jean Cornbutte's Project

As soon as the young girl, confided to the care of the sympathizing friends, had left the ship, André Vasling, the mate, apprised Jean Cornbutte of the dreadful event which had deprived him of his son, narrated in the ship's journal as follows: —

"At the height of the Maelstrom, on the 26th of April, the ship, putting for the cape, by reason of bad weather and southwest winds, perceived signals of distress made by a schooner to the leeward. This schooner, deprived of its mizzen-mast, was running towards the gulf, without sails. Captain Louis Cornbutte, seeing that this vessel was hastening into imminent danger, resolved to go on board her. Despite the remonstrances of his crew, he had the long-boat lowered into the sea, and got into it, with the sailor Comtois and the helmsman Pierre Nouquet. The crew watched them until they disappeared in the fog. Night came. The sea became more and more boisterous. The 'Jeune-Hardie,' drawn by the currents m those parts, was in danger of being ingulfed by the Maelstrom. She was obliged to fly before the wind. For several days she hovered near the place of the disaster, but in vain. The long-boat, the schooner, Captain Louis, and the two sailors did not reappear. André Vasling then called the crew together, took command of the ship, and set sail for Dunkirk."

After reading this dry narrative, Jean Cornbutte wept for a long time; and if he had any consolation, it was the thought that his son had died in attempting to save his fellow-men. Then the poor father left the ship, the sight of which made him wretched, and returned to his desolate home.

The sad news soon spread throughout Dunkirk. The many friends of the old sailor came to bring him their cordial and sincere sympathy. Then the sailors of the "Jeune-Hardie" gave a more particular account of the event, and André Vasling told Marie, at great length, of the devotion of her betrothed to the last.

Jean Cornbutte reflected, after having wept, and the next day after the ship's arrival, when André came to see him, said, —

"Are you very sure, André, that my son has perished?"

"Alas, yes, Monsieur Jean," replied the mate.

"And you made all possible search for him?"

"All, Monsieur Cornbutte. But it is unhappily but too certain that he and the two sailors were swallowed up in the whirlpool of the Maelstrom."

"Would you like, André, to keep the second command of the ship?"

"That will depend upon the captain, Monsieur Cornbutte."

"I shall be the captain," replied the old sailor. "I am going to discharge the cargo with all speed, make up my crew, and sail in search of my son."

"Your son is dead!" said André, obstinately.

"It is possible, André," replied Jean Cornbutte, sharply, "but it is also possible that he saved himself. I am going to rummage all the ports of Norway whither he might have been driven, and when I am fully convinced that I shall never see him again, I will return here to die!"

André Vasling, seeing that this decision was irrevocable, did not insist further, but went away.

Jean Cornbutte at once apprised his niece of his intention, and he saw a few rays of hope glisten across her tears. It had not seemed to the young girl that her lover's death might be doubtful; but scarcely had this new hope entered her heart, than she abandoned herself to it without reserve.

The old sailor determined that the "Jeune-Hardie" should put to sea without delay. The ship, solidly built, had no need of repairs. Jean Cornbutte gave his sailors notice that if they wished to re-embark, no change in the crew would be made. He alone replaced his son in the command of the brig. None of the comrades of Louis Cornbutte failed to respond to his call, and there were hardy tars among them,—Alaine Turquiette, Fidèle Misonne the carpenter, Penellan the Breton, who replaced Pierre Nouquet as helmsman, and Gradlin, Aupic, and Gervique, courageous and well-tried mariners.

Jean Cornbutte again offered André Vasling his old rank on board. The second mate was an able officer, who had proved his skill in bringing the "Jeune-Hardie" into port. Yet, from what motive could not be told, André made some difficulties and asked time for reflection.

"As you will, André Vasling," replied Cornbutte. "Only remember that if you accept, you will be welcome among us."

Jean had a devoted sailor in Penellan the Breton, who had long been his fellow-voyager. In times gone by, little Marie was wont to pass the long winter evenings in the helmsman's arms, when he was on shore. He felt a fatherly friendship for her, and she had for him an affection quite filial. Penellan hastened the fitting out of the ship with all his energy, all the more because, according to his opinion, André Vasling had not perhaps made every effort possible to find the castaways, although he was excusable from the responsibility which weighed upon him as captain.

Within a week the "Jeune-Hardie" was ready to put to sea. Instead of merchandise, she was completely provided with salt meats, biscuits, barrels of flour, potatoes, pork, wine, brandy, coffee, tea, and tobacco.

The departure was fixed for the 22d of May. On the evening before, André Vasling, who had not yet given his answer to Jean Cornbutte, came to his house. He was still undecided, and did not know which course to take.

Jean was not at home, though the house door was open. André went into the hall, next to Marie's chamber, where the sound of an animated conversation struck his ear. He listened attentively, and recognized the voices of Penellan and Marie.

The discussion had no doubt been going on for some time, for the young girl seemed to be stoutly opposing what the Breton sailor said.

"How old is my uncle Cornbutte?" said Marie.

"Something about sixty years," replied Penellan.

"Well, is he not going to brave danger to find his son?"

"Our captain is still a sturdy man," returned the sailor. "He has a body of oak and muscles as hard as a bar of spare. So I am not afraid to have him go to sea again!"

"My good Penellan," said Marie, "one is strong when one loves! Besides, I have full confidence in the aid of Heaven. You understand me, and will help me."

"No!" said Penellan. "It is impossible, Marie. Who knows whither we shall drift, or what we must suffer? How many vigorous men have I seen lose their lives in these seas!"

"Penellan," returned the young girl, "if you refuse me, I shall believe that you do not love me any longer."

André Vasling understood the young girl's resolution. He reflected a moment, and his course was determined on.

"Jean Cornbutte," said he, advancing towards the old sailor, who now entered, "I will go with you. The cause of my hesitation has disappeared, and you may count upon my devotion."

"I have never doubted you, André Vasling." replied Jean Cornbutte, grasping him by the hand. "Marie, my child!" he added, calling in a loud voice.

Marie and Penellan made their appearance.

"We shall set sail to-morrow at daybreak, with the outgoing tide," said Jean. "My poor Marie, this is the last evening that we shall pass together."

"Uncle!" cried Marie, throwing herself into his arms.

"Marie, by the help of God, I will bring your lover back to you!"

"Yes, we will find Louis," added André Vasling.

"You are going with us, then?" asked Penellan, quickly.

"Yes, Penellan, André Vasling is to be my first mate," answered Jean.

"Oh, oh!" ejaculated the Breton, in a singular tone.

"And his advice will be useful to us, for he is able and enterprising."

"And yourself, captain," said André. "You will set us all a good example, for you have still as much vigor as experience."

"Well, my friends, good by till to-morrow. Go on board and make the final arrangements. Good by, André; good by, Penellan."

The mate and the sailor went out together. Jean and Marie remained alone with each other. Many bitter tears were shed during that sad evening. Jean Cornbutte, seeing Marie so wretched, resolved to spare her the pain of separation by leaving the house on the morrow without her knowledge. So he gave her a last kiss that evening, and at three o'clock next morning was up and away.

The departure of the brig had attracted all the old sailor's friends to the pier. The curé, who was to have blessed Marie's union with Louis, came to give a last benediction on the ship. Rough grasps of the hand were silently exchanged, and Jean went on board.

The crew were all there. André Vasling gave the last orders. The sails were spread, and the brig rapidly passed out under a stiff northwest breeze, whilst the curé, upright in the midst of the kneeling spectators, committed the vessel to the hands of God.

Whither goes this ship? She follows the perilous route upon which so many castaways have been lost! She has no certain destination. She must expect every peril, and be able to brave them without hesitating. God alone knows where it will be her fate to anchor. May God guide her!

Chapter III

A Ray of Hope

At that time of the year the season was favorable, and the crew might hope promptly to reach the scene of the shipwreck.

Jean Cornbutte's plan was naturally traced out. He counted on stopping at the Feroe Islands, whither the north-wind might have carried the castaways; then, if he was convinced that they had not been received in any of the ports of that locality, he would continue his search beyond the Northern Ocean, ransack the whole western coast of Norway as far as Bodoe, the place nearest the scene of the shipwreck; and, if necessary, farther still.

André Vasling thought, contrary to the captain's opinion, that the coast of Iceland should be explored; but Penellan observed that, at the time of the catastrophe, the gale came from the west; which, while it gave hope that the unfortunates had not been forced towards the gulf of the Maelstrom, gave ground for supposing that they might have been thrown on the Norwegian coast.

It was determined, then, that this coast should be followed as closely as possible, so as to recognize any traces of them that might appear.

The day after sailing, Jean Cornbutte, intent upon a map, was absorbed in reflection, when a small hand touched his shoulder, and a soft voice said in his car, —

"Have good courage, uncle."

He turned, and was stupefied. Marie embraced him.

"Marie, my daughter, on board!" he cried.

"The wife may well go in search of her husband, when the father embarks to save his child."

"Unhappy Marie! How wilt thou support our fatigues? Dost thou know that thy presence may be injurious to our search?"

"No, uncle, for I am strong."

"Who knows whither we shall be forced to go, Marie? Look at this map. We are approaching places dangerous even for us sailors, hardened though we are to the difficulties of the sea. And thou, frail child?"

"But, uncle, I come from a family of sailors. I am used to stories of combats and tempests. I am with you and my old friend Penellan!"

"Penellan! It was he who concealed you on board?"

"Yes, uncle; but only when he saw that I was determined to come without his help."

"Penellan!" cried Jean.

Penellan entered.

"It is not possible to undo what you have done, Penellan; but remember that you are responsible for Marie's life"

"Rest easy, captain," replied Penellan. "The little one has force and courage, and will be our guardian angel. And then, captain, you know my idea. that all is for the best in this world."

The young girl was installed in a cabin, which the sailors soon got ready for her, and which they made as comfortable as possible.

A week later the "Jeune-Hardie" stopped at the Feroë Islands, but the most minute search was fruitless. No castaway, shipwrecked vessel had come upon these coasts. Even the news of the event was quite unknown. The brig resumed its voyage, after a stay of ten days, about the 10th of June. The sea was calm, and the winds were favorable. The ship sped rapidly towards the Norwegian coast, which it explored without better result.

Jean Cornbutte determined to proceed to Bodoë. Perhaps he would there learn the name of the shipwrecked schooner to the succor of which Louis and the sailors had sacrificed themselves.

On the 30th of June the brig cast anchor in that port.

The authorities of Bodoë gave Jean Cornbutte a bottle found on the coast, which contained a document bearing these words: —

"This 26th April, on board the 'Frooern,' after being accosted by the long-boat of the 'Jeune-Hardie,' we were drawn by the currents towards the ice. God have pity on us!"

Jean Cornbutte's first impulse was to thank Heaven. He thought himself on his son's track. The "Frooern" was a Norwegian sloop of which there had been no news, but which had evidently been drawn northward.

Not a day was to be lost. The "Jeune-Hardie" was at once put in condition to brave the perils of the polar seas. The faithful Misonne, the carpenter, carefully examined her, and assured himself that her solid construction might resist the shock of the ice-masses.

Penellan, who had already engaged in whale-fishing in the arctic waters, saw to it that woollen and fur coverings, many sealskin moccasins, and wood for the making of sledges with which to cross the ice-fields were put on board. The amount of provisions was increased, and spirits and charcoal were added; for it might be that they would have to winter at some point on the Greenland coast. They also procured, with much difficulty and at a high price, a quantity of lemons, for preventing or curing the scurvy, that terrible disease which decimates crows in the icy regions. The ship's hold was filled with salt meat, biscuits, brandy, etc., as the steward's room no longer sufficed. They provided themselves, moreover, with a large quantity of "pemmican," an Indian preparation which concentrates a great deal of nutrition within a small volume.

By order of the captain, some saws were put on board, for cutting the ice-fields, as well as picks and wedges for separating them. The captain determined to procure some dogs, for drawing the sledges on the Greenland coast.

The whole crew was engaged in these preparations, and displayed great activity. The sailors Aupic, Gervique, and Gradlin zealously obeyed Penellan's orders; and he admonished them not to accustom themselves to woollen garments, though the temperature in this latitude, situated just above the polar circle, was very low.

Penellan, though he said nothing, narrowly watched every action of André Vasling. This man was Dutch by birth, came from no one knew whither, but was at least a good sailor, having made two voyages on board the "Jeune-Hardie." Penellan would not as yet accuse him of anything, unless it was that he kept near Marie too constantly, but did not let him out of his sight.

Thanks to the energy of the crew, the brig was equipped by the 16th of July, a fortnight after its arrival at Bodoe. It was then the favorable season for attempting explorations in the Arctic seas. The thaw had been going on for two months, and the search might be carried farther north. The "Jeune-Hardie" set sail, and directed her way towards Cape Brewster, on the eastern coast of Greenland, near the seventieth degree of latitude.

Chapter IV

In the Passes

About the 23d of July a reflection, raised above the sea, announced the first icebergs, which, emerging from Davis Straits, advanced into the ocean. From this moment a vigilaznt watch was ordered to the lookout men, for it was important not to come into collision with these enormous masses.

The crew was divided into two watches. The first was composed of Fidèle Misonne, Gradlin, and Gervique, and the second of André Vasling, Aupic, and Penellan. These watches were to last only two hours, for in those cold regions a man's force is diminished one half. Though the "Jeune-Hardie" was not yet beyond the sixty-third degree of latitude, the thermometer already stood at nine degrees Centigrade below zero.

Rain and snow often fell abundantly. On fair days, when the wind was not too violent, Marie remained on deck, and her eyes became accustomed to the uncouth scenes of the polar seas.

On the 1st of August she was promenading aft, and talking with her uncle, Penellan, and André Vasling. The ship was then entering a channel three miles wide, across which broken masses of ice were descending rapidly southward.

"When shall we see land?" asked the young girl.

"In three or four days at the latest," replied Jean Cornbutte.

"But shall we find there fresh traces of my poor Louis?"

"Perhaps so, my daughter; but I fear that we are still far from the end of our voyage. It is to be feared that the 'Frooern' was driven farther northward."

"That may be," added André Vasling, "for the squall which separated us from the Norwegian boat lasted three days, and in three days a ship makes good headway, when it is no longer able to resist the wind."

"Permit me to tell you, Monsieur Vasling," replied Penellan, "that that was in April, that the thaw had not then begun, and that therefore the 'Frooern' must have been soon arrested by the ice."

"And no doubt dashed into a thousand pieces," said the mate, "as her crew could not manage her."

"But these ice-fields," returned Penellan, "gave her an easy means of reaching land, from which she could not have been far distant."

"Let us hope so," said Jean Cornbutte, interrupting the discussion, which was daily renewed between the mate and the helmsman. "I think we shall see land before long."

"There it is!" cried Marie. "See those mountains!"

"No, my child," replied her uncle. "Those are mountains of ice, the first we have met with. They would shatter us like glass, if we got entangled between them. Penellan and Vasling, overlook the men."

These floating masses, more than fifty of which now appeared at the horizon, came nearer and nearer to the brig. Penellan took the helm, and Jean Cornbutte, mounted on the gallant, indicated the route to take.

Towards evening the brig was entirely surrounded by these moving ledges, the crushing force of which is irresistible. It was necessary, then, to cross this fleet of mountains, for prudence prompted them to keep straight ahead. Another difficulty was added to these perils; the direction of the ship could not be accurately determined, as all the surrounding points constantly changed position, and thus failed to afford a stationary perspective. The darkness soon increased with the fog. Marie descended to her cabin, and the whole crew, by the captain's orders, remained on deck. They were armed with long boat-hooks with iron spikes, to preserve the ship from collision with the ice.

The ship soon entered a strait so narrow that often the ends of her yards were grazed by the mountains adrift, and her booms seemed about to be driven in. They were even forced to weather the great yard so as to touch the shrouds. Happily these precautions did not deprive the vessel of any of its speed, for the wind could only reach the upper sails, and these sufficed to carry her forward rapidly. Thanks to her slender hull, she passed through these valleys, which were filled with whirlpools of rain, whilst the icebergs crushed against each other with sharp cracking and splitting.

Jean Cornbutte returned to the deck. His eyes could not penetrate the surrounding darkness. It became necessary to furl the upper sails, for the ship threatened to ground, and if she did so, she was lost.

"Cursed voyage!" growled André Vasling among the sailors, who, forward, were avoiding the most menacing ice-blocks with their boat-hooks.

"The fact is, that if we escape, we shall owe a fine candle to Our Lady of the Ice!" replied Aupic.

"Who knows how many floating mountains we have got to pass through yet?" added the mate.

"And who can guess what we shall find beyond them?" replied the sailor.

"Don't talk so much, prattler," said Gervique, "and look out on your side. When we have got by them, it 'll be time to grumble. Look out for your boat-hook!"

At this moment an enormous block of ice, in the narrow strait through which the brig was passing, came rapidly down upon her, and it seemed impossible to avoid it; for it barred the whole width of the channel, and the brig could not heave to.

"Do you feel the tiller?" asked Cornbutte of Penellan.

"No, captain. The ship does not steer any longer."

"*Ohé*, boys!" cried the captain to the crew; "don't be afraid, and buttress your hooks against the gunwale"

The block was nearly sixty feet high, and if it threw itself upon the brig, she would be crushed. There was an undefinable moment of suspense, and the crew retreated backward, abandoning their posts despite the captain's orders.

But at the instant when the block was not more than half a cable's length from the "Jeune-Hardie," a dull sound was heard, and a veritable waterspout fell upon the stem of the vessel, which then rose on the back of an enormous billow.

The sailors uttered a cry of terror; but when they looked before them, the block had disappeared, the passage was free, and beyond an immense plain of water, illumined by the rays of the declining sun, assured them of an easy navigation.

"All is for the best!" cried Penellan. "Let's trim our topsails and mizzen!"

A very common incident in those parts had just occurred. When these masses are detached from one another in the thawing season, they float in a perfect equilibrium; but on reaching the ocean, where the water is relatively warmer, they are speedily undermined at the base, which melts little by little, and which is also shaken by the shock of other ice-masses. There comes a moment when the centre of gravity of these masses is displaced, and then they are completely overturned. Only, if this block had turned over two minutes later, it would have fallen on the brig, and carried her down in its fall.

Chapter V

Liverpool Island

The brig now sailed in a sea which was almost entirely open. At the horizon only, a whitish light, this time motionless, indicated the presence of immovable plains.

Jean Cornbutte now directed the "Jeune-Hardie" towards Cape Brewster. They were already approaching the regions where the temperature is excessively cold, for the sun's rays only reach them very feebly, owing to their obliquity.

On the 3d of August the brig confronted immovable and united ice masses. The passages were seldom more than a cable's length in width, and the ship was forced to make many turnings, which sometimes placed her heading the wind.

Penellan watched over Marie with paternal care, and, despite the cold, prevailed upon her to spend two or three hours every day on deck, for exercise had become one of the indispensable conditions of health.

Marie's courage did not falter. She even comforted the sailors with her cheerful talk, and all of them became warmly attached to her. André Vasling showed himself more attentive than ever, and seized every occasion to be in her company; but the young girl, by a sort of presentiment, accepted his services with a certain coldness. It may be easily conjectured that André's conversation referred more to the future than to the present, and that he did not conceal the slight probability there was of saving the castaways. He was convinced that they were lost, and the young girl ought thenceforth to confide her existence to some one else.

Marie had not as yet comprehended André's designs, for, to his great disgust, he could never find an opportunity to talk long with her alone. Penellan had always an excuse for interfering, and destroying the effect of André's words by the hopeful opinions he expressed.

Marie, meanwhile, did not remain idle. Acting on the helmsman's advice, she set to work on her winter garments; for it was necessary that she should completely change her clothing. The cut of her dresses was not suitable for these cold latitudes. She made, therefore, a sort of furred pantaloons, the bottoms of which were furnished with sealskin; and her narrow skirts came only to her knees, so as not to be in contact with the layers of snow with which the winter would cover the ice-fields A fur mantle, fitting closely to the figure and supplied with a hood, protected the upper part of her body.

In the intervals of their work, the sailors also made up clothing with which to shelter themselves from the cold. They fashioned a quantity of high sealskin boots, with which to cross the snow during their explorations. They worked thus all the time that the navigation in the straits lasted.

André Vasling, who was an excellent shot, several times brought down aquatic birds with his gun; innumerable flocks of these were always careering about the ship. A sort of eider-ducks provided the crew with very palatable food, which relieved the monotony of the salt meat.

At last the brig, after many turnings, came in sight of Cape Brewster. A long-boat was put to sea. Jean Cornbutte and Penellan reached the coast, which was entirely deserted.

The ship at once directed its course towards Liverpool Island, discovered in 1821 by Captain Scoresby, and the crew gave a hearty cheer when they saw the natives running along the shore. Communication was speedily established with them, thanks to Penellan's knowledge of a few words of their language, and some phrases which the natives themselves had learned of the whalers who frequented those parts.

These Greenlanders were small and squat; they were not more than four feet six inches high; they had red, round faces, and low foreheads; their hair, flat and black, fell over their shoulders; their teeth were decayed, and they seemed to be affected by the sort of leprosy which is peculiar to ichthyophagous tribes.

In exchange for pieces of iron and brass, of which they are extremely covetous, these poor creatures brought bear furs, the skins of sea-calves, sea-dogs, sea-wolves, and all the animals generally known as seals. Jean Cornbutte obtained these at a low price, and they were certain to become most useful.

The captain then made the natives understand that he was in search of a shipwrecked vessel, and asked them if they had heard of it. One of them immediately drew a kind of ship on the snow, and indicated that a vessel of some sort had been carried northward three months before: he also managed to make it understood that the thaw and breaking up of the ice-fields had prevented the Greenlanders from going in search of it; and, indeed, their very light canoes, which they managed with paddles, could not go to sea at that time.

This news, though meagre, restored hope to the hearts of the sailors, and Jean Cornbutte had no difficulty in persuading them to advance farther in the polar seas.

Before quitting Liverpool Island, the captain purchased a pack of six Esquimaux dogs, which were soon acclimated on board. The ship weighed anchor on the morning of the 10th of August, and entered the northern straits under a brisk wind.

The longest days of the year had now arrived; that is, the sun, in these high latitudes, did not set, and reached the highest point of the spirals which it described above the horizon.

This total absence of night was not, however, very apparent, for the fog, rain, and snow sometimes enveloped the ship in real darkness.

337

Jean Cornbutte, who was resolved to advance as far as possible, began to take measures of health. The space between decks was securely enclosed, and every morning care was taken to ventilate it with fresh air. The stoves were installed. and the pipes so disposed as to yield as much heat as possible. The sailors were advised to wear only one woollen shirt over their cotton shirts, and to hermetically close their seal cloaks. The fires were not yet lighted, for it was important to reserve the wood and charcoal for the most intense cold.

Warm beverages, such as coffee and tea, were regularly distributed to the sailors morning and evening; and as it was important to live on meat, they shot ducks and teal, which abounded in these parts.

Jean Cornbutte also placed at the summit of the mainmast a "crow's-nest," a sort of cask staved in at one end, in which a lookout remained constantly to observe the ice-fields.

Two days after the brig had lost sight of Liverpool Island, the temperature became suddenly colder under the influence of a dry wind. Some indications of winter were perceived. The ship had not a moment to lose, for soon the way would be entirely closed to her. She advanced across the straits, between which lay ice-plains thirty feet thick.

On the morning of the 3d of September, the "Jeune-Hardie" reached the top of Gaël-Hamkes Bay. Land was then thirty miles to the leeward. It was the first time that the brig had stopped before a mass of ice which offered no outlet, and which was at least a mile wide. The saws must now be used to cut the ice. Penellan, Aupic, Gradlin, and Turquiette were chosen to work the saws, which had been carried outside the ship. The direction of the cutting was so determined that the current might carry off the pieces detached from the mass. The whole crew worked at this task for nearly twenty hours. They found it very painful to remain on the ice, and were often obliged to plunge into the water up to their middle; their sealskin garments protected them but imperfectly from the dampness.

Besides, all excessive toil in those high latitudes is soon followed by an overwhelming weariness; for the breath soon fails, and the strongest are forced to rest at frequent intervals.

At last the navigation became free, and the brig was towed beyond the mass which had so long obstructed her course.

Chapter VI
The Quaking of the Ice

For several days the "Jeune-Hardie" struggled against formidable obstacles. The crew were almost all the time at work with the saws, and often powder had to be used to blow up the enormous blocks of ice which closed the way.

On the 12th of September the sea offered but one solid plain, without issue or passage, surrounding the vessel on all sides, so that she could neither advance nor retreat. The temperature remained at an average of sixteen degrees below zero. The winter season had come, with its sufferings and dangers.

The "Jeune-Hardie" was then near the twenty-first degree of longitude west and the seventy-sixth degree of latitude north, at the entrance of Gael-Hamkes Bay.

Jean Cornbutte made his preliminary preparations for wintering. He first searched for a creek whose position would shelter the ship from the wind and breaking up of the ice. Land, which was probably thirty miles west, could alone offer him secure shelter, and he resolved to attempt to reach it.

He set out on the 12th of September, accompanied by André Vasling, Penellan, and the two sailors Gradlin and Turquiette. Each man carried provisions for two days, for it was not likely that their expedition would occupy a longer time, and they were supplied with skins on which to sleep.

Snow had fallen in great abundance and was not yet frozen over; and this delayed them seriously. They often sank to their waists, and could only advance very cautiously, for fear of falling into crevices. Penellan, who walked in front, carefully sounded each depression with his iron-pointed staff.

About five in the evening the fog began to thicken, and the little band were forced to stop. Penellan looked about for an iceberg which might shelter them from the wind, and after refreshing themselves, with regrets that they had no warm drink, they spread their skins on the snow, wrapped themselves up, lay close to each other, and soon dropped asleep from sheer fatigue.

The next morning Jean Cornbutte and his companions were buried beneath a bed of snow more than a foot deep. Happily their skins, perfectly impermeable, had preserved them, and the snow itself had aided in retaining their heat, which it prevented from radiating without.

The captain gave the signal of departure, and about noon they at last descried the coast, which at first they could scarcely distinguish. High ledges of ice, cut perpendicularly, rose on the shore; their variegated summits, of all forms and shapes, reproduced on a large scale the phenomena of crystallization. Myriads of aquatic fowl flew about at the approach of the party, and the seals, lazily lying on the ice, plunged hurriedly into the depths.

"I' faith!" said Penellan, "we shall not want for either furs or game!"

"Those animals," returned Cornbutte, "give every evidence of having been already visited by men; for in places totally uninhabited, they would not be so wild."

"None but Greenlanders frequent these parts," said André Vasling.

"I see no trace of their passage, however; neither any encampment nor the smallest hut," said Penellan, who had climbed up a high peak. "O captain!" he continued, "come here! I see a point of land which will shelter us splendidly from the northeast-wind."

"Come along, boys!" said Jean Cornbutte.

His companions followed him, and they soon rejoined Penellan. The sailor had said what was true. An elevated point of land jutted out like a promontory, and curving towards the coast, formed a little inlet of a mile in width at most. Some moving ice-blocks, broken by this point, floated in the midst, and the sea, sheltered from the colder winds, was not yet entirely frozen over.

This was an excellent spot for wintering. It remained to carry the ship thither. Jean Cornbutte remarked that the neighboring ice-field was very thick, and it seemed very difficult to cut a canal to bring the brig to its destination. Some other creek, then, must be found; it was in vain that he explored northward. The coast remained straight and abrupt for a long distance, and beyond the point, it was directly exposed to the attacks of the east-wind. The circumstance disconcerted the captain all the more that André Vasling essayed to show how bad the situation was. Penellan found it difficult to convince himself, in this dilemma, that all was for the best.

But one chance remained,—to seek a shelter on the southern side of the coast. This was to return on their path, but hesitation was useless. The little band returned rapidly in the direction of the ship, as their provisions had begun to give out. Jean Cornbutte searched for some practicable passage or at least some fissure by which a canal might be cut across the ice-fields, all along the route, but in vain.

Towards evening the sailors came to the same place where they had encamped over night. There had been no snow during the day, and they could recognize the imprint of their bodies on the ice. They again disposed themselves to sleep with their furs.

Penellan, much disturbed by the bad success of the expedition, was sleeping restlessly, when, at a waking moment, his attention was attracted by a dull rumbling. He listened attentively, and the rumbling seemed so strange that he nudged Jean Cornbutte with his elbow.

"What is that?" said the latter, whose mind, according to a sailor's habit, was awake as soon as his body.

"Listen, captain."

The noise increased, with perceptible violence.

"It can only be thunder, in so high a latitude," said Cornbutte, rising.

"I think we have to do with some white bears," replied Penellan.

"The devil! We have not seen any yet."

"Sooner or later, we must have expected a visit from them. Let us give them a good reception."

Penellan, armed with a gun, lightly crossed the lodge which sheltered them. The darkness was very dense; he could discover nothing; but a new incident soon betrayed to him the cause of the noise, which did not proceed from their vicinity. Jean Cornbutte rejoined him, and they observed with terror that this rumbling, which wakened their companions, came from beneath them.

A new kind of peril menaced them. To the noise, which resembled peals of thunder, was added a distinct undulating motion of the ice-field. Several of the party lost their balance and fell.

"Attention!" cried Penellan.

"Yes!" some one responded.

"Turquiette! Gradlin! where are you?"

"Here I am!" responded Turquiette, shaking off the snow with which he was covered.

"This way, Vasling," cried Cornbutte to the mate. "And Gradlin?"

"Present, captain. But we are lost!" shouted Gradlin, in fright.

"No!" said Penellan. "Perhaps we are saved!"

Hardly had he uttered these words when a frightful cracking noise was heard. The ice-field broke clear through, and the sailors were forced to cling to the block which wavered just by them. Despite the helmsman's words, they found themselves in a most perilous position, for an ice-quake had occurred. The ice-masses had just "weighed anchor," as the sailors say. The movement lasted nearly two minutes, and it was to be feared that the crevice would yawn at the very feet of the unhappy sailors. They anxiously awaited daylight in the midst of continuous shocks, for they could not, without risk of death, move a step, and they remained stretched out at full length to avoid being engulfed.

As soon as it was daylight, a very different aspect presented itself to their eyes. The vast plain, a compact mass the evening before, was now separated in a thousand places, and the waves, raised by some submarine commotion, had broken the thick layer which sheltered them.

The thought of his ship occurred to Jean Cornbutte's mind.

"My poor brig!" he cried. "It must have perished!"

The deepest despair began to overcast the faces of his companions. The loss of the ship inevitably preceded their own deaths.

"Courage, my friends," said Penellan. "Reflect that this night's disaster has opened us a path across the ice, which will enable us to bring our ship to the bay for wintering! And, stop! I am not mistaken. There is the 'Jeune-Hardie,' a mile nearer to us!"

All hurried forward, and so imprudently that Turquiette slipped into a fissure, and would have certainly perished, had not Jean Cornbutte seized him by his hood. He got off with a rather cold bath.

The brig was indeed floating two miles away. After infinite trouble, the little band reached her. She was in good condition; but her rudder, which they had neglected to lift, had been broken by the ice.

Chapter VII

Settling for the Winter

Penellan was once more right; all was for the best, and this ice-quake had opened a practicable channel for the ship to the bay. The sailors had only to make skilful use of the currents to conduct her thither.

On the 19th of September, the brig was at last moored in her bay for wintering, two cables' lengths from the shore, securely anchored on a good bottom. The ice began, the next day, to form around her hull; it soon became strong enough to bear a man's weight, and they could establish a communication with land.

The rigging, as is customary in arctic navigation, remained as it was; the sails were carefully folded on the yards and covered with their casings, and the "crow's-nest" remained in place, as much to enable them to make distant observations as to attract attention to the ship.

The sun now scarcely rose above the horizon. Since the June solstice, the spirals which it had described descended lower and lower; and it would soon disappear altogether.

The crew hastened to make the necessary preparations. Penellan supervised the whole. The ice was soon thick around the ship, and it was to be feared that its pressure might become dangerous; but Penellan waited until, by reason of the going and coming of the floating ice-masses and their adherence, it had reached a thickness of twenty feet; he then had it cut around the hull, so that it united under the ship, the form of which it assumed; enclosed thus in a mould, the brig had no longer to fear the pressure of the ice, which could make no movement.

The sailors then elevated, along the wales, to the height of the net-tings, a snow wall five or six feet thick, which soon froze as hard as a rock. This envelope did not allow the interior heat to radiate outside. A canvas tent, covered with skins and hermetically closed, was stretched over the whole length of the deck, and formed a sort of walk for the sailors.

They also constructed on the ice a storehouse of snow, in which articles which embarrassed the ship were stowed away. The partitions of the cabins were taken down, so as to form a single vast apartment forward, as well as aft. This single room, besides, was more easy to warm, as the ice and humidity found fewer corners in which to take refuge. It was also less difficult to ventilate it, by means of canvas funnels which opened without.

Each sailor exerted great energy in these preparations, and about the 25th of September they were completed. André Vasling had not shown himself the least active in this task. He devoted himself with especial zeal to the young girl's comfort, and if she, absorbed in thoughts of her poor Louis, did not perceive this, Jean Cornbutte did not fail soon to remark it. He spoke of it to Penellan; he recalled several incidents which completely enlightened him regarding his mate's intentions; André Vasling loved Marie, and reckoned on asking her uncle for her hand, as soon as it was proved beyond doubt that the castaways were irrevocably lost; they would return then to Dunkirk, and André Vasling would be well satisfied to wed a rich and pretty girl, who would then be the sole heiress of Jean Cornbutte.

But André, in his impatience, was often imprudent. He had several times declared that the search for the castaways was useless, when some new indication contradicted him, and enabled Penellan to exult over him. The mate, therefore, cordially detested the helmsman, who returned his dislike heartily. Penellan only feared that André might sow seeds of dissension among the crew, and persuaded Jean Cornbutte to answer him evasively on the first occasion.

When the preparations for the winter were completed, the captain took measures to preserve the health of the crew. Every morning the men were ordered to air their berths, and carefully clean the interior walls, to deprive them of the night's dampness. They received boiling tea or coffee, which are excellent cordials to use against the cold, morning and evening; then they were divided into hunting-parties, who should procure as much fresh nourishment as possible for every day.

Each one also took healthy exercise every day, so as not to expose himself without motion to the cold; for in a temperature thirty degrees below zero, some part of the body might suddenly become frozen. In such cases, friction of the snow was used, which alone could heal the affected part.

Penellan also strongly advised cold ablutions every morning. It required some courage to plunge the hands and face in the snow, which had to be melted within. But Penellan bravely set the example, and Marie was not the last to imitate him.

Jean Cornbutte did not forget to have readings and prayers, for it was needful that the hearts of his comrades should not give way to despair or weariness. Nothing is more dangerous in these desolate latitudes.

The sky, always gloomy, filled the soul with sadness. A thick snow, lashed by violent winds, added to the horrors of their situation. The sun would soon altogether disappear. Had the clouds not gathered in masses above their heads, they might have enjoyed the moonlight, which was about to become really their sun during the long polar night; but, with the west-winds, the snow did not cease to fall. Every morning it was necessary to clear off the sides of the ship, and to cut a new stairway in the ice to enable them to reach the ice-field. They easily succeeded in doing this with snow-knives; the steps once cut, a little water was thrown over them, and they at once hardened.

Penellan had a hole cut in the ice, not far from the ship. Every day the new crust which formed over its top was broken, and the water which was drawn thence, from a certain depth, was less cold than that at the surface.

All these preparations occupied nearly three weeks. It was time to go forward with the search. The ship was imprisoned for six or seven months, and only the next thaw could open a new route across the ice. It was wise, then, to profit by this delay to extend their explorations northward.

Chapter VIII
Plan of the Explorations

On the 9th of October, Jean Cornbutte held a council to settle the plan of his operations, to which, that there might be union, zeal, and courage on the part of every one, he admitted the whole crew. Map in hand, he clearly explained their situation.

The eastern coast of Greenland advances perpendicularly northward. The discoveries of the navigators have given the exact boundaries of those parts. In the extent of five hundred leagues, which separates Greenland from Spitzberg, no land has been found. An island (Shannon Island) lay a hundred miles north of Gael-Hamkes Bay, where the "Jeune-Hardie" was going to winter.

If the Norwegian schooner, according to all the probabilities, had been driven in this direction, supposing that she could not reach Shannon Island, it was here that Louis Cornbutte and his comrades must have sought for a winter asylum.

This opinion prevailed, despite André Vasling's opposition; and it was decided to direct the explorations on the side towards Shannon Island.

Arrangements to this end were at once begun. A sledge like that used by the Esquimaux had been procured on the Norwegian coast. This was constructed of planks curved before and behind, and was made to slide over the snow and ice. It was twelve feet long and four wide, and could therefore carry provisions, if need there was, for several weeks Fidèle Misonne soon put it in order, working upon it in the snow storehouse, whither his tools had been carried. For the first tune a coal-stove was set up in this storehouse, without which all labor there would have been impossible. The pipe was carried out through one of the lateral walls, by a hole pierced in the snow; but a grave inconvenience resulted from this,—for the heat of the stove, little by little, melted the snow where it came in contact with it, and the opening visibly increased. Jean Cornbutte contrived to surround this part of the pipe with some metallic canvas, which is impermeable by heat. This succeeded completely.

While Misonne was at work upon the sledge, Penellan, aided by Marie, was preparing the clothing necessary for the expedition. Sealskin boots they had, fortunately, in plenty. Jean Cornbutte and André Vasling occupied themselves with the provisions. They chose a small barrel of spirits, intended to supply a portable chafing-dish; reserves of coffee and tea in ample quantity were packed; a small box of biscuits, two hundred pounds of pemmican, and some gourds of brandy completed the stock of aliments. The guns would bring down some fresh game every day. A quantity of powder was divided between several bags; the compass, sextant, and spy-glass were put carefully out of the way of injury.

On the 11th of October the sun no longer appeared above the horizon. They were obliged to keep a lighted lamp in the lodgings of the crew all the time. There was no time to lose; the explorations must be begun. This is why: In the month of January it would become so cold that it would be impossible to venture out without peril of life. For two months at least the crew would be condemned to the most complete imprisonment; then the thaw would begin, and would be prolonged to the time when the ship should quit the ice. This thaw would, of course, prevent any explorations. On the other hand, if Louis Cornbutte and his comrades were still in existence, it was not probable that they would be able to resist the severities of the arctic winter. They must therefore be saved beforehand, or all hope would be lost. André Vasling knew all this better than any one. He therefore resolved to put every possible obstacle in the way of the expedition.

The preparations for the journey were completed about the 20th of October. It remained to select the men who should compose the party. The young girl could not be deprived of the protection of Jean

Cornbutte or of Penellan; neither of these could, on the other hand, be spared from the expedition.

The question then was whether Marie could bear the fatigues of such a journey. She had already passed through rough experiences without seeming to suffer from them, for she was a sailor's daughter, used from infancy to the fatigues of the sea, and even Penellan was not dismayed to see her struggling in the midst of this severe climate, against the dangers of the polar seas.

It was decided, therefore, after a long discussion, that she should go with them, and that a place should be reserved for her, at need, on the sledge, on which a little wooden hut was constructed, hermetically closed in. As for Marie, she was delighted, for she dreaded to be left alone without her two protectors.

The expedition was thus formed: Marie, Jean Cornbutte, Penellan, André Vasling, Aupic, and Fidèle Misonne. Alaine Turquiette remained in charge of the brig, and Gervique and Gradlin stayed behind with him. New provisions of all kinds were carried, for Jean Cornbutte, in order to carry the exploration as far as possible, had resolved to establish depots along the route, at each seven or eight days' march. When the sledge was ready it was at once fitted up, and covered with a skin tent The whole weighed some seven hundred pounds, which a pack of five dogs might easily carry over the ice.

On the 22d of October, as the captain had foretold, a sudden change took place in the temperature. The sky cleared, the stars emitted an extraordinary light, and the moon shone above the horizon, no longer to leave the heavens for a fortnight. The thermometer descended to twenty-five degrees below zero.

The departure was fixed for the following day.

Chapter IX

The House of Snow

On the 23d of October, at eleven in the morning, in a fine moonlight, the caravan set out. Precautions were this time taken that the journey might be a long one, if necessary. Jean Cornbutte followed the coast, and ascended northward. The steps of the travellers made no impression on the glittering, hard ice. Jean was forced to guide himself by points which he selected at a distance; sometimes he fixed upon a hill bristling with peaks; sometimes on a vast iceberg which pressure had raised above the plain.

At the first halt, after going fifteen miles, Penellan prepared to encamp. The tent was erected against an ice-block. Marie had not suffered seriously with the extreme cold, for luckily the breeze had subsided, and was much more bearable; but the young girl had several times been obliged to descend from her sledge to avert numbness from impeding the circulation of her blood. Otherwise, her little hut, hung with skins, afforded her all possible comfort.

When night, or rather sleeping-time, came, the little hut was carried under the tent, where it served as a bedroom for Marie. The evening repast was composed of fresh meat, pemmican, and hot tea. Jean Cornbutte, to avert danger of the scurvy, distributed to each of the party a few drops of lemon-juice. Then all slept under God's protection.

After eight hours of repose, they got ready to resume their march. A substantial breakfast was provided to the men and the dogs; then they set out. The ice, exceedingly compact, enabled these animals to draw the sledge with rapid ease. The party sometimes found it difficult to keep up with them.

But the sailors soon began to suffer one discomfort,—the being dazzled. Ophthalmia betrayed itself in Aupic and Misonne. The moon's light, striking on these vast white plains, burned the eyesight, and gave the eyes insupportable pain.

There was thus produced a very singular effect of refraction. As they walked, when they thought they were about to put foot on a hillock, they stepped down lower, which often occasioned falls, happily so little serious that Penellan made them occasions for bantering. Still, he told them never to take a step without sounding the ground with the ferruled staff with which each was armed.

About the 1st of November, ten days after they had set out, the caravan had gone fifty leagues to the northward. Jean Cornbutte was painfully dazzled, and his sight sensibly changed. Aupic and Misonne had to feel their way, for their eyes, rimmed with red, seemed burned by the white reflection. Marie had been preserved from this misfortune by remaining within her hut, to which she confined herself as much as possible. Penellan, sustained by an indomitable courage, resisted all these fatigues. But it was André Vasling who bore himself best, and upon whom the cold and dazzling seemed to produce no effect. His iron frame was equal to every hardship; and he was secretly pleased to see the most robust of his companions becoming discouraged, and already foresaw the moment when they would be forced to retreat to the ship again.

On the 1st of November it became absolutely necessary to halt for a day or two. As soon as the place for the encampment had been selected, they proceeded to arrange it. It was determined to erect a house of snow, which should be supported against one of the rocks of the promontory. Misonne at once marked out the foundations, which measured fifteen feet long by five wide. Penellan, Aupic, and Misonne, by aid of their knives, cut out great blocks of ice, which they carried to the chosen spot and set up, as masons would have placed stone-walls. The sides of the foundation were soon raised to a height and thickness of about five feet; for the materials were abundant, and the structure was intended to be sufficiently solid to last several days. The four walls were completed in eight hours; an opening had been left on the southern side, and the canvas of the tent, placed on these four walls, fell over the opening and sheltered it. It only remained to cover the whole with large blocks, destined to form the roof of this temporary structure.

After three more hours of hard work the house was done, and they all went into it, overcome with weariness and discouragement. Jean Cornbutte suffered so much that he could not walk, and André Vasling so skilfully aggravated his gloomy feelings, that he forced from him a promise not to pursue his search farther in those frightful solitudes. Penellan did not know which saint to invoke. He thought it unworthy and craven to give up to reasons which had little weight, and tried to destroy them; but in vain.

Meanwhile, though it had been decided to return, rest had become so necessary that for three days no preparations for departure were made.

On the 4th of November Jean Cornbutte began to bury, on a point of the coast, the provisions for which there was no use. A stake indicated the place of the deposit, in the improbable event that new explorations should be made in that direction. Every day since they had set out similar deposits had been made, so that they were assured of ample sustenance on the return.

The departure was fixed for ten in the morning, on the 5th. The most profound sadness filled the little band. Marie with difficulty restrained her tears, when she saw her uncle so completely discouraged. So many useless sufferings! So much labor lost! Penellan himself became ferocious in his ill-humor; he devoted everybody to the nether regions, and did not cease to wax angry at the weakness and cowardice of his comrades, who were more timid and tired, he said, than Marie, who would have gone to the end of the world without complaint.

André Vasling could not disguise the pleasure which this decision gave him. He showed himself more attentive than over to the young girl, to whom he even held out hopes that a new search should be made when the winter was over; knowing well that it would then be too late!

Chapter X
Buried Alive

The evening before the departure, just as they were about to take supper, Penellan was breaking up some empty casks for firewood, when he was suddenly suffocated by a thick smoke. At the same instant the snow-house was shaking as if by a quaking of the earth. The party uttered a cry of terror, and Penellan hurried outside.

It was entirely dark. A frightful tempest—for it was not a thaw—was raging, whirlpools of snow careered around, and it was so exceedingly cold that the helmsman felt his hands rapidly freezing. He was obliged to go in again, after rubbing himself violently with snow.

"It is a tempest," said he. "May Heaven grant that our house may withstand it, for, if the storm should destroy it, we should be lost!"

At the same time with the gusts of wind, a noise was heard beneath the frozen soil; icebergs, broken from the promontory, dashed away noisily, and fell upon one another; the wind blew with such violence, that it seemed sometimes as if the whole house moved from its foundation; phosphorescent lights, inexplicable in that latitude, flashed across the whirlpools of the snow.

"Marie! Marie!" cried Penellan, seizing the young girl's hands.

"We are badly caught!" said Misonne.

"And I know not whether we shall escape," replied Aupic.

"Let us quit the snow-house! said André Vasling.

"It is impossible!" returned Penellan. "The cold outside is terrible; perhaps we can bear it by staying here."

"Give me the thermometer," demanded Vasling.

Aupic handed it to him. It showed ten degrees below zero inside the house, though the fire was lighted. Vasling raised the canvas which covered the opening, and pushed it aside hastily; for he would have been lacerated by the fall of ice which the wind hurled around, and which fell in a perfect hail-storm.

"Well, Vasling," said Penellan, "will you go out, then? You see that we are more safe here."

"Yes," said Jean Cornbutte; "and we must use every effort to strengthen the house on the interior."

"But a still more terrible danger menaces us," said Vasling.

"What?" asked Jean.

"The wind is breaking the ice against which we are propped, just as it has that of the promontory, and we shall be either driven hence or submerged!"

"That seems doubtful," said Penellan, "for it is freezing hard enough to ice over all liquid surfaces. Let us see what the temperature is."

He raised the canvas so as to pass out his arm, and with difficulty found the thermometer again, in the midst of the snow; but he at last succeeded in seizing it, and, holding the lamp to it, said, —

"Thirty-two degrees below zero! It is the coldest we have seen here yet!"

"Ten degrees more," said Vasling, "and the mercury will freeze."

A mournful silence followed this remark.

About eight in the morning Penellan essayed a second time to go out to judge of their situation. It was necessary to give an escape to the smoke, which the wind had several times repelled into the hut. The sailor wrapped his cloak tightly about him, made sure of his hood by fastening it to his head with a handkerchief, and raised the canvas.

The opening was entirely obstructed by a resisting snow. Penellan took his staff, and succeeded in plunging it into the compact mass; but terror froze his blood when he perceived that the end of the staff was not free, and was checked by a hard body!

"Cornbutte," said he to the captain, who had come up to him, "we are buried under this snow!"

"What say you?" cried Jean Cornbutte.

"I say that the snow is massed and frozen around us and over us, and that we are buried alive!"

"Let us try to clear this mass of snow away," replied the captain.

The two friends buttressed themselves against the obstacle which obstructed the opening, but they could not move it. The snow formed an iceberg more than five feet thick, and attached itself solidly to the house. Jean could not suppress a cry, which awoke Misonne and Vasling. An oath burst from the latter, whose features contracted. At this moment the smoke, thicker than ever, poured into the house, for it could not find an issue.

"Malediction!" cried Misonne. "The pipe of the stove is sealed up by the ice!"

Penellan resumed his staff, and took down the pipe, after throwing snow on the embers to extinguish them, which produced such a smoke that the light of the lamp could scarcely be seen; then he tried with his staff to clear out the orifice, but he only encountered a rock of ice! A frightful end, preceded by a terrible agony, seemed to be their doom. The smoke, penetrating the throats of the unfortunate party, caused an insufferable pain, and air would soon fail them altogether!

Marie here rose, and her presence, which inspired Cornbutte with despair, imparted some courage to Penellan. He said to himself that it could not be that the poor girl was destined to so horrible a death.

"Ah!" said she, "you have made too much fire. The room is full of smoke!"

"Yes, yes," stammered Penellan.

"It is evident," resumed Marie, "for it is not cold, and it is long since we have felt too much heat."

No one dared to tell her the truth.

"See, Marie," said Penellan, "help us get breakfast ready. It is too cold to go out. Here is the chafing-dish, the spirit, and the coffee. Come, you others, a little pemmican first, as this wretched storm forbids us from hunting."

These words stirred up his comrades.

"Let us first eat," added Penellan, "and then we shall see about getting off."

Penellan set the example and devoured his share of the breakfast. His comrades imitated him, and then drank a cup of boiling coffee, which somewhat restored their spirits. Then Jean Cornbutte decided energetically that they should at once set about devising means of safety.

André Vasling now said, —

"If the storm is still raging, which is probable, we must be buried ten feet under the ice, for we can hear no noise outside."

Penellan looked at Marie, who now understood the truth, and did not tremble. The helmsman first heated, by the flame of the spirit, the iron point of his staff, and successfully introduced it into the four walls of ice, but he could find no issue in either. Cornbutte then resolved to cut out an opening in the door itself. The ice was so hard that it was difficult for the knives to make the least impression on it. The pieces which were cut off soon encumbered the hut. After working hard for two hours, they had only hollowed out a space three feet deep.

Some more rapid method, and one which was less likely to demolish the house, must be thought of; for the farther they advanced, the more violent became the effort to break off the compact ice. It occurred to Penellan to make use of the chafing-dish to melt the ice in the desired direction. It was a hazardous method, for, if their imprisonment lasted long, the spirit, of which they had but little, would be wanting when needed to prepare the meals. Nevertheless, the idea was welcomed on all hands, and was put in execution. They first cut a hole three feet deep by one in diameter, to receive the water which would result from the melting of the ice; and it was well that they took this precaution, for the water soon oozed out under the action of the fire, and Penellan advanced across the mass of ice. The opening widened little by little, but this kind of work could not be long continued; for the water, covering their clothes, penetrated to their bodies here and there. Penellan was obliged to pause in a quarter of an hour, and to withdraw the chafing-dish with which to dry himself. Misonne then took his place, and worked sturdily at the task.

In two hours, though the opening was five feet deep, the points of the staffs could not yet find an issue without.

"It is not possible," said Jean Cornbutte, "that snow could have fallen in such abundance. It must have been gathered on this point by the wind. Perhaps we had better think of escaping in some other direction."

"I don't know," replied Penellan; "but if it were only not to discourage our comrades, we ought to continue to pierce the wall where we have begun. We must find an issue erelong."

"Will not the spirit fail us?" asked the captain.

"I hope not. But let us, if necessary, dispense with coffee and hot drinks. Besides, that is not what most alarms me"

"What is it, then, Penellan?"

"Our lamp is going out, for want of oil, and we are fast exhausting our provisions.—At last, thank God!"

Penellan went to replace André Vasling, who was vigorously working for the common deliverance.

"Monsieur Vasling," said he, "I am going to take your place; but look out well, I beg of you, for every tendency of the house to fall, so that we may have time to prevent it."

The time for rest had come, and when Penellan had added one more foot to the opening, he lay down beside his comrades.

Chapter XI

A Cloud of Smoke

The next day, when the sailors awoke, they were surrounded by complete darkness. The lamp had gone out. Jean Cornbutte roused Penellan to ask him for the tinder-box, which was passed to him. Penellan rose to light the fire, but, in getting up, his head struck against the ice ceiling. He was horrified, for on the evening before he could still stand upright. The chafing-dish being lighted up by the dim rays of the spirit, he perceived that the ceiling was a foot lower than before.

Penellan resumed work with desperate energy.

At this moment the young girl observed, by the light which the chafing-dish cast upon Penellan's face, that despair and will were struggling in his rough features for the mastery. She went to him, took his hands, and tenderly pressed them.

"She cannot, must not die thus!" he cried.

He took his chafing-dish, and once more attacked the narrow opening. He plunged in his staff, and felt no resistance. Had he reached the soft layers of the snow? He drew out his staff, and a bright ray penetrated to the house of ice!

"Here, my friends!" he shouted.

He pushed back the snow with his hands and feet, but the exterior surface was not thawed, as he had thought. With the ray of light, a violent cold entered the cabin and seized upon everything moist, to freeze it in an instant. Penellan enlarged the opening with his cutlass, and at last was able to breathe the free air. He fell on his knees to thank God, and was soon joined by Marie and his comrades.

A magnificent moon lit up the sky, but the cold was so extreme that they could not bear it. They re-entered their retreat; but Penellan first looked about him. The promontory was no longer there, and the hut was now in the midst of a vast plain of ice. Penellan thought he would go to the sledge, where the provisions were. The sledge had disappeared!

The cold forced him to return. He said nothing to his companions. It was necessary, before all, to dry their clothing, which was done with the chafing-dish. The thermometer, held for an instant in the air, descended to thirty degrees below zero.

An hour after, Vasling and Penellan resolved to venture outside. They wrapped themselves up in their still wet garments, and went out by the opening, the sides of which had become as hard as a rock.

"We have been driven towards the northeast," said Vasling, reckoning by the stars, which shone with wonderful brilliancy.

"That would not be bad," said Penellan, "if our sledge had come with us."

"Is not the sledge there?" cried Vasling. "Then we are lost!"

"Let us look for it," replied Penellan.

They went around the hut, which formed a block more than fifteen feet high. An immense quantity of snow had fallen during the whole of the storm, and the wind had massed it against the only elevation which the plain presented. The entire block had been driven by the wind, in the midst of the broken icebergs, more than twenty-five miles to the northeast, and the prisoners had been carried with their floating prison. The sledge, supported by another iceberg, had been turned another way, for no trace of it was to be seen, and the dogs must have perished amid this frightful tempest.

André Vasling and Penellan felt despair taking possession of them. They did not dare to return to their companions. They did not dare to announce this fatal news to their comrades in misfortune. They climbed upon the block of ice in which the hut was hollowed, and could perceive nothing but the white immensity which encompassed them on all sides. Already the cold was beginning to stiffen their limbs, and the humidity of their garments was being transformed into icicles which hung about them.

Just as Penellan was about to descend, he looked towards André. He saw him suddenly gaze in one direction, then shudder and turn pale.

"What is the matter, Vasling?" he asked.

"Nothing," replied the other. "Let us go down and urge the captain to leave these parts, where we ought never to have come, as quickly as possible."

Instead of obeying, Penellan ascended again, and looked in the direction which had drawn the mate's attention. A very different effect was produced on him, for he uttered a shout of joy, and cried, —

"Blessed be God!"

A light smoke was rising in the northeast. There was no possibility of deception. It indicated the presence of animate beings. Penellan's cries of joy reached the rest below, and all were able to convince themselves with their eyes that he was not mistaken.

Without thinking of their want of provisions or the severity of the temperature, wrapped in their hoods, they were all soon advancing towards the spot whence the smoke arose in the northeast. This was evidently five or six miles off, and it was very difficult to take exactly the right direction. The smoke now disappeared, and no elevation served as a guiding mark, for the ice-plain was one united level. It was important, nevertheless, not to diverge from a straight line.

"Since we cannot guide ourselves by distant objects," said Jean Cornbutte, "we must use this method. Penellan will go ahead, Vasling twenty steps behind him, and I twenty steps behind Vasling. I can then judge whether or not Penellan diverges from the straight line."

They had gone on thus for half an hour, when Penellan suddenly stopped and listened. The party hurried up to him.

"Did you hear nothing?" he asked.

"Nothing," replied Misonne.

"It is strange," said Penellan. "It seemed to me I heard cries from this direction."

"Cries?" replied Marie. "We are perhaps near our end, then."

360

"That is no reason," said Andreé Vasling. "In these high latitudes and cold regions sounds may be heard to a great distance."

"However that may be," replied Jean Cornbutte, "let us go forward, or we shall be frozen."

"No!" cried Penellan. "Listen!"

Some feeble sounds, quite perceptible, however, were heard. They seemed to be cries of distress. They were twice repeated. They seemed like cries for help. Then all became silent again.

"I was not mistaken," said Penellan. "Forward!"

He began to run in the direction whence the cries had proceeded. He went thus two miles, when, to his utter stupefaction, he saw a man lying on the ice. He went up to him, raised him, and lifted his arms to heaven in despair.

André Vasling, who was following close behind with the rest of the sailors, ran up and cried, —

"It is one of the castaways! It is our sailor Courtois!"

"He is dead," replied Penellan. "Frozen to death!"

Jean Cornbutte and Marie came up beside the corpse, which was already stiffened by the ice. Despair was written on every face. The dead man was one of the comrades of Louis Cornbutte!

"Forward!" cried Penellan.

They went on for half an hour, in perfect silence, and perceived an elevation which seemed without doubt to be land.

"It is Shannon Island," said Jean Cornbutte.

A mile farther on they distinctly perceived smoke, escaping from a snow-hut, closed by a wooden door. They shouted. Two men rushed out of the hut, and Penellan recognized one of them as Pierre Nouquet.

"Pierre!" he cried.

Pierre stood still as if stunned, and unconscious of what was going on around him. André Vasling looked at Pierre Nouquet's companion with anxiety mingled with a cruel joy; for he did not recognize Louis Cornbutte in him.

"Pierre! it is I!" cried Penellan. "These are all your friends!"

Pierre Nouquet recovered his senses, and fell into his old comrade's arms.

"And my son,—and Louis!" cried Jean Corubutte, in an accent of the most profound despair.

Chapter XII

The Return to the Ship

At this moment a man, almost dead, dragged himself out of the hut and along the ice.

It was Louis Cornbutte.

"My son!"

"My beloved!"

These two cries were uttered at the same time, and Louis Cornbutte fell fainting into the arms of his father and Marie, who drew him towards the hut, where their tender care soon revived him.

"My father! Marie!" cried Louis, "I shall not die without having seen you!"

"You will not die!" replied Penellan, "for all your friends are near you."

André Vasling must have hated Louis Cornbutte bitterly, not to extend his hand to him; but he did not.

Pierre Nouquet was wild with joy. He embraced everybody; then he threw some wood into the stove, and soon a comfortable temperature was felt in the cabin.

There were two men there whom neither Jean Cornbutte nor Penellan recognized.

They were Jocki and Herming, the only two sailors of the crew of the Norwegian schooner who had been left.

"My friends, we are saved!" said Louis. "My father! Marie! You have exposed yourselves to so many perils!"

"We do not regret it, my Louis," replied his father. "Your brig, the 'Jeune-Hardie,' is securely anchored in the ice sixty leagues from here. We will rejoin her all together."

"When Courtois comes back, he'll be mightily pleased," said Pierre Nouquet.

A mournful silence followed this, and Penellan apprised Pierre and Louis of their comrade's death by cold.

"My friends," said Penellan, "we will wait here until the cold decreases. Have you provisions and wood?"

"Yes; and we will burn what is left of the 'Frooern.' "

The "Frooern" had indeed been driven to a place forty miles from where Louis Cornbutte had taken up his winter quarters. She was broken up by the icebergs floated by the thaw, and the castaways were carried, with a part of the débris of their cabin, on the southern shores of Shannon Island.

They were then five in number,—Louis Cornbutte, Courtois, Pierre Nouquet, Jocki, and Herming. As for the rest of the Norwegian crew, they had been submerged with the long-boat at the moment of the wreck.

When Louis Cornbutte, drawn in among the ice, saw this close around him, he took every precaution for passing the winter. He was an energetic man, very active and courageous; but despite his firmness, he had been subdued by this horrible climate, and when his father found him, he had given up all hope of life. He had not only had to contend with the elements, but with the ugly temper of the two Norwegian sailors, who owed him their existence. They were a sort of savages, almost inaccessible to the most natural emotions. When Louis had the opportunity to talk to Penellan, he advised him to watch them carefully. In return, Penellan told him of André Vasling's conduct. Louis could not believe it; but Penellan convinced him that after his disappearance, Vasling had always acted so as to secure Marie's hand.

The whole day was employed in rest and the pleasures of reunion. Misonne and Pierre Nouquet killed some sea-birds near the hut, whence it was not prudent to stray far. These fresh provisions and the replenished fire raised the spirits of the weakest. Louis Cornbutte got visibly better. It was the first moment of happiness these brave people had experienced. They celebrated it with enthusiasm in this wretched hut, six hundred leagues from the North Sea, in a temperature of thirty degrees below zero!

This temperature lasted till the end of the moon, and it was not until about the 17th of November, a week after their meeting, that Jean Cornbutte and his party could think of setting out. They only had the light of the stars to guide them, but the cold was less extreme, and even some snow fell.

Before quitting this place, a grave was dug for poor Courtois. It was a sad ceremony, which deeply affected his comrades; he was the only one who would not again see his native land.

Misonne had constructed, with the planks of the cabin, a sort of sledge for carrying the provisions, and the sailors drew it by turns. Jean Cornbutte led the expedition by the ways already traversed. Camps were established with great promptness, when the times for repose came. Jean Cornbutte hoped to find his deposits of provisions again, as they had become wellnigh indispensable by the addition of four persons to the party. He was therefore very careful not to diverge from the route by which ho had come.

By good fortune he recovered his sledge, which had stranded near the promontory where they had all run so many dangers. The dogs, after eating their straps to satisfy their hunger, had attacked the provisions in the sledge. These had sustained them, and they served to guide the party to the sledge, where there was a considerable quantity of provisions left. The little band resumed its march toward the bay. The dogs were harnessed to the sleigh, and no event of interest attended the return.

It was observed that Aupic, André Vasling, and the Norwegians kept aloof and did not mingle with the others; but, unbeknown to themselves, they were narrowly watched. This germ of dissension more than once aroused the fears of Louis Cornbutte and Penellan.

About the 7th of December, twenty days after the discovery of the castaways, they perceived the bay where the "Jeune-Hardie" was lying. What was their astonishment to see the brig perched four yards in the air, on blocks of ice! They hurried forward, much alarmed for their companions, and were received with joyous cries by Gervique, Turquiette, and Gradlin. All of them were in good health, though they too had been subjected to formidable dangers.

The tempest had made itself felt throughout the polar sea. The ice had been broken and displaced, crushed one piece against another, and had seized the bed on which the ship rested. Its specific weight tending to carry it under water, the ice had acquired an incalculable force, and the brig had been suddenly raised up out of the sea.

The first moments were given up to the happiness inspired by the safe return. The exploring party were rejoiced to find everything in good condition, which assured them a supportable though it might be a rough winter. The ship had not been shaken by her sudden elevation, and was perfectly tight. When the season of thawing came, they would only have to slide her down an inclined plane, to launch her, in a word, in the once more open sea.

But a bad piece of news spread gloom on the faces of Jean Cornbutte and his comrades. During the terrible gale the snow storehouse on the coast had been quite demolished; the provisions which it contained were scattered, and it had not been possible to save a morsel of them. When Jean and Louis Cornbutte learned this, they visited the hold and steward's room, to ascertain the quantity of provisions which still remained.

The thaw would not come until May, and the brig could not leave the bay before that period. They had therefore five winter months before them, to pass amid the ice, during which fourteen persons were to be fed. Having made his calculations, Jean Cornbutte found that he would at most be able to keep them alive till the time for departure, by putting each and all on half-rations. Hunting for game became compulsory to procure food in larger quantity.

For fear that they might again run short of provisions, it was decided to deposit them no longer in the ground. All of them were kept on board, and beds were disposed for the new-comers in the common lodging. Turquiette, Gervique, and Gradlin, during the absence of the others, had hollowed out a flight of steps in the ice, which enabled them to easily reach the ship's deck.

Chapter XIII
The Two Rivals

André Vasling had been cultivating the good – will of the two Norwegian sailors. Aupic also made one of their band, and held himself apart, with loud disapproval of all the new measures taken; but Louis Cornbutte, to whom his father had transferred the command of the ship, and who had become once more master on board, would listen to no objections from that quarter, and in spite of Marie's advice to act gently, made it known that he intended to be obeyed on all points.

Nevertheless, the two Norwegians succeeded, two days after, in getting possession of a box of salt meat. Louis ordered them to return it to him on the spot, but Aupic took their part, and André Vasling declared that the measures relative to the food could not be any longer enforced.

It was useless to attempt to show these men that these measures were for the common interest, for they knew it well, and only sought a pretext to revolt.

Penellan advanced towards the Norwegians, who drew their cut-lasses; but, aided by Misonne and Turquiette, he succeeded in snatching the weapons from their hands, and gamed possession of the salt meat. André Vasling and Aupic, seeing that matters were going against them, did not interfere. Louis Cornbutte, however, took the mate aside, and said to him, —

"André Vasling, you are a wretch! I know your whole conduct, and I know what inspires it, but as the safety of the whole crew is confided to me, if any man of you thinks of conspiring to destroy them, I will stab him with my own hand!"

"Louis Cornbutte," replied the mate, "it is allowable to you to act the master; but remember that absolute obedience does not exist here, and that the strongest alone here makes the law."

Marie had never trembled before the dangers of the polar seas, but she was terrified by this hatred, of which she was the cause, and the captain's vigor hardly reassured her

Despite this declaration of war, the meals were partaken of in common and at the same hours. Hunting furnished some ptarmigans and white hares; but this resource would soon fail them, amid the approaching terrible cold weather. This began at the solstice, on the 22d of December, on which day the thermometer fell to thirty-five degrees below zero The men experienced pain in their ears, noses, and the extremities of their bodies. They were seized with a mortal torpor, mixed with headache, and their breathing became more and more difficult.

In this state they had no longer any courage to go hunting or to take any exercise. They remained crouched around the stove, which gave them but a meagre heat; and when they went away from it, they perceived that their blood suddenly cooled.

Jean Cornbutte's health was seriously impaired, and he could no longer quit his lodging Symptoms of scurvy manifested themselves in him, and his legs were soon covered with white spots. Marie was well, however, and occupied herself tending the sick ones with the zeal of a sister of charity. The honest fellows blessed her from the bottom of their hearts.

The 1st of January was one of the gloomiest of these winter days. The wind was violent, and the cold insupportable. They could not go out, except at the risk of being frozen. The most courageous were fain? to limit themselves to walking on deck, sheltered by the tent. Jean Cornbutte, Gervique, and Gradlm did not leave their beds. The two Norwegians, Aupic, and André Vasling, whose health was good, cast ferocious looks at their companions, whom they saw wasting away.

Louis Cornbutte led Penellan on deck, and asked him how much fire material was left.

"The coal was exhausted long ago," replied Penellan, "and we are about to burn our last pieces of wood."

"If we are not able to keep off this cold, we are lost," said Louis.

"There still remains a way," said Penellan,—"to burn what we can of the brig, from the barricading to the water-line, and we can even, if need be, demolish her entirely, and rebuild a smaller craft."

"That is an extreme means," replied Louis, "which it will be full time to employ when our men are well. For," he added in a low voice, "our force is diminishing, and that of our enemies seems to be increasing. That is extraordinary."

"It is true," said Penellan; "and unless we took the precaution to watch night and day, I know not what would happen to us."

"Let us take our hatchets," returned Louis, "and make our harvest of wood."

Despite the cold, they mounted on the forward barricading, and cut off all the wood which was not indispensably necessary to the ship; then they returned with this new provision. The fire was started afresh, and a man remained on guard to prevent it from going out.

Meanwhile Louis Cornbutte and his friends were soon tired out. They could not confide any detail of the life in common to their enemies. Charged with all the domestic cares, their forces were soon exhausted. The scurvy betrayed itself in Jean Cornbutte, who suffered intolerable pain. Gervique and Gradlin showed symptoms of the same disease. Had it not been for the lemon-juice with which they were abundantly furnished, they would have speedily succumbed to their sufferings. This remedy was not spared in relieving them.

But one day, the 15th of January, when Louis Cornbutte was going down into the steward's room to get some lemons, he was stupefied to find that the barrels in which they were kept had disappeared. He hurried up and told Penellan of this misfortune. A theft had been committed, and it was easy to recognize its authors. Louis Cornbutte then understood why the health of his enemies continued so good! His friends were no longer strong enough to take the lemons away from them, though his life and that of his comrades depended on the fruit; and he now sank, for the first time, into a gloomy state of despair.

Chapter XIV

Distress

On the 20th of January the larger part of the crew had not the strength to leave their beds. Each, independently of his woollen coverings, had a buffalo-skin to protect him against the cold; but as soon as he put his arms outside the clothes, he felt a pain which obliged him quickly to cover them again.

Meanwhile, Louis having lit the stove fire, Penellan, Misonne, and André Vasling left their beds and crouched around it. Penellan prepared some boiling coffee, which gave them some strength, as well as Marie, who joined them in partaking of it.

Louis Cornbutte approached his father's bedside; the old man was almost motionless, and his limbs were helpless from disease. He muttered some disconnected words, which carried grief to his son's heart.

"Louis," said he, "I am going to die. O, how I suffer! Save me!"

Louis took a decisive resolution. He went up to the mate, and, controlling himself with difficulty, said, —

"Do you know where the lemons are, Vasling?"

"In the steward's room, I suppose," returned the mate, without stirring.

"You know they are not there, as you have stolen them."

"You are the master, Louis Cornbutte, and may say and do anything."

"For pity's sake, André Vasling, my father is dying! You can save him,—answer!"

"I have nothing to answer," replied André Vasling.

"Wretch!" cried Penellan, throwing himself, cutlass in hand, on the mate.

"Help, friends!" shouted Vasling, retreating.

Aupic and the two Norwegian sailors jumped from their beds and placed themselves behind him. Turquiette, Penellan, and Louis prepared to defend themselves. Pierre Nouquet and Gradlin, though ill, rose to second them.

"You are still too strong for us," said Vasling. "We do not wish to fight on an uncertainty."

The sailors were so weak that they dared not attack the four rebels, for, had they failed, they would have been lost

"'André Vasling," said Louis Cornbutte, in a gloomy tone, "if my father dies, you will have murdered him; and I will kill you as if you were a dog!"

Vasling and his confederates retired to the other end of the cabin, and did not reply.

It was then necessary to renew the supply of wood, and, in spite of the cold, Louis went on deck and began to cut away a part of the barricading, but was obliged to retreat in a quarter of an hour, for he was in danger of falling, overcome by the freezing air. As he passed, he cast a glance at the thermometer left outside, and saw that the mercury was frozen. The cold, then, exceeded forty-two degrees below zero. The weather was dry, and the wind blew from the north.

On the 26th the wind changed to the northeast and the thermometer outside stood at thirty-five degrees. Jean Cornbutte was in agony, and his son had searched in vain for some remedy with which to relieve his pain. On this day, however, throwing himself suddenly on Vasling, he managed to snatch a lemon from him which he was about to suck. Vasling made no attempt to recover it. He seemed to be awaiting an opportunity to accomplish his wicked designs.

The lemon-juice somewhat relieved old Cornbutte, but it was necessary to continue the remedy. Marie begged Vasling on her knees to produce the lemons, but he did not reply, and soon Penellan heard the wretch say to his accomplices, —

"The old fellow is dying. Gervique, Gradlin, and Nouquet are not much better. The others are daily losing their strength. The time is near when their lives will belong to us!"

It was then resolved by Louis Cornbutte and his adherents not to wait, and to profit by the little strength which still remained to them. They determined to act the next night, and to kill these wretches, so as not to be killed by them.

The temperature rose a little. Louis Cornbutte ventured to go out with his gun in search of some game.

He proceeded some three miles from the ship, and, often deceived by the effects of the mirage and refraction, he went farther away than he intended. It was imprudent, for recent tracks of ferocious animals betrayed themselves. He did not wish, however, to return without some fresh meat, and continued on his route; but he then experienced a strange feeling, which turned his head. It was what is called "white vertigo."

The reflection of the ice hillocks and fields affected him from head to foot, and it seemed to him that the dazzling color penetrated him and caused an irresistible nausea. His eye was impregnated, his sight became wandering. He thought he should go mad with the whiteness. Without fully understanding this terrible effect, he advanced on his way, and soon raised a ptarmigan, which he eagerly pursued. The bird soon fell, and in order to reach it Louis leaped from an ice-block and fell heavily; for the leap was at least ten feet, and the refraction made him think it was only two. The vertigo then seized him, and, without knowing why, he began to call for help, though he had not been injured by the fall. The cold began to take him, and he painfully rose, urged by the sense of self-preservation.

Of a sudden, without being able to account for it, he smelt an odor of boiling fat. As he was in the wind coming from the ship, he supposed that this odor proceeded from her, and could not imagine why they should be cooking fat; this being a dangerous thing to do, as likely to attract thither the white bears.

Louis returned towards the ship, absorbed in reflections which soon inspired his excited mind with terror. It seemed to him as if colossal masses were moving on the horizon, and he asked himself if there was not still a quaking of the ice. Several of these masses interposed themselves between him and the ship, and appeared to rise about its sides. He stopped to gaze at them more attentively, when he recognized a herd of gigantic bears.

These animals had been attracted by the odor of grease which had surprised Louis. He sheltered himself behind a hillock, and counted three which were scaling the blocks on which the "Jeune-Hardie" was resting.

Nothing led him to suppose that this danger was known on the interior of the ship, and a terrible anguish oppressed his heart. How resist these redoubtable enemies? Would André Vasling and his confederates unite with the rest on board in the common peril? Could Penellan and the others, half starved, benumbed with cold, resist these formidable beasts, made wild by unassuaged hunger? Would they not be surprised by an unlooked-for attack?

Louis made these reflections rapidly. The bears had crossed the blocks, and were mounting to the assault of the ship. He might then quit the block which protected him; he went nearer, clinging to the ice, and could soon see the enormous animals tearing the tent with their paws and leaping on the deck. He thought of firing his gun to give his comrades notice; but if these came up without arms, they would inevitably be torn in pieces, and nothing indicated that they were aware of their new danger.

Chapter XV

The White Bears

After Louis Cornbutte's departure, Penellan had carefully shut the cabin door, which opened at the foot of the deck steps. He returned to the stove, which he took it upon himself to watch, whilst his companions regained their berths in search of a little heat.

It was then six in the evening, and Penellan set about preparing supper. He went down into the steward's room for some salt meat, which he wished to soak in the boiling water. When he returned, he found André Vasling in his place, cooking some pieces of grease in a basin.

"I was there before you," said Penellan, roughly; "why have you taken my place?"

"For the same reason that you claim it," returned Vasling. "Because I want to cook my supper."

"You will take that off at once, or we shall see!"

"We shall see nothing," said Vasling; "my supper shall be cooked in spite of you."

"You will not eat it, then," cried Penellan, rushing upon Vasling, who seized his cutlass, crying, —

"Help, Norwegians! Help, Aupic!"

These, in the twinkling of an eye, sprang to their feet, armed with pistols and daggers.

Penellan precipitated himself upon Vasling, to whom, no doubt, was confided the task to fight him alone; for his accomplices rushed to the beds where lay Misonne, Turquiette, and Nouquet. The latter, ill and defenceless, was delivered over to Herming's ferocity. The carpenter seized a hatchet, and, leaving his berth, hurried up to encounter Aupic. Turquiette and the Norwegian Jocki struggled fiercely. Gervique and Gradlin, suffering horribly, were not even conscious of what was passing around them.

Nouquet soon received a stab in the side, and Herming turned to Penellan, who was fighting desperately. André Vasling had seized him around the body.

At the beginning of the affray the basin had been upset on the stove, and the grease, spreading on the burning coals, impregnated the atmosphere with its odor. Marie rose with cries of despair, and hurried to the bed of old Jean Cornbutte.

Vasling, less strong than Penellan, soon perceived that the latter was getting the better of him. They were too close together to make use of their weapons. The mate, seeing Herming, cried out, —

"Help, Herming!"

"Help, Misonne!" shouted Penellan, in his turn.

But Misonne was rolling on the ground with Aupic, who was trying to stab him with his cutlass. The carpenter's hatchet was of little use to him, for he could not wield it, and it was with the greatest difficulty that he parried the lunges which Aupic made with his knife.

Meanwhile blood flowed amid the groans and cries. Turquiette, thrown down by Jocki, a man of immense strength, had received a wound in the shoulder, and he tried in vain to clutch a pistol which hung in the Norwegian's belt. The latter held him as in a vise, and it was impossible for him to move.

At Vasling's cry for help, he being held by Penellan close against the door, Herming rushed up. As he was about to stab the Breton's back with his cutlass, the latter felled him to the earth with a vigorous kick. His effort to do this enabled Vasling to disengage his right arm; but the door, against which they pressed with all their weight, suddenly yielded, and Vasling fell over.

Of a sudden a terrible growl was heard, and a gigantic bear appeared on the steps. Vasling saw him first. He was not four feet away from him. At the same moment a detonation was heard, and the bear, wounded or frightened, retreated. Vasling, who had succeeded in regaining his feet, set out in pursuit of him, abandoning Penellan.

Penellan then replaced the door, and looked around him. Misonne and Turquiette, tightly garroted by their antagonists, had been thrown into a corner, and made vain efforts to break loose. Penellan rushed to their assistance, but was overturned by the two Norwegians and Aupic. His exhausted strength did not permit him to resist these three men, who so clung to him as to hold him motionless. Then, at the cries of the mate, they hurried on deck, thinking that Louis Cornbutte was to be encountered.

André Vasling was struggling with a bear, which he had already twice stabbed with his knife. The animal, beating the air with his heavy paws, was trying to clutch Vasling. He, retiring little by little on the barricading, seemed to be doomed, when a second denotation was heard. The bear fell. André Vasling raised his head and saw Louis Cornbutte in the ratlines of the mizzenmast, his gun in his hand. Louis had shot the bear in the heart, and he was dead.

Hate overcame gratitude in Vasling's breast; but before satisfying it, he looked around him. Aupic's head was broken by a paw-stroke, and lay lifeless on deck. Jocki, hatchet in hand, was with difficulty parrying the blows of the second bear, which had just killed Aupic. The animal had received two wounds, and still struggled desperately.

A third bear was directing his way towards the ship's prow. Vasling paid no attention to him, but, followed by Herming, went to the aid of Jocki; but Jocki, seized by the beast's paws, was crushed, and when the bear fell under the shots of the other two men, he held only a corpse in his shaggy arms.

"We are only two, now," said Vasling, with gloomy ferocity, "but if we yield, it will not be without vengeance!"

Herming reloaded his pistol without replying. Before all, the third bear must be got rid of. Vasling looked forward, but did not see him. On raising his eyes, he perceived him erect on the barricading, clinging to the ratlines and trying to reach Louis. Vasling let his gun fall, and directed it towards his enemy, while a fierce joy glittered in his eyes.

"Ah," he cried, "you owe me that vengeance!"

Louis took refuge in the top of the mast. The bear kept mounting, and was not more than six feet from Louis, when he raised his gun and pointed it at the animal's heart.

Vasling raised his weapon to shoot Louis if the bear fell.

Louis fired, but the bear did not appear to be hit, for he leaped with a bound towards the top. The whole mast shook.

Vasling uttered a shout of exultation.

"Herming," he cried, "go and find Marie! Go and find my betrothed!"

Herming descended the cabin stairs.

Meanwhile the furious beast had thrown himself upon Louis, who was trying to shelter himself on the other side of the mast; but at the moment that his enormous paw was raised to break his head, Louis, seizing one of the backstays, let himself slip down to the deck, not without danger, for a ball hissed by his ear when he was half-way down. Vasling had shot at him, and missed him. The two adversaries now confronted each other, cutlass in hand.

The combat was about to become decisive. To entirely glut his vengeance, and to have the young girl witness her lover's death, Vasling had deprived himself of Herming's aid. He could now reckon only on himself.

Louis and Vasling seized each other by the collar, and held each other with iron grip. One of them must fall dead. They struck each other violently. The blows were only half parried, for blood soon flowed from both. Vasling tried to clasp his adversary about the neck with his arm, to bring him to the ground. Louis, knowing that he who fell was lost, prevented him, and succeeded in grasping his two arms; but in doing this he let fall his cutlass.

Piteous cries now assailed his ears; it was Marie's voice. Herming was trying to drag her up. Louis was seized with a desperate rage. He stiffened himself to bend Vasling's loins; but at this moment the combatants felt themselves seized in a powerful embrace. The bear, having descended from the mast, had fallen upon the two men. Vasling was pressed against the animal's body. Louis felt his claws entering his flesh. The bear was strangling both of them.

"Help! help! Herming!" cried the mate.

"Help! Penellan!" cried Louis.

Steps were heard on the stairs. Penellan appeared, loaded his pistol, and discharged it in the bear's ear; he roared; the pain made him relax his paws for a moment, and Louis, exhausted, fell motionless on the deck; but the bear, closing his paws tightly in a supreme agony, fell, dragging down the wretched Vasling, whose body was crushed under him.

Penellan hurried to Louis Cornbutte's assistance. No serious wound endangered his life; he had only lost his breath for a moment.

"Marie!" he said, opening his eyes.

"Saved!" replied Penellan. "Herming is lying there with a knife-wound in his stomach."

"And the bears —"

"Dead, Louis, dead, like our enemies! But for those beasts we should have been lost. Truly, they came to our succor. Let us, then, thank Providence!"

Louis and Penellan descended to the cabin, and Marie fell into their arms.

Chapter XVI
Conclusion

Herming, mortally wounded, had been carried to a berth by Misonne and Turquiette, who had succeeded in getting free. He was already at the last gasp of death; and the two sailors occupied themselves with Nouquet, whose wound was not, happily, a serious one.

But a greater misfortune had overtaken Louis Cornbutte. His father no longer gave any signs of life. Had he died of anxiety for his son, delivered over to his enemies? Had he succumbed in presence of these terrible events? They could not tell. But the poor old sailor, broken by disease, had ceased to live!

At this unexpected blow Louis and Marie fell into a sad despair; then they kneeled at the bedside and wept, and prayed for Jean Cornbutte's soul. Penellan, Misonne, and Turquiette left them alone in the cabin, and went on deck. The bodies of the three bears were carried forward. Penellan decided to keep their skins, which would be of no little use; but he did not think for a moment of eating their flesh. Besides, the number of men to feed was now much decreased. The bodies of Vasling, Aupic, and Jocki, thrown into a hole dug on the coast, were soon rejoined by that of Herming. The Norwegian died during the night, without repentance or remorse, foaming at the mouth with rage.

The three sailors repaired the tent, which, torn in several places, permitted the snow to fall on the deck. The temperature was exceedingly cold, and lasted till the return of the sun, which did not reappear above the horizon till the 8th of January.

Jean Cornbutte was buried on the coast. He had left his native land to find his son, and had died in these terrible regions! His grave was dug on an eminence, and the sailors placed over it a simple wooden cross.

From that day, Louis Cornbutte and his comrades passed through many other trials; but the lemons, which they found, restored them to health.

Gervique, Gradlin, and Nouquet were able to rise from their berths a fortnight after these terrible events, and to take a little exercise.

Soon hunting for game became more easy and its results more abundant. The water-birds returned in large numbers. They often brought down a kind of wild duck which made excellent food. The hunters had no other deprivation to deplore than that of two dogs, which they lost in an expedition to reconnoitre the state of the ice-fields, twenty-five miles to the southward.

The month of February was signalized by violent tempests and abundant snows. The mean temperature was still twenty-five degrees below zero, but they did not suffer in comparison with past hardships. Besides, the sight of the sun, which rose higher and higher above the horizon, rejoiced them, as it forecast the end of their torments. Heaven had pity on them, for warmth came sooner than its wont. The ravens appeared in March, careering about the ship. Louis Cornbutte captured some cranes which had wandered thus far northward. Flocks of wild birds were also seen in the south.

The return of the birds indicated a diminution of the cold; but it was not safe to rely upon this, for with a change of wind, or in the new or full moons, the temperature suddenly fell; and the sailors were forced to resort to their most careful precautions to protect themselves against it. They had already burned all the barricading, the bulkheads, and a large portion of the bridge. It was time, then, that their wintering was over. Happily the mean temperature of March was not over sixteen degrees below zero. Marie occupied herself with preparing new clothing for the advanced season of the year.

After the equinox, the sun had remained constantly above the horizon. The eight months of perpetual daylight had begun. This continual sunlight, with the increasing though still quite feeble heat, soon began to act upon the ice.

Great precautions were necessary in launching the ship from the lofty layer of ice which surrounded her. She was therefore securely propped up, and it seemed best to await the breaking up of the ice; but the lower mass, resting on a bed of already warm water, detached itself little by little, and the ship gradually descended with it. Early in April she had reached her natural level.

Torrents of rain came with April, which, extending in waves over the ice-plain, hastened still more its breaking up. The thermometer rose to ten degrees below zero. Some of the men took off their sealskin clothes, and it was no longer necessary to keep a fire in the cabin stove day and night. The provision of spirit, which was not exhausted, was used only for cooking the food.

Soon the ice began to break up rapidly, and it became imprudent to venture upon the plain without a staff to sound the passages; for fissures wound in spirals here and there. Some of the sailors fell into the water, with no worse result than a pretty cold bath.

The seals returned, and they were often hunted, and their grease utilized.

The health of the crew was fully restored, and the time was employed in hunting and preparations for departure. Louis Cornbutte often examined the channels, and decided, in consequence of the shape of the southern coast, to attempt a passage in that direction. The breaking up had already begun here and there, and the floating ice began to pass off towards the high seas. On the 25th of April the ship was put to rights. The sails, taken from their sheaths, were found to be perfectly preserved, and it was with real delight that the sailors saw them once more swaying in the wind. The ship gave a lurch, for she had found her floating line, and though she would not yet move forward, she lay quietly and easily in her natural element.

In May the thaw became very rapid. The snow which covered the coast melted on every hand, and formed a thick mud, which made it wellnigh impossible to land. Small heathers, rosy and white, peeped out timidly above the lingering snow, and seemed to smile at the little heat they received.

Twenty miles off, the ice-masses, entirely separated, floated towards the Atlantic Ocean. Though the sea was not quite free around the ship, passes opened by which Louis Cornbutte wished to profit.

On the 21st of May, after a parting visit to his father's grave, Louis at last set out from the bay. The hearts of the honest sailors were filled at once with joy and sadness, for one does not leave without regret a place where a friend has died. The wind blew from the north, and favored their departure. The ship was often arrested by ice-banks, which were cut with the saws; icebergs not seldom confronted her, and it was necessary to blow them up with powder. For a month the way was full of perils, which sometimes brought the ship to the verge of destruction; but the crew was sturdy, and used to these dangerous exigencies. Penellan, Pierre Nouquet, Turquiette, Fidèle Misonne, did the work of ten sailors, and Marie had smiles of gratitude for each.

The "Jeune-Hardie" at last passed beyond the ice in the latitude of Jean-Mayer Island. About the 25th of June she met ships going north-ward for seals and whales. She had been nearly a month emerging from the Polar Sea.

On the 16th of August she came in view of Dunkirk. She had been signalled by the lookout, and the whole population flocked to the jetty. The sailors of the ship were soon clasped in the arms of their friends. The old cure received Louis Cornbutte and Marie with patriarchal arms, and of the two masses which he said on the following day, the first was for the repose of Jean Cornbutte's soul, and the second to bless these two lovers, so long united in misfortune.

Master Zacharius:
The Clockmaker Who
Lost His Soul

Chapter I

A Winter's Night

The city of Geneva is situated at the western extremity of the lake to which it gives—or owes—its name. The Rhone, which crosses the city on emerging from the lake, divides it into two distinct quarters, and is itself divided, in the centre of the city, by an island rising between its two banks. This topographical situation is often to be observed in the great centres of commerce or industry. Doubtless the earliest inhabitants were seduced by the facilities of transportation afforded by the rapid arms of the rivers,—"those roads which advance of themselves," as Pascal says. In the case of the Rhone, they are roads which run. At the period when new and regular buildings had not as yet been erected on this island, anchored like a Dutch gahot in the midst of the river, the wonderful mass of houses huddled the one against the other offered to the eye a confusion full of charms. The small extent of the island had forced some of these buildings to perch upon piles, fastened pell-mell in the strong currents of the Rhone. These big timbers, blackened by time and worn by the waters, looked like the claws of an immense crab, and produced a fantastic effect. Some yellowed nets, real spiders' webs stretched amid these venerable substructures, shivered and trembled in the shade as if they had been the foliage of these old oaks, and the river, engulfing itself in the midst of this forest of piles, foamed with melancholy groans.

One of the habitations on the island struck the observer by its strange appearance of extreme age. It was the residence of the old clockmaker, Master Zacharius, his daughter Gerande, Aubert Thun, his apprentice, and his old servant, Scholastique.

What an original personage was this Zacharius! His age seemed incalculable. The oldest inhabitants of Geneva could not have told how long his lean and picked head had wavered on his shoulders, nor the first day on which he had been seen walking along the streets of the town, his long white locks floating waywardly in the wind. This man did not live. He oscillated after the manner of the pendulums of his clocks. His features, dry and cadaverous, affected sombre tints. Like the pictures of Leonardo di Vinci, he had put black in the foreground.

Gerande occupied the best room in the old house; whence, through a narrow window, her gaze rested sadly upon the snowy summits of the Jura. But the bedroom and shop of the old man were in a sort of cellar, situated on a level with the river, and the flooring of which rested on the piles themselves. From an immemorial period Master Zacharius had not been known to emerge thence, except at meal-time, and when he went forth to regulate the different clocks of the city. He passed the rest of the time at a bench covered with numerous clockmaking instruments, which, for the most part, he had himself invented.

For he was a man of talent. His works were very popular throughout France and Germany. The most industrious workmen in Geneva freely admitted his superiority, and that he was an honor to the city. They pointed him out, saying, "To him is due the glory of having invented the escapement!"

Indeed, it is from this invention, which the labors of Zacharius will later make clear, that is to be dated the birth of the real science of clockmaking.

Well, after having worked long and marvellously, Zacharius slowly put his tools in their places, covered with light glass the delicate pieces he had just adjusted, and consigned his wheel, in its turn, to repose; then he raised a peephole, fashioned in the flooring of his hovel, and there, leaning over it for hours together, while the Rhone gurgled and rushed beneath him, he intoxicated himself with its misty vapors.

One winter's evening old Scholastique was serving supper, in which, according to ancient usage, she was aided by the young apprentice.

Though carefully prepared dishes were offered to Master Zacharius in fine blue-and-white porcelain, he ate nothing. He scarcely replied to the soft questionings of Gerande, who was visibly affected by the gloomy silence of her father; and the garrulousness of Scholastique herself only struck his ear like the grumblings of the river, to which he no longer paid attention. After this silent repast the old clockmaker left the table without embracing his daughter, nor did he, as usual, bid the rest "good evening." He disappeared through the narrow door which conducted to his retreat, and the staircase fairly creaked under his heavy tread.

Gerande, Aubert, and Scholastique remained silent for some moments. The weather was gloomy; the clouds dragged themselves heavily along the Alps, and threatened to dissolve in rain; the severe temperature of Switzerland filled the soul with melancholy, while the midland winds prowled among the hills and whistled drearily.

"Do you know, my dear demoiselle," said Scholastique at last, "that our master has kept wholly to himself for some days? Holy Virgin! I see he has not been hungry, for his words have remained in his stomach, and the Devil himself would be adroit to force one out of him!"

"My father has some secret trouble which I cannot even guess," replied Gerande, a sad anxiety betraying itself in her countenance.

"Mademoiselle, do not permit so much sadness to overshadow your heart. You know the singular habits of Master Zacharius. Who can read his secret thoughts in his face? Something annoying has no doubt happened to him, but he will have forgotten it by to-morrow, and will repent having made his daughter anxious."

It was Aubert who spoke thus, glancing at Gerande's lovely eyes. Aubert was the first apprentice whom Master Zacharius had ever admitted to the intimacy of his labors, for he appreciated his intelligence, discretion, and goodness of heart; and this young man had attached himself to Gerande with that mysterious faith which presides over heroic denouements.

Gerande was eighteen years of age. The oval of her face recalled that of the artless Madonnas, whom veneration still displays at the street corners of the antique towns of Brittany. Her eyes betrayed an infinite simplicity. She was beloved as the most delicate realization of a poet's dream. Her apparel was of modest colors, and the white linen which was folded about her shoulders had the tint and perfume peculiar to the linen of the church. She led a mystical existence at Geneva, which had not as yet been delivered over to the dryness of Calvinism.

Whilst, night and morning, she read her Latin prayers in her iron-clasped missal, Gerande also discovered a hidden sentiment in Aubert Thun's heart, and comprehended what a profound devotion the young workman had for her. Indeed, the whole world in his eyes was condensed in this old house of the clockmaker, and he passed all his time near the young girl, when, the hours of work over, he left her father's workshop.

Old Scholastique saw all this, but said nothing. Her loquacity exhausted itself in preference on the evils of the times, and the little worries of the household. Nobody tried to stop its course. It was with her as with the musical snuff-boxes which they made at Geneva; once wound up, you must have broken her, but she would play all her airs through.

Finding Gerande absorbed in a melancholy silence, Scholastique left her old wooden chair, fixed a taper on the end of a candlestick, lit it, and placed it near a small waxen Virgin, sheltered in her niche of stone. It was the family custom to kneel before this protecting Madonna of the domestic hearth, and to beg her kindly watchfulness during the coming night; but on this evening, Gerande remained silent in her seat.

"Well, well, dear demoiselle," said the astonished Scholastique, "supper is over, and it is time to go to bed. Why do you tire your eyes by sitting up late? Ah, Holy Virgin! It's much better to sleep, and to get a little comfort from happy dreams! In these detestable times in which we live, who can promise herself a fortunate day?"

"Ought we not to send for a doctor for my father?" asked Gerande.

"A doctor!" cried the old domestic. "Has Master Zacharius ever listened to their fancies and pompous sayings? He might accept medicines for the watches, but not for the body!"

"What shall we do?" murmured Gerande. "Has he gone to work, or has he retired?"

"Gerande," answered Aubert, softly, "some mental trouble annoys your father, and that is all."

"Do you know what it is, Aubert?"

"Perhaps, Gerande."

"Tell us, then," cried Scholastique, eagerly, prudently extinguishing her taper.

"For several days, Gerande," said the young apprentice, "something absolutely incomprehensible has been going on. All the watches which your father has made and sold for some years have suddenly stopped. Very many of them have been brought back to him. He has carefully taken them to pieces; the springs were in good condition, and the wheels well set. He has put them together yet more carefully; but, despite his skill, they have refused to go."

"The devil's in it!" cried Scholastique.

"Why say you so?" asked Gerande. "It seems very natural to me. All things are limited in the world. The infinite cannot be fashioned by the hands of men."

"It is none the less true," returned Aubert, "that there is in this something very mysterious and extraordinary. I have myself been helping Master Zacharius to search for the cause of this derangement of his watches; but I have not been able to find it, and more than once I have despairingly let my tools fall from my hands"

"But why undertake so vain a task?" resumed Scholastique. "Is it natural that a little copper instrument should go of itself, and mark the hours? We ought to have kept to the sun-dial!"

"You will not talk thus, Scholastique," said Aubert, "when you learn that the sun-dial was invented by Cain."

"O Lord! what are you telling me?"

"Do you think," asked Gerande, simply, "that we might pray to God to give life to my father's watches?"

"Without doubt," replied Aubert.

"Good! These will be useless prayers," grumbled the old servant, "but Heaven will pardon them for their good intent."

The taper was relighted. Scholastique, Gerande, and Aubert knelt down together upon the flags of the room. The young girl prayed for her mother's soul, for a blessing for the night, for travellers and prisoners, for the good and the wicked, and more earnestly than all for the unknown misfortunes of her father.

Then the three devout souls rose with somewhat of confidence in their hearts, for they had laid their sorrow in God's bosom.

Aubert repaired to his own room; Gerande sat pensively by the window, whilst the last lights were disappearing from the city streets; and Scholastique, having poured a little water on the flickering embers, and shut the two enormous bolts on the door, threw herself upon her bed, where she was soon dreaming that she was dying of fright.

Meanwhile the terrors of this winter's night had increased. Sometimes, with the whirlpools of the river, the wind engulfed itself among the piles, and the whole house shivered and shook, but the young girl, absorbed in her sadness, thought only of her father. After hearing what Aubert told her, the malady of Master Zacharius took fantastic proportions in her mind; and it seemed to her as if his dear existence, become purely mechanical, moved now with pain and effort on its exhausted pivots.

Suddenly the shutters, impelled by the squall, struck against the window of the room. Gerande shuddered, without understanding the cause of the noise which thus disturbed her revery. When she became a little calmer she opened the sash. The clouds had burst, and a torrent-like rain pattered on the surrounding roofs. The young girl leaned out of the window to draw to the shutter shaken by the wind, but she feared to do so. It seemed to her that the ram and the river, confounding their tumultuous waters, were submerging the frail house, the planks of which were creaking in every direction. She would have flown from her chamber, but she saw below the flickering of a light which appeared to come from Master Zacharius's retreat, and in one of those momentary calms, during which the elements keep a sudden silence, her ear caught plaintive sounds. She tried to shut her window, but could not. The wind violently repelled her, like a villain who was introducing himself into a dwelling.

Gerande thought she would go mad from terror. What was her father doing? She opened the door, and it escaped from her hands, and shook loudly under the attack of the tempest. Gerande then found herself in the dark supper-room, succeeded in gaining, on tiptoe, the staircase which led to her father's shop, and, pale and fainting, glided down.

The old watchmaker was upright in the middle of the room, which was filled with the groans of the river. His bristling hair gave him a sinister aspect. He was talking and gesticulating, without seeing or hearing anything. Gerande arrested her steps on the threshold.

"It is death!" said Master Zacharius, in a thick voice; "it is death! Why should I live longer, now that I have dispersed my existence over the earth? For I, Master Zacharius, am really the creator of all the watches that I have fashioned! It is a part of my very soul that I have shut up in each of these boxes of iron, silver, or gold! Every time that one of these accursed watches stops, I feel my heart cease beating, for I have regulated them with its pulsations!"

As he spoke in this strange way, the old man cast his eyes on his bench. There lay all the pieces of a watch that he had carefully taken apart. He took up a sort of hollow cylinder, called a barrel, in which the spring is enclosed, and removed the steel spiral, which, instead of relaxing itself, according to the laws of its elasticity, remained coiled on itself, like a sleeping viper. It seemed knotted, like those impotent old men whose blood has long been congealed. Master Zacharius vamly essayed to uncoil it with his thin fingers, the outlines of which were exaggerated on the wall; but he tried in vain, and soon, with a terrible cry of anguish and rage, he threw it through the peephole into the boiling Rhone.

Gerande, her feet riveted to the floor, stood breathless and motionless. She wished to approach her father, but could not. Giddy hallucinations took possession of her. Suddenly she heard, in the shade, a voice murmur in her ears, —

"Gerande, dear Gerande! grief still keeps you awake! Go in again, I beg of you; the night is cold."

"Aubert!" whispered the young girl. "You!"

"Ought I not to be disturbed by what disturbs you?"

These soft words sent the blood back into the young girl's heart. She leaned on Aubert's arm, and said to him, —

"My father is very ill, Aubert! You alone can cure him, for this disorder of the mind would not yield to his daughter's consolings. His mind is attacked by a very natural delusion, and in working with him, repairing the watches, you will bring him back to reason. Aubert," she continued, "it is not true, is it, that his life confounds itself with that of his watches?"

Aubert did not reply.

"But it must be a calling reproved of God,—that of my father?"

"I know not," returned the apprentice, warming the cold hands of the girl with his own. "But go back to your room, my poor Gerande, and with sleep, recover hope!"

Gerande slowly returned to her chamber, and remained there till daylight; sleep did not weigh down her eyelids. Meanwhile, Master Zacharius, always mute and motionless, gazed at the river as it rolled turbulently at his feet.

Chapter II
The Pride of Science

The severity of the Geneva merchant in business matters has become proverbial He is rigidly honorable, and excessively just. What must, then, have been the shame of Master Zacharius, when he saw these watches, which he had so carefully constructed, returning to him from every direction?

It was certain that these watches had suddenly stopped, and without any apparent reason. The wheels were in a good condition and firmly fixed, but the springs had lost all elasticity. Vainly did the watchmaker try to replace them; the wheels remained motionless. These unaccountable derangements were greatly to the old man's discredit. His noble inventions had many times brought upon him suspicions of sorcery, which now seemed confirmed. These rumors reached Gerande, and she often trembled for her father, when she saw malicious glances directed towards him.

Yet on the morning after this night of anguish, Master Zacharius seemed to resume work with some confidence. The morning sun inspired him with some courage. Aubert hastened to join him in the shop, and received an affable "good day."

"I am getting on better," said the old man. "I don't know what strange troubles of the head attacked me yesterday, but the sun has quite chased them away, with the clouds of the night"

"In faith, master," returned Aubert, "I don't like the night for either of us!"

"And thou art right, Aubert. If you ever become a superior man, you will understand that day is as necessary to you as food. A man of merit owes himself to the homage of the rest of mankind!"

"Master, it seems to me that the pride of science has possessed you."

"Pride, Aubert! Destroy my past, annihilate my present, dissipate my future, and then it will be permitted to me to live in obscurity! Poor boy, who comprehends not the sublime things to which my art is wholly devoted! Art thou not but a tool in my hands?"

"Yet, Master Zacharius," resumed Aubert, "I have more than once merited your praise for the manner in which I adjusted the most delicate pieces of your watches and clocks."

"No doubt, Aubert; thou art a good workman, such as I love; but when thou workest, thou thinkest thou hast in thy hands but copper, silver, gold; thou dost not perceive these metals, which my genius animates, palpitating like living flesh! Thus thou wouldst not die, with the death of thy works!"

Master Zacharius remained silent after these words, but Aubert essayed to keep up the conversation.

"Indeed, master," said he, "I love to see you work so unceasingly! You will be ready for the festival of our corporation, for I see that the work on this crystal watch is going forward famously."

"No doubt, Aubert," cried the old watchmaker, "and it will be no slight honor for me to have been able to cut and shape the crystal to the durability of a diamond! Ah, Louis Berghem did well to perfect the art of diamond-cutting, which has enabled me to polish and pierce the hardest stones!"

Master Zacharius was holding several small watch pieces of cut crystal, and of exquisite work-manship. The wheels, pivots, and box of the watch were of the same material, and he had employed remarkable skill in this very difficult task.

"Would it not be fine," said he, his face flushing, "to see this watch palpitating beneath its transparent envelope, and to be able to count the beatings of its heart?"

"I will wager, sir," replied the young apprentice, "that it will not vary a second in a year."

"And you would wager on a certainty! Have I not imparted to it all that is purest of myself? And does my heart itself vary?"

Aubert did not dare to lift his eyes to his master's face.

"Tell me frankly," said the old man, sadly. "Have you never taken me for a fool? Do you not think me sometimes subject to dangerous folly? Yes; is it not? In my daughter's eyes and yours, I have often read my condemnation. Oh!" he cried, as if in pain, "to be not understood by those whom one most loves in the world But I will prove victoriously to thee, Aubert, that I am right! Do not bow thy head, for thou wilt be stupefied. The day on which thou understandest how to listen to and comprehend me, thou wilt see that I have discovered the secrets of existence, the seciets of the mysterious union of the soul with the body!"

As he spoke thus, Master Zacharius appeared superb in his vanity. His eyes glittered with a supernatural fire, and his pride illumined every feature. And truly, if ever vanity was excusable, it was that of Master Zacharius!

The watchmaking art, indeed, down to his time, had remained almost in its infancy. From the day when Plato, four centuries before the Christian era, invented the night watch, a sort of clepsydra which indicated the hours of the night by the sound and playing of a flute, the science had continued nearly stationary. The masters paid more attention to the arts than to mechanics, and it was the period of beautiful watches of iron, copper, wood, silver, which were richly engraved, like one of Cellini's ewers. They made a masterpiece of chasing, which measured time very imperfectly, but was still a masterpiece. When the artist's imagination was not directed to the perfection of modelling, it sought to create clocks with moving figures and melodious sounds, which were put in operation in a very diverting fashion. Besides, who troubled himself, in those days, with regulating the advance of the hours? The delays of the law were not as yet invented; the physical and astronomical sciences had not as yet established their calculations on scrupulously exact measurements; there were neither establishments which were shut at a given hour, nor trains which departed at a precise moment. In the evening the curfew bell sounded; and at night the hours were cried amid the universal silence. Certainly people did not live so long, if existence is measured by the amount of business done, but they lived better. The mind was enriched with the noble sentiments born of the contemplation of masterpieces. They built a church in two centuries, a painter painted but few pictures in the course of his life, a poet only composed one great work; but these were so many masterpieces.

When the exact sciences began at last to make some progress, watch and clock making followed in their path, though it was always arrested by an insurmountable difficulty,—the regular and continuous measurement of time.

It was in the midst of this stagnation that Master Zacharius invented the escapement, which enabled him to obtain a mathematical regularity by submitting the movement of the pendulum to a constant force. This invention had turned the old man's head. Pride, swelling in his heart, like mercury in the thermometer, had attained the height of transcendent folly. By analogy he had allowed himself to be drawn to materialistic conclusions, and as he constructed his watches, he fancied that he had surprised the secrets of the union of the soul with the body.

So it was that, on this day, perceiving that Aubert listened to him attentively, he said to him in a tone of simple conviction, —

"Dost thou know what life is, my child? Hast thou comprehended the action of those springs which produce existence? Hast thou examined thyself? No; and yet, with the eyes of science, thou mightst have seen the intimate relation which exists between God's work and my own, for it is from his creature that I have copied the combinations of the wheels of my clocks."

"Master," replied Aubert, eagerly, "can you compare a copper or steel machine with that breath of God which is called the soul, which animates our bodies, as the breeze lends motion to the flowers? What mechanism could be so adjusted as to inspire us with thought?"

"That is not the question," responded Master Zacharius, gently, but with all the obstinacy of a blind man walking towards an abyss. "In order to understand me, thou must recall the object of the escapement which I have invented. When I saw the irregular working of clocks, I understood that the movements shut up in them did not suffice, and that it was necessary to submit them to the regularity of some independent force. I then thought that the balance-wheel might accomplish this, and I succeeded in regulating the movement! Now, was it not a sublime idea that came to me, to return to it its lost force by the action of the clock itself, which it was charged with regulating?"

Aubert assented by a motion.

"Now, Aubert," continued the old man, growing animated, "cast thine eyes upon thyself! Dost thou not understand that there are two distinct forces in us, that of the soul and that of the body, that is, a movement and a regulator? The soul is the principle of life; that is, then, the movement. Whether it is produced by a weight, by a spring, or by an immaterial influence, it is none the less at the heart. But without the body this movement would be unequal, irregular, impossible! Thus the body regulates the soul, and, like the balance-wheel, it is submitted to regular oscillations. And this is so true, that one falls ill when one's drink, food, sleep—in a word, the functions of the body—are not properly regulated! As in my watches, the soul renders to the body the force lost by its oscillations. Well, what produces this intimate union between soul and body, if not a marvellous escapement, by which the wheels of the one work into the wheels of the other? This is what I have divined, applied; and there are no longer any secrets for me in this life, which is, after all, but an ingenious mechanism!"

Master Zacharius was sublime to see in this hallucination, which transported him to the ultimate mysteries of the infinite. But his daughter Gerande, standing on the threshold of the door, had heard all. She rushed into her father's arms, and he pressed her convulsively to his breast.

"What is the matter with thee, my daughter?" he asked.

"If I had only a spring here," said she, putting her hand on her heart, "I would not love you as I do father."

Master Zacharius looked intently at Gerande, and did not reply. Suddenly he uttered a cry, carried his band eagerly to his heart, and fell fainting on his old leathern chair.

"Father, what is the matter?"

"Help!" cried Aubert. "Scholastique!"

But Scholastique did not come at once. Some one was knocking at the front door; she had gone to open it, and when she returned to the shop, before she could open her mouth, the old watchmaker, having recovered his senses, spoke: —

"I divine, my old Scholastique, that you bring me still another of those accursed watches which have stopped."

"O Lord, it is true enough!" replied Scholastique, handing a watch to Aubert.

"My heart could not be mistaken!" said the old man, with a sigh.

Aubert now carefully readjusted the watch, but it would not go.

Chapter III

A Strange Visit

Poor Gerande would have lost her life with that of her father, had it not been for the thought of Aubert, who still attached her to the world.

The old watchmaker was, little by little, passing away. His faculties evidently grew more feeble, as he concentrated them on a single thought. By a sad association of ideas, he referred everything to his monomania, and a human existence seemed to have departed from him, and given place to the extra-natural existence of the intermediate powers. Moreover, certain malicious rivals revived the hostile rumors which had spread concerning his labors.

The news of the strange derangements which his watches betrayed had a prodigious effect upon the master clockmakers of Geneva. What signified this sudden inertia of their wheels, and why these strange relations which they seemed to have with the old man's life? These were the kind of mysteries which people never contemplate without a secret terror. In the various classes of the town, from the apprentices to the great lords who used his watches, there was no one who could not himself judge of the singularity of the fact. The citizens wished, but in vain, to penetrate to Master Zacharius. He fell very ill; and this enabled his daughter to withdraw him from incessant visits, which thereupon degenerated into reproaches and recriminations.

Medicines and physicians were powerless in presence of this organic wasting away, the cause of which could not be discovered. It sometimes seemed as if the old man's heart had ceased to beat; then the pulsations were resumed with an alarming irregularity.

A custom existed, in those days, of submitting the works of the masters to the judgment of the people. The heads of the various corporations sought to distinguish themselves by the novelty or the perfection of their productions, and it was among these that the condition of Master Zacharius excited the most lively, because most interested, commiseration. His rivals pitied him the more willingly, the less he was to be feared. They never forgot the old man's success, when he exhibited his magnificent clocks with moving figures, his striking watches, which provoked the general admiration, and commanded such high prices in the cities of France, Switzerland, and Germany.

Meanwhile, thanks to the constant and tender care of Gerande and Aubert, his strength seemed to return a little, and in the tranquillity in which his convalescence left him, he succeeded in detaching himself from the thoughts which had absorbed him. As soon as he could walk, his daughter lured him away from the house, which was still besieged with dissatisfied intruders. Aubert remained in the shop, vainly adjusting and readjusting the rebel watches: and the poor boy, completely mystified, sometimes covered his face with his hands, fearful that he, like his master, might go mad.

Gerande led her father towards the more pleasant promenades of the town. With his arm resting on hers, she conducted him sometimes through the quarter of Saint Antoine, the view from which extends towards Cologny and on the lake; on fine mornings they caught sight of the gigantic peaks of Mount Buet against the horizon. Gerande pointed out these spots to her father, who had wellnigh forgotten even their names. His memory wandered, and he took a childish interest in learning anew what had passed from his mind. Master Zacharius leaned upon his daughter, and the two heads, one white as snow and the other covered with rich golden tresses, were confounded in the same sun's ray.

So it came about that the old watchmaker at last perceived that he was not alone in the world. As he looked upon his young and lovely daughter, himself old and broken, he reflected that after his death she would be left alone, without support. Many of the young mechanics of Geneva had already sought to win Gerande's love; but none of them had succeeded in gaining access to the impenetrable retreat of the watchmaker's household. It was natural, then, that during this lucid interval the old man's choice should fall on Aubert Thun. Once struck with this thought, he remarked to himself that this young couple had been brought up with the same ideas and the same beliefs, and the oscillations of their hearts seemed to him, as he said one day to Scholastique, "isochronal."

The old servant, literally delighted with the word, though she did not understand it, swore by her holy patron saint that the whole town should hear it within a quarter of an hour. Master Zacharius found it difficult to calm her, but made her promise to keep on this subject a silence which she never was known to observe.

So, though Gerande and Aubert were ignorant of it, all Geneva was soon talking of their speedy union. But it happened also that, while the worthy folk were gossiping, a strange chuckle was often heard, and a voice saying, "Gerande will not wed Aubert."

If the gossipers turned round, they found themselves facing a little old man who was quite a stranger to them.

How old was this singular being? No one could have told. People conjectured that he must have existed for several centuries, and that was all. His big flat head rested upon shoulders the width of which was equal to the height of his body; this was not above three feet. This personage would have figured well on a pendulum fulcrum, for the dial would have naturally been placed on his face, and the balance-wheel would have oscillated at its ease in his chest. His nose might readily be taken for the style of a sun-dial, for it was small and sharp; his teeth, far apart, resembled the gearing of a wheel, and ground themselves between his lips; his voice had the metallic sound of a bell, and you could hear his heart beat like the tick-tick of a clock. This little man, whose arms moved like the needles on a dial, walked with jerks, without ever turning round. If any one followed him, it was found that he walked a league an hour, and that his course was nearly circular.

This strange being had not long been seen wandering, or rather circulating, around the town; but it had already been observed that, every day, at the moment when the sun passed the meridian, he stopped before the Cathedral of Saint Pierre, and resumed his course after the twelve strokes of midday had sounded. Excepting at this precise moment, he seemed to become a part of all the conversations in which the old watchmaker was talked of, and people asked each other, in terror, what relation could exist between him and Master Zacharius. It was remarked, too, that he never lost sight of the old man and his daughter while they were taking their promenades.

One day Gerande perceived this monster looking at her with a hideous smile. She clung to her father with a frightened motion.

"What is the matter, my Gerande?" asked Master Zacharius.

"I do not know," replied the young girl.

"But thou art changed, my child Art thou going to fall ill in thy turn? Ah, well," he added, with a sad smile, "then I must take care of thee, and I will do it tenderly."

"O father, it will be nothing. I am cold, and I imagine that it is—"

"What, Gerande?"

"The presence of that man, who always follows us," she replied in a low tone.

Master Zacharius turned towards the little old man.

"Faith, he goes well," said he, with a satisfied air, "for it is just four o'clock. Fear nothing, my child; it is not a man, it is a clock!"

Gerande looked at her father in terror How could Master Zacharius read the hour on this strange creature's visage?

"By the by," continued the old watchmaker, paying no further attention to the matter, "I have not seen Aubert for several days."

"He has not left us, however, father," said Gerande, whose thoughts turned into a gentler channel.

"What is he doing, then?"

"He is working."

"Ah!" cried the old man. "He is at work repairing my watches, is he not? But he will never succeed; for it is not repairs they need, but a resurrection!"

Gerande remained silent.

"I must know," added the old man, "if they have brought back any of those damned watches, upon which the Devil has imposed an epidemic!"

After these words Master Zacharius fell into absolute taciturnity, till he knocked at the door of his house, and for the first time since his convalescence descended to his shop, while Gerande sadly repaired to her chamber.

At the moment when Master Zacharius crossed the threshold of his shop, one of the many clocks suspended on the wall struck five o'clock. Usually the bells of these clocks—admirably regulated as they were—struck simultaneously, and this rejoiced the old man's heart; but on this day the bells struck one after another, so that for a quarter of an hour the car was deafened by the successive noise. Master Zacharius suffered terribly; he could not remain still, but went from one clock to the other, and beat the measure for them, as an orchestra leader who has no longer control over his musicians.

When the last had ceased striking, the door of the shop opened, and Master Zacharius shuddered from head to foot to see before him the little old man, who looked fixedly at him and said, —

"Master, may I not speak with you a few moments?"

"Who are you?" asked the watchmaker, abruptly.

"A colleague I am charged with regulating the sun."

"Ah, you regulate the sun?" replied Master Zacharius, eagerly, without wincing. "I can scarcely compliment you upon it. Your sun goes badly, and in order to make ourselves agree with it, we have to keep advancing and retarding our clocks!"

"And, by the Devil's cloven foot," cried this weird personage, "you are right, my master! My sun does not always indicate midday at the same moment as your clocks; but some day it will be known that this is because of the inequality of the movement of the earth's transfer, and a mean midday will be invented which will regulate this irregularity!"

"Shall I live till then?" asked the old man, with glistening eyes.

"Without doubt," replied the little old man, laughing. "Can you believe that you will ever die?"

"Alas! I am very ill."

"Ah, let us talk of that. By Beelzebub! that will lead to just what I wish to speak to you about."

Saying this, the strange being leaped upon the old leather chair, and carried his legs one under the other, after the fashion of the bones which the painters of funeral hangings cross beneath skulls. Then he resumed, in an ironical tone, —

"See, Master Zacharius, what is going on in this good town of Geneva? They say that your health is failing, that your watches have need of a doctor!"

"Ah, do you believe that there is an intimate relation between their existence and mine?" cried Master Zacharius.

"Why, I imagine that these watches have faults, even vices. If these wantons do not preserve a regular conduct, it is right that they should bear the consequences of their irregularity. It seems to me that they have need of reforming a little!"

"What do you call faults?" asked Master Zacharius, reddening at the sarcastic tone in which these words were uttered "Have they not a right to be proud of their origin?"

"Not too proud, not too proud," replied the little old man. "They bear a celebrated name, and an illustrious signature is graven on their cases, it is true, and theirs is the exclusive privilege of being introduced among the noblest families; but for some time they have become deranged, and you can do nothing about it, Master Zacharius; and the stupidest apprentice in Geneva could prove it to you!"

"To me, to me!" cried Master Zacharius, with a flush of outraged pride.

"To you, Master Zacharius,—you, who cannot restore life to your watches!"

"But it is because I have a fever, and so have they also!" replied the old man, as a cold sweat broke out upon him.

"Very well, they will die with you, since you are prevented from imparting a little elasticity to their springs."

"Die! No, for you yourself have said it! I cannot die,—I, the first watchmaker in the world; I, who, by means of these pieces and diverse wheels, have been able to regulate the movement with absolute precision! Have I not subjected time to exact laws, and can I not dispose of it like a despot? Before a sublime genius had disposed regularly these wandering hours, in what vast waste was human destiny plunged? At what certain moment could the acts of life be connected with each other? But you, man or devil, whatever you may be, have never considered the magnificence of my art, which calls every science to its aid! No, no! I, Master Zacharius, cannot die, for, as I have regulated time, time would end with me! It would return to the infinite, whence my genius has rescued it, and it would lose itself irreparably in the gulf of chaos! No, I can no more die than the Creator of this universe, submitted to its laws! I have become his equal, and I have partaken of his power! If God has created eternity, Master Zacharius has created time!"

402

The old watchmaker now resembled the fallen angel, defiant in the presence of the Creator. The little old man gazed at him, and even seemed to breathe into him this impious transport.

"Well said, master," he replied "Beelzebub had less right than you to compare himself with God! Your glory must not perish! So your servant desires to give you the method of controlling these rebellious watches."

"What is it? what is it?" cried Master Zacharius.

"You shall know on the day after that on which you have given me your daughter's hand."

"My Gerande?"

"Herself!"

"My daughter's heart is not free," replied Master Zacharius, who seemed neither astonished nor angry at the strange demand.

"Bah! She is not the least beautiful of watches; but she will end by stopping also —"

"My daughter,—my Gerande! No!"

"Well, return to your watches, Master Zacharius. Adjust and readjust them. Get ready the marriage of your daughter and your apprentice. Temper your springs with your best steel. Bless Aubert and the pretty Gerande. But remember, your watches will never go, and Gerande will not wed Aubert!"

Thereupon the little old man disappeared so quickly that Master Zacharius could not hear six o'clock strike in his breast.

Chapter IV
The Church of St. Pierre

Meanwhile Master Zacharius became more feeble in mind and body every day An unusual excitement, indeed, impelled him to continue his work more eagerly than ever, nor could his daughter entice him from it.

His pride was still more aroused after the scene in which his strange visitor had so deeply agitated him, and he resolved to overcome, by the force of genius, the malign influence which weighed upon his work and himself. He first repaired to the various clocks of the town which were confided to his care. He made sure, by a scrupulous examination, that the wheels were in good condition, the pivots firm, the counter-weights exactly balanced. Every part, even to the bells, was examined with the minute attention of a physician studying the breast of a patient. Nothing indicated that these clocks were on the point of being affected by inertia.

Gerande and Aubert often accompanied the old man on these visits. He would no doubt have been pleased to see them eager to go with him, and certainly he would not have been so much absorbed in his approaching end, had he thought that his existence was to be prolonged by that of these cherished ones, and had he not understood that something of the life of a father always remains in his children.

The old watchmaker, on returning home, resumed his labors with feverish zeal. Though persuaded that he would not succeed, it yet seemed to him impossible that this could be so, and he unceasingly took apart and readjusted the watches which were brought to his shop.

Aubert tortured his mind in vain to discover the causes of the evil.

"Master," said he, "this can only come from the wear of the pivots and gearing."

"It gives you pleasure, then, to kill me little by little?" replied Master Zacharius, violently. "Are these watches child's work? Have I not forged these pieces of copper myself, so as to obtain a greater strength? Are not these springs tempered to a rare perfection? Could anybody have used finer oils than mine? You must yourself agree that it is impossible, and you avow, in short, that the devil is in it!"

From morning till night discontented purchasers besieged the house, and they got access to the old watchmaker himself, who knew not which of them to listen to.

"This watch is too slow, and I cannot succeed in regulating it," said one.

"This," said another. "Is absolutely obstmate, and stands still, as did Joshua's sun"

"If it is true," said most of them, "that your health has an influence on that of your watches, Master Zacharius, get well as soon as possible."

The old man gazed at these people with haggard eyes, and only replied by shaking his head, or by a few sad words —

"Wait till the first fine weather, my friends. The season is coming which revives existence in wearied bodies. The sun must come to warm us all!"

"A fine thing, if my watches are to be ill through the winter!" said one of the most angry. "Do you know, Master Zacharius, that your name is inscribed in full on their faces? By the Virgin, you do little honor to your signature!"

It happened at last that the old man, abashed by these reproaches, took some pieces of gold from his old trunk, and began to buy back the damaged watches. At news of this, the customers came in a crowd, and the poor watchmaker's money fast melted away; but his honesty remained intact. Gerande warmly praised his delicacy, which was leading him straight towards ruin; and Aubert soon offered his own savings to his master.

"What will become of my daughter?" said Master Zacharius, now and then clinging, in the shipwreck. to his paternal love.

Aubert dared not answer that he was full of hope for the future and of deep devotion to Gerande. Master Zacharius would have that day called him his son-in-law, and thus refuted the sad prophecy, which still buzzed in his ears, —

"Gerande will not wed Aubert."

The watchmaker at last succeeded in entirely despoiling himself. His antique vases passed into the hands of strangers; he deprived himself of the richly carved panels which adorned the walls of his house; some primitive pictures of the early Flemish painters were soon disposed of, and everything, even to the precious tools that his genius had invented, were sold to indemnify the clamorous customers.

Scholastique alone refused to listen to reason on the subject; but her efforts failed to prevent the unwelcome visitors from reaching her master, and from soon departing with some valuable object. Then her chattering was heard in all the streets of the neighborhood, where she had long been known. She eagerly denied the rumors of sorcery and magic on the part of Master Zacharius, which gained currency; but as at bottom she was persuaded of their truth, she said her prayers over and over again to redeem her pious falsehoods.

It had been noticed that for some time the old watchmaker had neglected his religious duties. Time was, when he had accompanied Gerande to church, and had seemed to find in prayer the intellectual charm which it imparts to thoughtful minds, as it is the most sublime exercise of the imagination. This voluntary neglect of holy practices, added to the secret habits of his life, had in some sort confirmed the accusations levelled against his labors. So, with the double purpose of drawing her father back to God and to the world, Gerande resolved to call religion to her aid. She thought that it might give some vitality to his dying soul; but the dogmas of faith and humility had to combat, in the soul of Master Zacharius, an insurmountable pride, and came into collision with that vanity of science which connects everything with itself, without rising to the infinite source whence first principles flow.

It was under these circumstances that the young girl undertook her father's conversion, and her influence was so effective that the old watchmaker promised to attend high mass at the Cathedral on the following Sunday. Old Scholastique could not contain her joy, and at last found irrefutable arguments against the gossiping tongues, which accused her master of impiety. She spoke of it to her neighbors, her friends, her enemies, to those whom she knew not as well as to those whom she knew.

"In faith, we scarcely believe what you tell us, dame Scholastique," they replied; "Master Zacharius has always acted in concert with the devil!"

"You have n't counted, then," replied the old servant, "the fine bells which strike for my master's clocks? How many times they have struck the hours of prayer and the mass!"

"No doubt," they would reply. "But has he not invented machines which go all by themselves, and which actually do the work of a real man?"

"Could a child of the devil," exclaimed dame Scholastique, wrathfully, "have executed the fine iron clock of the château of Andernatt, which the town of Geneva was not rich enough to buy? A pious motto appeared at each hour, and a Christian who obeyed them would have gone straight to Paradise! Is that the work of the devil?"

This masterpiece, made twenty years before, had carried Master Zacharius's fame to its acme: but even then there had been accusations against him of sorcery. At least, the old man's visit to the Cathedral would reduce malicious tongues to silence.

Master Zacharius, doubtless having forgotten the promise made to his daughter, had returned to his shop. After being convinced of his powerlessness to give life to his watches, he resolved to try if he could not make some new ones. He abandoned all these inert bodies, and devoted himself to the completion of the crystal watch, which he intended to be his masterpiece; but in vain did he use his most perfect tools, and employ rubies and diamonds for resisting friction.

The watch fell from his hands the first time that he attempted to adjust it!

The old man concealed this circumstance from every one, even from his daughter; but from that time his health rapidly declined. There were only the last oscillations of a pendulum, which goes slower when nothing restores its primitive force. It seemed as if the laws of gravity, acting directly upon him, were dragging him irresistibly down to the grave.

The Sunday so ardently anticipated by Gerande at last arrived. The weather was fine, and the temperature inspiriting. The people of Geneva were passing quietly through the streets, gayly chatting about the return of spring. Gerande, tenderly taking the old man's arm, directed her steps towards the Cathedral, while Scholastique followed behind with the prayer-books. People looked curiously at them as they passed. The old watchmaker permitted himself to be led like a child, or rather like a blind man. The faithful of Saint Pierre were almost frightened when they saw him cross the threshold, and shrank back at his approach.

The chants of high mass were already resounding through the church. Gerande advanced to her accustomed bench, and kneeled with profound and simple reverence. Master Zacharius remained standing beside her.

The ceremonies continued with the majestic solemnity of that pious age, but the old man had no faith. He did not implore the pity of Heaven with cries of anguish of the "Kyrie"; he did not, with the "Gloria in Excelsis," sing the splendors of the celestial heights; the reading of the Testament did not draw him from his materialistic revery, and he forgot to join in the homage of the "Credo." This proud old man remained motionless, as insensible and silent as a stone statue; and even at the solemn moment when the bell announced the miracle of transubstantiation, he did not bow his head, but gazed directly at the sacred host which the priest raised above the heads of the faithful. Gerande looked at her father, and a flood of tears moistened her missal. At this moment the clock of Saint Pierre struck half past eleven. Master Zacharius turned quickly towards this ancient clock which still spoke. It seemed to him as if its face was gazing steadily at him; the figures of the homs shone as if they had been engraved in lines of fire, and the hands darted forth electric sparks from their sharp points.

The mass ended. It was customary for the "Angelus" to be said at noon, and the priests, before leaving the altar, waited for the clock to strike the hour of twelve. In a few moments this prayer would ascend to the feet of the Virgin.

But suddenly a harsh noise was heard. Master Zacharius uttered a piercing cry.

The large hand of the clock, having reached twelve, had abruptly stopped, and the clock did not strike the hour.

Gerande hastened to her father's aid. He had fallen down motionless, and they carried him outside the church.

"It is the death-blow!" murmured Gerande, sobbing.

When he had been borne home, Master Zacharius lay upon his bed utterly crushed. Life seemed only to still exist on the surface of his body, like the last whiffs of smoke about a lamp just extinguished.

When he came to his senses, Aubert and Gerande were leaning over him. At this supreme moment the future took in his eyes the shape of the present. He saw his daughter alone, without support.

"My son," said he to Aubert, "I give my daughter to thee."

So saying, he stretched out his hand towards his two children, who were thus united at his death-bed.

But soon Master Zacharius lifted himself up in a paroxysm of rage. The words of the little old man recurred to his mind.

"I do not wish to die!" he cried; "I cannot die! I, Master Zacharius, ought not to die! My books,—my accounts!"

He sprang from his bed towards a book in which the names of his customers, and the articles which had been sold to them, were inscribed. He seized it and rapidly turned over its leaves, and his emaciated thumb fixed itself on one of the pages.

"There!" he cried, "there! this old iron clock, sold to Pittonaccio! It is the only one that has not been returned to me! It still exists,—it goes,—it lives! Ah, I wish for it,—I must find it! I will take such care of it that death will no longer seek me!"

And he fainted away.

Aubert and Gerande knelt by the old man's bedside, and prayed together.

Chapter V

The Hour of Death

Several days passed, and Master Zacharius, though almost dying, rose from his bed and returned to active life, under a supernatural excitement. He lived by pride. But Gerande did not deceive herself; her father's body and soul were forever lost.

The old man got together his last resources, without thought of those who were dependent upon him. He betrayed an incredible energy, walking, ferreting about, and mumbling strange, incomprehensible words.

One morning Gerande went down to his shop. Master Zacharius was not there. She waited for him all day. Master Zacharius did not return.

Gerande wept bitterly, but her father did not reappear.

Aubert searched everywhere through the town, and soon came to the sad conviction that the old man had left it.

"Let us find my father!" cried Gerande, when the young apprentice told her this sad news.

"Where can he be?" Aubert asked himself.

An inspiration suddenly came to his mind. He remembered the last words which Master Zacharius had spoken. The old man only lived now in the old iron clock that had not been returned! Master Zacharius must have gone in search of it.

Aubert spoke of this to Gerande.

"Let us look at my father's book," she replied.

They descended to the shop. The book was open on the bench. All the watches or clocks made by the old man, and which had been returned to him out of order, were stricken out, excepting one.

"Sold to M. Pittonaccio, an iron clock, with bell and moving figures; sent to his château at Andernatt."

It was this "moral" clock of which Scholastique had spoken with so much enthusiasm.

"My father is there!" cried Gerande.

"Let us hasten thither," replied Aubert. "We may still save him!"

"Not for this life," murmured Gerande, "but at least for the other."

"By the grace of God, Gerande! The château of Andernatt stands in the gorge of the 'Dents-du-Midi,' twenty hours from Geneva. Let us go!"

That very evening Aubert and Gerande, followed by the old servant, set out on foot by the road which skirts Lake Leman. They accomplished five leagues during the night, stopping neither at Bessinge nor at Ermance, where rises the famous château of the Mayors. They with difficulty forded the torrent of the Dranse; and everywhere they went they inquired for Master Zacharius, and were soon convinced that they were on his track.

The next morning, at daybreak, having passed Thonon, they reached Evian. whence the Swiss territory may be seen extended over twelve leagues. But the travellers did not even perceive the enchanting prospect. They went straight forward, urged on by a supernatural force. Aubert, leaning on a knotty stick, offered his arm alternately to Gerande and to Scholastique; and he exerted a supreme energy to sustain his companions. All three talked of their sorrow, of their hopes, and thus passed along the beautiful road by the water-side, and across the narrow plateau which unites the borders of the lake with the eminences of the Chalais. They soon reached Bouveret, where the Rhone enters Lake Leman.

On leaving this town they diverged from the lake, and their weariness increased amid these mountain districts. Vionnaz, Chesset, Collombay, half-lost villages, were soon left behind. Meanwhile their knees bent, their feet were lacerated by the sharp points which covered the ground like granite bushes. No trace of Master Zacharius!

He must be found, however, and the two young people did not seek repose either in the isolated hamlets or at the château of Monthay, which, with its dependencies, formed the appanage of Margaret of Savoy. At last, late in the day, they reached the hermitage of Notre-Dame-du-Sex, which is situated at the base of the Dents-du-Midi, six hundred feet above the Rhone. They were nearly dead with fatigue.

The hermit received the wanderers as night was falling. They could not have gone another step, and here they must needs rest.

The hermit could give them no news of Master Zacharius. They could scarcely hope to find him still living amid these sad solitudes. The night was dark, the wind howled amid the mountains, and the avalanches roared down from the summits of the broken crags.

Aubert and Gerande, crouching before the hermit's hearth, told him their melancholy tale. Their mantles, covered with snow, were drying in a corner; and without, the hermit's dog barked lugubriously, and mingled his voice with that of the tempest.

"Pride," said the hermit to his guests, "has lost an angel created for good. It is the obstacle against which the destinies of man strike. You cannot oppose reasoning to pride, the principal of all the vices, since, by its very nature, the proud man refuses to listen to it. It only remains, then, to pray for your father!"

All four knelt down, when the barking of the dog redoubled, and some one knocked at the door of the hermitage.

"Open, in the name of the devil!"

The door yielded under the blows, and a dishevelled, haggard, ill-clothed man appeared.

"My father!" cried Gerande.

It was Master Zacharius.

"Where am I?" said he. "In eternity! Time is ended,—the hours no longer strike,—the hands have stopped!"

"Father!" returned Gerande, with so piteous an emotion that the old man seemed to return to the world of the living.

"Thou here. Gerande?" he cried: "and thou. Aubert? Ah, my dear betrothed ones, you are going to be married in our old church!"

"Father," said Gerande, seizing him by the arm, "come home to Geneva,—come with us!"

The old man tore away from his daughter and hurried towards the door, on the threshold of which the snow was falling in large flakes.

"Do not abandon your children!" cried Aubert.

"Why return," replied the old man, sadly, "to those places which my life has already quitted, and where a part of myself is forever buried?"

"Your soul is not dead!" said the hermit, solemnly.

"My soul? O no,—its wheels are good! I perceive it beating regularly—"

"Your soul is immaterial,—your soul is immortal!" replied the hermit, sternly.

"Yes,—like my glory! But it is shut up in the château of Andernatt, and I wish to see it again!"

The hermit crossed himself; Scholastique became almost inanimate. Aubert held Gerande in his arms.

"The château of Andernatt is inhabited by one who is damned," said the hermit, "one who does not salute the cross of my hermitage."

"My father, go not thither!"

"I want my soul! My soul is mine—"

"Hold him! Hold my father!" cried Gerande.

But the old man had leaped across the threshold, and plunged into the night, crying, "Mine, mine, my soul!"

Gerande, Aubert, and Scholastique hastened after him. They went by difficult paths, across which Master Zacharius sped like a tempest, urged by an irresistible force. The snow raged around them, and mingled its white flakes with the froth of the tumbling torrents.

As they passed the chapel erected in memory of the massacre of the Theban legion, they hurriedly crossed themselves. Master Zacharius was not to be seen.

At last the village of Evionnaz appeared in the midst of this sterile region. The hardest heart would have been moved to see this hamlet, lost among these horrible solitudes. The old man sped on, and plunged into the deepest gorge of the Dent-du-Midi, which pierce the sky with their sharp peaks.

Soon a ruin, old and gloomy as the rocks at its base, rose before him.

"It is there—there!" he cried, still more frantically hastening his pace.

The château of Andernatt was a ruin even then. A thick, crumbling tower rose above it, and seemed to menace with its downfall the old gables which reared themselves below. The vast piles of jagged stones frowned gloomily to the right. Several dark halls appeared amid the débris, with caved-in ceilings, now become the abode of vipers.

A low and narrow postern, opening upon a ditch choked with rubbish, gave access to the château. No doubt some margrave, half lord, half brigand, had inherited it; to the margrave had succeeded bandits or counterfeiters, who had been hung on the scene of their crime. The legend went that, on winter nights, Satan came to lead his diabolical dances on the slope of the deep gorges in which the shadow of these ruins was engulfed.

But Master Zacharius was not dismayed by their sinister aspect. He reached the postern. No one forbade him to pass. A spacious and gloomy court presented itself to his eyes. He passed along the kind of inclined plane which conducted to one of the long corridors, the arches of which seemed to banish daylight from beneath their heavy springings. His advance was unresisted. Gerande, Aubert and Scholastique closely followed him.

Master Zacharius, as if guided by an irresistible hand, seemed sure of his way, and strode along with rapid step. He reached an old worm?-eaten door, which fell before his blows, whilst the bats described oblique circles around his head.

An immense hall, better preserved than the rest, was soon reached. High sculptured panels, on which larves, ghouls, and other strange figures seemed to agitate themselves confusedly, covered its walls. Several long and narrow windows shivered beneath the bursts of the tempest.

Master Zacharius, on reaching the middle of this hall, uttered a cry of joy.

On an iron support, fastened to the wall, stood the clock in which now resided his entire life. This unequalled masterpiece represented an ancient Roman church, with its heavy bell-tower, where there was a complete chime for the anthem of the day, the "Angelus," the mass, and vespers. Above the church door, which opened at the hour of the ceremonies, was placed a "rose," in the centre of which two hands moved, and the archivolt of which reproduced the twelve hours of the face sculptured in relief. Between the door and the rose, just as Scholastique had said, a maxim, relative to the employment of every moment of the day, appeared on a copper plate. Master Zacharius had regulated this succession of devices with a really Christian solicitude; the hours of prayer, of work, of repast, of recreation, and of repose followed each other according to the religious discipline, and were to infallibly insure salvation to him who scrupulously observed their commands.

Master Zacharius, intoxicated with joy, went forward to take possession of the clock, when a frightful roar of laughter resounded behind him.

He turned, and by the light of a smoky lamp recognized the little old man of Geneva.

"You here?" cried he.

Gerande was afraid. She drew closer to Aubert.

"Good day, Master Zacharius," said the monster.

"Who are you?"

"Signor Pittonaccio, at your service! You have come to give me your daughter! You have remembered my words,—'Gerande will not wed Aubert."

The young apprentice rushed upon Pittonaccio, who escaped from him like a shadow.

"Stop, Aubert!" cried Master Zacharius.

"Good night," said Pittonaccio; and he disappeared.

"My father, let us fly from this hateful place!" cried Gerande. "My father!"

Master Zacharius was no longer there. He was pursuing the phantom of Pittonaccio across the rickety corridors. Scholastique, Gerande, and Aubert remained, speechless and fainting, in the large gloomy hall. The young gul had fallen upon a stone seat; the old servant knelt beside her and prayed; Aubert remained erect, watching his betrothed. Pale lights wandered in the darkness, and the silence was only broken by the movements of the little animals which range among old wood, and the noise of which marks the hours of "the clock of death."

When daylight came, they ventured upon the endless staircase which wound beneath these ruined masses; for two hours they wandered thus, without meeting a living soul, and hearing only a far-off echo responding to their cries. Sometimes they found themselves buried a hundred feet below the ground, and sometimes they reached places whence they could overlook the surrounding mountains.

Chance brought them at last back again to the vast hall, which had sheltered them during this night of anguish. It was no longer empty. Master Zacharius and Pittonaccio were talking there together, the one upright and rigid as a corpse, the other crouching over a marble table.

Master Zacharius, when he perceived Gerande, went forward and took her by the hand, and led her towards Pittonaccio, saying, "Behold your lord and master, my daughter. Gerande, behold your husband!"

Gerande shuddered from head to foot.

"Never!" cried Aubert, "for she is my be trothed."

"Never!" responded Gerande, like a plaintive echo.

Pittonaccio began to laugh.

"You wish me to die, then?" exclaimed the old man. "There, in that clock, the last which goes of all which have gone from my hands, my life is shut up; and this man tells me, 'When I have thy daughter, this clock shall belong to thee. And this man will not adjust it. He can break it, and plunge me into chaos. Ah, my daughter, you no longer love me!"

"My father!" murmured Gerande, recovering consciousness.

"If you knew what I have suffered, far away from this principle of my existence!" resumed the old man. Perhaps its springs were left to wear out, its wheels to get clogged. But now, in my own hands, I can nourish this health so dear, for I must not die,—I, the great watchmaker of Geneva. Look, my daughter, how these hands advance with certain step. See, five o'clock is about to strike. Listen well, and look at the maxim which is about to be revealed."

Five o'clock struck with a noise which resounded sadly in Gerande's soul, and these words appeared in red letters: —

"YOU MUST EAT OF THE FRUITS OF THE TREE OF SCIENCE."

Aubert and Gerande looked at each other stupefied. These were no longer the pious sayings of the Catholic watchmaker. The breath of Satan must have passed there. But Zacharius paid no attention to this, and resumed: —

"Dost thou hear, my Gerande? I live, I still live! Listen to my breathing,—see the blood circulating in my veins! No, thou wouldst not kill thy father, and thou wilt accept this man for thy husband, so that I may become immortal, and at last attain the power of God!"

At these blasphemous words old Scholastique crossed herself, and Pittonaccio laughed aloud with joy.

"And then, Gerande, thou wilt be happy with him. See this man,— he is Time! Thy existence will be regulated with absolute precision. Gerande, since I gave thee life, give life to thy father!"

"Gerande," murmured Aubert, "I am thy betrothed."

"He is my father!" replied Gerande, fainting.

"She is thine!" said Master Zacharius. "Pittonaccio, thou wilt keep thy promise!"

"Here is the key of the clock," replied the horrible man.

Master Zacharius seized the long key, which resembled an uncoiled snake, and ran to the clock, which he hastened to wind up with fantastic rapidity. The creaking of the spring jarred upon the nerves. The old watchmaker wound and wound the key, without stopping a moment, and it seemed as if the movement were beyond his control. He wound more and more quickly, with strange contortions, until he fell from sheer weariness.

"There it is, wound up for a century!" he cried.

Aubert rushed from the hall as if he were mad. After long wandering, he found the outlet of the hateful château, and hastened into the open air. He returned to the hermitage of Notre-Dame-du-Sex, and talked so desperately to the holy recluse, that the latter consented to return with him to the château of Andernatt.

If, during these hours of anguish, Gerande had not wept, it was because her tears were exhausted.

Master Zacharius had not left the hall. He ran every moment to listen to the regular beating of the old clock.

Meanwhile the clock had struck, and to Scholastique's great terror, these words had appeared on the silver face: —

"MAN OUGHT TO BECOME THE EQUAL OF GOD."

The old man had not only not been shocked by these impious maxims, but read them deliriously, and was pleased with these thoughts of pride, whilst Pittonaccio kept close by him.

The marriage-contract was to be signed at midnight. Gerande, almost unconscious, saw or heard nothing. The silence was only broken by the old man's words, and the chuckling of Pittonaccio.

Eleven o'clock struck. Master Zacharius shuddered, and read in a loud voice: —

"MAN SHOULD BE THE SLAVE OF SCIENCE, AND SACRIFICE TO IT RELATIVES AND FAMILY."

"Yes!" he cried, "there is nothing but science in this world!"

The hands slipped over the face of the clock with the hiss of a serpent, and the movement beat with accelerated strokes.

Master Zacharius no longer spoke. He had fallen to the floor, he rattled, and from his oppressed bosom came only these half-broken words: "Life—science!"

The scene had now two new witnesses, the hermit and Aubert. Master Zacharius lay upon the floor; Gerande was praying beside him, more dead than alive.

Of a sudden a dry, hard noise was heard, proceeding from the striking-apparatus.

Master Zacharius sprang up.

"Midnight!" he cried.

The hermit stretched out his hand towards the old watchmaker,— and midnight did not sound.

Master Zacharius uttered a terrible cry, when these words appeared: —

"WHOEVER SHALL ATTEMPT TO MAKE HIMSELF THE EQUAL OF GOD SHALL BE FOREVER DAMNED!"

The old clock burst with a noise like thunder, and the spring, escaping, leaped across the hall with a thousand fantastic contortions; the old man rose, ran after it, trying in vain to seize it, and exclaiming, "My soul,—my soul!"

The spring bounded before him, first on one side, then on the other, and he could not reach it.

At last Pittonaccio seized it, and, uttering a horrible blasphemy, ingulfed himself in the earth.

Master Zacharius fell over. He was dead.

The old watchmaker was buried in the midst of the peaks of Andernatt.

Then Aubert and Gerande returned to Geneva, and during the long life which God accorded to them, they imposed it on themselves to redeem by prayer the soul of the castaway of science.